I0629279

THE DEVIL'S GREENHOUSE

ERIK
SHEIN
MELISSA
DAVIS
KAREN
FULLER

The Devil's Greenhouse is a work of fiction. While the story, characters, and locations depicted in this work are products of the author's imagination, the narrative is inspired by and adapted from real-life events. Any resemblance to actual persons, living or dead, or to real events or locales is purely coincidental. The author and publisher make no claims regarding the accuracy of any real-life elements reference and assert that this work is intended solely for entertainment purposes.

World Castle Publishing, LLC
Pensacola, Florida
Copyright © 2024 Shein Partnership, LLC
Authors: Erik Shein, Melissa Davis & Karen Fuller
Paperback ISBN: 9798891263048
eBook ISBN: 9798891262683
First Edition World Castle Publishing, LLC, October 29, 2024
http://www.worldcastlepublishing.com

Licensing Notes

All rights reserved. The Devil's Greenhouse and Universe are Trademarks of Shein Partnership, LLC. No part of this publication may be reproduced, stored in a retrieval system, or transmitted in any form or by any means — electronic, Digital, mechanical, photocopying, recording, or any other — except for brief quotations in printed reviews without the prior permission of the publisher. The publisher does not have any control over and does not assume any responsibility for the author or third party's websites and their content. Requests for information should be addressed to:
Shein Partnership, LLC
4766 East Eden Drive
Cave Creek, AZ 85331

Cover Art: Cover Designs by Karen
Cover-designs-by-karen.com

Evil wears no face, knows neither mercy nor compassion, feels neither love nor joy. How can it stand then, against the very best of humanity?

CHAPTER 1
THE PRIEST'S UNHOLY REVELATION

The Church of the Holy Redeemer was a sacred haven illuminated by the ethereal light of dawn. The pews lay empty, but to Father Alex Corbin's eyes, they were filled with ghostly figures swaying in silent reverence. Wrinkled and weathered, his face told the story of a lifetime devoted to God. As he adorned himself in his priestly garments, his bony fingers caressed a faded photograph of his parents. With a solemn gesture, he traced the sign of the cross over their faces, seeking comfort in their memory before beginning his holy duties.

Father Alex emerged into the grand chapel, taking in a deep breath and relishing the hallowed stillness that surrounded him. Rays of sunlight streamed through the stained glass, casting a kaleidoscope of colors on the ancient stone floor. The air was thick with the fragrance of incense and aged timber, filling him with a sense of awe and reverence.

Alex began his daily ritual, moving with a graceful intensity towards the altar. Each candle he lit seemed to cast out the shadows, their flickering flames dancing in an ethereal breeze. As he performed each deliberate action, it was as if he was communing with a higher power in a sacred trance.

He eventually settled onto a hard wooden pew and lowered his head in prayer. Suddenly, a low growl rattled through the chapel, shaking loose centuries of dust from the rafters above. Alex's eyes flew open as the stained glass windows shuddered violently, their brilliant colors swirling madly against the ancient stone walls. The growling grew into a deafening roar, accompanied by a fierce wind that erupted through the chapel, snuffing out every candle on the altar in one savage breath.

Alex cowered behind his arms as the debris whipped around him, the wind howling like a furious demon. As sudden as it had begun, the tempest abruptly ceased, leaving only an eerie stillness. Alex cautiously scanned the dimly lit room, searching for any signs of disturbance. Had one of the doors been forced open? Though everything looked undisturbed, a gnawing sense of dread crept through his body.

A foreboding feeling consumed him. The shadows slithered and twisted, taunting his senses. A palpable evil hung in the air as if a malevolent entity was waiting just beyond the veil of darkness. Alex's body trembled involuntarily. This chapel, once a source of solace and peace after all these years, now seemed tainted and unclean to him. Doubt and uncertainty crept into his mind, disrupting his unwavering devotion.

"Hello?" His voice echoed eerily in the empty space. "Is someone there?"

There was no response, only a menacing stillness. But Alex couldn't shake the feeling of being scrutinized by some malevolent entity. His nerves frayed, he hastily finished lighting the final candle. Whispers of a prayer escaped his lips as the flames erupted with intensity for a fleeting moment before flickering ominously.

Silence was shattered by the forceful blast of the sanctuary's grand entrance, its solid doors flung open with such a clamor that it echoed through every corner of the vast space. Father Alex spun on his heels, his pulse racing, but saw no one in sight, and the doors remained firmly shut. He made the sign of the cross and took a trembling breath, surveying the room for any signs of disturbance. But all was eerily still as if nothing had happened at all.

Alex shuddered, clutching his rosary with a death grip. He could sense the presence of pure malevolence within these sacred walls.

Gently setting the ornate chalice upon the ancient altar, Alex gingerly retrieved his weathered Bible. A soft sigh escaped his lips as he flipped to the well-loved page, his voice a hushed whisper in the vast cathedral. With a reverent hand, he traced the sign of the cross on the surface of the water, the sound of his words reverberating off the cold, stone walls.

"Holy Lord...sanctify this gift of water..."

As Alex dipped his fingers into the chalice, a frown creased his brow. A viscous film coated the water's surface, reflecting an eerie glow that seemed to defy all logic. As he swirled the liquid, he intensified his prayers, desperate to ward off the rising sense of dread within him. "...let it be a sign of your purity and blessing..."

As his hand rose, Alex's pulse quickened, and he felt a wave of terror wash over him. His once pure fingers were now tainted by an ominous blackness that seemed to seep from within. Gazing into the chalice, he saw the holy water had been corrupted into a thick, malevolent liquid that devoured all light in its path.

With a mounting sense of terror, Alex frantically traced the sign of the cross over the water, his prayers spilling forth in frantic tremors. His typically unwavering voice now shook with desperation and fear. But no matter how fervently he begged the Almighty, the water remained a corrupted shadow of its once pristine state.

"No...Lord have mercy..." The words escaped Alex's lips in a horrified whisper, barely audible even in the silent church.

He staggered back, unable to look away from the defiled chalice. The rituals he had clung to for centuries now felt futile and weak against this unfathomable contamination. As the first golden rays of dawn filtered through the stained glass windows, Father Alex stood alone in his holy refuge, his unwavering beliefs crumbling beneath him.

Father Alex gazed in terror at the murky liquid, his thoughts spiraling out of control. How could this happen? The sacred chalice, the blessed water, the very sanctity of this holy ground — all debased by a malevolence beyond his understanding.

He recoiled from the holy altar, his gaze frantically scanning the dimly lit corners of the hallowed church. What malevolent entity had infiltrated these sacred walls? The dancing candle flames seemed to mock him with phantom figures and elusive movements. But no tangible danger presented itself.

Alex's heart raced with ferocity, the blood thundering in his ears. He knew he must gather his wits and focus. Clutching his rosary like a shield, he steeled himself for the battle ahead. As a devout servant of God, it was his duty to protect his people from the forces of darkness. He would not let evil triumph over good.

Alex inhaled deeply, his gaze shifting back to the ornate altar. He crossed himself again and began reciting a prayer of exorcism, his tone resolute and commanding. The ancient Latin words reverberated through the hallowed halls, filled with divine power and conviction.

As Alex chanted the ancient incantation, a chilling breeze began to swirl up from the depths of the ancient stones beneath his feet. The flickering candlelight seemed to falter and fade, casting a foreboding darkness over the church interior. Undeterred, he clutched his rosary beads tightly in his trembling fingers.

As he raised the defiled chalice in a solemn gesture, the tainted liquid inside began to boil and churn with an otherworldly rage. Alex let out a howl of despair as putrid froth sprayed over the sacred altar, coating everything in its path, including his once-pristine vestments.

The pungent, tar-like substance oozed down the altar as Father Alex gazed in utter shock. In all his years of devoted service, he had never laid eyes on such an abomination. He stepped back cautiously, unable to tear his gaze away from the chalice as the foul liquid overflowed and seeped onto the cold stone floor.

An eerie aura radiated from the depths as if some dark force was fueling its infernal contents. Noxious fumes billowed, carrying a foul stench of decay and brimstone. Father Alex gripped his crucifix, struggling against a wave of revulsion. This could only be the work of the devil himself.

As if by dark magic, the liquid in the chalice began to take on a life of its own. Sinister shapes emerged from the bubbling depths, with eerie letters etched into their surface as if carved by an otherworldly force. Father Alex's brow furrowed in deep concentration as his mind struggled to make sense of the ancient symbols before him.

"This cannot be," he whispered. "It's not possible."

But there it was, revealed with terrifying clarity — a prophecy of the impending doomsday, the inevitable ascension of the Antichrist forewarned in enigmatic yet undeniable terms. The sacred chalice slipped from Father Alex's trembling grasp, crashing upon the unforgiving stone tiles below. As it shattered, its contents vanished in a swirl of malodorous fumes, leaving behind only a blemish of malevolence on the once-pure altar.

Father Alex crumbled to the ground, the heaviness of the unspeakable horrors he had just witnessed threatening to shatter his very essence. How could he possibly combat a darkness so relentless that it could corrupt even the holiest of objects within the church?

His attention was suddenly drawn to a subtle shifting in the corner of his vision. He spun on his heel, eyes landing on a marble depiction of the Blessed Mother. His expression hardened as he noticed an otherworldly glyph engraved into its pedestal. With trepidation, he inched closer, studying the intricately hewn symbols adorning the Virgin's garments and shroud. A sharp intake of breath escaped him as he realized their significance.

The profanity seemed to infect everything, reaching far beyond the statue. Everywhere Alex looked, he saw blasphemous symbols and graffiti scrawled across holy objects. Even the ancient statues, relics, and stained glass windows were tainted with wicked markings that seemed to originate from a realm beyond our own. As Alex took in the desecration of all he held dear, a wave of terror washed over him like a dark baptism.

With a trembling hand, he timidly reached out to caress the symbol engraved on the baptismal font. As soon as his fingers grazed the cool stone, he recoiled in horror as if scorched by the fires of hell.

His gaze flickered to the crucifix, where a dark liquid oozed from the wound in Christ's side. It was a profane mockery of the sacred blood spilled for humanity's salvation. The revulsion consumed Father Alex, and he could not bear to look upon the defiled representation of his Redeemer any longer. He turned away, unable to stomach the sight any further.

He struggled to suppress the roiling sickness in his gut, bile clawing its way up his throat. This was a desecration beyond anything he could have imagined. The revered statues, holy artifacts, even the likeness of Christ Himself — all had been tainted by an insidious and malevolent presence.

Father Alex stumbled weakly towards the imposing doors of the chapel, desperate to break free from the oppressive darkness. He craved light, clean air, anything to rid his senses of the putrid stench of malevolent forces that lingered in the depths of his mind.

With a guttural growl, he thrust open the heavy doors, but instead of being greeted by the dawn's first light, he was met with an inky blackness that seemed to devour everything in its path. The once clear sky was now shrouded in ominous storm clouds, obscuring the moon and stars. The air was thick with the stench of decay and despair, like a putrid bog ready to engulf the entire city.

Alex raised his gaze to the distant horizon, where an eerie red glow cast an otherworldly light upon the spires and rooftops of Savannah. It was as if the heavens themselves had been set ablaze, tainted by the spilled blood of countless innocents. The foretold apocalypse had come to pass, signaling the commencement of mankind's downfall.

With wide, unblinking eyes, Father Alex crumpled to the ground in despair. Though his faith burned strong within him, a cold fear took root in his heart. He had pleaded for the fortitude to defy the forces of darkness, but as the end drew near, he questioned if any mortal could resist the impending evil that threatened to consume them all.

He couldn't simply stand idly by and allow this atrocity to occur. Without a moment's hesitation, he turned and sprinted back into the towering cathedral. The heavy oak doors slammed shut with a deafening thud, enclosing him in the sacred space. Desperation writhed within Alex's very being as he frantically searched for any solution. His trembling fingers grasped onto an ancient leather-bound tome, desperately flipping through its pages with feverish determination. But despite his efforts, the answer remained elusive, and his heart sank with dread. Throwing the book down in exasperation, his mind raced with both desperation and terror.

"Deliver us from evil..." The words fell from his lips, a prayer and a plea.

Alex stood in solitude, surrounded by desecrated remnants of his beliefs. The insidious presence of an indescribable danger loomed over him, testing his unwavering devotion. His priestly robes swished delicately as he approached the altar, each footfall resonating through the ominous stillness.

He approached the basin of holy water, a sacred act he had carried out countless times before. Yet as he dipped his fingers and traced the cross, the water hissed against his flesh. Alex recoiled in astonishment, his gaze darting around the room. The bowl erupted into a frenzy, its contents churning and bubbling with an otherworldly energy.

Stumbling backward, he scanned the dark corners of the church. "Reveal yourself!" he whispered, his voice trembling.

The room was still, not even a whisper to break the eerie silence. Alex steeled himself, lighting the incense. Its familiar aroma usually brought him solace, but today, it seemed to cling to his skin like a sinister cloud. He began chanting in ancient Latin, each word falling from his lips with practiced ease. Yet, as he waved the incense with rhythmic precision, the smoke grew thick and suffocating. It filled his lungs with a burning sensation, but he refused to falter in his ritual. The heavy smoke engulfed him, forcing him to his knees. In a fit of coughing and choking, he dropped the incense censer to the ground, its clattering sound echoing in the empty room.

Tears streaming down his face, he gazed up at the towering crucifix looming over the altar. The once serene face of Christ now twisted into a sinister grin, taunting him from above. "Why have you forsaken me?" The question hung in the air, unanswered. Alex's shoulders slumped in defeat. He looked up to the cross once more. "Why have you forsaken this place?"

His grasp on the crucifix tightened, the white-knuckled strain revealing his inner turmoil. Tears welled up in his eyes as the very core of his faith trembled under the weight of doubt. "Give me the strength, O Lord..." The desperate supplication drifted away into the darkness, tainted by the insidious presence that surrounded him. The holy relic in his trembling hand grew dull, defiled by the malevolent forces at play. With a resounding clang, the metal cross slipped from his fingers, and Alex recoiled in terror. Sinister murmurs invaded the sanctuary, planting seeds of doubt in his already troubled mind.

"You are nothing...God has abandoned you..." The voices tormented him, questioning his life's purpose.

Alex pressed his hands over his ears, but he couldn't shut out the whispers. Blood oozed from the religious icons, intensifying the desecration. In that moment, surrounded by the corruption of all he held dear, Father Alex faced the terrifying possibility that his faith might not be enough to save him from the darkness closing in.

CHAPTER 2
A GRISLY DISCOVERY

In the heart of Savannah, where moss-draped oaks whispered tales of Southern charm, a rain-soaked alley now spoke of something far more sinister. Its darkness was pierced only by the determined beams of two detectives' flashlights and the glint of something that should not be there.

The alley stretched before them, slick with recent rain. Broken streetlights cast eerie shadows along the grime-covered walls. Each step brought them deeper into the unknown, their shoes squelching against the damp ground.

Detective Mara Lawson strode down the dim passageway, the stench of rot and decay assaulting her nostrils. Her partner, Terry, stood by her side, his unwavering presence lending her strength as she kept one hand close to her gun, alert to any potential threats.

The grimy alley pulsed with an undercurrent of tension, a stark microcosm of the city's underbelly. Shadows danced in the feeble glow of streetlights, conspiring to conceal secrets best left unspoken. A sudden flurry of movement shattered the eerie stillness – a mouse, nature's unwitting messenger, darted across weathered concrete.

Mara's reaction was instinctive, honed by years on these merciless streets. Her hand flew to her weapon, a reflex born of countless encounters where hesitation meant the difference between life and death.

"Shit!" she hissed.

But Terry, her partner in this nightly dance with darkness, steadied her with a touch that spoke volumes about their complicated dynamic. "Easy there," he murmured, his voice a mix of concern and amusement. His teasing grin cut through the tension, a futile attempt to lighten the oppressive atmosphere.

Mara pulled away sharply, her voice edged with irritation. "Save it, Terry. Next time, I'll let the rabid rat bite you."

Terry's response was quick, his humor a desperate grasp at normalcy. "Rabid rats? In this economy? It's probably just looking for affordable housing like the rest of us."

The city's economic despair became a punchline, a bitter acknowledgment of the decay that surrounded them. "Hilarious," Mara retorted. "Next stand-up night, you're buying the drinks." Her flashlight beam cut through the gloom, landing on a grimy dumpster ahead. She pointed, all business now. "Who called this in, anyway?"

Terry's response was matter-of-fact, belying the gravity of what awaited them. "Some homeless guy. Dispatch said he was pretty shaken up."

As they approached their grim discovery, the air grew thick with foreboding. The mutilated corpse, adorned with arcane symbols, represented more than just another statistic. It was a harbinger, a grotesque canvas hinting at horrors yet to come.

Mara recoiled, her face hardening as she covered her nose with her sleeve. Her eyes met Terry's, conveying volumes in a single glance. "Cult shit," she declared, her voice tight with recognition and dread.

Terry, still clinging to levity like a lifeline, quipped, "What, no 'hello' for our friend here?" But his humor fell flat in the face of such grotesque violence.

Mara cut him a sharp glance, her patience wearing thin. "Cut the jokes. This isn't just some tweaker. These symbols... I've seen them before."

Her certainty clashed with Terry's attempts at rationalization, their usual dynamic fraying under the weight of this macabre discovery.

Terry crouched, shining his light closer to the body, examining the carvings. His voice strained for normalcy. "C'mon,

Mara. You know how creative the street crowd gets when they're high."

But Mara's eyes narrowed, her instincts screaming warnings that Terry's pragmatism couldn't silence. Pulling on a pair of latex gloves, she knelt, studying the symbols intently. "My gut's screaming this is bigger," she insisted, her voice low and intense.

The faint wail of sirens in the distance grew louder, heralding the approach of a system ill-equipped to comprehend the magnitude of what they'd stumbled upon.

Terry stood, sighing in frustration. "Your gut needs to lay off the true crime podcasts. We deal in evidence, remember?"

Mara ignored his remark, her focus laser-sharp on the gruesome tableau before them. "There's a pattern here, Terry. A message."

Terry gestured toward the scene with exaggerated casualness, his flippancy a thin veneer over growing unease. "Yeah, and it says 'PCP is one hell of a drug.'"

Mara stood abruptly, ripping off her gloves, frustration evident in every line of her body. "Mock me all you want, but when this blows up into something bigger, remember this moment."

She strode purposefully toward a group of homeless people, her determination palpable.

Terry lingered, conflicted, torn between his partner's conviction and his own desperate need to cling to the familiar. Mara paused, looking back over her shoulder. Her words cut through his indecision:

"You coming to interview witnesses or staying here to trade quips with our friend?"

As Terry hesitated, glancing back at the body, he swallowed hard. The weight of the moment, the potential enormity of what they'd stumbled upon, settled heavily upon him. With a barely perceptible nod, he followed Mara, stepping into the unknown.

Mara approached the group of homeless people huddled

around a barrel fire, the flames casting flickering shadows across their weathered faces. The fire's warmth was a stark contrast to the chill of dread that had settled in her stomach. Terry followed behind, his notebook clutched in hand like a talisman against the unknown.

"Folks, we need to talk about last night. Anyone see anything unusual?" Mara's voice cut through the crackle of the fire, sharp and authoritative.

From the huddle, a weathered woman stepped forward. Her eyes darted nervously between Mara and Terry as if weighing which detective might be more receptive to her tale. "Lights, Detective," she offered, her voice quivering. "Not normal ones. Like...the sky was having a seizure."

Terry stifled a laugh, the sound dying in his throat as Mara leaned in, her focus laser-sharp on the woman's words. "What kind of lights? What else did you see?" Mara pressed, her intensity drawing more of the group from their reticence.

A grizzled man pushed forward, his voice low and rough, as if the very act of speaking pained him. "Voices," he growled. "Not human. Like...the devil himself was gargling glass."

The absurdity of the statement was too much for Terry. He rolled his eyes, flipping his notebook shut with a sharp snap that echoed in the tense atmosphere. "Right, and you were completely sober when you heard Satan's greatest hits?"

The homeless man tensed, muscles coiling as he prepared to lunge at Terry. But Mara was faster, stepping between them, her voice a harsh whisper directed at her partner. "For Christ's sake, Terry!"

The confrontation had drawn the attention of a vagrant teen, his eyes wide with a fear that seemed to go beyond the immediate tension. He edged closer to Mara as if seeking protection. "They say the old cults never left," he murmured, his voice barely above a whisper. "Just went underground. Literal underground."

Terry, unable to contain himself, smirked and shook his

head. "What's next, kid? Bigfoot DJ'd the whole thing?"

His words were the spark that ignited the powder keg. The group surged forward, hands raised, a cacophony of shouts directed at Terry. The scene teetered on the edge of chaos.

Mara reacted instinctively, pushing Terry back and stepping in front of him. Her voice, honed by years on the force, cut through the noise like a blade. "HEY! We're here to help! But you've gotta give us something solid. One at a time!"

The crowd grumbled, a wave of discontent slowly receding as they backed down. Terry, finally sensing the gravity of his misstep, looked sheepish, carefully avoiding Mara's piercing glare. She leaned in close, her voice low and dangerous. "One more word, Terry, and I'll let them feed you to whatever demons they think they saw."

The barrel fire cast long shadows that seemed to dance with malevolent glee. As Mara turned back to the group, determination etched on her face, it was clear that this investigation had taken a turn into territory far darker and more treacherous than either detective had anticipated. The truth, it seemed, lurked in the shadows, whispering of horrors that defied rational explanation.

CHAPTER 3
MARKED BY EVIL

The morgue's fluorescent lights cast a cold glare over the scene. As Mara and Terry entered, the sharp scent of disinfectant mingled with the underlying odor of decay. Medical equipment cluttered every surface. Along one wall, crime scene photos hung on a dated chalkboard. In the center stood stainless steel autopsy tables, their surfaces reflecting the harsh light. The coroner, a seasoned veteran, stood next to one table, reaching for a scalpel as he acknowledged their presence. The atmosphere was heavy with dread and clinical detachment. Here, death was just another puzzle to solve.

The coroner, his pristine coat gleaming against the cold steel, beckoned them closer to the body. "Glad you both could make it. Let's get to it." He unveiled the white sheet covering the corpse. Terry's features contorted in disgust, but Mara leaned in, her eyes sparkling with unsettling fascination. The corpse's pallid skin seemed to glow under the harsh light.

The coroner gestured towards the savage lacerations on the victim's abdomen. "Observe the wounds across the abdomen." His gloved finger traced the intricate symbol etched into the skin. "These align with the obscure pagan symbols found at the crime scene."

Mara shot Terry an 'I told you so' look, her eyes blazing with vindication. Terry folded his arms tightly, returning her glare. The coroner, oblivious to their wordless battle, continued.

"But the real kicker? Tox screen showed heavy concentrations of Psilocybin in his system."

Terry frowned. "Psilocy-what now?"

"Hallucinogenic mushroom compounds." The coroner

handed Terry the toxicology report. "Enough to induce a delirious psychotropic state."

Mara's brow furrowed as she made the connection, a gasp escaping her lips as her hands clenched into fists. "Like... a mind-altering ritual sacrament?" The coroner nodded solemnly.

Terry scoffed, arms crossed. "Or some punk dealer's dosing his junkies with bad shit. No need to go putting more crazy ideas in my partner's head."

Mara's jaw tightened at his narrow-minded skepticism. The coroner sighed, his aged features impassive.

He took the report from Terry. "Believe what you want, Detective Jones. I'm just giving you the facts." His tone was weary. "I have reports to complete. I'll be at my desk if you have any further questions."

As the coroner's plodding steps faded into the distance, Mara's unwavering stare fixated on the lifeless form before her. Every grisly detail seared into her consciousness. She meticulously dissected the body, her sharp eyes scanning each inch with thoroughness and fascination. A palpable tension hung in the air, broken only by the monotonous buzzing of overhead lamps and the repulsive squelching beneath Mara's latex gloves as she probed the arcane markings.

"These symbols, the mushrooms...this was no random homicide."

Her companion stood rigidly behind her, arms folded and foot tapping, radiating pent-up irritation. "Come on, Mara. We gotta get back, file the report—"

"Someone did this intentionally, for some dark purpose," she continued, ignoring him. Her delicate fingertips lightly grazed the mysterious markings etched into the deceased man's chest. "You saw the crime scene...this was ritualistic."

With a pained expression, Terry watched as Mara's eyes sparkled with intense curiosity while she studied the lifeless corpse. He couldn't believe her determination to reach a final verdict so quickly. "Ritualistic? It was some junkie carved up by a dealer. Let's stick to the facts here."

Mara's emerald gaze narrowed, a flash of irritation dancing within them as she whirled to confront him. "The facts are telling me this was occult-related. You can't ignore the evidence — "

Terry threw out his hands in frustration. "There's not enough evidence to go off of." He rolled his eyes impatiently. "While you're making absurd hypotheses, we've got other cases piling up. We got a job to do."

Mara let out a contemptuous scoff, her eyes refusing to leave the inert form before her, drawn to it as if under a bewitching spell. "My instincts are telling me something sinister is happening here." Her voice was low and determined. "And I'm going to find out what."

As Mara's eyes traced the dead man's features, the corpse's eyes abruptly flicked open, opaque and sightless. The emptiness within them struck her with a wave of visceral dread, her skin prickling with an icy chill. She stumbled backward, gasping as her heart hammered against her ribs. The pungent stench of death enveloped her, threatening to overwhelm her senses.

She couldn't look away from the lifeless figure, his skin ashen and icy like cold marble. His skeletal fingers seemed to reach out, imploring for aid from beyond the veil. Her mind reeled with fear and disbelief as she struggled to comprehend the impossible scene unfolding before her.

Terry, completely unaware of her shock, impatiently glanced at his watch. Mara took a deep, calming breath, trying to steady her racing heart. The body lay still before them, its once-opened eyes now shut. But the haunting image was forever burned into her mind. Was it a mere figment of her imagination?

"Let's go — " her voice steadier than she felt " — we've got a killer to catch."

Shaking off the eerie encounter, she turned her back on the cold slab and the body that lay upon it. Taking a moment to collect herself, she brushed past a confused Terry, leaving the room without another word. The sterile smell of the morgue gave way to the neutral scent of the hallway as she made her way to the exit, her mind already racing with the implications of what she'd witnessed.

Mara exploded through the morgue's double doors, her mind a maelstrom of fractured theories and relentless doubts. The warm late morning air hit her face, a stark contrast to the sterile chill inside. She strode purposefully toward her car, keys jingling in her trembling hand.

Terry's urgent footsteps echoed behind her, and he slid into the passenger seat with a rush of displaced air before she could protest. Mara's fingers tightened on the steering wheel, her knuckles white with tension.

Terry inhaled deeply, his voice cautious. "Look, I know you wanna do right by the victim."

Mara whipped around to face him, her eyes blazing with an intensity that made Terry flinch. "Believe what you want, but I'm going to get to the bottom of this." Her voice was low and filled with conviction. "No matter what it takes."

Her promise lingered between them, heavy with unspoken implications. Mara's gaze returned to the road ahead, but the fire in her eyes remained undimmed. It burned with an intensity that bordered on obsession, a dangerous glint that revealed just how far she was willing to go.

She revved the engine. Despite the bright sun, shadows seemed to deepen around them as if drawn to Mara's determination. But Mara was unafraid, resolved to immerse herself in that darkness at any cost, even if it meant losing her sanity or her very soul.

The drive back to the station was silent, the tension between them palpable. As she parked, Mara glanced up at the towering structure, its windows reflecting the encroaching darkness like obsidian mirrors, beckoning her deeper into the mystery that lay ahead.

She stepped out of the car, her thoughts consumed by the case's grisly intricacies. Terry trailed in her wake like a lost soul as she strode towards the entrance.

Mara sat on the edge of her desk, fully absorbed in the macabre crime scene photos spread before her. The victim's gruesome remains churned her stomach, but the mysterious occult symbols etched into the flesh held her captive. Each intricate line and curve seemed to move before her, imprinting themselves in her mind with a malevolent force. The air around her grew heavy with dread, as if the sinister symbols still lingered, casting their dark influence. Yet Mara couldn't look away, muttering, "There's something here...some message. If I could just decipher it."

The dull scrape of shoes against linoleum signaled Terry's approach. As he leaned over to examine the photos, his brow furrowed, and his lips curved into a skeptical frown. He perused the images with a discerning gaze, searching for flaws or discrepancies. "I told you to let this go, Mara. We've got nothing to link this to any ritualistic cult."

Mara shook her head vehemently, swiping her hand dismissively. "You're not looking deep enough. There's more here than meets the eye."

Terry snatched his jacket from the back of his chair, his irritation evident in the forceful motion. He shrugged into the sleeves and thrust a finger at Mara, his voice biting. "Don't go tilting at windmills, Lawson. Stick to the evidence, or the Captain will have your badge."

Terry's footsteps receded. Mara's resolve strengthened as she returned to the photographs, her determination unwavering. "There's something here. I know it. I just have to keep looking," she muttered, her fingers tracing the edges of a particularly disturbing image.

Hours bled into night, leaving the station abandoned, devoured by encroaching shadows. Mara stood alone, a solitary beacon of light amidst the gloom. The photos, meticulously arranged in a sinister pattern, seemed to whisper forbidden knowledge. Fatigue clouded her mind, breeding insidious doubts that coiled through her thoughts.

"Is Terry right — am I losing my mind, chasing phantoms?" The question hung in the air, unanswered.

She shook her head, banishing the doubt. "No. Trust your instincts, Mara," she muttered. "Terry's wrong. There's more to this."

With renewed determination, she grasped the photo showcasing the ominous symbol carved deep into the victim's chest. The intricate lines seemed to twist and turn under her intense scrutiny. Suddenly, a startling realization dawned upon her.

"Wait a minute...I've seen this before." Her eyes widened as memories flooded back. This symbol had haunted her for years, since her days as a rookie cop investigating another murder. The victim's body had been grotesquely posed, arcane symbols carved into pallid flesh like a macabre canvas. While cynical investigators dismissed it as the work of a madman, Mara's intuition had whispered of darker forces at play.

Now, faced with the same sinister markings, that whisper grew to a roar. Something more was at work here — something she was determined to uncover, no matter the cost.

With obsessive fervor, Mara delved into the forbidden realm of occult symbols. Days blurred together as she immersed herself in ancient tomes, their musty pages whispering forgotten secrets. One volume captivated her, its pages teeming with esoteric images that mirrored the sinister markings etched upon the victim's body.

Mara eagerly presented her findings to the lead detective, convinced of a breakthrough. But he scoffed, accusing her of fabricating connections. Higher authorities swiftly closed the case, labeling it a solitary occurrence. Yet Mara sensed something more nefarious at play. That was fifteen years ago.

The familiar symbol awakened something primal within Mara, a dormant instinct roused after years of slumber. It was a sign from the mysterious forces that had guided her since childhood. She carefully stowed the haunting crime scene photos in her aged leather bag, determined to uncover the hidden truth. This refined city concealed a malevolent secret, and Mara vowed to expose it, letting nothing stand in her way as she sought retribution for the tormented victims.

Her hand trembled as she extracted a tattered tome from her bag, its title reading "Demonology and the Occult." The coarse leather cover seemed to pulse beneath her fingers. As she thumbed through the pages, they whispered sinister secrets. Her heart quickened until, finally, she found what she sought within the aged text.

The words pulsated with dark power, and Mara gasped, "The Mark of Mephistopheles?"

"What if I'm wrong?" she muttered, slamming the book shut. "Or worse...what if I'm right?" She drew a shuddering breath, anxiety gnawing at her resolve. "Please," she whispered to the empty room, "if there's anyone out there listening...please let me be wrong."

Mara reclined in her chair, her mind racing as she plotted her next move. The chilling truth she had unearthed only stoked the fires of her determination. With a steady hand, she collected the gruesome crime scene photos, each one a fragment of a macabre jigsaw puzzle. "Whatever you've unleashed here, I'll stop it. I'll find the truth. No matter what it takes."

She paused, her hand lingering on the worn leather cover of the tome before carefully sliding it back into her satchel. The soft glow of her laptop beckoned, promising answers and knowledge. Her fingers trembled as they hovered over the keyboard, hesitant to delve deeper into the darkness that awaited. But with a determined exhale, she began her research, relying on modern technology to uncover truths that even the ancient text couldn't reveal.

As the night dragged on, shadows engulfed the room. The pale light of Mara's laptop cast an otherworldly aura on her face as she leaned closer, fixated on the screen. A labyrinth of occult symbols and dark rituals unfurled before her, each click drawing her deeper into a realm of forbidden knowledge.

Arcane sigils and grotesque illustrations danced across the screen, each more disturbing than the last. Mara's brow furrowed, her mind reeling as she tried to process the deluge of occult information.

From the digital abyss, a name suddenly blazed across her screen: HUNTER ELDRITCH. The words "reclusive demonologist" and "expert on the occult" accompanied the name, piquing Mara's interest. Her heart quickened as she clicked the link, her eyes scanning Hunter's impressive credentials and published articles. Perhaps here, at last, lay the key to unlocking the sinister mystery that had consumed her.

Mara's eyes flickered with brief indecision, but her hesitation was fleeting. In the stillness of the near-empty station, the weight of her decision bore down on her. With a determined gleam in her eye, she grasped her phone with conviction.

Her hand trembled as she punched in the number from Hunter's website. Each ring stretched into eternity, tension mounting with every passing second. At last, the call connected, her heart racing. "Hello, is this Hunter Eldritch?" Mara's voice was steady, masking the anxiety churning within her.

She held her breath, absorbing the gravelly voice on the other end. Her face, inscrutable in the shadowy room, gave nothing away. "Yes, Detective Lawson," she nodded, her grip tightening on the phone. "I need your help."

With those words, Mara knew she had sealed her fate. The shadows in the precinct seemed to deepen, silent witnesses to her descent into the abyss of darkness she had chosen to embrace.

CHAPTER 4
WHISPERS OF THE DEVIL'S GREENHOUSE

Mara's footsteps echoed through the expansive, oak-lined hallway. She paused at the entrance to Hunter Eldritch's private library. As she pushed open the elaborate wrought iron door, a wave of rich scents enveloped her. The sharp tang of decaying pages mingled with the sweet aroma of melting wax, creating a hypnotic and almost intoxicating atmosphere.

Mara's eyes slowly acclimated to the dim light. Flickering candles scattered haphazardly around the room cast eerie shadows that danced and swayed. The walls were adorned with towering shelves, overflowing with ancient grimoires and mysterious artifacts. A sense of foreboding washed over her as she realized this was no ordinary library — it was a gateway into a world of dark magic and forbidden knowledge. Each shadowy recess seemed to harbor its own whispered mysteries.

She scanned the vast chamber, taking in the towering shelves laden with ancient tomes bound in supple leather. Mysterious glyphs adorned the walls, their intricate patterns appearing to writhe in the wavering glow of candlelight sconces. With each step, Mara felt herself descending deeper into a supernatural realm where anything could manifest at any moment.

As she ventured further into the chamber, a figure emerged from the inky darkness. It was Hunter Eldritch, a towering and slender man enveloped in opulent garments. Each piece was embellished with ancient symbols and runes, granting him an ethereal aura. But it was his kind smile and gentle gaze that soothed Mara's nerves, a stark contrast to the ominous setting surrounding them.

Hunter gestured towards a tattered velvet armchair. Its plush cushions seemed to beckon Mara. As she settled into the seat, she marveled at Hunter's movements. Every motion exuded a supernatural elegance, as if he were an ethereal being.

"Welcome to my humble abode, Detective Lawson," he said softly. "How may I assist you in your quest for truth?"

Mara's piercing gaze roamed restlessly, absorbing every detail from the ornate wall carvings to the enigmatic relics displayed throughout the room. She gracefully rose and took a cautious step forward as if afraid to disturb the room's ancient stillness. When her eyes finally met Hunter's, they were filled with wonder and fascination.

In that moment, she felt like an intrepid explorer stumbling upon a forgotten culture or a cunning detective unraveling a cryptic riddle from centuries past. "I've never seen anything like this before," she breathed. The room's atmosphere enveloped her, its secrets whispering tantalizing promises that begged to be unraveled.

A low, throaty laugh escaped from Hunter's mouth, the sound both alluring and unsettling. "It's a world seldom seen by mortal eyes," he explained, "a realm of hidden knowledge and forgotten truths. But fear not, for you have ventured here seeking answers, and answers you shall find."

Mara's eyes widened, both enamored and fearful of the ancient secrets before her. She was drawn to the decaying book on its elaborate stand, unable to resist its powerful allure. Her fingertips grazed the rough, aged leather. The intricate symbols seemed to pulse with centuries of untold stories. With each touch, she felt the weight of history seeping into her very being, a sensation both thrilling and terrifying.

As she stood entranced by the ancient tome, Hunter silently glided towards her. His ethereal aura seemed to transcend time itself, his voice a mere whisper laden with ancient wisdom. "That tome," he intoned solemnly, pointing at the book, "holds the story of an age long past — a tale of darkness and redemption forever intertwined. But be warned, Detective," his eyes glinted with hidden knowledge, "for the truths it reveals are not for the faint of heart. They may shake your very core and change everything you thought you knew."

Mara's pulse quickened at his words, a mix of anticipation and unease washing over her. Brushing away her lingering doubts, she deftly extracted a stack of crime scene photos from her bag. She arranged them carefully in front of Hunter on the table, observing as he leaned in with intense curiosity and an unmistakable trace of dread etched onto his face.

"These symbols were painted in blood at the latest crime scene," Mara explained, her voice steady despite the gruesome nature of the images. "We've never seen anything like it. Can you make any sense of them?"

Hunter's eyes widened, revealing his astonishment and bewilderment. He leaned in closer to the photographs, his gaze piercing and unwavering as he analyzed them. The candlelight caught his crystal blue eyes, revealing an unsettling, otherworldly glimmer. It was as if Mara could glimpse something ancient and malevolent lurking within their depths.

Hunter's hand glided over the mysterious symbols on the photographs. An air of solemnity descended upon the room. He wore a grave expression, one that betrayed his recognition of a profound truth. When he spoke, his hushed words carried intense emotion. "I wish I couldn't...but these are unmistakable." He paused, his eyes transfixed on the haunting symbols before him. The atmosphere thickened with ominous tension. "These symbols...they harbor dark intentions."

His face darkened as he pointed to a specific symbol, his voice dropping to a foreboding whisper. "This is more than just a mere design. It's a sigil, a calling card for something malevolent."

Mara edged closer, her eyes widening with morbid fascination as his chilling words sank in. "What does it mean? Is it connected to something...sinister?" Her heart pounded with anticipation, her mind racing with possibilities.

Hunter's intense stare bore into her, his face etched with the weight of his thoughts. "This symbol is tied to a forbidden ritual, a summoning of darkness that transcends mortal realms. We are standing on the precipice of something ancient and evil."

Mara hesitated before revealing the final image, fearing his response. The photo depicted a gruesome scene. The victim's chest bore a blood-red trident etched over a ring. Its three prongs eerily resembled the towering spires of Caina.

"I need to make a confession," Mara said, her voice barely above a whisper. "I've seen this symbol before." Hunter's eyes widened as she handed him the image. "When I was a rookie cop, we found another victim similar to this one. The department brushed it under the rug as a singular incident and closed the case." Mara took a deep breath. "That case has haunted me for fifteen years. The two victims share this same symbol carved over their hearts."

A dark frown marred Hunter's face as he studied the symbol. "This is rare indeed," he murmured.

"It's the Mark of Mephistopheles," Mara said. Her finger trembled as it traced the symbol in the picture. "I couldn't find much written about him. I was hoping you could help."

Hunter's troubled gaze met hers. "Mephistopheles embodies evil and temptation. Though absent from the Bible, I believe he's both real and deeply feared. Some say he was among the fallen angels cast from Heaven during Lucifer's rebellion. He's believed to be the Devil's messenger, tasked with luring souls to eternal damnation."

Hunter paused, his expression grim. "A crossroads demon, if you will, who preys on vanity and ambition, offering worldly power and pleasure in exchange for one's eternal soul. His symbol is rarely seen; allegiance to Mephistopheles is often a closely guarded secret."

Mara frowned, confusion etching her features. "A crossroads demon? Aren't they usually a threat to the desperate or greedy? But why sacrifice a body and carve this symbol into the chest? It doesn't add up."

Hunter let out a heavy sigh, his eyes darkening. "Little is known about this demon, shrouded as he is in secrecy. I fear he may be far more formidable than legends suggest."

Mara watched Hunter closely, troubled by his reaction. "Clearly, this group is after something far beyond a mere crossroads demon." Hunter nodded. "What exactly are they invoking? Do you know who we're dealing with?"

Hunter's response confirmed her fears. "Forces beyond most people's comprehension. An ancient cult...one that worships demonic entities. They call themselves The Devil's Greenhouse."

"Demons? Cults?" Mara's mind reeled, struggling to process the bewildering information. "I need more than myths to solve these murders. Something concrete. My partner Terry already thinks I'm crazy for going down this rabbit hole."

Hunter's intense gaze met Mara's, his eyes burning with determination. "I've devoted my life to studying these so-called myths. This cult is real. And if they are invoking Mephistopheles or other entities, I fear they are..." He trailed off, his expression grave.

The unfinished thought loomed over them, heavy with unspoken dread.

Mara's breath caught, her hand instinctively rising to her chest. "If they are...what? What happens then?"

Hunter's response was chilling in its simplicity. "Then may God have mercy on us all."

An air of unease settled between them. Mara and Hunter locked gazes, each feeling the weight of his words. Mara stood firm, her voice laden with determination. "Tell me everything you know about them."

Hunter grimly nodded, his slender fingers reaching for an ancient leather-bound tome. The cover groaned as Hunter opened it, brittle pages revealing long-forgotten secrets. Mara braced herself, anticipating the imminent revelation of the cult's sinister past and the true peril they now faced.

"These symbols are not mere coincidence," Hunter began. "They are the calling card of an insidious cult that has thrived in the shadows for centuries, devoted to summoning demonic entities."

Mara gnawed her lower lip, torn between dread and desperation. Anticipation hung thick in the air. "Continue..."

Hunter nodded gravely. "The cult's intentions are nefarious, their powers dark and formidable. We must act swiftly to prevent their next move."

Mara's expression shifted, a mix of unease and fascination. The detective within her craved explanations, but a primal instinct whispered of inexplicable dangers.

Hunter turned a page in the old journal. "They're on the brink of a catastrophic invocation — a ritual that could unleash unimaginable horrors upon this world." Mara's eyes widened, her mind racing to comprehend the gravity of the situation. "They seek to summon a malevolent demonic entity, a force of darkness beyond mortal comprehension."

Mara's sharp intake of breath echoed through the room as she grasped the full extent of the cult's plans. The room seemed to chill. Mara shook her head, struggling to accept the reality of the situation.

Hunter placed his warm hand over hers. "You must understand, Detective, the stakes couldn't be higher. If they succeed, the consequences for humanity will be dire." He paused, allowing his words to sink in. "We are racing against time, and failure is not an option. We must stop them before it's too late."

Mara's discomfort intensified, the gravity of the situation weighing heavily on her. "If what you say is true...we're facing a threat beyond anything I've encountered before."

Hunter met Mara's eyes, a silent acknowledgment of the impending threat passing between them. In that moment, the air seemed thick with shared responsibility and unspoken dread.

Hunter released her hand and stood, pacing the room with restless energy. His gaze swept over the shadowed chamber, his mind clearly racing with possibilities.

Mara watched him, her heart pounding. She took a deep breath, steeling herself. "Alright," she said, determination replacing fear in her voice. "What's our first move?"

Hunter ran a hand through his unruly hair. "I have more research to do. I wasn't prepared for what you've shown me tonight."

Mara grabbed her bag and the crime scene photos. "I'll leave you to it." She handed him her card. "I'll go back to my apartment and do the same. If you're even partially right, it'll take both of us to stop this. Call me if you find anything."

Hunter nodded, returning the photo they had been examining. "I'll contact you as soon as I have more information, Detective."

"Mara," she corrected, tucking the photo away. "Call me Mara. It looks like we'll be working closely together on this."

Hunter inclined his head. "Very well, Mara, it is. I'm sure we'll be speaking again soon."

Mara slipped on her jacket and headed out to her apartment. Despite the late hour, she knew sleep would elude her. Thankfully, it was Friday night, and she didn't have to worry about an early return to the precinct.

The heavy door creaked shut behind Mara as she stepped into the cold night air. She slid into her sleek black car, starting the engine as her mind raced. City lights blurred past as she drove, her mind in turmoil.

By the time she unlocked her apartment door, she had replayed their conversation at least a dozen times. She didn't want to believe it. Part of her longed for her mundane routine, where she was just a cop out to catch the bad guys. Now, the world around her seemed transformed into something more sinister and foreboding.

The implications of a larger conflict between good and evil weighed heavily on her mind. Could she handle this responsibility? Did she have any real choice in the matter? If

Hunter's words were true — and she hoped they weren't — they could be facing an unprecedented catastrophe.

She sat at her desk and powered up her laptop, the apartment's shadows seeming more ominous than usual. The dim light from her desk lamp cast strange patterns across her face, highlighting her furrowed brow. Hunter's revelations threatened to shatter the foundations of her rational skepticism, leaving her grappling with a new, unsettling reality.

Vivid images flashed through Mara's mind: Hunter's library, the crime scene, the mysterious symbols. His grave warnings echoed in her ears, accompanied by glimpses of the eerie artifacts from his study. The crime scene symbols danced before her eyes, their meanings tantalizingly out of reach.

Her hand hovered over the photos, fingers tense. Mara struggled to reconcile her logical training with the supernatural implications of the case. Her internal voice wavered with uncertainty:

"Am I ready to accept the supernatural? Or am I losing my grip on reason by entertaining these impossible notions?"

The room felt smaller, mirroring the pressure of her impending decision. Mara's gaze fixed upon the occult symbols, her expression a mix of fascination and unease. The air seemed to thicken as if reality itself awaited her next move.

With each passing moment, the line between rationality and the unknown blurred further. Mara felt poised on the edge of a vast, unfathomable abyss. The symbols on the page seemed to blur, their strange forms captivating her attention and challenging her understanding of reality.

Taking a deep, steadying breath, Mara steeled herself against the onslaught of doubt and fear. Her expression hardened with newfound resolve. In that moment, she made her choice, ready to plunge into the darkness that awaited her.

With a swift, decisive motion, she grasped the photos. The symbols seemed to pulse under her touch, their cryptic allure drawing her in. After a final glance at her once-familiar surroundings, she packed up her materials and left for the police station. The weekend would ensure an empty department, giving her ample time to work undisturbed.

Mara's desk groaned under the weight of her obsession. Stacks of yellowed newspaper clippings teetered precariously. Dusty tomes on demonology lay open, their arcane symbols seeming to shift in the flickering fluorescent light. Hunched over her cluttered workspace, the detective scanned the pages of an ancient book with intense focus. The rhythmic sound of turning pages filled the stale air, keeping time with Mara's growing unease.

Her brow furrowed as she absorbed the cryptic knowledge. Each symbol and ritual description sent a shiver through her, but she couldn't look away. The weight of her investigation pressed down on her, heavier than the mountain of papers surrounding her.

As the sun sank lower, Mara sought refuge in the dimly lit public library. The expansive table before her disappeared under ancient books and manuscripts. Her hand moved quickly, pen flying across parchment as she pieced together fragments of knowledge. In the library's silence, only the soft turning of pages and the scratch of her pen could be heard.

As night fell, Mara hunched over a dusty computer in a secluded corner of the library. The monitor's glow illuminated her tired face as she researched the occult. Her fingers flew across the keys, revealing sinister sigils, sacrificial rites, and grisly historical accounts. Each discovery added to the puzzle, revealing a disturbing pattern of cult activity.

Back at the station, Mara's desk had become an island in a sea of paper. She stood before it, eyes darting from file to file, connecting invisible threads between past cult activities and recent murders. The desk lamp cast shifting shadows across her face, accentuating her dark-ringed eyes and grim expression. As the pieces fell into place, a cold dread settled in her stomach.

As the night deepened, Mara delved into the newspaper

archives, uncovering long-buried stories. The whir of the microfilm machine pierced the silence, its drone contrasting with her quickening pulse. Article after article flashed before her — bizarre occurrences, unexplained disappearances, and whispered rumors of the impossible. Her face cycled through shock, disgust, and finally, grim determination as hidden truths emerged.

Exhausted, Mara returned to her apartment, needing time to process her findings. Suddenly, her eyes widened in realization. The final piece of the puzzle clicked into place, revealing the full, terrifying picture. With renewed purpose, she approached the large corkboard next to her computer desk, pen in hand. She worked feverishly, pinning articles and connecting them with red string, creating a web of malevolence spanning years.

Stepping back to survey her work, the weight of her discovery settled on her. The cult's influence reached further and deeper than she had imagined, and she knew with chilling certainty that this was only the beginning.

CHAPTER 5
DESCENT INTO DARKNESS

Mara stretched languidly, arms reaching skyward, a long-drawn yawn escaping her lips. Her fingertips brushed against the stacks of paperwork littering her desk. Friday's pre-dawn body discovery had robbed her of much-needed rest, and fatigue now weighed heavily upon her. Terry's towering frame loomed over her, his presence radiating unspoken menace. A palpable tension hung between them, both ready to strike at any moment.

As Mara pored over the case files, she felt the weight of Terry's disapproving stare. She felt compelled to meet his gaze, and as their eyes locked, his demeanor shifted palpably. Gone was the usual warmth and kindness that emanated from him, replaced instead by a chilling sense of doubt.

Terry crossed his arms tightly, his eyes meeting hers with a chilly, unyielding stare of steel. "Mara, we need to talk. Your focus on this cult obsession is leading us down dead ends. We should investigate the victim's criminal ties, not chase phantoms."

Mara's fingers clenched, her body tensing as Terry's words hung heavy in the air. She locked eyes with him, her gaze unflinching, refusing to back down under his accusatory expression. "These so-called 'shadows' are not dead ends, Terry. They're threads in a tapestry of darkness we cannot ignore. The evidence points us in that direction."

Terry's brow furrowed as he shook his head in disbelief. He gestured towards Mara's desk, where an organized chaos of papers covered in strange symbols and grainy photographs of blood-soaked crime scenes lay strewn about. The scene resembled a hauntingly beautiful exhibit of the macabre. "You're diving into this occult nonsense while real leads slip through our fingers. We need concrete facts, not fantasies, to solve this case."

Terry's words cut deep, but Mara's resolve hardened. She rose, her spirit unyielding, a fiery confidence blazing within her. The forces she investigated seemed to rally beside her, urging her to stand her ground and defend her beliefs. "This is not fantasy, Terry. This is a pattern, a connection that goes beyond mere criminal ties. These symbols, these rituals — they hold significance. We can't overlook them."

Terry's mouth twisted into a scowl, betraying a mix of worry and irritation. He exhaled heavily, raking his fingers through his disheveled locks, frustration consuming him. "Mara, I get it. But we need to approach this practically. The department demands solid proof, not wild theories. You're risking your credibility by veering off course like this."

Mara's face hardened, fierce determination radiating from her gaze as she squared her shoulders. The stakes towered beyond Terry's comprehension. Their very existence hung on her resolve. But she dared not reveal the truth to him yet; his jaded mind would struggle to fathom the true danger without tangible evidence. "I'll follow every lead, Terry. Even if it means venturing into uncharted territory. I trust my instincts and won't ignore what's right in front of us."

Mara's voice resonated with unwavering certainty. Terry appeared doubtful, always the logical one. But this was not a moment for wavering. Her conviction and devotion to their mission intensified. Uncertainty flickered in his gaze, and she knew she must persuade him of their path to triumph. "I know you've always followed procedure, Terry. You trust in the system, in the rules. And that has served you well," Mara continued, her voice softening as she appealed to his sensibilities. "But sometimes, facing the darkness means coloring outside the lines. I'm not asking you to abandon logic or protocol. I'm asking you to open your mind to possibilities beyond the ordinary because ordinary measures won't suffice."

Terry studied Mara's face, taking in the set of her jaw

and the fierce glint in her eyes. She had always possessed a keen intuition, a wild soul that rebelled against his rigid nature. Their constant clash made them both alluring and formidable. Yet, despite this, he hesitated. "What if you're wrong, Mara? What if this is just a distraction from the truth?"

Mara stepped closer, placing a hand on his arm. Her touch was gentle yet electrifying. "I'm willing to take that risk if it means stopping evil from spreading. But I can't do this alone, Terry. I need my partner, the one person I trust to have my back no matter what."

Mara's voice cracked slightly as she finished pleading, but she refused to back down. She met Terry's gaze head-on, silently willing him to understand the gravity of their situation. This was about more than just solving a case or upholding the law; it was about plumbing the depths of human depravity and the supernatural forces that lurked in the shadows. Mara knew all too well what they were up against, and she needed her partner's support now more than ever.

Terry looked away for a moment, his jaw clenched as he wrestled with his doubts. Though his rational mind railed against it, he couldn't deny his unshakable trust in Mara. They'd been through too much together, and he knew she wouldn't ask this of him lightly. Sighing heavily, he finally looked back at her and nodded once, an unspoken agreement passing between them. "All right, Mara," he said reluctantly. "I'll follow your lead...for now." His eyes narrowed with an afterthought. "But if there's no hard evidence tying these rituals or cults to our case after a week, we go back to basics, agreed?"

A grin of relief and gratitude spread across Mara's face. "Agreed, and thanks, Terry."

With a final, determined glance at her partner, Mara grabbed her coat and strode out of the office. The crisp late afternoon air nipped at her skin as she navigated the city streets, symbols and rituals swirling in her mind. Rounding a corner, the faint glow of candlelight caught her attention. She had arrived at her destination.

The small bell above the door tinkled as Mara entered the Occult Bookshop. Heavy black curtains covered the windows, blocking out the daylight and casting the shop in a mysterious dimness. Shelves upon shelves of dusty tomes lined the walls, their spines illuminated by flickering candlelight. The air was thick with the scent of musty pages and pungent incense, making it feel as though she had stepped into another world.

Mara's eager gaze swept across the shelves, entranced by the eclectic collection of relics. Ancient spell books bound in black, supple skin caught her eye, seeming to radiate with mysterious energy. Ethereally glowing stones beckoned to her, their otherworldly light captivating. Jars filled with enigmatic concoctions lined the shelves, their contents defying all logic and fueling Mara's insatiable curiosity. She felt herself being pulled deeper into this surreal and enchanted realm before her.

Mara's senses heightened as she ventured deeper into the shop, her skin prickling with foreboding. The walls loomed ominously, their ancient symbols carved into the very essence of the building, thrumming with an otherworldly energy. With every step, trepidation and intrigue enveloped her. She trod carefully, watching the symbols with wary eyes as they tracked her every move. The shop itself seemed a living, breathing entity — one that held secrets and knowledge far beyond her mortal comprehension.

A figure materialized from the shadows. The bizarre bookshop owner fixed Mara with a penetrating gaze, delving into the very essence of her being. A knowing smile played across their lips as they spoke. "Welcome, seeker of truths. What draws you to this realm of secrets?"

The cryptic voice unnerved her, but she steeled her resolve. This was why she had come. She needed answers. She approached, eyes gleaming with intrigue and determination. "I seek knowledge," Mara said softly. "Knowledge of the shadows lurking in our city. Knowledge about a cult that treads the line between myth and reality."

The owner's smile widened, recognition sparking in their eyes. "We all seek truths, Detective Mara Lawson. But beware, some truths shatter mortal minds."

Mara's breath caught in her throat. How did the shopkeeper know her identity? Another perplexing detail in a case defying rational explanation. Her hand trembled slightly as she retrieved a photograph from her coat pocket. It was carefully selected, shielding others from the crime scene's gruesome reality. Mara delicately traced the symbol etched into the victim's skin. She held out the photo, gesturing towards the intricate markings. Leaning in close, she whispered, "Tell me about the cult responsible for this. Their rituals. Their intentions. What lies behind the symbols carved into the victims' flesh?"

"Let me see what I can find for you." The owner's gnarled fingers skimmed the spines of ancient tomes, caressing each one as if greeting an old friend. "The cult...they dance with forces beyond our understanding. Their practices date back to eras long forgotten. To know them is to embrace the abyss."

With an almost theatrical flourish, the owner produced a grimoire. The book's presence seemed to devour the shop's meager light. Bound in unearthly leather, its cover was adorned with sigils that hurt Mara's eyes to look upon directly. Her breath caught in her throat as she accepted the tome. It weighed impossibly heavy in her hands, as if it contained more than just paper and ink. With trembling fingers, she opened it.

Each page unveiled nightmares that surpassed Mara's darkest imaginings. Twisted beliefs scrawled in known and unknowable languages leapt from the pages. Rituals that defied the laws of nature and sanity sprawled across the parchment. In the shadows lurked a sense of something monstrous and unfathomable that the cult was hellbent on unleashing upon the unsuspecting world.

The owner bowed slightly, their voice reverent. "May this tome guide you on the path you walk, Detective. But remember, once you venture into the shadows, they never truly let you go."

Mara's fingers clenched tightly around the grimoire, its malevolent energy seeping into her being. The ancient book pressed against her chest, heavy with powerful secrets. Dread and determination surged through her veins, urging her forward in her quest. This was it. The key to unraveling the mystery that had consumed her for so long. Whispers and murmurs seemed to emanate from the pages, enticing her to unlock its secrets and embrace the darkness within. But she would not falter. This was her destiny, immovable and inexorable. "Thank you. I will."

As Mara turned to leave, the symbols on the walls writhed and danced in her peripheral vision. She knew, with a certainty that chilled her to her core, that she was stepping across an invisible threshold. And whatever awaited her on the other side would change her forever.

With a final nod to the shop owner, Mara paid for the book, tucked the grimoire under her arm, and stepped out into the late afternoon. The city's cacophony jarred her after the shop's quiet. She walked back towards the police station, her mind racing with visions of arcane revelations. Clutching the book tighter, Mara strode through the flashing city lights, the grimoire a dark beacon guiding her pursuit of truth.

Mara stood in the dimly lit police archives room, surrounded by towering stacks of dusty files. The sickly yellow glow from the overhead lights barely illuminated the space as her nimble fingers sifted through the cold case folders. The musty scent of old paper and forgotten secrets hung heavy in the air.

As she scanned the labels on each file, one in particular leapt out at her: "Cold Case — Ritualistic Killings." With trembling hands, Mara yanked the folder from its resting place, her heart racing as she began to rifle through its pages. Each sheet unveiled a nightmare of unsolved murders, the victims' bodies defiled with occult symbols meticulously carved into their cold flesh. Mara's eyes widened as she absorbed every horrific detail, a mix of revulsion and morbid fascination washing over her.

The grisly images seared themselves into her mind, fueling a determination to unravel the twisted mystery that lay before her.

As she delved deeper, eerie similarities emerged between the cases. Arcane symbols, strange fungi, and herbs were present at each crime scene, like a malevolent force's breadcrumb trail. The dark puzzle pieces snapped into place with sickening clarity.

Crime scene images assaulted her mind's eye unbidden. Each photograph opened a window into a world of dark rituals, visually chronicling atrocities committed for unspeakable evil. The cult's long history of terror unfolded before her, each image more haunting than the last.

Mara's lips parted, her voice barely a whisper in the oppressive silence of the archives. "It's all connected," she breathed, "a trail of darkness leading back through time." The words hung heavily in the air, laden with ominous implications. Her gaze remained fixed on the horrific evidence before her, reflecting a potent mixture of dread and determination. With chilling certainty, Mara knew she had stumbled upon something far more sinister than she could have ever imagined. Despite the shroud of darkness that seemed to envelop her, Mara steeled herself to follow the path ahead, resolute in her pursuit of the truth, no matter where it might lead her.

CHAPTER 6
THE OCCULTIST'S INFERNAL BARGAIN

Savannah, Georgia 1856

The humid summer air hung heavy over Savannah's cobblestone streets, lending an oppressive weight to the lingering shadows. Though the sun had set hours ago, a faint orange glow still clung to the horizon as if reluctant to relinquish its grasp on the old city. The gas lamps did little to pierce the gloom, their flickering flames seeming to taunt the darkness rather than conquer it.

On the edges of Forsyth Park, the moss-draped oaks swayed gently, their limbs creaking with menace. The wispy Spanish moss undulated like ghostly tendrils in the faint breeze, reaching out as if to ensnare any poor soul wandering the deserted lanes. Somewhere in the distance, the lonesome cry of a marsh bird echoed through the stillness.

Savannah's stately mansions and townhomes stood sentinel, their white columns and intricate ironwork balconies now taking on an air of decay. Peeling paint, cracked windowpanes, and rusting gates hinted at the slow erosion of time. An ominous energy charged the night air as if the old city's dark past still lurked in its shadows.

Here and there, orange candlelight glowed from behind shuttered windows. But few dared to walk the streets past nightfall when Savannah relinquished itself to far older forces. Something sinister stirred in the swampy wilderness beyond the city's edge, an unseen presence that had haunted this land long before the first European settlers arrived.

Balor Payne's occult study was a realm of flickering shadows and arcane mystery. The dim candlelight danced across walls lined with ancient tomes, their leather bindings cracked and worn from years of use. Strange symbols and sigils adorned every surface, glowing with otherworldly energy that seemed to pulse with a life of its own. An oil lamp, its wick burning low, sat on the old ornate desk next to Balor's stacks of research. Hunched over a weathered grimoire, the intense and driven occult practitioner, now in his sixties, traced gnarled fingers across the cryptic text with an air of deep concentration and determination. The musty smell of ancient knowledge filled the air, mingling with the faint scent of brimstone and incense.

"The secrets of eternity...the whispers of the dark..." Balor's voice was barely a whisper, his eyes alight with fervent obsession.

With a trembling hand, Balor reached for a nearby parchment and began etching eldritch sigils with feverish precision. The sharp tip of his quill scratched against the aged paper, leaving behind intricate symbols that seemed to pulse with an ethereal energy. Each stroke drew him deeper into a realm of forbidden knowledge, luring him with promises of untold power and secrets beyond mortal understanding. As he continued to write, his breath caught in his throat, a sudden revelation unfurling before him like a dark and dangerous flower. Deciphering the hidden meaning within the arcane text filled Balor with equal parts awe and trepidation. He knew that following this path would lead him down a road of darkness and destruction, yet the allure of its power was impossible to resist, drawing him ever closer to its embrace.

"At last...the key to unlocking the veil between worlds," he exclaimed, exultation dripping from every syllable. Up until now, he had only heard dark rumors about the existence of this ritual. Now, it was finally within his grasp.

As the moon rose higher in the sky, Balor lit black candles and arranged them in a precise circle. His hands trembled with excitement and fear as he placed a human heart, still warm and dripping, at the center of the ritual space. He carefully traced ancient symbols in blood on the ground and positioned severed animal heads around the edges. This was no ordinary ceremony — this would change his fate forever. Balor had never felt more alive as he prepared for the ritual that would determine his ultimate destiny.

Standing tall and solid, Balor rooted his feet into the ground as if drawing strength from the earth itself. With a commanding presence, he lifted his arms towards the sky in a grand gesture of invocation. His deep voice reverberated off the walls of his dark chamber, filling the space with a sense of power and mystique. "Mephistopheles," he called out with unwavering reverence, his words seeming to carry weight beyond their physical form. "Hear my call."

A whisper of wind stirred the pages of the ancient tome as if in response to his summons. Undeterred, Balor continued, his voice growing stronger. "The veil shall part. Mephistopheles, hear my call."

Tendrils of fear coiled around his heart as he grasped the ritual dagger, its blade glinting with malice in the dim, flickering candlelight. With each ceremony, Balor's descent into darkness and madness grew more pronounced, consuming him whole. The once noble rituals had twisted into something cruel and macabre, pushing the boundaries of what was considered sane and moral. Each step took him further down the path of his own destruction until, finally, he found himself at the bottom of a deep, inky abyss, lost to the darkness that now consumed him. The air was thick with the stench of decay and corruption, a fitting atmosphere for the depravity unfolding before him.

As the ritual reached its zenith, unearthly whispers filled the air. Shadows seemed to flicker and dance around Balor, their movements unnatural and deeply unsettling. The sense of impending dread was palpable, thick enough to choke on.

Balor's eyes blazed with determination as he stood in the center of a dimly lit circle. "Mephistopheles, I summon thee!" Balor's voice rose to a fever pitch. "Grant me the power I seek!"

The candles around him flickered as a sinister breeze blew through the room, and Balor could feel an otherworldly presence growing stronger with each passing second.

In that spine-chilling moment, reality itself seemed to warp and twist. An ominous gateway materialized before Balor, its dark energies coalescing into a form that defied mortal comprehension. The manifestation of Mephistopheles filled the chamber — a towering, malevolent presence wreathed in living shadows. His eyes, twin infernos of unholy fire, locked onto Balor with an intensity that froze the blood in his veins.

Mephistopheles, with fiery red skin and horns protruding from his forehead, towered over Balor. His voice echoed through the dark chamber, sending a chill down Balor's spine. "Balor Payne, mortal seeker of forbidden truths," Mephistopheles intoned, his voice a symphony of damnation. "Your summons has been heard. What do you offer in exchange for the knowledge and power you seek?"

The light in Balor's eyes turned from wonder to a sinister glint, and his lips curved into a predator's smile. He leaned in close to the altar, his fingers twitching with anticipation as he prepared to speak the forbidden words that would seal his eternal fate. "Tonight, I offer my soul to the abyss. Tonight, I bind myself to the darkness eternal."

Balor's hands trembled uncontrollably as he raised the ceremonial dagger, its blade glinting with an ethereal luminescence in the dim light of the summoning chamber. His unwavering gaze locked onto Mephistopheles, a look of solemn determination etched deeply into his features. A tempest of dark energy swirled around him, crackling with an unholy power that threatened to consume his very being. The chamber walls shuddered and groaned as if alive while shadows coalesced into spectral forms, their eerie whispers carrying ancient secrets in forgotten tongues. The air grew heavy with anticipation, each passing moment drawing Balor closer to the precipice of a fate from which there would be no return.

Triumph blazed in Balor's eyes as he spoke his final vow. "I pledge myself to you, Mephistopheles. Grant me the power I seek, and in return, I offer my eternal servitude."

Mephistopheles towered over Balor Payne, his deep crimson eyes piercing into his soul. "Your offering has been accepted," he announced with a sinister grin. "From this moment on, your fate is sealed. Your soul belongs to me for all eternity."

With a swift, decisive motion, Balor raised the silver dagger and pressed the sharp tip against his chest. He closed his eyes and took a deep breath, steeling himself for what was to come. As he plunged the blade into his own flesh, a ribbon of crimson bloomed, marking the final step in his descent into darkness. The chamber trembled with unseen forces as the pact was sealed in blood, binding him to the dark entity that had promised power and vengeance.

Mephistopheles, a figure with burning eyes, extended a hand towards Balor. The occultist, now marked by a newfound aura of malevolent power, bowed before his dark benefactor. As he did so, a miraculous and terrifying transformation took place. The years melted away from Balor's form, leaving him a man in his prime — no older than his thirties.

A chilling smile spread across Balor's newly youthful face. "I am reborn in darkness, immortal and indomitable."

The price had been paid. The bargain was struck. And in that moment, a new chapter of horror was written into the annals of history.

Balor rose from his kneeling position, regarding the demon Mephistopheles with newfound reverence. He could feel the dark energy coursing through his veins, granting him renewed vitality and sinister purpose. The ritual had worked — his pact was sealed. Now, the real work could begin.

Balor's eyes widened as the energy surged through his body, causing a tingling sensation in his fingertips. "I can feel it," Balor murmured. "This power, it's beyond anything I could have imagined."

Mephistopheles towered over the mortal, his dark figure casting eerie shadows in the dimly lit room. He nodded once, and wisps of shadow seemed to curl from his body. "Our bargain is struck," he intoned, his voice deep and menacing. "You have my protection and patronage. But beware, use your new gifts wisely."

Balor's eyes glinted with a dangerous excitement as he sat in his dimly lit office, surrounded by maps and charts of the city. The possibilities seemed endless now that Mephistopheles had become his benefactor. With the demon's support, his cult could finally gain the power and control they had been seeking for so long. Balor reveled in the thought of the authorities, who had always interfered with their plans, being rendered powerless against them. A wicked grin spread across his face as he realized that the time had finally come for their reign of terror to truly begin. The city would soon tremble before their might, and nothing would stand in their way.

Balor stood tall and proud, his voice carrying across the room with unwavering confidence. "I will not fail you," he said. "This city will kneel before our power. I will see Savannah reborn in the image of true darkness."

"See that you honor our arrangement," Mephistopheles rumbled. Already, the demon's form was dissipating, the summoning at an end. "Provide the promised sacrifices, and you shall keep what I have given."

"It shall be done," Balor vowed. The demonic presence faded back through the gateway between worlds, leaving Balor alone in the ritual chamber. He glanced down at the dagger still buried in his chest, the wound already sealing itself with preternatural swiftness.

As the ominous portal closed, leaving only flickering candles and dissipating shadows as witnesses to the infernal bargain just struck, Balor felt a sudden wave of unease wash over him. The weight of his actions began to settle in, but it was quickly replaced by an intoxicating rush of power and an insatiable hunger for more. His newfound immortality and dark gifts would enable him to achieve feats he had only dared to dream of before. The possibilities stretched out before him like an endless, twisted path, beckoning him to explore the depths of his own potential. With a wicked smile playing across his lips, Balor embraced the darkness that now flowed through his veins, ready to unleash his newfound power upon the unsuspecting world.

Rising to his feet, Balor surveyed the chamber with renewed purpose. The bloodstained altar, the discarded parchments bearing ancient sigils, and the dagger that had sealed his pact with Mephistopheles all bore testament to the gravity of his choice. His transformation was complete; he was reborn as an agent of the underworld, destined to walk between the realms of men and monsters.

"The price has been paid," Balor muttered, a dark smile curling his lips. "Now the games begin."

With newfound energy coursing through his veins, Balor set about fulfilling his half of the bargain. He knew the stakes all too well: should he fail to provide the souls Mephistopheles demanded, his own would be forfeit. The thought spurred him on, propelling him into action.

Balor strode through the darkened streets of Savannah, the night cloaking him. Though the district was usually bustling with visitors and revelers even at this late hour, an unnatural stillness had settled over the city. Balor's very presence seemed to leech the life and spirit from his surroundings.

He made his way towards Wright Square, the public park that was the site of the gallows where convicted witches were put to death. Now, it would serve again as an altar upon which sacrifices could be offered to Mephistopheles.

Balor had already sent word to his followers, instructing them to bring an offering — someone who would not be missed. As he entered the square, the darkness seemed to coalesce around him. He could feel Mephistopheles' presence, the demon watching, waiting to see if his new acolyte would prove worthy of the power he had been granted.

One by one, robed figures emerged from the shadows. The cultists encircled their leader, clutching the bound and gagged sacrifices they had procured. Mephistopheles' rasping voice echoed in Balor's mind.

"Here is your chance to prove yourself, mortal. Carry out the ritual I taught you. Offer these souls up to me."

Balor smiled cruelly. It was time to embrace his destiny.

***

Savannah, Georgia, present day.

The torches flickered, casting writhing shadows across the walls of the gathering place. Darkness clung to every corner as if it were a living, breathing entity. In the center of this ominous space stood Balor Payne, his black hooded robe melding with the surrounding gloom. The essence of youth still graced his features, thanks to a deal struck nearly two centuries ago. His piercing gaze swept over the assembled cultists, their faces a conflicted canvas of reverence and barely concealed terror.

As Balor stepped onto the stage, the crowd instinctively gravitated towards him, their eyes drawn to his presence like moths to a flickering flame. When he began to speak, his voice seemed to emanate from all directions at once, echoing with an otherworldly power that left his audience entranced. The very shadows appeared to shift and swirl around him, enhancing his enigmatic aura and commanding the attention of all who witnessed his performance. "My faithful," he declared, his words dripping with promise and temptation, "behold the dawn of our new reign. Our allegiance to the shadows shall be rewarded beyond measure." The air crackled with anticipation as Balor's followers hung on his every word, their hearts filled with a fervent desire to follow him into the depths of darkness.

A hushed murmur rippled through the crowd, a blend of awe and trepidation. Despite their fear, their loyalty remained unshakable, their eyes fixed upon their dark messiah.

Balor's lips curled into a sinister smile as he continued, "Tonight, we sow the seeds of our devotion, nurturing the darkness that dwells within each of us. The time approaches for our grand design to come to fruition." He paused, allowing the weight of his words to settle over the assembly. The air grew thick with anticipation, the very atmosphere pulsing with a malevolent energy that seemed to emanate from Balor himself. His voice dropped to a whisper, yet it carried across the room with alarming clarity. "Embrace the shadows, my disciples, for they shall guide our path to glory. Together, we shall unleash untold darkness upon the mortal realm, and none shall stand in our way."

The cultists nodded fervently, their eyes gleaming with a disconcerting mixture of fear and fanatical devotion. The flickering torchlight danced across their faces, transforming their features into grotesque masks of shifting shadows and eerie, unnatural light. In that moment, it seemed as if the darkness itself had taken on a physical form, poised to spill forth from their unholy sanctuary and engulf the unsuspecting world beyond. The cultists reveled in the promise of power and chaos, their hearts consumed by the allure of the shadows that now bound them together in unholy communion.

CHAPTER 7
REBORN IN FLAMES

The vinyl floor tiles were cracked and peeling, revealing decades of dirt and grime. The lingering odor of fried food clung to every surface in the small diner. Lilith slouched against the chipped countertop, her red mien of tangled hair falling over her tired face. Her eyes, once filled with hope, now held no spark. The noisy hustle and bustle of the diner only added to the weight of her thoughts as she sunk deeper into despair.

Lilith's gaze shifted from her menu to the looming figure above her. The waitress stood tall, hands on hips and a frown etched across her face. Lilith could feel the disapproval radiating from her.

"You're maxed out, honey. Gonna need cash."

Lilith's heart raced as she frantically dug through her purse, scattering its contents on the table. Her trembling fingers brushed past crumpled receipts and old tissues until they finally found a few coins at the bottom, accompanied by lint-covered mints. The waitress's eyes narrowed in annoyance as Lilith's panic continued to rise. Her fingers trembled as she carefully counted out the small pile of coins on the counter. She sighed, her heart dropping with each one. Her eyes scanned the sparse shelves, looking for anything she could afford with her meager savings. But it was never enough. Never enough to ease the gnawing hunger in her stomach.

The waitress leaned in close, her breath hot on Lilith's cheek. "Either pay up, or I call the cops."

Lilith's face burned with shame, her cheeks turning a deep shade of red. She couldn't bring herself to meet anyone's gaze in the crowded diner. Hurriedly, she pushed herself off the stool and shuffled towards the door, head down. The tinkling of the bell above the door rang loudly in her ears as she stepped out into the frigid, inhospitable night. The darkness seemed to swallow her up as she left the warmth and light of the diner behind.

The bustling street overwhelmed her senses — the stench of rotting garbage and the harsh glare of neon signs lining every storefront. Homeless figures huddled in doorways, their wary eyes tracking her as she briskly moved through the crowds. A drug dealer leaned casually against a graffiti-covered wall, surrounded by scantily-clad girls who clung to his every word, seeming lost and searching for direction. The scene was chaotic and unsettling, making her feel as though she had entered a different world entirely.

Lilith's feet carried her to a dilapidated apartment building, its façade crumbling like her dreams. She climbed the creaking stairs, each step an effort.

The door to her studio apartment groaned open, revealing a tableau of squalor. Empty liquor bottles littered the floor, glinting dully in the dim light. Lilith's gaze was drawn to the dresser drawer, and she knew what lay hidden within – a junkie's treasure trove of needles and spoons.

Only one spot of brightness pierced the gloom: a framed photograph on the nightstand. A smiling couple gazed out from behind the dusty glass, their joy a stark contrast to the misery surrounding it.

Lilith collapsed onto the bare mattress, curling into herself as if to shield against the world's cruelty. Her eyes fixed on the water-stained ceiling above. "Please..." she whispered, her voice cracking. "Someone help me."

A sudden, inexplicable sense of unease gripped Lilith as a shadow seemed to flit across her vision. She bolted upright, her heart pounding frantically in her chest, eyes darting to every corner of the room in search of the unseen threat. But only stillness greeted her, the silence as oppressive and suffocating as a sealed tomb. Lilith's breath came in short, ragged gasps as she tried to calm her frayed nerves, the irrational fear slowly loosening its hold on her mind.

Her thoughts drifted back to when she first arrived in Savannah a mere two years ago, at the tender age of 24. Wide-eyed and full of dreams, Lilith had been eager to make her mark on the world. However, fate had other plans, and she soon found herself entangled with the wrong crowd. The memories of those early days flooded back, a bittersweet reminder of the path that had led her to this moment, alone and haunted by the shadows of her past.

She was fresh off the bus from a small town up north, eager to start over in a new city. The glittering lights and Southern charm lured her in, promising adventure and opportunity around every corner. She found a tiny studio apartment downtown and took a waitressing job at a 24-hour diner, thinking it all seemed so glamorous compared to her sleepy hometown.

But the glamour soon faded beneath the gritty underbelly of life on those Savannah streets. The long night shifts wore her down, leaving her exhausted as she dragged herself home each morning to her dingy apartment. She started spending time with a rough group who hung around outside the diner, recognizing the same loneliness and disillusionment in their eyes that she saw in her own reflection.

They introduced her to vices she had never known before — liquor to numb the pain, pills to escape reality. Her addiction spiraled out of control, costing her job and draining her savings until she was left utterly destitute. She lost touch with the friends from her old life, too ashamed for them to see how far she had fallen. Alone and desperate, she contemplated ending it all.

Lilith slumped on the weathered park bench, a solitary figure adrift in a sea of lush urban greenery. Her once neat clothes were now wrinkled and stained, her tangled hair a reflection of her disheveled state. With her head bowed in defeat, she seemed to radiate an aura of despair that pushed away any passersby who dared to come near. It was as if an invisible force field surrounded her, shielding her from the world.

From the corner of her eye, she caught movement. A man approached, his gait smooth and purposeful. He settled onto the bench beside her, close enough to converse but not so near as to crowd her. Something about his presence set her nerves on edge.

"Rough day?" His voice was velvet-soft, a stark contrast to the harsh whispers of self-doubt echoing in Lilith's mind.

She risked a glance upward, then quickly averted her gaze. The man's eyes held a glimmer of understanding that threatened to unravel her carefully constructed walls.

"It's alright. We've all been there. Sometimes life kicks us while we're down." His words hung in the air between them, heavy with unspoken empathy. Lilith shifted uncomfortably, her fingers twisting the frayed hem of her shirt. The stranger allowed the silence to stretch, giving weight to his next words. "But it doesn't have to stay that way. My family, we look after each other. Give purpose to life."

Something in his tone caught Lilith's attention. She found herself meeting his gaze, searching for any sign of deception. Instead, she saw only a lifeline thrown to a drowning soul.

"It starts with little steps. Come to a meeting. See what we're about. No obligations."

Lilith hesitated, her mind a battlefield of warring emotions. Hope and suspicion clashed, leaving her teetering on the edge of decision.

The man leaned in slightly, his voice dropping to a conspiratorial whisper. "Our rituals give meaning, structure. Help people find their way when all seems lost. What do you say?"

Time seemed to slow as Lilith weighed her options. The world around them faded into a grey blur, leaving only this moment of choice. Finally, almost imperceptibly, she nodded.

A smile spread across the stranger's face, transforming his features. He extended a hand, palm up — an invitation and a promise rolled into one. "You'll see. Everything will be fine now."

Lilith's fingers trembled as she placed her hand in his. As he helped her to her feet, she caught sight of his eyes once more. For a fleeting instant, she thought she saw something ancient and hungry lurking in their depths.

They walked away together, leaving the bench behind. Lilith glanced back one last time, a shiver of apprehension running through her. But she continued on, following her mysterious benefactor into an uncertain future, the park fading into the distance like a half-remembered dream.

As they left the park, the man led her through winding streets, his stride confident and sure. The cityscape gradually changed from familiar to foreign, the buildings growing older and more decrepit. They finally stopped in front of a tall iron gate, beyond which lay a sprawling compound. His hand on her back was a steady pressure, guiding her forward as they stepped into a new world.

Lilith stepped into the cult compound, her heart racing with a mixture of anticipation and trepidation. The air buzzed with an eerie energy as smiling members swarmed around her, their eyes gleaming with an unsettling intensity. Hands reached out to touch her, pat her back, and squeeze her shoulders. The attention was overwhelming, almost suffocating.

A woman with glassy eyes and a plastered-on grin leaned in close. "We're so happy you're here. You're part of our family now."

The words should have been comforting, but they filled Lilith with a growing sense of unease. As she was led deeper into the compound, whispers and meaningful glances followed her. The members spoke in hushed tones about the outside world, painting it as a hostile, unforgiving place.

The same woman who had welcomed her continued, her voice dripping with manufactured sympathy, "Out there, they'll never understand you like we do."

As night fell, Lilith found herself standing among a sea of swaying figures, all draped in identical robes. The flickering bonfire cast long, dancing shadows across their faces, transforming them into grotesque masks. The air was thick with smoke and the metallic tang of something Lilith couldn't quite place.

A hush fell over the gathering as a figure emerged from the darkness. Balor, the cult leader, his eyes reflecting the flames like twin infernos. His voice, when he spoke, seemed to reverberate through Lilith's very bones.

"My children...tonight, we welcome into our family one who has walked through the darkness and emerged to see the light." He paused, his gaze sweeping across the assembled crowd before landing on Lilith. "Lilith, come forward."

Her legs felt like lead as she took hesitant steps toward Balor. She had never liked being the center of attention and now wasn't any different. The weight of dozens of eyes bored into her back.

Balor's lips curled into what might have been a smile on anyone else. On him, it looked predatory. "You have overcome your demons, Lilith. Cast off the last chains of your painful past and truly join us."

Lilith's fingers tightened around the bag she clutched to her chest. It contained the last vestiges of her old life — photos, trinkets, memories made tangible. With trembling hands, she began to withdraw the items one by one.

As she tossed a photo into the hungry flames, the world around her seemed to blur. Suddenly, she was a child again, her mother's laughter ringing in her ears as they chased each other through a sun-dappled garden. The memory was so vivid she could almost smell the grass and feel the warmth on her skin.

Balor's hand on her shoulder yanked her back to reality. The photo that she had been clutching with trembling hands curled and blackened in the raging fire, taking with it the last echo of her mother's voice. More items followed, each igniting a flash of memory that seared through Lilith's mind before being consumed by the flames. A teddy bear from her childhood. A ticket stub from her first concert. Her high school diploma. With each memento turned to ash, Lilith felt a piece of herself crumble away.

The fire crackled and popped, sending sparks spiraling into the night sky. Around her, the cult members began to chant, their voices rising in a discordant chorus that seemed to pulse with the flickering flames.

Lilith took a deep, shuddering breath. The acrid smell of burning memories filled her lungs. She turned to Balor, seeking... something. Approval? Comfort? She wasn't sure anymore.

His arms engulfed her, and his voice rumbled in her ear. "Welcome home, child."

The crowd erupted into ecstatic cheers, the sound overwhelming Lilith. As she stood there, wrapped in Balor's embrace and surrounded by her new "family," a small, quiet part of her wondered if she had made a terrible mistake. But that voice grew fainter with each passing second, drowned out by the roar of the fire and the exultant cries of the cult members.

She was home now. Wasn't she?

As the cheers died down, Balor released her from his embrace and led her towards a hidden door. The transition from the open night to the dimly lit chamber was disorienting, but she followed him without question. The symbols on the walls seemed to come alive in the flickering candlelight, whispering promises of a new beginning.

The occult chamber pulsed with otherworldly energy, its walls adorned with ancient symbols that whispered secrets of rebirth and transformation. Flickering candles cast dancing shadows across the room, their eerie light glinting off an ornate dagger and torch resting on a central altar.

Robed figures moved with solemn purpose, their faces hidden in the depths of their hoods. They parted to reveal Lilith, her eyes glazed and unfocused as if peering into some unseen realm. Gone was the woman she had once been; in her place stood a vessel ready to be filled with dark purpose.

At the head of the gathering loomed Balor, the cult's

charismatic leader. His presence seemed to draw the very shadows closer, his voice a serpentine whisper that slithered into the minds of his followers.

"Tonight, we free you from the burdens of your past," he intoned, his words dripping with sinister promise. "You shall be reborn anew!"

The cultists presented Lilith with a cloth effigy, its crude features an unsettling mockery of her former self. Balor's eyes glittered with anticipation as he continued the ritual.

"With invocation, imbue this vessel with your lingering essence. Let all that binds you to your former existence pass into this fetish."

Lilith's chest rose and fell as she drew in a deep breath. With mechanical precision, she leaned forward, exhaling into the fabric doll. The air seemed to thicken, charged with unseen forces.

"Now, my child..." Balor's voice dropped to a near-whisper, "let the final rebirth begin!"

He pressed the ornate torch into Lilith's waiting hand. The assembled cultists began to chant, their voices a discordant symphony that grew in volume and urgency. Lilith stood frozen, the effigy clutched in one hand, the torch in the other. For a moment, a flicker of doubt passed across her face. But as the weight of expectant gazes bore down upon her, that last spark of hesitation was extinguished. With a swift, decisive motion, Lilith brought the torch to the effigy.

Flames leapt hungrily across the cloth, devouring the last tangible link to her past. Lilith's eyes reflected the inferno, wide and unblinking, as she watched her former self reduced to cinders. The chanting swelled to a fevered pitch, drowning out the crackle of the fire.

As the last embers fell at her feet, something fundamental shifted within Lilith. The woman she had been was gone, consumed by the flames of rebirth. In her place stood a creature of the cult's making, baptized in fire and shadow.

CHAPTER 8
UNRAVELING ALLIANCES

Captain Franklin's office was a picture of stark order, a sharp contrast to the chaotic bundle Mara carried in her arms. She clutched ancient tomes and evidence bags, which threatened to overflow and slip from her grasp. As she burst through the door, the weight of her discovery teetered precariously, on the verge of spilling onto the polished floor.

Franklin, a man in his fifties with a face marked by years of hardened pragmatism, watched without emotion as Mara dumped her macabre cargo onto his immaculate desk. Papers fluttered, crime scene photos scattered across the surface, and the musty scent of old books filled the air.

Franklin's hands were on his hips, and his eyes were fixed on the cluttered desk in front of him. His voice was flat, but a slight furrow in his brow gave away his exhaustion as he asked, "What is all this?"

Mara's emerald eyes blazed with fervor as she laid out the evidence before Franklin. "It's all here," she insisted, her voice tinged with urgency. "Grisly crime scenes depicting ritual carnage, autopsy reports riddled with arcane mutilations. It all points to one thing: sinister entities being summoned through dark rituals." Her fingers danced across the gruesome tableau, each photograph more horrific than the last. Mutilated bodies, their flesh carved with arcane symbols, and shadows that seemed to writhe even in the stillness of the images. Mara stabbed at the autopsy reports, willing Franklin to see the truth hidden beneath the cold, clinical language.

Franklin leaned back in his chair, the soft creaking sound filling the momentary silence between them. He regarded Mara with a mixture of concern and skepticism. "Detective Lawson," he began, his tone measured and firm, "I appreciate your dedication to this case, but this talk of demonic forces and ancient cults is crossing a line. We deal with facts and evidence here, not fantastical tales or superstitions." He folded his hands on the desk, his gaze unwavering as he met Mara's intense stare. "If we want to solve these crimes, we need to focus on the tangible leads and follow the proper procedures, not chase after shadows and ghost stories."

Mara took a deep breath, attempting to rein in her frustration. The week that she and Terry had agreed upon was almost up, and she desperately needed the captain's support to continue working on this case. Only she and Hunter truly understood the significance of these signs. She had to convince the captain that this was a serious matter, one that demanded their full attention and resources. "Captain," she began, her voice steady despite the urgency she felt, "this is the work of demonic forces." Mara raked her fingers through her hair, the gesture betraying her mounting frustration. "These murders are only the beginning. Mephistopheles and his acolytes will stop at nothing to unleash doom upon this city. We have to act now before it's too late."

A flicker of something – perhaps ambition or a deeper cynicism – glinted in Franklin's eyes as he regarded the scattered evidence before him. He leaned forward, his hands clasped tightly on the desk, and fixed Mara with a stern gaze. "Detective, you're letting this case get the better of you," he cautioned, his tone a mixture of concern and admonishment. "We need hard proof, not wild theories about the supernatural." Franklin's expression hardened, the lines around his mouth deepening into a mask of stern authority. "If you want to pursue this investigation, you'll need to bring me concrete evidence, something that will stand up in court. Until then, I suggest you focus on more tangible leads and follow proper protocol."

Undeterred by Franklin's skepticism, Mara seized an

ancient text, its pages brittle and yellowed with age. She thrust it towards the captain, her finger jabbing at a passage scrawled in an eldritch script. "These are not mere shadows, Captain," she insisted, her voice filled with conviction. "This is a threat that we cannot ignore. Lives are on the line, and I will do whatever it takes to uncover the truth and stop this evil from spreading."

Her hand darted to a crime scene photograph, the image searing itself into her mind even though she had seen it a hundred times before. A young woman, her life snuffed out in an act of unspeakable cruelty, lay contorted across a blood-soaked pentagram. "This girl was someone's daughter!" Mara exclaimed, her voice trembling with a mixture of anger and despair. "Who knows how many more innocent lives will be lost if we don't act now?"

Franklin's hand sliced through the air, dismissing her pleas with a casual gesture that struck Mara deeply. "Detective Lawson," he warned, his tone cold and condescending, "we follow protocol here, not your intuition. Tread carefully."

Mara's eyes widened in indignation, a hot flush of anger rising to her cheeks. Her being a woman had nothing to do with her dedication to the case or her ability to uncover the truth. If anything, Franklin's sexist remark only fueled her determination to press on and prove him wrong. "Captain, you have to listen to me," she pleaded, her voice steady despite the frustration bubbling inside her. "This goes beyond a regular case; we are facing a danger unlike anything we've encountered before. If we don't take action now, the consequences could be catastrophic."

Franklin's face remained expressionless, his jaw clenched as he stared at her with unflinching eyes. Despite the frantic energy radiating from her, he stood tall and unmoved, a stoic wall blocking her desperate pleas. "Detective Lawson, your fixation on these supernatural elements is clouding your judgment."

Mara felt a mix of emotions swirling within her. Frustration and helplessness battled for control, each threatening to break her resolve. She knew she needed to make Franklin understand the gravity of the situation, but finding the right words seemed impossible. The looming horror over their city weighed heavily on her mind, adding to the conflicted feelings that consumed her. "These occult symbols and rituals are not coincidences. People's lives are at stake here, and I can't just stand by and watch!"

Franklin's knuckles turned white as he clenched his fists, tension radiating from his body. His voice quivered with barely contained frustration as he uttered a single word that seemed to reverberate through the small office: "Enough!"

Mara flinched at the sudden outburst, the silence that followed deafening in its intensity. Franklin's jaw tightened, the muscles working beneath his skin as he prepared to deliver the crushing blow. "Your obsession with this case has led to a gross misuse of departmental resources," he stated, his tone cold and unforgiving. "As of this moment, you are suspended without pay, effective immediately."

Mara's heart plummeted at the words, her mind struggling to process the truth of what she was hearing. She wanted desperately to deny it, to argue her case and make Franklin see reason, but deep down, she knew that her worst fears were slowly unraveling before her very eyes. "You can't do this," she protested, her voice barely above a whisper. "I'm on to something here, something big. If we don't pursue this lead, more lives will be lost."

Franklin leaned back in his chair, his expression a mask of stern resolve. "I've made my decision, Detective Lawson," he said, his words carrying an air of finality. "Turn in your badge and gun. Until further notice, you are not to involve yourself in any official police business. Is that clear?"

Franklin remained unmoved, a statue of bureaucratic authority, his eyes fixed upon Mara with an unwavering resolve. "You've left me no choice, Detective Lawson," he said, his voice devoid of any sympathy or understanding. "Turn in your badge and gun. This is not up for negotiation."

Mara felt a sense of defeat creeping over her, threatening

to consume her very being. The weight of the suspension pressed down upon her shoulders, a heavy burden that seemed almost impossible to bear. But even in the face of such overwhelming darkness, she couldn't let go of the fire that burned within her — the fierce determination to see this case through, no matter the personal cost.

With a heavy heart and a profound sense of disappointment, Mara reluctantly complied with the suspension, placing her gun and badge on the captain's desk. As she did, the weight of responsibility for the lives at stake pressed down on her, refusing to let go. A part of her wanted to surrender to the hopelessness that now loomed over her. But another part, the part that had driven her to become a detective in the first place, held on, clinging to the belief that justice would prevail in the end.

"I will solve this case, with or without your approval," Mara declared, her voice barely above a whisper yet filled with an unshakable conviction. "You're making a grave mistake, Captain, and I pray that you realize it before it's too late."

With those final words, Mara turned and walked out of the office, her heart heavy with the knowledge that the battle ahead would be fought alone, but her spirit unbroken and her resolve as strong as ever.

As Mara turned to leave, her mind already racing with plans, Franklin's cold voice lingered in the air, haunting her steps. "Do as you please, Detective. But mark my words, there will be consequences if you choose to tread this dangerous path alone."

The door closed behind Mara with a soft click, but to her, it sounded like the sealing of a tomb, a final, ominous note that marked the beginning of a solitary battle against the encroaching darkness. The path ahead had just become infinitely more challenging, but she would face it alone if necessary. The fate of the city — perhaps even the world — depended on her success.

Stepping out into the cool night air, Mara's eyes hardened with resolve, a steely determination settling over her features. She knew exactly where she needed to go: Hunter Eldritch's library.

If anyone could help her proceed with the investigation, it was Hunter. As she drove her car down the long, lonely road, the city lights fading behind her, Mara's mind racing, already preparing for the challenges that lay ahead.

Upon entering Hunter's library, Mara's heart raced, the weight of her mission pressing heavily upon her. The air hung thick with the familiar scent of aged parchment and hidden knowledge, a testament to the countless secrets that lay within these walls. Shadows danced across the room, cast by the dim candlelight that struggled to illuminate the pervasive darkness.

As if drawn by Mara's presence, Hunter emerged from the shadows, his form appearing with an almost otherworldly quality. An eerie glow seemed to radiate from him, casting haunting highlights across his angular features and giving him an aura of mystery and power.

Mara's voice wavered slightly as she addressed her enigmatic ally. "We have to be careful, Hunter," she cautioned, her words tinged with a mixture of apprehension and determination. "We're treading dangerous waters, and the consequences of our actions could be dire."

Hunter's piercing gaze met hers, his eyes filled with an unwavering resolve that mirrored her own. "Fear not, Mara," he reassured her, his voice a low, compelling whisper. "We are but servants of truth, and in this noble pursuit, we must cast aside the constraints of convention and forge our own path to justice."

A maelstrom of emotions swirled within Mara's eyes — determination warring with uncertainty. Her jaw tensed as she struggled to resolve the conflicting emotions within her. She knew what she had to do, but the thought of it filled her with dread. "I can't let them get away with this. We need to unravel the cult's plans, even if it means going against the rules."

"Your courage is commendable, Mara," Hunter intoned, his voice a low rumble that seemed to resonate through the room, filling the space with a palpable sense of gravity. "The path we walk is treacherous, fraught with dangers both known and unseen, but together, we shall navigate the shadows with purpose and determination."

Mara's mind wavered, a flicker of uncertainty dancing across her thoughts as she contemplated the enormity of the task before them. As Hunter stepped closer, his imposing figure seemed to bring a sense of safety and danger all at once, a paradoxical mix that left her feeling both comforted and unnerved. She knew she needed to stay strong, to maintain her resolve in the face of the challenges ahead, but his presence made it difficult to keep her composure.

"I, too, have faced the darkness that lurks beyond mortal understanding," Hunter continued, his voice a soothing balm to her frayed nerves. "It is not a path for the faint-hearted, nor for those who would shy away from the truth, no matter how terrible it may be. But fear not, for I will be your guide, your steadfast companion as we venture into the unknown."

Mara's guarded expression softened, a glimmer of trust sparking in her eyes as she held Hunter's steady gaze. The tension between them seemed to melt away, replaced by a silent understanding that transcended words. "If this is the only way to stop them, to prevent more innocent lives from being lost, then I'll follow you into the shadows, Hunter. Together, we'll face whatever horrors await us."

Hunter nodded solemnly, his features etched with the weight of untold secrets and the burden of knowledge that few could bear. "Then let it be known that we are bound by more than mere mortal laws," he declared, his voice a hushed whisper that carried the weight of a sacred oath. "Together, we embark on a path unseen by most, seeking justice in the veiled realms of the arcane, where the line between light and darkness blurs."

Mara sank into a chair at a nearby table, its surface laden with ancient tomes and cryptic manuscripts that seemed to whisper their secrets to her. Her fingers brushed over cracked leather bindings, tracing the intricate patterns that adorned their covers as she spoke. "So, these victims...they're part of a pattern, a larger ritual unfolding over time, aren't they?"

Hunter's silent nod confirmed her suspicions, sending a chill through her very core, a cold realization that settled in the pit of her stomach. "Each murder is a piece in the cult's grand design," he explained, his voice tinged with a mixture of fascination and dread. "A twisted tapestry woven from the threads of innocent lives, all in service to their dark masters. We must decipher their next move, anticipate their actions before it is too late."

Mara's gaze fell upon a weathered map spread across the table, its surface marked with cryptic symbols and arcane sigils. Her fingers traced invisible lines connecting the gruesome crime scenes, a macabre constellation that seemed to pulse with an unseen energy. "If we overlay the crime scenes with ley lines and historical cult centers, we might be able to predict their next target, to stay one step ahead of their malevolent plans."

As Mara spoke, Hunter's attention was drawn to a peculiar artifact nestled among the arcane paraphernalia scattered across the table. The small, intricately carved talisman pulsed with a faint, otherworldly energy that seemed to call to him, beckoning him to unravel its secrets. With practiced ease, he murmured a soft incantation, his words imbued with ancient power as he awakened the talisman's dormant energy. "This talisman could reveal hidden energies, providing insights beyond the mortal realm," he explained, his voice tinged with a mix of reverence and curiosity.

Mara watched in awe as tendrils of ethereal light danced around the activated artifact, casting an eerie glow that seemed to pierce the shadowed recesses of the library. The weight of their undertaking pressed upon her, a tangible presence that settled in the pit of her stomach, and she voiced her growing unease. "There's a thin veil separating us from the abyss, isn't there? A fragile barrier that keeps the darkness at bay."

Hunter's gaze locked with hers, a silent understanding passing between them, a shared acknowledgment of the perilous path they now trod. "We stand at the precipice of a darkness few dare to confront," he replied, his voice a hushed whisper that carried the weight of untold secrets. "But together, we shall pierce the shadows, delving into the heart of the unknown to unearth the truth that lies hidden within."

Mara nodded, her expression a mixture of determination and trepidation, a reflection of the conflicting emotions that warred within her. The enormity of their task loomed before her like an insurmountable mountain, a daunting challenge that threatened to overwhelm her resolve. "We need a plan — one that exhausts every lead, mundane or otherwise. No stone can be left unturned in this pursuit of justice, no avenue unexplored."

As the words left her lips, Mara felt the weight of their unholy crusade settle upon her shoulders, a heavy burden that she knew she must bear. The library's oppressive atmosphere seemed to close in around them, a stark reminder of the otherworldly forces they now dared to challenge, the unseen entities that lurked just beyond the veil of reality.

With a shared nod of resolve, they dove into the research, their hands dancing over the ancient texts and cryptic symbols that held the keys to unlocking the mysteries before them. Hours slipped by unnoticed as they pieced together clues, their minds working in perfect tandem, a symphony of intellect and intuition. The library's silence was only broken by the occasional murmur of revelation or the rustle of turning pages, the soft sounds of two determined souls on a quest for truth.

The heavy oak door burst open, shattering the library's silence and jolting Mara from her intense focus on the ancient tome. Terry stormed in, his face a mix of fury and concern, his presence a disruptive force in the sanctuary of forbidden knowledge. Hunter's eyes narrowed, watching the newcomer warily, his body tensing in readiness for any potential threat.

"Mara, we need to talk," Terry declared, his voice echoing off the book-lined walls, a harsh demand that brooked no argument.

Mara's heart raced, a frantic drumbeat that pounded in her ears as she struggled to compose herself. She hadn't expected Terry to find her here, in this hidden haven of arcane secrets. The realization that he knew of this place's existence sent a chill down her spine. "Terry. What are you doing here?" she asked, her voice barely above a whisper.

Terry's jaw tightened, the muscles in his face taut with a combination of seething anger and desperate longing. His eyes blazed with intensity, reflecting the turbulent emotions swirling within him, a tempest of conflicting desires. "Trying to stop you from ruining your career over this nonsense," he snapped, throwing out his hands in frustration. "You got suspended, Mara. You're off the force unless you get your head straight."

"You have to know that I'm not happy about my suspension, Terry. I love my job," Mara said, sighing heavily as she sat forward in her chair, her shoulders slumping under the weight of her words. Her gaze locked on his, unwavering and determined, a silent plea for understanding. "But I'm finally seeing things clearly for the first time," she continued, gesturing around their surroundings with a sweep of her hand. "There are forces at work here that you can't possibly understand, powers that threaten to consume us all if we don't stand against them."

Terry's gaze shifted to Hunter, who stood silently in the shadows, a figure cloaked in mystery and secrets. "You mean the ramblings of your new partner, Hunter, here?" he scoffed, his voice dripping with sarcasm. "Chasing ghosts and shadows instead of evidence that'll stand up in court?"

Hunter's lips curled into a sardonic smile, his eyes glinting with a knowing amusement. "There are truths your courts cannot comprehend, detective. Realities that lie beyond the narrow confines of your legal system."

Terry's patience snapped, his composure shattering. He rounded on Hunter, eyes blazing with barely contained fury. "Can it, Hunter. This is between partners." He turned back to Mara, his voice softening, a plea woven into his words. "We've been through hell together, Mara. Does our code mean nothing to you anymore?"

Mara felt the pull of their shared history, the weight of countless cases, and late nights spent in pursuit of justice. She met Terry's gaze, her resolve wavering under the intensity of his stare. "Of course it does, Terry. But lives are at stake here. I can't ignore that, no matter the personal risk."

Terry reached out, his hand hovering in the space between them, a bridge spanning the growing chasm that separated their worlds. His eyes pleaded silently, begging Mara to reconsider, to step back from the precipice. "And I can't watch you throw away everything we've built on the word of some...occult fanatic."

Hunter scoffed, the sound dripping with disdain, a sharp retort to Terry's accusation. "Fanatic? I've devoted my life to understanding these forces, to unraveling the mysteries that threaten to consume us all while you bury your head in the sand, content to remain ignorant."

Mara's mind raced, flashing through a montage of blood-soaked crime scenes and arcane symbols carved into flesh. "Hunter's research is solid, Terry. I've seen the evidence firsthand, the ritualistic nature of these killings. There are dark forces at work here, things that lie beyond the grasp of conventional law."

Terry's face contorted in disbelief, his features twisting into a mask of incredulity. "Don't tell me you buy into this bizarro mumbo jumbo, Mara. We're officers of the law sworn to uphold justice based on facts and evidence. Not folk tales and fortune-telling."

Mara could see where Terry was coming from and could understand his skepticism in the face of the unbelievable. But she couldn't ignore her gut instinct, the nagging feeling that there was more to this case than met the eye. "I wish it were that simple, Terry. But what we're facing defies simple explanation, challenges everything we thought we knew about the world."

"Then help me understand!" Terry's voice cracked with emotion, a desperate plea for connection, for understanding.

"Don't cut me out for this crackpot, Mara. Let me in. Let me help you."

Mara's heart ached a dull pain that throbbed in her chest. She wanted nothing more than to shield Terry from the horrors she'd glimpsed, to protect him from the darkness that threatened to engulf them all. "I'm trying to protect you, Terry. The less you know, the safer you'll be. Please, just trust me on this."

Terry shook his head, his expression a mix of hurt and frustration, a man torn between loyalty and doubt. "I want to trust you, Mara. But you're on a dangerous path here, one that could destroy everything we've worked for. For both our sakes... come back while you still can."

Mara's gaze darted between Terry and the evidence surrounding her, the ancient texts, cryptic symbols, and gruesome crime scene photos forming a tapestry of the unthinkable. She felt torn between two worlds, each pulling at her with equal force, demanding her allegiance. "I'm sorry, Terry. I have to see this through, no matter where it leads."

Terry stared at Mara, betrayal etched across his features, a deep wound that cut to the very core of his being. Without another word, he turned and stormed out, his footsteps echoing through the library. The door slammed shut behind him, the sound reverberating through the room.

Mara sank back into her chair, the weight of her decision pressing down on her, a heavy burden that settled deep in her bones. She sighed, feeling the chasm between her old life and her new purpose widening with each passing moment, an irreversible divide.

Hunter's voice cut through the silence, a sharp contrast to the emotional turmoil that hung in the air. "He doesn't understand the true nature of what we're facing, the forces we're up against."

Mara rubbed her temples, feeling a headache building behind her eyes, a dull throb that pulsed in time with her racing thoughts. "Oh, Terry understands how serious this problem is, Hunter. He just doesn't believe in the supernatural, in the existence of things that defy rational explanation. He thinks it's all just smoke and mirrors, a trick of the mind."

Hunter's eyes gleamed with a mix of pity and anticipation, a knowing look that hinted at the horrors to come. "If I'm right, and I believe I am, he's in for a rude awakening, Mara. Everyone is. The veil between worlds is thinning, and soon, the truth will be impossible to ignore."

Hunter's words hung heavily in the air, filling the room with a sense of foreboding that made it hard for Mara to breathe. She stood, suddenly overwhelmed by the oppressive atmosphere, the urge to escape becoming irresistible. Grabbing her jacket from the back of the chair, the cool leather against her skin, Mara headed for the door. "I'm exhausted, Hunter. I need to go home and clear my head."

As Mara stepped out into the night, she couldn't shake the feeling that she was walking a tightrope between two realities, balancing precariously on the edge of the unknown. One false step, one misjudgment, and everything she knew, everything she held dear, would come crashing down around her, lost forever to the shadows that lurked just beyond the veil.

***

The night air was thick with unspoken tension as Terry stood before Mara's apartment door, his heart pounding. His face, marked by deep lines of concern, revealed the internal struggle waging within him — a battle between loyalty and doubt. For a moment, he hesitated, his hand hovering, ready to knock. The gravity of what lay ahead pressed down on him, a burden he wasn't sure he was prepared to bear.

Finally, mustering his resolve, Terry rapped his knuckles against the door, the sound sharp and insistent. The noise reverberated through the quiet hallway, seeming to echo the turbulent emotions coursing through his veins, a cacophony of fear, frustration, and desperate hope.

The door creaked open, revealing Mara standing in the threshold. Her expression was a mask of guarded expectation, her eyes searching Terry's face for any hint of what was to come, any clue as to the purpose of his unexpected visit. Without a word, Terry stepped inside, the air between them thick with unspoken tension, a palpable electricity that crackled in the confined space. "Mara, we need to talk about what happened today," Terry said, his voice low and grave, a somber declaration that hung in the air.

Mara's solemn nod was barely perceptible in the dim light of her apartment, a subtle acknowledgment of the gravity of the situation.

Terry continued, his words laced with a mixture of frustration and genuine concern, a potent cocktail of emotions that threatened to overwhelm him. "I can't stand by and watch you throw everything away, Mara. You're walking into uncharted territory, risking it all for...for what? For darkness, for the unknown?"

Mara's gaze locked onto Terry's, her eyes blazing with a combination of defiance and unwavering resolve, a fire that refused to be extinguished. The silence stretched between them, pregnant with unspoken accusations and pleas, a chasm that widened with each passing second. "Terry, you've been my partner for years, and I value that more than anything," Mara finally said, her voice steady despite the storm of emotions raging behind her eyes. "But this...this goes beyond our history, beyond our partnership. Lives are at stake, and I can't ignore that, no matter the cost."

Terry's shoulders drooped under the heavy strain of their shared past. "But what about the evidence, Mara? What about the rules, the procedures we've sworn to uphold? We can't just abandon reason for...for fairy tales and superstitions. That's not who we are, not what we stand for."

Mara's response came without hesitation, her conviction palpable in every word, a testament to the strength of her beliefs. "The evidence is pointing me in a direction you can't see yet, Terry. It's leading me down a path that defies conventional wisdom that challenges everything we thought we knew. I have to follow this path, no matter where it leads, no matter how dark the journey may be."

Terry's face contorted with a mixture of disbelief and anguish, a reflection of the turmoil that raged within him. "This isn't you, Mara. This isn't the partner I know, the friend I've trusted with my life. You're sacrificing everything we've worked for, everything we've believed in, for what? For a hunch, for a feeling?"

"This is who I am now," Mara countered, her voice tinged with a hint of sadness but unyielding in its determination. "I've seen things, Terry, things that have changed me, that have opened my eyes to a reality I can no longer ignore. I have to see this through, even if it means...even if it means leaving it all behind, leaving our partnership, our friendship, in the past."

The effect of her words was unmistakable on Terry's face, breaking something deep within him. He flinched, eyes wide with shock and hurt as if Mara's declaration had wounded him. When he spoke again, his voice was barely above a whisper, raw with emotion, a fragile thread on the verge of snapping. "You're choosing this...this madness, over everything we've shared, everything we've built together?"

Mara's response was laden with regret, a heavy burden that weighed upon her soul. But even in the face of Terry's anguish, her resolve remained unshaken, a pillar of determination that refused to crumble. "I have to, Terry. I can't turn my back on the truth, no matter how painful it may be."

Terry's face hardened, his hurt morphing into a simmering anger that bubbled just beneath the surface. His next words came out in a rush, sharp and biting, a verbal assault that cut deep into Mara's heart. "Fine, Mara. You want to risk everything for this... this obsession? You want to throw away years of partnership, of friendship, for some twisted crusade? Go right ahead. But when it all comes tumbling down, when you're left alone in the darkness, don't expect me to be there to pick up the pieces."

With that, Terry turned on his heel and stormed out of the apartment, his footsteps heavy with the weight of his anger and betrayal. Mara watched him go, her eyes following his retreating form until he disappeared from sight, swallowed up by the shadows of the hallway. The slam of the door echoed through the apartment, a final punctuation to their fractured partnership, a resounding declaration of the chasm that now divided them.

In the silence that followed, Mara stood alone, the weight of her choices settling around her. The path ahead was uncertain, fraught with danger and darkness, a treacherous journey into the unknown. But she had made her decision, had chosen to follow the truth wherever it might lead, no matter the cost. There was no turning back now, no retreat from the battle that lay before her. With a heavy heart and a steely resolve, Mara prepared herself for the trials to come, knowing that she would face them alone, a solitary figure standing against the rising tide of darkness.

CHAPTER 9
CONVERGENCE OF FATES

Age-old wisdom slumbered in the cobweb-covered tomes in Hunter's library. Mara and Hunter leaned in close, their features etched in intense focus as they delved into the occult scriptures before them. Mara reached over and tugged a star chart from the top of the stack of books on the table in front of her. Her finger traced the constellations on a weathered star chart, her eyes widening as connections sparked in her mind. "These astrological patterns...they align perfectly with the cult's recent activities."

Hunter's gaze snapped to the map, his pupils dilating as realization dawned. "It's all converging...the signs, the symbols, the portents. We're standing at the edge of a precipice."

Mara nodded silently in agreement. With a steady hand, she reached for the ancient leather-bound tome. The spine creaked as she pried it open, revealing yellowed pages that seemed to hold secrets from centuries past. She found the desired passage and placed the book between them on the crowded table, its presence adding to the somber atmosphere. "This passage... it speaks of a cosmic event that mirrors the ritual the cult is preparing for."

Hunter leaned in closer, his breath catching as he deciphered the ancient words. The weight of their discovery settled over them, heavy and oppressive. When he spoke, his voice was thick with foreboding. "The planets align as prophesied in these archaic texts. The hour of reckoning approaches. The end times are upon us."

The library walls felt oppressive, as if the shadows themselves were alive and drawing near, drawn to their unsettling discovery. The air grew heavy with a sense of impending doom, pregnant with the promise of cosmic horrors waiting to be unleashed. Mara and Hunter exchanged a glance, their expressions grave as they realized they were on the edge of a darkness beyond their wildest imaginings.

Mara and Hunter were so engrossed in the ancient texts that they failed to hear the library door creak open. A tall, slender figure slipped inside, moving with graceful, almost supernatural ease between the dusty bookshelves. He wore a long black coat that seemed to absorb all light, blending him into the shadows. Only the gleam of his pale grey eyes gave away his presence as he watched the pair hunched over the forbidden tomes.

The man moved silently towards them, his footsteps making no sound on the wooden floorboards. He came up behind Mara, leaning down until his lips nearly brushed her ear. "You're meddling in affairs far beyond your comprehension," he whispered.

Mara jerked back with a gasp, nearly falling out of her chair before Hunter caught her arm to steady her. They both turned to face the intruder, whose thin lips curled into a cruel smile.

"Who are you?" Hunter demanded, instinctively moving to shield Mara.

The man tilted his head, regarding them with an amused, predatory glint in his pale eyes. "Let's just say I'm a...concerned party. And your amateur investigations threaten to upset some very delicate plans."

Mara's instincts, sharpened by years of detective work, warned her that the stranger was a dangerous predator. His voice dripped with sinister intent, setting her nerves on edge. Hunter, her loyal companion and guardian, tensed beside her, poised to either attack or retreat at a moment's notice.

The man chuckled softly. "Please, don't let me interrupt your studies. By all means, keep digging. Perhaps you'll uncover the truth right before it comes crashing around you."

Mara and Hunter exchanged wary glances as the strange man circled the table, his fingers brushing over the ancient texts. His cryptic words lingered in the air, casting a shadow over the room.

"Who sent you?" Mara asked, forcing steel into her voice. Though her pulse raced, she kept her gaze locked on the intruder.

He paused, tilting his head as if amused by the question. "No one sent me. I'm here for the same reason you are — to witness the awakening."

"The awakening of what?" Hunter pressed, eyes narrowed.

The man leaned in, breath cold on their faces. "Of forces beyond your comprehension. But you've both touched the void, haven't you?" His grin widened. "You've heard its call."

Mara recoiled. This man, if that's what he was, knew too much. Knew things no one should.

Hunter stood abruptly, chair scraping back. "I think it's time for you to leave."

Their visitor held up his hands in mock surrender. "As you wish. But heed this warning — tread carefully in these final days. The shadows are stirring, and they know your names."

With that ominous threat lingering, he melted back into the darkness between the shelves. Mara hurried to lock the library door behind him. She turned to Hunter, heart pounding.

"Who was that?"

Hunter shook his head grimly. "I don't know. But I suspect we're on the right path if we've attracted such dark attention."

Mara felt her blood run cold at the stranger's cryptic warning. She turned to Hunter, a question on her lips, but he cut her off with an upraised hand, eyes darting around the shadowy library. Wordlessly, he began gathering up the ancient texts scattered across the table, his movements urgent.

Mara followed his lead, helping stack the fragile books and charts. Her mind raced with unanswered questions, but she remained silent, trusting her partner's instincts. They worked swiftly, neither uttering a sound in the oppressive hush that had fallen over the library.

The last book packed away, Hunter snatched up an old oil lamp and lit it with a match. Its flickering glow cast dancing shadows across his pallid features. Beckoning Mara with a tilt of his head, he led the way through the dusty stacks towards a rear corner shrouded in darkness.

There, nestled between shelves laden with esoteric tomes, a narrow door was set into the exposed brick. Mara had never noticed it before. Producing an old iron key, Hunter unlocked it to reveal a cramped staircase winding down into subterranean blackness. Cobwebs brushed Mara's face as she followed him down the creaking steps into the forgotten vault below the library's main floor.

At the bottom, Hunter set the lamp on a rough-hewn wooden table. Its weak light revealed an underground room stacked to the ceiling with strange artifacts — ancient relics, crumbling scrolls, and piles upon piles of books bound in cracking leather and stained vellum.

The air was dank and heavy as if the collected knowledge of centuries past pressed down upon them. Mara ran her fingers along the spines of the mysterious tomes, these dark archives hidden beneath the mundane world above.

"What is this place?" she whispered.

Hunter busied himself, lighting candles set in rusting iron sconces along the clammy brick walls. "My private collection. Pieces deemed too heretical or dangerous for the library's public shelves. But knowledge too potent to destroy."

He turned, his angular features thrown into dramatic relief by the flickering candlelight. "We tread treacherous ground, Mara. Each step takes us deeper into the abyss, closer to secrets that should perhaps remain buried."

Mara met his piercing gaze unflinchingly. "Then we descend together. The light of truth is our torch against the darkness."

Hunter's gaze searched her eyes before he gave a single nod. He turned and retrieved an ancient text from the cluttered desk, its faded symbols barely legible. "This tome details a prophecy that warns of the cosmic alignment we've discovered," he said, his voice low and gravelly. "I believe the answers we seek lie within these pages."

He passed a volume to Mara, who handled the crumbling parchment gingerly. They took seats at the rough table and began to translate the mysterious texts by candlelight, delving deeper into the occult secrets coiled below the sedate streets of Savannah.

A charge seemed to pass between them, a shared understanding of the gravity of their undertaking. "We begin," he said simply, and together they turned to the first page.

Mara and Hunter delved deeper into their research, the room charged with frantic energy. Dusty tomes lay scattered across the desk, their yellowed pages brittle with age. They moved with feverish intensity, flipping through ancient texts and unrolling celestial maps that crackled under their touch.

Mara's eyes darted across cryptic symbols, her brow furrowed in concentration. A growing sense of dread filled the air, thick and oppressive. Hunter aligned star charts on his laptop, its soft glow casting eerie shadows across his face.

As the pieces began to fall into place, a horrifying picture emerged. Mara's breath caught in her throat as she connected the final dots. Her voice, barely above a whisper, broke the tense silence. "You were right, Hunter. These symbols...they aren't just random markings. They're building towards something much larger, more sinister."

Hunter's gaze snapped up from his work, locking onto Mara's pale face. The gravity of her words hung heavy in the air between them.

"The cult's plans are more catastrophic than we ever imagined," he said, his voice rough with tension. He paused, swallowing hard before continuing. "The convergence of rituals, alignments, it all points to the apocalyptic prophecy I told you about."

A chill swept through the room, raising goosebumps on their skin. The weight of their discovery pressed down on them, making it hard to breathe. "We're not just dealing with a cult," she whispered, her voice trembling. "We're on the brink of a cosmic catastrophe."

Hunter's face was a mask of grim determination, but fear danced in the depths of his eyes. He ran a shaking hand through his disheveled hair, his next words making Mara's blood run cold. "The stars are aligning for something beyond our understanding."

The room fell silent once more, save for the ominous ticking of the clock on the wall. Outside, storm clouds gathered on the horizon as if nature itself sensed the impending doom that loomed over them all.

Just then, a soft knock at the door startled them both. Mara exchanged a wary glance with Hunter before cautiously climbing the stairs and approaching the library's main entrance. Hunter stood right behind her. She slowly turned the knob, the door creaking open to reveal a figure cloaked in shadow. Mara instinctively reached for her gun, heart pounding, as the stranger stepped into the light.

"It's been a long time, Mara," said a familiar voice. Mara's eyes widened in disbelief as the hood was lowered, revealing the face of a woman from her past.

"Serafine?" Mara gasped. "I thought you were..."

"Dead?" Serafine finished with a sly smile. "The rumors were not entirely unfounded."

Mara stood frozen, unable to process this ghost from her past. Serafine had been like a sister to her growing up. They had bonded over their shared fascination with the supernatural before Serafine had disappeared years ago.

"What happened to you?" Mara finally managed.

"That is a long story," Serafine replied cryptically. "One I wish we had time for. But there are more pressing matters at hand." Her expression turned grim as she glanced between Mara and Hunter. "I take it you know about the coming alignment and the cult's plans to bring about the end times."

Mara nodded mutely, unnerved by Serafine's apparent

knowledge. She stared at Serafine in stunned silence, her mind racing to make sense of this sudden reappearance. After years with no word, here Serafine was, speaking of apocalyptic prophecies as if she were simply picking up a paused conversation.

Hunter stepped forward, eyeing the newcomer warily. "You seem to know much about our current situation," he said slowly. "But you have us at a disadvantage. How is it you come to be here now, Serafine?"

Serafine turned her hooded gaze on Hunter, her eyes glinting in the light. "In good time, Hunter. But know that I come as an ally." She gestured to the tomes on the shelves around them. "You have unlocked part of the mystery, but there are things hidden even from your underground collections."

Mara's shock was fading, replaced by a simmering anger. "An ally? You vanished without a word! For years I thought you were dead, and now you reappear speaking of the end times?"

Serafine's expression softened. "Dearest Mara, not a day has gone by that I haven't regretted the pain of my departure. But forces were in motion that you could not yet understand." She stepped closer, her voice urgent. "I know you feel betrayed, but you must trust that I am here to help stop the coming darkness."

Hunter held up a hand. "Let us move this conversation somewhere more secure." He began gathering up the materials on the desk. "I know of a location where we can speak freely."

Mara eyed Serafine warily as they descended the narrow staircase to Hunter's underground sanctum, flickering candles casting dancing shadows along the stone walls. Despite Serafine's reassuring words, doubt and hurt still warred within Mara's heart.

Hunter opened another door in the underground sanctum, which led them into a small, windowless room lined with ancient texts and occult artifacts. Turning to Serafine, he broke the tense silence. "You claim to possess vital knowledge about the cult's plans. Tell us what you know."

Serafine lowered her hood, her piercing eyes reflecting the

candlelight. "As you have discovered, the cult seeks to harness cosmic forces beyond comprehension to bring about the end of this world. I have learned they now stand poised to complete the rituals needed to summon the Chaos Bringer."

Mara sucked in a sharp breath, exchanging an alarmed look with Hunter. "Another demon? I thought they were bringing forth Mephistopheles."

"Believe me, they are one and the same. This being," Serafine continued, "exists outside the boundaries of our reality, in the dark abyss between dimensions. If summoned, it would unleash total annihilation."

"How do you know all this?" Mara asked sharply, arms folded across her chest.

Serafine met her gaze. "After I left, I was drawn into their circle. I've seen their depravity firsthand, their insane devotion to cosmic annihilation." Her voice dropped to a haunted whisper. "I barely escaped with my life and soul intact."

She turned her focus to Hunter. "You know the prophecies. The fatal alignment draws near. Together, we may be able to prevent the ritual and stop The Devil's Greenhouse."

Mara felt her anger toward Serafine soften slightly, but wariness still lingered. She shared a tense look with Hunter before speaking.

"Even if what you say is true, we're still facing impossible odds. This 'Devil's Greenhouse' seems to have influence everywhere. How can a few of us hope to stop their apocalyptic plans?"

Hunter's eyes glinted with fervent intensity in the candlelight. "We may be outmatched in numbers and resources, but we possess something they do not — knowledge. My occult research has uncovered rituals and talismans to help protect us from their dark magic."

He gestured to the ancient texts lining the walls. "And with Serafine's inside information, we can strategically target their operations."

Serafine nodded. "Hunter speaks wisdom. United, our unique skills can thwart the completion of their sinister rituals across the city."

Mara bit her lip, considering their words. Her detective's mind turned over the possibilities, weighing risks against the apocalyptic consequences of failure. Finally, she met their expectant gazes and gave a determined nod. "Very well. We do this together, as a team." She turned to Serafine. "But I'll be watching you closely. Betray us again, and you'll answer to me."

Serafine bowed her head solemnly. "You have my word, Mara. We end this threat...or die trying."

The three exchanged resolute looks in the candlelit darkness.

CHAPTER 10
CONVINCING THE COMMISSIONER

Mara pored over the yellowed pages of ancient texts, her fingers tracing the arcane symbols as she tried to unravel their meaning. Across the room, Hunter scribbled furiously, his pen scratching against parchment amid a cluttered array of bizarre artifacts and occult objects.

Mara's thoughts kept wandering back to her encounter with Serafine the previous night. Her old friend had appeared like a specter, materializing unexpectedly after being presumed dead for years. Serafine claimed she had returned to help stop the evil overtaking Savannah, but Mara wasn't sure she could be trusted.

Breaking the silence, Mara cleared her throat. "So, Serafine's back."

Absorbed in an ancient scroll depicting demonic entities, Hunter didn't look up. "It would seem so," he murmured.

"And you don't find that the least bit suspicious?" Mara pressed. "She disappears for years and then just shows up out of the blue?"

Finally glancing up, Hunter met Mara's gaze, his blue eyes glinting. "Of course, it's suspicious. But we know little of where she's been or what she's learned. According to you, Serafine has always been...an enigma. Her knowledge could prove useful if she's truly here to help."

Hunter steepled his long, pale fingers together contemplatively. "And certain signs do align with her claims — the blood moon omen, the unearthed ritual site, the disturbed spirits...something is awakening, whether she is complicit or not."

Mara frowned, unconvinced. She still keenly remembered how Serafine had abandoned her, leaving a hole in her life when she'd needed her most. She sighed and ran her fingers through her hair in frustration. "I just don't know if I can trust her again. She was my best friend, and when she disappeared...it broke something in me."

Hunter regarded her thoughtfully. "Trust must be earned, not freely given. But consider that people often change in profound ways during long absences. The Serafine who has returned may not be the same person who left."

Mara turned away, gazing out the dusty window at the live oaks swaying in the humid breeze. Savannah seemed cloaked in a deeper gloom since Serafine's return, as if the city itself was unsettled.

"We cannot ignore the signs," Hunter continued softly. "Ancient forces are stirring, things long buried now clawing their way to the surface. Serafine may provide insight into the rising darkness."

Mara crossed her arms, conflicted. As a detective, she knew she couldn't afford to turn away any source of information, no matter how questionable. But as a woman, she struggled to silence the hurt that still ached from Serafine's betrayal.

"Evil feeds on division and mistrust," cautioned Hunter, as though reading her thoughts. "Your history makes you wary, and rightly so. But for now, we face this threat united."

Mara turned back to Hunter, meeting his piercing gaze. She knew they needed whatever occult knowledge Serafine possessed. The safety of Savannah depended on it. She sighed deeply, her breath seeming to carry the weight of her internal conflict. She knew Hunter was right — any personal feelings about Serafine needed to be set aside for the sake of their larger mission. This darkness rising in Savannah threatened them all, and they desperately needed more insight.

"Okay," Mara finally said. "I'll try to keep an open mind about Serafine for now. But I intend to watch her closely. If I sense even a hint of deception, I won't hesitate to confront her."

Hunter nodded. "A wise approach. Trust, yet verify as the saying goes." He glanced down at the ancient text before him, his brow furrowing. "Now, let us continue our research. I believe I am close to deciphering the nature of the entity behind these disturbances."

Mara turned her focus back to the dusty tomes and strange artifacts surrounding her. She could feel the occult mystery deepening. What they were facing seemed older than Savannah itself — an ancient evil that predated human memory. She shivered, wondering if they were prepared for the secrets soon to be unearthed.

Just then, a raven cawed outside the window, its cry piercing the heavy air. Hunter and Mara exchanged an uneasy glance. Both could sense the occult forces gathering like an approaching storm. The raven's cry echoed in Mara's mind — a dark omen warning of impending danger. But she steeled her nerves, more determined than ever to uncover the truth.

The sudden creak of the door shattered their concentration. Both heads snapped up as a wild-eyed man stumbled into the room, his matted hair and tattered clothes reeking of the streets. Fear radiated from him in palpable waves, causing Mara and Hunter to exchange apprehensive glances.

"The shadows!" the man raved, his voice cracking with hysteria. "I've seen them crawling from the depths! The old ones with their thousand faces! The catacombs, the rituals, the screams echoing through the stone. Blood offerings under the full moon. I saw them! I saw them all!"

Mara's breath caught in her throat as she locked eyes with Hunter. The air in the room seemed to grow colder, charged with an electric tension that prickled across her skin.

Mara swallowed hard, forcing her voice to remain steady. "What did you see? Where?"

The man's eyes bulged, darting around the room as if expecting horrors to materialize from the shadows. "Below the city, where the bones of the dead whisper. Where they gather to call forth the End. The vermin, the storms — it's already begun!" His voice rose to a fever pitch. "Can't you hear the screams on the wind?"

As the man's ravings grew more frantic, Hunter approached him cautiously. He gently grasped the trembling man's arm, his voice low and soothing. "It's alright. Try to calm yourself." Hunter began guiding him towards the door. "We'll get you somewhere safe."

The old man's body went rigid, resisting Hunter's efforts. His eyes, wide with terror, locked onto Mara. "No one is safe! Not while they prepare His coming!" He thrashed against Hunter's grip. "Only you can stop Them now. The shadows...the shadows will swallow us all!"

With a final push, Hunter managed to usher the man out of the room. The door clicked shut, leaving behind a deafening silence. Mara stood frozen, the man's words echoing in her mind. Her chest tightened as the implications of what she'd heard sank in.

"My god," she whispered, her voice barely audible. "If what he saw is real..." Mara's fists clenched at her sides, a steely determination settling over her features. "We're out of time."

Mara turned to Hunter, her jaw set with grim resolve. "We need to investigate the catacombs beneath the city immediately. If there are occult rituals happening down there, we have to stop them."

Hunter nodded gravely, already gathering supplies into a worn leather satchel. "I concur. The old man's ravings align too closely with my research to be a mere coincidence. An ancient evil is awakening in the tunnels below Savannah."

He slung the bag over his shoulder and met Mara's gaze. "We must maintain constant vigilance. The forces we face are cunning and deceptive. They will attempt to exploit any weakness."

Mara checked her gun and flashlight, steeling her nerves.

She had investigated many disturbing cases during her career, but this time felt different — more personal, more ominous.

As she and Hunter descended into the dank catacombs, the stale air seemed alive with unseen forces. Mara could feel the hairs on her neck prickling. The beam of her flashlight carved a narrow tunnel through the oppressive darkness. Ancient stone walls glistened with foul moisture. Mara tried to ignore the scurrying of claws and slithering of scales echoing from the blackness.

Up ahead, a faint light flickered, casting twisting shadows down the passage. Mara exchanged a silent nod with Hunter. They crept forward, hands poised on their weapons. The passage opened into a vast chamber illuminated by the ghostly glow of candles. A cloaked circle of figures stood chanting before a blood-stained altar.

The old man suddenly reappeared from the shadows. His frantic eyes darted around as he spoke in hushed, urgent tones. "You must listen. It's too late for me, but maybe not for you. The tunnels, the rituals — it was all a ruse. They wanted you to come down here. They're waiting for you to make you part of their sacrifice."

Mara felt her blood turn to ice. She exchanged an alarmed look with Hunter. All of his occult research had pointed to this location. Could they have been so easily deceived?

The old man was trembling violently now, peering into the shadows as if expecting an attack at any moment. His voice dropped to an ominous whisper. "You must go before it's too late. I will draw them off, buy you some time. But hurry!"

With that, the man turned and scurried back down the tunnel, disappearing into the darkness. Mara strained her ears, hearing the faint echo of chanting and strange unnatural sounds drifting up the passage. Mara stood frozen, her mind racing through their options. This was clearly a trap meant to lure them in. But the occult ritual sounded dangerously close to completion. If they turned back now, would they have another chance to stop it?

She turned to Hunter, who was scrutinizing the dark tunnel ahead, his expression unreadable. "We can't leave yet," Mara said firmly. "We have to at least assess the situation, see if there's any way we can intervene before it's too late."

Hunter nodded slowly, his piercing blue eyes reflecting the beam of her flashlight. "Agreed. But we must be strategic. A direct confrontation would be unwise."

Mara thought for a moment. "We need help. Someone on the inside who can get close without raising suspicion." Her eyes lit up. "Serafine. She knows the occult underworld here. If we can convince her, maybe she can infiltrate the ritual, gather intel, and buy us more time."

"A dangerous proposition," Hunter murmured. "But Serafine's knowledge could prove invaluable." He rifled through his satchel and produced a battered book. "I will attempt to learn what I can from this grimoire. It may reveal weaknesses we can exploit."

Mara felt a swell of hope. They had the beginnings of a plan. "Alright, let's get out of here. We'll regroup and figure out our next move."

Mara's mind turned to the police commissioner. If she could make him understand the gravity of the threat, maybe she could get official support. But convincing him would be difficult — he was a pragmatist, dismissive of anything occult.

As Mara and Hunter emerged from the tunnels, she took a deep breath, steeling herself. Time was running short. She had to act quickly. Mara turned to Hunter as they climbed the stone steps leading out of the underground tunnels and back to the streets of Savannah. "We need to convince the police commissioner about what's happening down there. If I can get him to understand the danger, he might be able to send backup."

Hunter nodded, his expression grave. "Yes, though few possess minds open enough to accept such ominous truths. Still, we must make the attempt."

Mara quickened her pace as they emerged into the misty night air. The city seemed to be unnaturally still, as if holding its breath. Mara suppressed a shiver, trying not to imagine what malevolent forces might be stirring in the shadows.

A few hours later, Mara stood before Commissioner John O'Neill's imposing desk, her heart pounding with urgency. The aging police commissioner, his face etched with the lines of decades on the force, peered skeptically at the array of photos and documents spread before him.

Mara leaned forward, her voice tight with desperation. "Sir, all the evidence conclusively points to an imminent apocalyptic event being planned by this cult. In our city. We have to act now before it's too late."

O'Neill's weathered face creased with disdain. "This is nonsense, Detective. Ancient prophecies and magic spells? Do you know how insane this sounds?"

She'd anticipated his disbelief, but the stakes were too high to back down now. "I thought so, too, at first. But we can't ignore where the evidence is leading."

With trembling fingers, she opened a thick file folder. Crime scene photos spilled out, each one emblazoned with arcane symbols that seemed to writhe and twist before their eyes. "And these decoded communications between cult members directly reference summoning their demon god to cleanse the earth," Mara continued, her voice barely above a whisper.

O'Neill's face flushed with frustration. "Come on, Mara. This is grasping at straws, not real detective work."

Anger flared in Mara's chest. "You're wrong! The connections are real if you just open your mind."

Before O'Neill could protest further, Mara produced a small tablet. The screen flickered to life, revealing grainy footage that made the hair on the back of her neck stand on end. Shadows danced and coalesced into impossible shapes as an unearthly wail filled the office.

O'Neill's eyes widened, a flicker of unease crossing his

face as he watched.

"Explain that away," Mara challenged. "This is all tied to cosmic events and prophecies coming to pass now. You need to trust me!"

The Commissioner slumped back in his chair, rubbing his temples. "Where did you even get all this nonsense?"

Mara hesitated, knowing how it would sound. "I've been working with an occult expert named Hunter Eldritch. He predicted this years ago."

"Of course you have," O'Neill scoffed. "More crazies."

Desperation clawed at Mara's insides. She leaned across the desk, her voice raw with emotion. "We're running out of time! You have to authorize a serious investigation into these cult activities before their doomsday ritual happens! Please, sir, I'm begging you. Lives depend on it." She paused, searching O'Neill's face for any sign of understanding. "I know it seems unbelievable, sir. But we have to trust what's right in front of us. Lives are at stake."

The silence stretched between them, heavy with the weight of unseen forces. Finally, O'Neill's shoulders sagged in resignation. "You're right, detective. We need to take action. I'll authorize a formal investigation into these...disturbing allegations."

Relief flooded through Mara, but it was short-lived. "With all due respect, a standard investigation won't cut it. We need an elite task force with special jurisdiction to get ahead of this threat."

O'Neill's brow furrowed. "That's a tall order, detective. The resources, the authority we'd have to grant..."

Mara cut him off, her words tumbling out in a desperate rush. "Sir, we're facing a fanatical cult on the verge of catastrophe. Half-measures won't work. I'm talking about protecting the world from apocalypse." The weight of her words hung in the air. O'Neill's face was grave as he considered the implications.

"Alright," he said at last. "I'll approve the formation of

an elite Cult Crimes Task Force under your command, whatever resources you need. But this occult business..."

Mara saw her opening and seized it. "We'll need expertise there. My civilian consultant, Hunter Eldritch. He understands what we're up against."

O'Neill nodded reluctantly. "Very well. Stopping these lunatics is priority one. What's your plan?"

Mara's mind raced, piecing together fragments of Hunter's warnings and her own instincts. "Locate their ritual sites. Disrupt their operations. Prevent this 'Summoning' at all costs. We're venturing into the unknown here. But failure is not an option."

The Commissioner reached into his desk drawer, producing an official-looking credential. He held it out to Mara, his expression solemn. "Then Godspeed in this war, detective. The world is counting on you now."

As Mara's fingers closed around the badge, she felt the weight of responsibility settle onto her shoulders. It was a burden she'd carry gladly if it meant averting catastrophe.

Her voice was steel as she met O'Neill's gaze. "Let's go save the damn world."

CHAPTER 11
BLOODIED BUT UNBROKEN

As the autumn wind whipped through the alley, sending leaves dancing at his feet, an unsettling sensation washed over Terry. Savannah's once humid air now bit at his skin, causing his hair to stand on end beneath layers that suddenly felt constricting. A stray cat darted out from behind a nearby dumpster, its eyes flashing like fireflies in the dusk. Terry tried to shake off the uneasiness that gripped him, refusing to succumb to superstitions.

"Get it together," he muttered under his breath, his jaw clenched. He couldn't let emotions get in the way. This lead was crucial and potentially case-breaking. He had to stay focused on the facts.

As he approached the alley's end, the scent of decay hung thick in the air. He paused, hand hovering over the old peeling doorknob. Calling for backup flashed through his mind, but the thought of appearing weak to his colleagues, especially Mara, tightened his gut. Taking a breath, he grasped the rusty handle. The aged hinges screamed as the door swung inward.

"Police! Anyone here?" Terry's shout echoed unanswered through the dingy space. Shattered glass, graffitied walls, and rotting furniture filled the room — a stark contrast to the order in which he usually found comfort in. Sweeping his flashlight beam across the darkness, he ventured deeper, senses on high alert.

A wave of dread washed over him, seeming to leech the warmth from his very bones. Whipping around, he searched for the source of the unnatural chill. A figure lurked in the shadows, face obscured beneath a hood. Strange runes adorned the skeletal hand they raised, guttural words whispering into the darkness.

"Who are you?" He fought to keep the tremors from his

voice. "What do you want?"

"Your demise." The figure's distorted hiss scraped at his ears. With a flick of their wrist, eldritch energy erupted forth.

He dove to the side, pulses hammering as the blast sizzled past. Scrambling up, his mind reeled, struggling to comprehend the impossible. Spells? Curses? But magic was the stuff of myths...wasn't it?

He aimed his gun with quivering hands. "Stay back!"

The assailant only cackled, a sickening sound oozing malevolence. They hurled more darkness, the unnatural energy prickling over his skin.

Terry dove behind crumbling drywall, his chest heaving as he struggled to process the impossible. His assailant glided towards him, an evil power swirling from their outstretched palms. Terry's mind reeled — magic couldn't be real. His logical worldview lay shattered at his feet.

A pulse of energy sizzled over his head, filling the air with the acrid scent of ozone. He clenched his jaw. There were forces beyond his comprehension threatening everything he sought to protect. But he couldn't afford to dwell on impossibilities. Lives were at stake. Right now, it was his own.

Jaw set with determination, he channeled the icy fear in his veins into fuel. Criminals he could handle, but this spectral foe was something else entirely. Backup and standard methods were useless here. This was a battle for truth and survival. Peering around the crumbling sheetrock, he surveyed his enemy. Their fluid motions seemed otherworldly and unencumbered as they glided nearer, darkness swirling from outstretched palms. Terry's heart slammed against his ribs. There had to be a weakness somewhere...

"Is this what you want, detective?" His foe's voice oozed malevolence. "To see true darkness?"

Terry gritted his teeth as blood and sweat dripped down his temple. He was out of his depth — dangerously so.

The warehouse door swung open with a thundering crash.

Hunter burst into the warehouse, eyes narrowing as they fixed on the spectral figure. Terry glimpsed recognition in his primal snarl — this foe was no ordinary criminal tapping into forbidden power. This was an agent of chaos itself.

Hunter's fingers sliced arcs through the air, movements swift and precise. Ancient syllables spilled from his lips as he worked to unravel the pulsing darkness. Crackling energy enveloped him, the aura of a master practitioner.

Sensing the threat, the hooded figure turned, malice etched beneath its hood. It unleashed a barrage of hissing hexes, each more potent than the last. But Hunter was no stranger to the malevolent arts. He moved with preternatural grace, shattering each attack mid-flight with dazzling counter runes.

The warehouse thrummed with the symphony of their duel — ethereal lights flashing, energy crackling. Two wielders locked in an ancient battle between order and oblivion.

Awe gripped Terry as he watched Hunter dance with darkness itself. His gun felt useless in his white-knuckled grip — bullets were no match for supernatural foes. Instead, he poised himself to assist Hunter, ready to react to any openings.

The warehouse became a battleground of flickering light and swirling blackness. The hooded figure's attacks grew increasingly desperate and uncontrolled, their frustration evident in each wild strike. In contrast, Hunter moved with effortless precision, anticipation guiding his motions as if he had fought such battles for centuries.

Terry's mind reeled, struggling to integrate magic's reality into his worldview. What he had dismissed as fantasy and folklore now crackled to life before his eyes, the rules he thought governed reality crumbling. This was a realm beyond logic, the existence of forces both wondrous and terrifying.

As spells continued ricocheting off the walls, Terry steeled himself. If he and Hunter were to rein in these arcane threats, he would need to expand his perspective. There were mysteries left to unravel that he had sworn to illuminate.

In a decisive moment, Hunter seized an opening in the spectral barrage. Channeling crackling energy into his palms, he unleashed a brilliant lance of light. It speared through swirling darkness to strike the hooded figure at its core. An agonized wail pierced the air as its form flickered, strength fading like a guttering candle.

But defeat did not come swiftly. With malicious tenacity, the weakened figure hurled one final blast toward Terry. He dove behind crumbling masonry, the black energy exploding against the stone. Debris pelted down around him.

Rising, Terry's eyes caught on something glinting amidst the rubble — a shard of broken glass. His own reflection peered back, fragmented and distorted. Terry clasped it tightly, this strange mirror seeming to reflect the cracks forming in his understanding of everything.

Jaw set, he stepped up beside Hunter, shard in hand. If they were to defeat this darkness, he would need to reshape his perspective. Together, they faced the wavering figure that threatened everything Terry had sworn to protect.

As the warehouse trembled, Hunter gripped Terry's arm, urgency in his voice. "We need to go — now!"

"Who — what was that?" Terry gasped as they hurried from the crumbling warehouse, his mind still struggling to process the impossibilities.

Hunter's gaze was grave, determination etched on his face. "The enemy we've hunted has finally emerged. But they're just the beginning — things will get worse before it gets better."

Terry grappled with the implications even as his feet pounded the pavement. Magic, spells, a man capable of battling the arcane...it was too much. But he had no choice but to trust Hunter now.

"Okay, let's go," Terry managed, voice quavering. The warped reality seemed to peel back as they fled, the familiar streets settling around them once more.

But Terry still felt the encounter's malevolence clinging

to his senses. Shadows still danced with ominous intent no matter how far they ran. The night air tasted bitter, the lingering resonance of the magic setting his teeth on edge. This was a world he no longer recognized. Its once-solid foundations crumbled away to reveal the nightmares seething beneath.

"Can you explain while we move?" Terry's hands quivered with adrenaline as they hurried through the city streets. His wide eyes darted about, grasping for any anchor of normalcy amidst the chaos.

"Sure." Urgency laced Hunter's steady tone. "Savannah is under threat from forces beyond anything you've faced — supernatural beings that have infiltrated and gained power."

Terry's mind reeled, struggling to integrate the impossible concept. Dark presences in his city? It defied everything he thought he knew, yet the truth now stared him down, daring him to deny it after what he'd just witnessed.

"Fine." His jaw tightened. "Then we need to stop them."

"Agreed, but caution is critical. They are far more dangerous than you grasp." Hunter's voice dropped, barely above a murmur. As they slipped through the shadows, Terry sensed the unseen world shifting around them, stirring with sinister intent.

They turned a corner, and Terry glimpsed their hooded foe — hunched and muttering guttural syllables, form flickering between human and something far more sinister. Ancient instincts screamed at the nightmarish visage.

"Down!" Hunter shoved Terry behind a sedan. Adrenaline flooded his veins, banishing doubt. This was real — there was no retreating from the truth now.

"Who are they?" Terry risked another glimpse at the morphing figure.

"Servants of Balor. The ancient demon, Mephistopheles, is their true master." Hunter's gaze remained locked on the target. "Their presence means he nears his apocalyptic goal."

Terry's knuckles whitened on his gun. "Then we'll stop

them. Together."

"Good." Grim determination etched Hunter's face. "Let's end this."

Energy prickled over Terry's skin—the twisting figure's magic seemed to stain the very air. He knew then with chilling certainty: a reckoning was at hand.

Hunter hurtled forth, hurling scintillating runes. They seared the creature's flesh, wrenching agonized howls into the night. But it refused defeat, lashing back with throbbing waves of darkness that drove Hunter back.

Refusing to stand idle, determination flooded Terry's veins — love for his city and desire to protect it from encroaching oblivion. His eyes desperately scoured the debris-choked alley until they landed upon salvation — a discarded pipe glinting in the stillness. Terry snatched it up, the cold metal an extension of his will.

Gripping his makeshift weapon, Terry charged into the maelstrom. He wove between lashing tendrils of shadow, each narrowly missing his pounding heart. Above, Hunter's magic cascaded down, bursts of brilliance that momentarily peeled back the demon's defenses.

In those flashes of light, Terry glimpsed his opening. Putting all his momentum behind the pipe, he swung with wild abandon at the core of the writhing abyss. The pipe collided against the demon's armored flesh with a resounding clang, sending shockwaves shuddering through its body. Though the blow barely damaged the hideous form, it stalled the creature's advance. Hunter seized the opportunity, blasting forth torrents of elemental fury — fire and lightning cascading over the writhing void.

In perfect sync, they fought. Magician and warrior united. As scintillating magic scorched at the demon's defenses, Terry struck with cold precision, pipe cracking down whenever its focus wavered. He wove seamlessly between throbbing pulses of shadow, striking again and again, forcing the creature back step by step.

But exhaustion weighed heavy with each blistering spell, each jarring swing. They couldn't endure much longer. Sensing imminent defeat, Hunter cast a desperate counter-curse to force back the encroaching oblivion.

"Run!"

Terry hesitated only a heartbeat before turning to flee into the night, the truth now seared into his mind's eye — malevolent darkness threatening all he held dear and one man who could help stop it.

Beneath the bruised dusk sky, Terry's lungs burned as he and Hunter hurried through gloomy streets. The very air seemed stained by the lingering presence of unseen horrors now lurking behind every corner. Terry couldn't wipe the image of their twisted foe from his mind, its visage a testament to the malevolence they faced.

"Keep moving," Hunter urged, preternaturally calm despite the circumstances. "We can't risk another encounter."

Terry nodded wordlessly, knuckles white upon his useless sidearm. The hooded figure could strike again at any moment.

Nearing Terry's modest brick home, Hunter stopped, critically surveying the area. From his coat, he produced a small leather pouch, sprinkling chalky powder around the property's perimeter. Intricate symbols took form beneath his fingers.

"What are you doing?" Terry's words tumbled out in gasps.

"Wards. To shield us from dark forces." Hunter indicated the now-invisible runes ringing the home. Terry smelled traces of burnt herbs hanging in the air as the symbols melded with the concrete.

"It's done."

"Thank you." Relief washed over Terry as they stepped inside the familiar oak door. His home held warmth and comfort despite the occult threat weighing heavy on his mind.

Spreading yellowed case files across worn wood, Terry

tapped a grainy photo. "There's a pattern here — unsolved murders shrouded in mystery, events twisted by unnatural forces." He traced the ominous path carved through his files.

His analytical mind whirred, connecting the sinister web threaded through evidence he once dismissed. Cold realization crept into his bones. Subtle signs now glared up from beneath harsh lamplight, a trail of corruption tainting the city's hidden corners. Terry met Hunter's steel gaze.

"You were right. Darkness has infected Savannah like a disease. But now..." His jaw clenched tight. "We are going to excise it, no matter what it takes."

Hunter's gaze bored into the files, intensity etched on his face. "This isn't one man's work. It's an organized cult — The Devil's Greenhouse operates boldly under our very noses."

"Can we trust anyone at the station?" Terry's brow furrowed. "Surely others have noticed something amiss..."

Hunter steepled his fingers, considering. "Perhaps, but discretion is critical now. This knowledge endangers all who possess it."

"You're right." Jaw tightening, Terry met Hunter's piercing eyes. "We work in secret. And when the evidence is ironclad, we drag this cult's deeds into the light."

Admiration glinted behind Hunter's stare. "An admirable plan indeed." He leaned closer, curiosity piqued by Terry's determination. Their voices dropped to whispers as they traced the web of corruption strangling the city Terry had sworn to protect.

A heavy silence fell between the two men as they contemplated the harrowing path ahead. For Terry, it was a new reality — one devoid of reason or logic's comforting rhythms. But there was no retreating from the truth now. Together, they would stand against the spreading darkness.

Returning to the room, Terry placed a stack of files down with a thud. "These were Mara's before her suspension."

Hunter nodded slowly. "I spoke with her afterwards. She

seemed relieved someone was listening."

Terry's shoulders slumped. "I should have kept an open mind."

"Let's focus on what she found." Hunter's weathered hands opened a file, pages whispering.

They huddled over her findings as if sharing forbidden secrets. Terry's fingers ran over grainy photos, documenting aftermaths only the occult could produce.

"Here..." Terry tapped a report insistently. "Mara requested backup multiple times, but Captain Franklin denied her. Claimed lack of resources, low priority." His eyes flashed. "It has to be deliberate obstruction."

Frowning, Hunter leaned closer, perusing Carl's scrawled notes. "He was more invested in image than truth. This rot runs deeper than we assumed..."

"Exactly!" Anger laced Terry's words. "Captain Franklin must have suspected, yet he smothered Mara's investigation instead of supporting it."

Fear and exhilaration warred within Terry. Defying Captain Franklin was dangerous, but stopping the ritual and exposing the truth would be worth any risk. He pictured Mara — her tireless dedication evident in the dark circles rimming her eyes, her steadfast belief that they could make a difference keeping her going on little sleep.

Terry paused, the weight of their task bearing down upon him. So much darkness lurked beneath Savannah's genteel veneer, threatening the very soul of the city he had sworn to protect.

"We're dealing with forces beyond mortal comprehension," Hunter said solemnly. "But we must push on, no matter the cost."

Terry nodded. As much as it pained him to accept, this was no ordinary criminal conspiracy. Ancient, eldritch powers were at work, their tendrils coiled around the city's pillars. Still, a kernel of doubt remained lodged in Terry's mind. He had built his life upon reason and evidence. To confront the irrational and unknowable went against everything he believed in.

Hunter seemed to sense his reservation. "I know how difficult this is," he said quietly. "But you've seen too much now to turn back. The truth has already claimed you as its own."

Terry stared down at the occult symbols scrawled across the files. This was Mara's life's work, her desperate attempt to pull back the veil and reveal the darkness lurking beneath. Could he walk away, knowing what she had sacrificed? "I need some time to think."

Hunter stood to leave. "I understand. This is a lot to take in."

Terry's worried gaze met Hunter's steadfast resolve. "You have no idea..." He ran a shaky hand through his disheveled locks. "This goes against everything I've been taught to believe."

Hunter grabbed his leather satchel and slung the strap over his shoulder. "The wards should hold. I must go." He turned to leave. "Just remember that time is not a luxury right now. Decide quickly. We could use your help."

Terry watched the door close behind Hunter. He felt like the weight of the world now rested on his shoulders. After all he'd just witnessed, he needed a drink in the worst way.

The dive bar's grimy interior matched Terry's disheveled appearance as he nursed a glass of whiskey. Dark circles ringed his bloodshot eyes, a testament to his haunted thoughts. The amber liquid swirled in his glass, a poor substitute for the peace he sought.

The creak of the door barely registered as Mara entered. Her purposeful stride carried her to Terry's table, but he remained fixated on his drink, shoulders slumped. "Never thought I'd find you in a place like this."

Terry's gaze flickered up, then away. The weight of unspoken horrors seemed to press down on him. "Yeah, well. Things change."

Mara slid into the seat across from him, her eyes filled with concern. Terry avoided her searching look, taking a long pull from his glass. The whiskey burned, but it was nothing compared to the memories searing his mind.

"Talk to me, Terry. Please."

His voice was rough, defeated. "Nothing to talk about."

"That's bullshit. I know you saw something. Something you can't explain."

Terry shook his head, his fingers tightening around the glass. The din of the bar faded away, leaving only the pounding of his heart and Mara's insistent presence.

"You don't have to go through this alone. Let me help."

Finally, Terry met her gaze. His eyes were haunted pools, reflecting terrors beyond imagination. "You were right, okay? About...all of it. I didn't want to believe you, but now..."

He trailed off, emotion threatening to overwhelm him. Mara reached out, her touch on his hand a lifeline in a sea of darkness.

"I know how hard this is for you. But we don't have time for doubts anymore."

Dread coiled in Terry's gut. "Why? What's happening?"

Mara leaned in, her voice dropping to a whisper that seemed to carry the weight of the world. "We've discovered an apocalyptic cult. They're planning a ritual to unleash...something terrible."

"Jesus Christ." The words escaped Terry in a horrified breath.

"Which is why I need you, Terry. I've been tasked with leading a covert team to stop them. We have to face this threat together."

Terry's mind reeled. The whiskey in his glass suddenly seemed inadequate protection against the horrors Mara described. His face contorted, wrestling with the enormity of what she was asking.

"I don't know, Mara. I'm not sure I'm ready for something like this."

"Yes, you are. I've always trusted you. Now, I need you

to trust me."

The moment stretched, taut with tension. Terry's inner struggle played out across his features — fear, doubt, and finally, resolve. He met Mara's gaze, finding strength in her unwavering belief.

"Okay. Okay, I'm with you. Let's end these bastards."

Mara nodded, relief and gratitude softening her features. She stood, and Terry followed suit, leaving behind the false comfort of alcohol and isolation.

"Grab your things. We've got work to do."

Terry tossed some crumpled bills on the sticky table. As they headed for the exit, a sense of grim determination settled over them. United once more, they stepped out into the night, ready to face the darkness that threatened to consume the world.

CHAPTER 12
A FLICKER OF LIGHT

The church interior bore the scars of recent paranormal activity. Scorch marks marred the once-pristine walls, pews lay overturned like discarded toys, and holy objects and relics stood defiled, mocking their former sanctity.

Father Alex moved through the devastation, his clerical vestments a stark contrast to the chaos surrounding him. He swept debris with mechanical motions, his hands trembling as he attempted to clean the defaced altars. Grief etched deep lines into his face, exhaustion weighing heavily on his slumped shoulders.

His eyes taking in the damage with a heavy heart. The events of the past few days had shaken his faith to its core. Evil had invaded this holy place, the house of God left in ruins. Alex sighed deeply as he righted a toppled candelabra, carefully returning the bent candles to their holders.

As he worked, a strange sensation came over him, like a whisper at the edge of hearing. He stilled, tilting his head to listen. At first, he thought it was just the wind sighing through the broken stained glass windows. But no, this was something else. A voice seemed to echo from the very stones of the church, indistinct but urgent.

"Danger..." Alex murmured. "More danger to come?"

The hairs on the back of his neck prickled as the spectral voice continued its cryptic warning. Images flashed through Alex's mind — fire, blood, a swirling vortex opening to realms beyond mortal comprehension. He swayed on his feet, bracing himself against a fractured pew.

When the visions faded, Alex was left shaken. Was this a message from the divine or some trickery from the demonic entities he now knew to be real? Either way, he understood the meaning behind the ominous words. Their struggle was far from over. More evil was coming, and Alex had to prepare.

Strengthening his resolve, the priest turned his eyes heavenward. "I hear you," he whispered. "And I will be ready."

The work of restoring the church would be arduous, but Father Alex felt emboldened by the strange message he had received. Though evil had marred this holy place, goodness would prevail.

As he swept away the last of the debris, Alex said a silent prayer over the altar. Light began to filter through the broken stained glass windows, bathing the sanctuary in soft hues. The church still bore scars, but there was beauty here too.

Father Alex worked methodically through the morning, scrubbing away the sinister markings and righting the overturned pews. Though his spirit felt heavy with the weight of the church's desecration, he focused on the light that now streamed through the broken windows. It was a reminder that goodness still pierced even the darkest of days, though his mind was troubled. The dire warning continued to echo through his thoughts. More evil coming, greater than they had faced before. He shuddered at the memory of the visions — fire, blood, screams of torment. Whatever malevolent force had desecrated the church was not finished with its unholy work.

As he polished the altar rail, Alex felt the hairs on his neck stand up again. The whispering was back, slithering into his mind.

"It comes..." the voice hissed. "It comes again..."

He whirled around, half expecting to see some demonic figure lurking in the shadowed recesses of the church. But there was nothing. Only stillness and that faint warning reverberating against his consciousness.

Suddenly, the floor beneath Alex's feet began to vibrate, dust shaking loose from the rafters. The trembling intensified, pews rattling violently against the stone floor. The priest's eyes widened in alarm and understanding. The warning had come not a moment too soon.

An unnatural wind swept through the sanctuary, whistling between fractured walls. It coalesced into a dark vortex above the altar, crackling with malevolent energy. Alex shielded his eyes from the maelstrom, planting his feet firmly as debris swirled around him. He would not abandon this holy place.

With an ear-splitting blast, the occult forces unleashed their fury. What was left of the stained glass windows exploded inward, multi-colored shards scything through the air. Alex threw his arms up to shield his face as the stained glass rained down around him in a kaleidoscopic hailstorm. Jagged shards tore through the heavy fabric of his vestments, slicing into the skin beneath. Warm blood trickled down his arms, but he barely felt the pain over the maelstrom raging in the church.

The howling wind intensified, buffeting Alex as he struggled to remain standing. The dark vortex above the altar spun faster, a black hole threatening to swallow everything in its path. From its churning depths came an unearthly shriek that chilled Alex to his core. The demon had returned to finish its unholy work.

Gripping his rosary, Alex planted his feet and began to chant Latin prayers of exorcism and protection. His voice rang out strong and clear even against the screaming winds. The vortex shuddered and contracted, emitting an anguished, inhuman wail. Alex pressed forward, holding his ground both physically and spiritually.

With a deafening crack, a bolt of lightning erupted from the vortex, scorching the air as it arced toward Alex. At the last second he dove aside, the bolt blasting a smoking crater where he had stood. His exorcisms were weakening the demon, but Alex feared he alone did not have the power to banish it fully from this plane.

The temperature dropped sharply as an unnatural cold emanated from the portal. Frost crept across the floor and over the fractured pews. The wind whipped at Alex's clerical robes, threatening to tear them from his body. Still, the priest did not waver.

A form began to take shape within the portal's inky depths. Eyes as black as the void stared back at Alex, filled with ancient malice. The demon's body continued to manifest, blood-red skin wrapped tight over an emaciated frame. It perched on the altar, long claws gripping the edges.

"You have no power here, hellspawn," Alex shouted above the howling wind. His hand gripped the silver cross hanging around his neck.

The demon's lipless mouth cracked into a gruesome smile, revealing rows of jagged teeth. It leapt from the altar, bounding across the sanctuary on all fours like a feral beast. Alex stood paralyzed as the creature bore down on him, unsure if his faith would be enough to stop its advance.

At the last moment, he found his voice and began reciting the Rite of Exorcism. The Latin verses rang out clear and true despite the maelstrom. As the demon let out an unearthly shriek, Alex continued to recite the Rite of Exorcism with a newfound determination. The silver cross in his hand began to glow intensely, casting a blinding light that forced the creature back. It hissed and spat, its red skin blistering under the divine radiance.

Amidst the chaos, Father Alex felt a surge of strength coursing through his veins. He recognized it as a divine power, a response to his unwavering faith and devotion. Emboldened by this newfound energy, he advanced towards the demon, wielding the cross like a weapon against the encroaching darkness.

"*In nomine Dei nostri Iesu Christi, et eius Sanctissimae Matris Mariae, et omnium sanctorum Angelorum et Sanctorum defendemur in won praelio ut creaturae tuae rescueas ab omni potestate daemonis! I exorcizam te, immunde spiritus, per Deum Patrem omnipotentem!*" Alex shouted the ancient words with conviction, every fiber of his being resonating with the power of his belief.

The demon recoiled further, its form flickering and

wavering in the face of Alex's onslaught. The pews and debris around them creaked and settled as the unnatural storm began to abate. The demon's form flickered as Father Alex's unwavering faith held the darkness at bay. But behind those soulless black eyes, Alex saw the creature's rage growing. This was no mindless beast — an ancient, sinister intelligence was at work here.

Alex knew he couldn't banish it alone. Holding the glowing cross before him, he slowly retreated from the altar while continuing the exorcism rites. The demon followed, crawling spider-like along the fractured pews, its movements jerky and unnatural. Alex's skin crawled at the sight, but he did not falter.

Reaching the heavy oak doors of the church, he pushed them open with his shoulder, still facing the creature as it scuttled after him. As soon as he was through, Alex slammed the doors shut behind him. The demon crashed against the other side, unleashing an unearthly screech of frustration. The oak doors creaked under the assault but held fast.

Alex sagged against the doors, breathing heavily. But his respite was brief. The air grew bitterly cold as frost crept outward from the church in wispy tendrils. He could hear the demon thrashing inside, its shrieks muffled but no less chilling. More ominously, the whispering had returned in full force. Alex pressed his hands over his ears, but the sound reverberated inside his mind.

"It comes..." the voices taunted. "We will feast on your souls!" Images flooded Alex's mind. He opened the doors to confront the beast head-on. As he continued to recite the Rite of Exorcism, the silver cross in his hand glowed brighter and brighter, driving the demonic entity back. The very air around them seemed to crackle with divine energy as Alex's faith and determination grew.

"I *exorcizam te, immunde spiritus, per Deum Filium omnipotentem!*" he cried out, advancing further towards the demon that now cowered before him. The creature's red skin blistered and smoked under the relentless onslaught of holy light.

The demon let out a screech that echoed through the sanctuary as it retreated toward the closing portal. The dark vortex above the altar shuddered and contracted, no longer able to maintain its grip on this realm.

"*Abiago te*! Return to the pit from which you came! *In nomine Patris, et Filii, et Spiritus Sancti*!" Alex thundered the words of exorcism with all his might, and as he finished, he thrust the glowing cross towards the shrinking portal.

With a deafening roar, the demonic entity vanished in a whirlwind of black smoke, drawn back into the waiting maw of the collapsing portal. As it disappeared, an unearthly scream rent the air — a cry of rage and defeat.

With renewed conviction, Alex gathered his tools to begin repairs. The visions had warned of more danger to come, but he would face it without fear. Strengthening both body and spirit for the battles ahead, Alex let the light of faith guide his path. Evil would not claim this place — or those under his protection — without a fight.

The creak of the church door echoed through the hollow space. Mara entered, her footsteps hesitant on the debris-strewn floor. Alex turned, regarding her with a mixture of wariness and skepticism.

"Can I help you, child?" he asked, his voice hoarse.

Mara straightened, her posture shifting from cautious to determined. "Father Alex. I'm Detective Mara Lawson. We need to talk."

Alex's eyes narrowed, a flicker of resignation passing over his features. "The police have already been here regarding the... incidents. I've cooperated fully."

"This goes beyond those incidents, Father. Please, hear me out." Mara's tone held an urgency that gave Alex pause.

She reached into her bag, withdrawing a collection of case files and occult evidence. As she laid them out before him, Alex's eyes widened, horror and recognition battling for dominance in his expression.

"My God..." The words escaped him in a whisper.

Mara pressed on, her voice low and intense. "This cult plans to unleash forces beyond what any of us can comprehend. But we have a chance to stop them. With your help."

Alex stumbled back, his hand gripping a nearby pew for support. "I...I don't know if I'm worthy of this fight anymore. My faith has been shaken to the core. The evil here felt ancient beyond measure. I was powerless."

"That's exactly why we need you," Mara insisted, her eyes locked on his. "Your knowledge of the ancient traditions these fanatics are exploiting. Help us fight fire with fire."

Alex shook his head, conflict etched in every line of his face. "Using darkness against darkness will only breed more darkness, child."

"Please. We're out of options. Before this spreads even further." Desperation tinged Mara's words.

Silence fell between them, heavy with the weight of impending doom. Alex's gaze drifted over the ravaged church, lingering on the defaced symbols of his faith. His shoulders sagged, then straightened as resolve settled over him.

"If this evil has already reached even hallowed ground... you may be right. Drastic action may be required to prevent the spread of such wickedness."

With reverent movements, Alex retrieved a holy stole, draping it over his vestments. The fabric seemed to glow in the dim light, a beacon of hope in the darkness.

"I pray you stay in the light during this fight, child," he said, his voice gaining strength. "But you have my vow — my gifts shall serve the protection of this world to my last breath."

Mara nodded, gratitude and grim determination mingling in her expression. Together, they turned towards the church doors, united in their solemn purpose. As they stepped out into the fading daylight, the weight of their task settled around them, the fate of the world hanging in the balance of their unholy alliance.

Alex paused at the threshold of the church, his hand lingering on the weathered wood of the door frame. The building loomed behind him, a silent sentinel of stone and stained glass that had been his sanctuary for so long. Now, it felt like a tomb.

The air hung heavy with the scent of impending rain, matching the darkness that churned in Alex's gut. He turned, allowing his gaze to sweep over the familiar façade one last time. The Gothic spires reached skyward as if beseeching a God who had long since abandoned this place. Shadows danced across the intricate carvings, twisting them into grotesque masks that seemed to mock his decision.

With a shuddering breath, Alex tore his eyes away from the church. Mara's crusade called to him, promising vengeance and a terrible sense of purpose. He stepped forward, each footfall on the cracked pavement driving him further away from his former life.

As Alex walked away, the first drops of rain began to fall, pattering against the stone steps behind him. He didn't look back again, but he could feel the weight of the church's gaze on his shoulders, a silent judgment that would follow him into the gathering storm.

CHAPTER 13
THE NEWLY FORMED SHADOWGUARD

The newly formed underground Shadowguard compound buzzed with activity, a hive of purpose and preparation. High-tech surveillance equipment materialized on walls and counters, sleek monitors flickering to life under the deft hands of technicians. Encrypted networks hummed into existence, invisible threads of communication weaving through the air.

But amidst the modern marvels, ancient powers took root. Leather-bound tomes, their spines cracked with age, found homes on freshly installed shelves. Arcane symbols bloomed across walls and floors, each line and curve meticulously painted with reverent precision. The air thickened with the scent of old parchment and fresh paint, a heady mixture of past and present.

At every entrance, cutting-edge biometrics meshed with more esoteric psychic screening measures. The compound became a fortress, guarded against threats both mundane and mystical.

Banks of monitors cast their cold light across worried faces. Glimpses of cult activity flashed across the screens, each image a stark reminder of the looming threat. Concern etched itself into furrowed brows and tightened jaws.

From above, the fully outfitted staging ground revealed itself as a masterpiece of integration. The mystical and technological intertwined, neither dominating both essential. It was a bastion of hope in a world teetering on the brink of cosmic horror.

In one corner, a forensics lab emerged, a sleek blend of chrome and glass. Microscopes stood guard over humming servers, their lenses poised to uncover the hidden secrets of both science and sorcery. Nearby, a chamber of relics took form. An altar, its surface darkened by countless rituals, stood ready for the next invocation.

Mara led Serafine through the dimly lit tunnels underneath the old cathedral, their footsteps echoing off the cold stone walls. Though the ancient catacombs had long been sealed off, they now served as the headquarters for the Shadowguard.

Serafine looked around in quiet awe as they passed rooms filled with banks of monitors, high-tech weapons, and strange occult artifacts. It was a fusion of science fiction and the arcane — flickering electronics side by side with ancient tomes and ritual objects.

They entered the main hub, where Mara's fellow Shadowguard operatives were busy training, researching, and coordinating their covert missions against the forces of darkness. Serafine watched with fascination as a pair of operatives in tactical gear entered, fresh from training.

"Impressive, is it not?" Mara said, her green eyes glinting with pride. "We've come a long way from our days of makeshift investigations. Now we have access to resources we never dreamed of."

She led Serafine over to a set of display cases housing all manner of mystical weapons — blessed swords, chalices carved from angel bone, firearms loaded with consecrated mercury rounds. Nearby was an arsenal of more conventional firearms and body armor.

"I know it is a lot to take in," Mara said gently, noticing her friend's overwhelmed expression. "But we will need all of this and more for the battle ahead. The Devil's Greenhouse has grown beyond anything I could have imagined."

Serafine nodded slowly as she took it all in. "I understand the necessity," she said. "Though I admit, part of me had hoped we were past the need for such...implements."

She reached out and delicately touched an intricate ritual blade in one of the cases. "But the darkness is rising again. I have seen it with my own eyes within the Greenhouse."

Mara placed a hand on her shoulder. "Tell me everything you know. We need to move swiftly if we're to have any hope of stopping them."

Serafine's gray eyes narrowed, her expression growing grim. "Their power has expanded beyond the physical plane into realms beyond mortal comprehension. The rituals I witnessed..." She shook her head. "They are meddling with forces they do not understand, trying to tear a hole in the very fabric of reality."

"To what end?" Mara asked. Around them, other Shadowguard operatives paused their tasks, listening intently.

"The annihilation of everything," Serafine said bluntly. "The cult plans to fling open the gates between worlds, unleashing the Old Ones to consume all. Should they succeed, no earthly weapons will save us."

A hush fell over the room. Mara's jaw tightened. "We need to talk to Hunter."

Mara and Serafine made their way through the underground tunnels to the newly established occult library that Hunter had been busy setting up. As they entered the vast, cavernous room, they were awestruck by the sheer volume of arcane tomes, ancient artifacts, and mystical objects that now filled the endless rows of shelves and display cases.

Hunter could be seen up on a tall ladder, busily sliding heavy, leatherbound books into place while directing other Shadowguard members who were assisting him. "No, no, the Pnakotic Manuscripts need to go in the ForbiddenTexts section, and someone please handle that Obsidian Orb with care!" he called out in an irritated tone, not even glancing down from his task.

Mara cleared her throat loudly, and Hunter peered down, his eyes lighting up when he saw the two women standing there. "Mara, Serafine! You're just in time. We've acquired some fascinating new relics that I cannot wait to show you," he said enthusiastically as he clambered down the ladder.

Up close, his odd wardrobe was even more apparent, from his scuffed boots to the long, black leather coat and the mystical amulets that hung from chains around his neck. But his blue eyes glinted sharply with intelligence as he eagerly led Mara and Serafine through the library, raving about the rare occult treasures he had uncovered and how they might aid their fight.

Serafine glanced around nervously. "Have you discerned how to safely handle such dangerous artifacts?"

Hunter waved a hand dismissively, and Mara placed a hand on Hunter's arm, stopping his enthusiastic rambling. "As fascinating as these artifacts may be, we have more pressing concerns," she said gravely. "Serafine has brought dire news from the Greenhouse. Their plans have...escalated."

Hunter's expression shifted, his excitement fading. He turned his piercing blue eyes to Serafine. "Tell me everything."

Serafine recounted the cult's intentions — the rituals to open gates to other realms and unleash beings of unfathomable power. Hunter listened intently, brow furrowed.

"We always knew they dabbled in forces beyond their control," he said. "But this..." He trailed off, shaking his head.

"Can we stop them?" Mara asked. Around them, Shadowguard members continued their work, but an undercurrent of unease now tainted the purposeful air.

"I don't know." Hunter's admission sent a chill through the room. "But we must try. And I may know where we can start."

He led them to a table holding an ancient text, its pages cracked and yellowed. "The Librum Tenebrarum," he explained. "It mentions rituals similar to what Serafine described. If we can translate it, there may be clues about how to reverse the process."

Mara nodded. "Get whatever resources you need. We'll begin preparations to infiltrate the Greenhouse."

Father Alex entered the occult library, his gaze drifting upwards in wonder at the vast collection of mystical tomes and artifacts. Though initially shocked by the sheer volume of occult objects, his expression soon softened with understanding. This was a necessary evil in service of the greater good.

Mara stepped forward to greet him, a look of relief flashing across her face. "Father Alex, thank God you're here. We need your guidance now more than ever."

She quickly made introductions, though Father Alex was already familiar with several Shadowguard members from his work in the community. Hunter pumped his hand enthusiastically before launching into an explanation of his latest occult findings. Father Alex listened patiently, interjecting an occasional question or word of caution.

When Hunter finished, Father Alex let out a slow breath. "Extraordinary. I had heard rumors, but nothing as troubling as this." He turned his hazel eyes to Mara. "What can I do to help?"

Mara smiled gratefully. "We need access to the church basement. I believe there are tunnels connecting it to areas beneath the Greenhouse compound. It may provide a way to infiltrate undetected."

Father Alex nodded. "Of course. The church is at your disposal." He placed a gentle hand on Mara's shoulder. "Have faith. With God's help, we will stop this evil from spreading."

His calm assurance lifted the mood in the room. Serafine eyed him curiously, seeming surprised by his willingness to help. "You take this all rather well, Father, for a devout man of God."

Father Alex smiled gently at Serafine. "I have seen and heard many strange and troubling things in my ministry. While the occult is not my area of expertise, I know there are forces of darkness in this world that we do not fully comprehend."

He gestured around the room. "All of this may seem frightening or unnatural to the uninitiated. But I believe your intentions are good, and so I choose to have faith that God is working through each of you in the fight against evil."

Serafine considered his words silently. Mara stepped forward and clasped Father Alex's hand.

"Your faith and wisdom have been a light in the darkness for many of us," she said warmly. "We couldn't do this without you."

Father Alex shook his head modestly. "You give me too much credit. All I've done is provide spiritual guidance and a sympathetic ear." He looked around the room, meeting each person's eyes. "The true courage lies with all of you who face the darkness head-on to protect others."

A murmur of appreciation went through the gathered Shadowguard members. Father Alex had a gift for speaking from the heart in a way that inspired those around him.

Hunter cleared his throat awkwardly. "Right, yes, well said...now about accessing those tunnels..."

Mara suppressed a smile. Hunter always seemed slightly uncomfortable with overt shows of emotion.

"Of course," Father Alex said briskly. "Let me show you the entrance in the basement."

Father Alex led Mara, Serafine, and Hunter through a side door into the basement of the old stone church. The air was cool and damp, with the musty smell of centuries-old masonry. Shadows flickered across the rough walls from their flashlight beams as they descended the worn stone steps.

At the bottom was a large, open room cluttered with boxes and old furnishings covered in sheets. Father Alex wove through the maze, footsteps echoing on the hard floor until he reached a wooden door set into the far wall.

"Through here," he said, producing an old iron key that turned reluctantly in the lock. The door creaked open to reveal a cramped, earthen passage sloping down into darkness.

"As far as I know, these tunnels date back to the early 1700s when religious persecution was common," Father Alex explained, his voice hushed in the confined space. "They provided escape routes and connections between safe houses."

Mara shone her flashlight down the tunnel. Tree roots poked through the walls and ceiling, and the damp earth smelled of decay. She glanced at Serafine, who gave a subtle nod. They had explored crypts far more unsettling than this.

"Fascinating," breathed Hunter as he craned his neck to peer down the passage. "Who knows where these could lead? Or what occult relics might be hidden inside?" His eyes glinted with excitement.

Father Alex looked grave. "I cannot say for certain where the tunnels lead today. But I pray they offer us safe passage."

"Me too, Father. Okay, guys, let's see where these tunnels lead." Mara stepped cautiously into the tunnel, sweeping her flashlight beam along the crumbling earthen walls. She could feel the weight of centuries pressing down in the stale air. This sacred passage had likely not been tread for decades, if not longer.

Behind her, Serafine glided silently while Hunter seemed to vibrate with nervous energy, impatient to explore the forgotten darkness. Father Alex brought up the rear, murmuring a quiet prayer of protection.

"Keep sharp," Mara said quietly. "We don't know what might be lurking down here." Rat bones crunched under her boots and she noted gaps in the walls where other passages split off into void. She paused at each junction, shining her light down the options, searching for clues.

The main tunnel continued sloping downward at an uneasy angle, twisting and turning. The occasional dangling root brushed Mara's face with clammy fingers. The further they went, the heavier the air seemed to press down.

Then, the tunnel opened into a small chamber. Mara swept her light over crumbling brick walls that showed hints of strange symbols etched beneath layers of dirt and mold. Rusty manacles hung empty from iron rings set into the walls.

Hunter edged closer to one, squinting. "Some kind of holding cell?" he murmured. "Or perhaps a site of arcane rituals long forgotten..."

Mara shivered despite herself. She preferred a straight-up fight to unseen, lingering menace. What dark secrets did these buried chambers still hold?

Father Alex stepped forward, pointing into the shadows.

"There's another door." He used the iron key he still held and tried the lock. It turned with little protest. The door opened to more darkness. He crossed himself. "Our journey is not over."

Father Alex led the way into the dark tunnel, his footsteps cautious on the uneven earthen floor. Mara followed close behind, one hand trailing along the clammy stone wall to guide her steps. She glanced back to see Serafine just steps behind, her face unreadable in the dim glow of their flashlights. Hunter brought up the rear, already engrossed in examining the tunnel walls and murmuring excitedly to himself.

The air grew colder and more stagnant as they descended at a gradual slope. After several minutes, Mara felt the tunnel begin to level out. Father Alex slowed and held up a hand for them to stop. His flashlight illuminated a decrepit wooden door embedded in the wall just ahead. Iron bands bordered the warped oak planks, and a rusty iron ring hung from a nail at its center.

Father Alex grasped the ring and pulled. The door resisted at first, then slowly creaked open on protesting hinges. Beyond was another dark chamber. He turned back to the others, his face etched with solemn purpose.

Mara swept her flashlight beam across the chamber, revealing rough stone walls and a dirt floor. The air was heavy with the musty odor of age and abandonment. She saw no other doorways leading out — whatever this room contained, it seemed they had reached their destination.

She played her light over the walls, noticing strange symbols carved into the stone, interwoven with disturbing imagery that looked like creatures from a nightmare. Mara suppressed a shudder, wondering what foul rituals had once been carried out here.

"Fascinating," Hunter murmured as he moved closer to examine the markings. "Clearly some form of archaic runic script, though I cannot decipher it presently..."

Mara's light fell upon a wooden table along the back wall. It was the only furnishing in the empty chamber. She crossed to it, sweeping aside layers of dust and dirt with a gloved hand. Beneath lay a weathered leather book, its cover cracked with age.

"A journal," Mara said. She opened it gingerly, the old pages rustling. Scanning the faded, spidery handwriting, she saw it was a record of someone's exploration of these tunnels, perhaps decades ago. What secrets might it contain?

She turned to Father Alex and the others. "This could give us some answers. Let's get it back to the church where Hunter can study it properly."

Father Alex nodded. "Our work here is done for now. We should return above ground before anything unsavory finds us."

Mara tucked the journal securely in her pack. As they turned to leave the chamber, a low, rumbling sound echoed up the tunnel behind them. Mara spun around, her flashlight beam darting across the dark passage.

"What was that?" Hunter whispered.

The rumbling came again, louder this time. Loose dirt sifted down from the ceiling of the tunnel. Mara felt the ground vibrate faintly beneath her feet.

"We need to move, now!" she said urgently.

They hurried to the chamber entrance, Mara in the lead. As they passed through the doorway, a deafening crack resounded from the depths of the tunnel. A rush of cool air hit them, laced with the odor of damp earth. Mara's light revealed the tunnel walls starting to crumble as some ancient support gave way.

"Run!" Mara shouted. She grabbed Father Alex's sleeve, and they bolted down the passage. The ceiling was collapsing rapidly behind them in a cacophony of falling dirt and stone. They had only seconds to escape.

Mara's lungs burned but she didn't slow, dragging the priest behind her. She glimpsed Serafine just ahead, gliding swiftly and silently over the uneven ground. Behind them, Hunter struggled to keep pace as the rocks fell behind him.

The surface tunnel was just ahead. Mara could see the basement door tantalizingly close. With a final burst of speed, she shoved Father Alex through the doorway and lunged after him. Seconds later, Hunter stumbled through, coated in dirt.

Mara slammed the basement door shut, her heart pounding as the tunnel collapsed behind it in a deafening avalanche of stone and earth. Dust billowed up through the cracks around the door into the basement.

"Is everyone alright?" Mara coughed, waving the dust from her face.

Father Alex leaned heavily against the wall, catching his breath and nodding. Serafine stood silent and still, her gray eyes betraying no hint of fear from their narrow escape.

Hunter stumbled forward, covered in dirt, his eyes alight. "Remarkable! The structural instability of the tunnels implies they are even older than I hypothesized. We are fortunate to have made it out alive!"

Mara shook her head wryly. Trust Hunter to be excited by a near-death experience. She was simply relieved they had all made it through in one piece.

"We need to regroup and examine what we've found," Mara said. "Hunter, study the journal and see if you can decipher anything about the ritual chamber. We also need to alert the authorities so they can secure the area."

Father Alex straightened, having caught his breath. "Agreed. Let us reconvene at the church rectory. I believe we are facing a greater danger than we realized."

Mara nodded. She had hoped to find answers down in the tunnels. Instead, they had only uncovered more dark mysteries and occult threats lurking beneath Savannah's haunted past. But she knew one thing for certain.

Whatever evil force was rising, she and the Shadowguard would be ready to face it head-on.

***

A few days later, back in the church's basement, Hunter was studying the journal they found in the tunnel. It dated back to 1856. It was written by a man studying Balor's cult, The Devil's

Greenhouse.

Hunter pored over the ancient text, translating the elaborate cursive script. Many of the pages were damaged by water and mildew. The ink faded and smeared, but he could make out enough disturbing details.

The journal's author, Clarence Whitfield, had infiltrated the cult to expose their occult practices. In vivid detail, he described their gatherings in the old tunnel sanctuary — the chanting, the ritual sacrifices, the summoning of otherworldly entities. They worshipped Mephistopheles, a pagan deity referred to as the Ravenous God, who granted visions and dark powers.

One passage in particular gave Hunter chills:

"Last eve on All Hallows, I witnessed the cult's foulest ritual yet. Ten virgins were offered to Mephistopheles's ravenous jaws. His eye opened, terrible and burning, and the screaming ceased. His servants then took the blood and...I cannot put to page the vile acts that followed."

Hunter shook his head in dismay. Such evil had lurked beneath Savannah's streets over a century ago. And now history was repeating.

He turned the page carefully. The next entry described a dark priest named Balor, who led the cult and communed with Mephistopheles directly. Balor drew occult symbols on the tunnel walls to focus the demon's energy. Hunter's eyes widened as he read Whitfield's ominous words. A gateway to another realm, a breeding ground for darkness — if the cult succeeded in opening such a portal beneath Savannah, the consequences could be catastrophic.

He flipped through the remaining pages but found no further entries after that revelation. What had happened to Clarence Whitfield? Had the cult discovered his deception and silenced him? The questions nagged at Hunter as he closed the journal.

A knock at the door made him look up. Mara entered, her expression grim.

"The police searched the tunnels," she said. "The collapse destroyed most of the sanctuary chamber. But they did find something among the rubble."

She held out a charred scrap of parchment. Hunter took it delicately, smoothing out the fragile fibers. Scrawled in an archaic script were fragments of an incantation:

"When the stars align above the cypress grove, the way shall open... The Feaster from the Furthest Void shall come forth to claim..."

The rest was too damaged to read. But the foreboding words sent a shudder down Hunter's spine. This was some kind of ritual text, likely used by Balor's original cult. Which meant their dark purpose could be resurgent.

"We have to stop them," Mara said, her green eyes flashing with determination. "Before they can finish what was started over a century ago. Balor's legacy ends here and now."

Mara paced the church basement, her mind racing. The charred ritual text was the first real lead they had found, but it raised as many questions as it answered.

What did the stars aligning above the cypress grove signify? What foul entity was this 'Feaster from the Furthest Void'? And how exactly did Balor's cult plan to summon it forth into their world?

She glanced at Hunter, who was scribbling notes feverishly, cross-referencing the ritual against various occult tomes spread open on his desk. His unconventional expertise gave them an edge, but they were running out of time.

Mara thought back to Clarence Whitfield's long-lost journal and the virgins sacrificed in the tunnel sanctuary. Whatever the cult was planning, lives were on the line. But the police sweep of the underground chambers had turned up no evidence of recent activity.

Where were they gathering now? How had the cult survived over a century, passing down Balor's legacy in secret? And who was leading them today?

She thought of the families shopping and laughing only a few blocks away, oblivious to the occult forces converging unseen around them. And she thought of Father Alex, back at his church, quietly comforting his parishioners, preparing them for the coming storm.

This was her city. These were her people. She had to put a stop to this.

Mara paced the worn stone floor of the church basement, impatience and frustration brewing within her. Three days had passed since their harrowing escape from the collapsing tunnels. Three days, while Balor's cult continued their sinister preparations unimpeded somewhere in the city.

She paused to peer over Hunter's shoulder at the journal laid out on the table. "Have you learned anything more we can act on?" she asked sharply.

Hunter didn't look up, engrossed in painstakingly transcribing a damaged page of text. "Patience, Mara. We face an occult threat over a century in the making. If we are to thwart it, we must proceed with care."

Mara crossed her arms. "We don't have time for care. Every moment we delay, Balor gets closer to..."

She trailed off as Father Alex entered the basement, his expression grave. "What is it, Father?" she asked.

"Another young woman has gone missing," he said quietly. "That makes six in the past month."

Mara's jaw tightened. She knew what that likely meant — another sacrificial victim for Balor's insidious rituals.

"Did the police find anything?" she asked.

Father Alex shook his head. "Just like the others, no trace except..." He hesitated.

"Except what?" Mara pressed.

"Ravens," he said reluctantly. "Dozens of ravens perched around her apartment building, watching."

CHAPTER 14
INTO THE SERPENT'S LAIR

The briefing room crackled with tense energy as Shadowguard prepared for their mission. Mara stood authoritatively at the front, her piercing green eyes surveying each member seated before her.

Mara clicked a remote, and an image of an isolated compound appeared on the screen behind her. "This is the cult's gathering place, located on Savannah's outskirts. Thanks to Hunter's research and verification through Serafine, we've learned the ritual requires six additional human sacrifices to occur precisely at midnight on the planetary alignment. We cannot allow this to happen."

Hunter stood up, his piercing blue eyes surveying the room. In his hand, he held a weathered leather journal, its pages yellowed with age. "This is the lost journal of Clarence Whitfield," Hunter began, his voice low and ominous. "We found it a few days ago, hidden in a sealed chamber beneath the old tunnels that run under the city." He slowly paced the room as he continued. "Whitfield was an occultist who came to Savannah in the 1850s. He had heard rumors of mysterious rituals being performed out in the swamps by an ancient cult. What he documented in this journal is...beyond belief."

Hunter flipped open the book, gently turning the aged pages. "According to Whitfield, the cult worshiped the primordial entity Mephistopheles. Every seven years, Mephistopheles demanded a sacrifice — six lives given freely to sustain his connection to our world. For decades, this blood ritual was upheld, passed down through generations of followers."

He looked up, his face grim. "Now, all signs indicate The

Devil's Greenhouse intends to honor that original bargain. If they complete the ritual, Mephistopheles will walk the earth once more."

Hunter's eyes flashed with intensity. "They intended to open a permanent gate, allowing Mephistopheles to cross over into our world. The ritual required a willing vessel, someone depraved enough to allow the demon to possess their body. I believe they have that vessel."

He turned and stared at the image of the compound. "It seems history is poised to repeat itself. This 'Great Rite' aims to finish what was started over a century ago. If we don't stop it, our world will be plunged into eternal darkness."

Serafine leaned forward, the overhead lighting catching in her gray eyes. "This ritual is more perilous than you know," she said, her voice hushed yet resonant in the small room. "The Great Rite is not merely human sacrifice. It is a blasphemous imitation of the most sacred rite. Perverted thus, it will wrench open the gates between worlds with catastrophic results."

She swept her gaze over each member as if imparting some secret knowledge that only she fully grasped. "We must not underestimate the power arrayed against us. Dark forces stir in anticipation of this unholy event. I have seen it in my dreams."

Terry shifted uncomfortably in his seat, demons, sacrifices, rituals. It was almost more than he could bear.

Father Alex nodded solemnly, making the sign of the cross. "I fear Serafine speaks the truth. The spiritual darkness gathering over Savannah chills my soul."

Father Alex leaned forward, his brow furrowed with concern. "I'm afraid another young woman has gone missing," he said gravely. "That makes seven in the past month. All of them vanished without a trace, just like the others." He removed his glasses and rubbed his eyes wearily before continuing. "I've also been noticing a disturbing number of ravens gathering around the church. Their incessant cawing echoes day and night. It's as if they are drawn here by some malevolent force."

Alex sighed heavily. "In all my years as a priest, I've never encountered such palpable evil. It's seeping into every corner of Savannah, stirring up fear and madness. I fear what is to come when the stars align and the ritual begins."

He looked at each of them in turn. "But we cannot allow despair to take root in our hearts. As long as we stand together, there is hope. Faith and light can still triumph over darkness."

Serafine nodded slowly, her gray eyes clouded with foreboding. "I agree with Father Alex. My dreams have grown more vivid of late. I have witnessed unspeakable rituals in the decaying mansions along the riverfront. Seen visions of a great horned beast with eyes of fire presiding over blood-soaked orgies." She paused, gathering her thoughts. "But there are glimpses of hope as well. A lone warrior wielding a flaming sword against the shadows. An ancient symbol etched in light, banishing the darkness."

Serafine focused intently on Mara. "You and I have a shared destiny, old friend, whether you accept it or not. Our fates are intertwined with the coming battle. Without us, all is lost."

Mara tensed, old memories surfacing. A friendship severed, two paths diverging into the unknown. Could she trust Serafine now, after so long apart? But the recklessness of youth still flickered deep within her.

"I'm listening," Mara said quietly. "Tell me what you have in mind."

Serafine's eyes glinted knowingly. She unrolled a parchment map, markings and symbols barely visible in the dim light.

"There is an entrance here, by the river's edge," she said, indicating a location. "It will take us beneath the compound to the ritual chambers underground. We must traverse it carefully."

Mara listened intently as Serafine described the secret entrance by the river. Though wary, a familiar thrill coursed through her veins. This was the life she had turned away from, and despite the danger, part of her had missed the excitement.

"It won't be easy," Mara said. "We'll need to evade their sentries and magical wards. Do you really think we can stop the ritual in time?"

Serafine met her gaze steadily. "We have to try. The fate of this city and perhaps the world depends on it. I know our past is...complicated. But right now, we need each other."

Mara took a deep breath and nodded. "Okay. Let's do this."

Hunter and Terry looked at each other warily as Mara and Serafine outlined their plan.

"This is foolishness," Hunter said sharply. "That tunnel could be crawling with cultists and who knows what foul magics. At least let me create some protective talismans to shield you."

Terry nodded in agreement. "We should inform the department and get back up. Rushing in blind is too risky."

Mara's eyes flashed defiantly. "There's no time. The ritual could happen any night now. Serafine and I can slip in quietly without detection."

"Please listen to reason," Terry implored. "We're a team in this. We all want to stop the cult, but no one should go alone."

Serafine gave a cryptic smile. "Some paths must be walked without company. Mara and I have gifts...and debts to repay. This mission is ours."

Hunter slammed a fist down. "Confound it. I cannot allow you two to throw your lives away!" His usual detached mien was replaced by frantic concern.

But Mara and Serafine would not be deterred. As Terry and Hunter argued and cajoled, the two women calmly geared up in silence, old habits kicking in. Mara checked her guns while Serafine prepared charms and talismans.

Father Alex approached, his eyes full of compassion. "Be careful, my friends," he said softly. "Though we walk in darkness, God is with us." He made the sign of the cross over them. Mara bowed her head, accepting his blessing.

A tense energy filled the safehouse, everyone sensing the

gravity of the situation. The men could only watch helplessly as the pair slipped into the shadows and vanished into the night on their secret quest, alone against the gathering dark but united at last.

The cult's compound loomed on the outskirts of the city, an imposing edifice of dark stone surrounded by a wrought iron fence. Mara and Serafine made their way stealthily to the river's edge. Following Serafine's directions, they discovered a drainage tunnel half-submerged. They descended into the narrow tunnel, flashlights providing the only illumination against the oppressive darkness. The dank air was heavy with the scent of mildew and stagnant water. Somewhere in the distance, droplets echoed rhythmically.

Mara took point, gun drawn, while Serafine followed close behind. The occultist held a flickering candle, muttering incantations under her breath. Strange symbols marked the walls, barely visible in the dim light.

As they progressed deeper underground, the temperature dropped noticeably. Their breath came out in icy puffs as an unnatural cold permeated the tunnel. Mara felt an icy finger of dread creep down her spine. Whatever dark forces were gathered here, they knew of the intruders.

A scraping sound reverberated down the tunnel, followed by faint whispering just beyond the edge of hearing. Mara spun, gun raised, but saw nothing. The shadows seemed to creep and contort just outside the candlelight. Serafine's chanting grew more urgent.

"We're close now," she whispered. "I can feel the dark energy pulsating from beyond that passage." She gestured toward a yawning black archway, ancient symbols carved into the stonework.

Mara steeled herself. If the ritual was underway, there was no time to waste. With a final glance at each other, the two women plunged into the darkness.

Mara and Serafine crept through the twisting tunnels, the

oppressive darkness weighing down on them. The scraping and whispering grew louder, reverberating off the cold stone walls. Mara's heart pounded as she swept her flashlight beam ahead, desperate for any signs of the cult's activities.

Suddenly, the tunnel forked, one path sloping upward while the other descended deeper into the earth. Mara hesitated, glancing back at Serafine.

"We must split up," Serafine said, her voice echoing eerily. "I will go below and do what I can to halt the ritual. You find their leader and end this."

Mara opened her mouth to protest, but Serafine pressed a talisman into her hand. "Trust in your gifts, Mara. We will see each other again."

Before Mara could respond, Serafine glided swiftly down the dark passageway, her candle casting dancing shadows behind her. Mara wanted to call out, but she knew Serafine was right — there was no time to lose. Gripping her gun and the talisman, she steeled her nerves and headed up the sloping tunnel.

The scraping and whispers intensified, interspersed with chanting and unearthly shrieks. Mara's skin crawled at the unholy sounds. She emerged into a vast chamber, pillars carved with disturbing symbols soaring overhead. Across the open space was an arched doorway, and beyond it, she could see figures swaying and chanting around a fiery altar.

Mara ducked behind the stone pillar, peering into the massive chamber below. Flickering torchlight cast dancing shadows across the walls, illuminated dark figures swaying and chanting around the altar. At the center stood Balor Payne, arms raised as he led the ritual. His pale eyes reflected the hellish flames, a manic grin twisting his face.

Mara's breath caught in her throat as she spotted Serafine across the chamber, partially concealed behind another pillar. They locked eyes briefly before Serafine turned her gaze to Balor. With a subtle nod, Mara knew it was time to act. She tightened her grip on her gun and the talisman, bracing herself.

Suddenly, Serafine strode from the shadows, interrupting the ritual as she confronted Balor directly. "Your twisted games end here, Balor," she declared, arcane energy crackling around her. The cultists shrieked in alarm, but Balor only laughed.

"Serafine, my dear, you should not have come alone," he purred menacingly. Beckoning with clawed fingers, shadowy specters materialized around Serafine.

She stood firm, beginning a banishing incantation. The specters recoiled from her light, but more emerged from the darkness. Serafine raised her arms, summoning a protective barrier as the entities swirled around her.

Mara watched helplessly as more shadowy specters emerged, surrounding Serafine. She continued her incantations, arcs of light repelling the demonic entities. But they kept coming, endless wraiths crawling forth from the shadows. Serafine's strength was waning. Her barrier flickered as the specters pressed in. Clawed hands grasped at her clothes, shrieks and howls battering her concentration.

"Your magic cannot stop what comes, Serafine," Balor taunted. "You have only ensured your own doom."

***

Terry could not let Mara and Serafine go alone, no matter their objections. "We can't just sit here while they throw themselves into danger," he said to Hunter and Father Alex. Though the women had expressly forbid them from following, Terry's duty as Mara's partner compelled him to act.

"I'm with you," Hunter said, his voice resolute. "We'll keep our distance so they don't detect us, but I'll be damned if I let them face the cult on their own." He began gathering equipment — blessed blades, protective amulets, and ancient tomes of arcane lore.

Father Alex sighed, but did not argue. "I cannot condone you directly disobeying their wishes. But I will pray the Lord guides your steps. Here, take these." He offered Terry a rosary and a vial of holy water. "They will shield you from the evil ahead."

Terry accepted them with a grateful nod. He checked his gun one last time, the familiar weight steadying his nerves. "Let's move quickly but cautiously. I know a back way into the compound grounds."

The three men stole into the night, keeping to the shadows as they tracked Mara and Serafine's path. The full moon cast an eerie glow through the live oaks dripping with Spanish moss. An owl's mournful hoot sent a chill through Terry's bones. He could sense the malevolent forces converging as they neared the cult's lair.

They crept through the night, steely determination driving them forward even as unease gnawed at their guts. Terry took the lead, guiding them along lesser-used trails that wound circuitously toward the cult's compound, hoping to avoid detection.

The sickly, sweet stench of death hung heavy in the air as they drew nearer, sending a shudder through Terry's body. In the distance, faint chanting echoed, the cultists' voices rising and falling in twisted ritual. Terry caught glimpses of robed figures slipping furtively between crumbling mausoleums and moss-draped oak trees, barely visible in the gloom.

A snapping twig made Terry freeze, signaling for absolute silence. The seconds ticked by, pregnant with tension, as they listened for any sign they'd been spotted. After an agonizing wait, Terry waved them forward, nerves jangling.

They reached the perimeter of the compound. The secret entrance was right where Serafine had indicated on her map. Terry carefully pulled open the creaking metal door, just enough for them to slip through one by one. The dank tunnel beyond was swallowed in inky darkness. The chanting from somewhere deep within reverberated faintly off the stone walls. Terry felt for the mini flashlight in his coat pocket, flicking it on and shining the dim beam ahead to light their way.

The ground was slick with stagnant water and slime, the

fetid air heavy with the stench of decay. Strange symbols were etched into the stone, their meanings indecipherable but radiating an unnatural malice. The tunnel seemed to stretch on endlessly, sloping gradually downward, leading them to the rotten heart of the cult's lair.

Terry focused on keeping his breathing steady, pushing down his rising dread. He knew Mara was somewhere up ahead, walking straight into the viper's nest, and he had to reach her. Hunter and Father Alex followed close behind, tense and silent. The priest clutched his rosary, his lips moving in silent prayer to bolster them against the evil surrounding them.

A distant scream pierced the gloom, reverberating off the walls. Terry broke into a run, no longer caring for stealth, his flashlight carving a frenzied arc through the dark. The tunnel opened into a vast chamber, a towering black altar at its center. They ducked behind some rubble to avoid being seen. In the center of the room, surrounded by a circle of robed figures, was a raised dais. Chained upon it, stripped naked and bleeding, was Serafine. Terry had to clench his jaw to keep from crying out.

Beside him, Father Alex began whispering a fervent prayer under his breath. Hunter's face was grim as he studied the scene, mentally cataloging details. Terry's mind raced — where was Mara?

They inched closer, keeping to the shadows, straining to see any sign of Mara amidst the robed figures. The cultists swayed and chanted, their voices rising and falling hypnotically as Serafine thrashed against her chains. Fresh blood trickled down her wrists where the manacles bit deep.

Where was Mara? Had she already been captured? Sacrificed? Terry couldn't let his mind go there. He had to believe she was still out there, hidden somewhere, ready to strike.

At the head of the altar stood Balor Payne, arms raised as he led the ritual. His face was alight with fervent ecstasy, pale eyes reflecting the flickering braziers surrounding the dais. He seemed transported, caught up in dark rapture as he chanted words in a guttural language that clawed at their minds.

Terry's eyes desperately scanned the chamber, searching for any sign of Mara amidst the swaying cultists. He clenched his flashlight, ready to charge forward, when a hand grabbed his shoulder. He whirled to see Mara crouched behind him, eyes blazing with determination.

"Don't," she whispered. "Not yet. We have to wait for the right moment."

Terry sagged with relief at the sight of her, then tensed as angry shouts erupted from the cultists. His gaze shot back to the altar.

Balor stood over Serafine, curved dagger raised high. His lips peeled back in a grin, revealing teeth filed to points. With a final shout, he plunged the dagger down.

Serafine's screams echoed through the chamber. The cultists' chanting reached a fever pitch as Balor repeatedly stabbed downwards, face alight with demonic ecstasy. Blood pooled beneath Serafine's writhing body, her cries growing weaker.

"No!" Mara shouted, lurching forward. Terry grabbed her, holding her back. She fought him wildly, tears streaming down her face as she watched her friend murdered.

With a final twist of the blade, Balor stepped back, arms wide in triumph. Serafine gave a last rattling gasp and went still, eyes glassy and unseeing. The cultists fell silent, heads bowed.

"It is done," Balor proclaimed, voice resonating unnaturally. "Her blood prepares the way. Soon, our Dark Lord shall rise."

In a state of shock, the group turned to leave the tunnels, unable to comprehend what they had just witnessed. Mara was nearly catatonic, consumed by intense feelings of guilt and grief. Father Alex whispered prayers and continuously made the sign of the cross.

Hunter grasped onto Mara's shoulder, his typically calm demeanor now drained of color. "I'm sorry. We should have acted sooner." However, Mara seemed to be in her own world, not registering his words at all.

Terry took point, gun drawn, senses hyper alert for any sign they had been spotted. The tunnels wound on interminably, dimly lit by Terry's flashlight. Strange symbols were scrawled on the walls, exuding menace.

They had emerged into the dark night, the air thick with the smell of the nearby swamp. In the distance, they could hear the rise of the cultists' chant once again. Mara shuddered, her features twisted in agony.

"What do we do now?" Terry asked, speaking softly. "We need a new strategy. Balor must be stopped before..." His voice trailed off, unwilling to utter the unspeakable fate that awaited them.

Father Alex rested a gentle hand on Mara's shoulder. "Have faith, child. Evil cannot prevail if good souls stand against it." Mara took a deep breath, wiping her eyes fiercely. She turned to face the others, her expression hardening with determination. "Now that Serafina is gone, I know what I must do," she said resolutely. "I'll go in disguise as a new cult recruit and infiltrate them for information. It's the only way we'll learn their plans."

Terry shook his head vehemently. "Absolutely not. That's far too dangerous, Mara. We need to regroup and think this through." Hunter nodded in agreement, frowning.

"I'm with Terry on this," he said. "Blundering into the cult's lair is reckless, especially alone." Mara crossed her arms defiantly.

"It's the only way. I can't let Serafina's death be in vain," she insisted. Father Alex stepped forward, raising a placating hand.

"My child, I understand your desire for justice," he said gently. "But we must have faith that another path will present itself. One that does not put you in such peril." Mara's eyes flashed.

"We're running out of time!" she exclaimed. "The ritual is coming, and we still have no idea what they're planning."

She turned and started walking away. "I'm doing this, with or without your help."

Terry hurried after her. "Mara, wait..."

CHAPTER 15
SHADOWS AND SACRIFICE

Mara gazed intently at her reflection in the full-length mirror, her fingers expertly adjusting the collar of her worn leather jacket. The scars and tears on its edges spoke of a life steeped in danger and thrill. Her fingers ran through her tousled hair, transforming it into a wild and untamed mane that concealed her true identity. In that moment, she embodied the reckless and alluring persona that she was born to play.

Terry and Hunter stood at a distance, their faces contorted with trepidation. The tension in the room was thick, foreshadowing the impending doom that loomed over them. But Mara remained obstinate, refusing to heed their warnings.

Terry's voice cut through the silence, tinged with worry. "Mara, this is a huge risk. If anything goes wrong..."

Mara spun around, her piercing gaze flashing with a determined strength that allowed no opposition. The rigid line of her jaw conveyed her unwavering resolve. "We've been up against impossible odds before," she countered, her tone steady and sure. "This is just another gambit in the grand scheme of things. Trust me."

Hunter's brow furrowed, his concern evident in the tightness around his eyes. "We do trust you, Mara. It's just...the cult is unpredictable. We can't predict their every move."

A shadow of understanding flickered across Mara's face as she gave a curt nod, acknowledging the gravity of what lay ahead. "I know the risks," she admitted, her voice low and intense, "but going undercover is our best chance to get inside their operation and stop whatever they're planning. I won't let you down."

She drew in a deep breath, her chest expanding as she centered herself, mentally donning the armor of her new identity.

Hunter stepped forward, extending his hand. In his palm rested a small device, its smooth surface belying its critical importance. "This will mask your digital footprint and keep your cover secure," he explained, his voice tight with barely suppressed anxiety. "Make sure it's on at all times."

Mara's fingers closed around the device, the cool metal a stark reminder of the technological tightrope she would be walking. With practiced efficiency, she affixed it to her jacket, its presence a comforting weight against her chest.

"I've got this," she assured them, her voice steady despite the adrenaline beginning to course through her veins. "Keep the communications line open."

Terry and Hunter exchanged a final, loaded glance, their eyes conveying volumes of unspoken fear and hope. Mara observed their silent exchange, feeling the full weight of their trust and concern settle upon her shoulders.

As she turned back to the mirror, Mara steeled herself for the perilous task that lay ahead. The reflection that stared back at her was no longer just Mara—it was a weapon, honed and ready to plunge into the heart of darkness that awaited her beyond the safety of their underground sanctuary.

With a final nod to her comrades, Mara turned away, her boots echoing ominously in the silent room. She adjusted her jacket, feeling the device against her chest, and began to transform into Melanie. The journey to the cult compound was a blur of anticipation and resolve.

Cloaked in her undercover persona, she observed her surroundings as two robed acolytes led her into the heart of the cult compound. The cavernous room swallowed what little light dared to penetrate its depths, leaving her eyes straining to adjust to the oppressive darkness.

Ominous symbols adorned the walls, their jagged lines and arcane curves seeming to writhe in the torchlight. Artifacts of unknown origin and purpose littered the space, each exuding an aura of malevolence that made Melanie's skin crawl.

Bracing herself, she joined a group of new initiates whose dull eyes and lifeless expressions betrayed the suffering they had already endured.

One of the acolytes, his face hidden beneath a deep cowl, addressed the group in a voice as cold as the grave. "You are all vessels...ready to be emptied and remade in the image of Balor."

Melanie couldn't help but shiver at the words, but she kept up her façade of obedience as they were all ushered into seats. The sharp clanging of shackles being fastened could be heard throughout the chamber, a chilling finality that sent a new wave of terror coursing through her body. Without warning, the second acolyte activated some unseen mechanism. The world exploded into a cacophony of sensory assault. Harsh, strobing lights seared Melanie's retinas while discordant sounds assaulted her ears, threatening to shatter her very sanity.

Grotesque images flashed before her eyes: blood-soaked rituals, acts of unspeakable violence, and figures that defied the laws of nature and sanity alike. Through it all, a voice boomed, seeming to come from everywhere and nowhere at once.

"Obey...Surrender...Serve Balor..."

The words seared into Melanie's mind, relentless and scorching. Around her, the other recruits convulsed, their eyes rolling back as they succumbed to the overwhelming brainwashing. Melanie gritted her teeth, holding onto her true identity, her mission, anything to keep herself from slipping into the madness.

Just when she thought she could take no more, the barrage ceased. The sudden silence was almost as deafening as the cacophony had been. Melanie blinked away the spots dancing in her vision, her head pounding with residual pain.

The first acolyte's lips curled into a smile that held no warmth, no humanity. "The cleansing has begun. You will all be reborn."

As Melanie fought to catch her breath, she knew with grim certainty that this was only the beginning of the horrors that awaited her in the depths of this unholy place.

The heavy metal doors clanged shut, sealing the recruits into their barren cells. Melanie found herself alone in a cramped space barely larger than a closet, with only a cot for company. Darkness pressed in around her, thick and oppressive. Her heart raced as she fumbled in her pocket, fingers closing around the tiny object hidden there. With trembling hands, she withdrew the miniature camera, its presence both a comfort and a source of fear. If they found it... Melanie pushed the thought away, focusing instead on her surroundings. The stark concrete walls seemed to close in, suffocating in their emptiness. A faint, musty smell permeated the air, hinting at long years of disuse and neglect.

She raised the camera, its lens glinting dully in what little light seeped through the cracks around the door. Slowly, methodically, she panned it across the cell, capturing every bleak detail of her prison. When she was satisfied she had documented everything, Melanie leaned close to the device. Her voice was barely a whisper, hardly more than an exhale of breath:

"I'm in."

The words hung in the air, a promise and a prayer. She could only hope someone was listening on the other end, ready to come to her aid if things went wrong. Because in this place, surrounded by darkness and zealots, things could go very wrong indeed.

The next initiation came too soon as the heavy iron door creaked open, and Melanie was thrust into a chamber steeped in darkness. Flickering torchlight cast long, dancing shadows across the stone walls, illuminating the grotesque scene before her. Robed figures stood in a semicircle, their faces obscured by deep hoods. At the center of their unholy congregation stood an altar, its surface stained a deep crimson.

Melanie's heart pounded in her chest as she watched a struggling form being dragged towards the altar. The Recruit — a young man barely out of his teens — thrashed and pleaded as the unholy priests strapped him down with practiced efficiency. His wide, terrified eyes locked with Melanie's for a brief, haunting moment before a towering priest stepped forward, blocking her view.

The priest raised a jagged blade high above his head. Its wicked edge caught the candlelight, and Melanie could see dried blood caked in its serrations. Unable to bear the sight any longer, she squeezed her eyes shut and turned away. A wet, tearing sound filled the chamber, followed by an agonized scream that chilled Melanie to her very core. The Recruit's cries echoed off the stone walls, growing weaker with each passing second. Melanie bit her lip hard enough to draw blood, desperately fighting the urge to vomit.

As the screams faded to whimpers, then to silence, the unholy priests began to chant. Their voices, low and guttural, seemed to pulse with an otherworldly power. The words were unlike any language Melanie had ever heard, full of harsh consonants and impossible syllables that made her head spin.

The chanting grew louder, filling the chamber with a deafening roar. Melanie's knees buckled, and she collapsed onto the cold stone floor, her body shaking uncontrollably. The world around her spun, and she could feel herself losing consciousness. As the darkness claimed her, the last thing she heard was the ominous echo of the priest's chant.

As she emerged from her unconscious state, the claustrophobic walls of her previous prison closed in on her once again. She deduced that she had been forcibly returned to her cramped cell. Sitting up, she pressed herself against the unforgiving stone, shivering not from the frigid temperature but from the blood-curdling shrieks echoing throughout the compound. Each piercing cry seemed to sear into her very being, a ghastly reminder of the terrors lurking ahead.

Darkness swirled in the confined room, contorting into sinister shapes under the flickering glow of distant lanterns that filtered through the crevices. It was as if the shadows had a life of their own, pulsing with malicious intent, ready to swallow her whole. Suddenly, a metallic scrape pierced the gloom. A small slot in the door slid open with a rusty groan, revealing a pair of gleaming eyes. The Acolyte's face, half-hidden in shadow, leered at her through the opening.

"Sleep well," he sneered, his voice dripping with cruel amusement. "The real work begins tomorrow."

Melanie cowered, her back against the cold stone wall. The slot slammed shut with a deafening thud, sealing her in the darkness of her tiny cell. The sound reverberated through her bones, a finality that crushed any glimmer of hope she held onto.

Left alone once more, Melanie's gaze fixated on the impenetrable abyss before her. Her once vibrant eyes now reflected only the desolation and despair within. The unspeakable terrors she had endured and those yet to come had stripped away all traces of the woman she once was, leaving behind only a shattered husk.

As the night wore on, Melanie remained motionless, her mind reeling with terrifying possibilities of what "real work" might entail. The screams continued their infernal chorus, a grim lullaby for the damned souls trapped within the compound's walls. She feared that her failure could result in the world suffering the same cruel fate.

Morning came too soon as she descended the narrow stone staircase, her cult robes whispering against the rough-hewn steps. Two cultists flanked her, their faces obscured by deep hoods. Flickering torchlight cast writhing shadows across the damp walls, transforming the passage into a nightmarish throat, leading to some unspeakable maw.

She steeled herself, drawing in a deep breath that tasted of mold and decay. But as they descended deeper, Mara's vision began to swim. Reality fractured, replaced by a whirlwind of horrific images that assaulted her senses. A bloodied altar materialized before her, its stone surface slick with crimson. The glint of steel caught her eye — a ritual blade, perhaps — followed by a piercing scream that echoed through her skull.

The vision shifted. An emaciated body lay sprawled across the altar, its pallid skin adorned with arcane symbols etched in blood and ash. Before Mara could process the sight, it dissolved into a frenzy of movement. The wet, meaty sound of tearing flesh filled her ears. She blinked rapidly, desperate to banish the visions. But they only intensified, bombarding her faster than she could comprehend. A robed figure stood triumphant, holding aloft a still-beating heart. Its chambers pulsed obscenely in the torchlight, dripping gore onto the stone floor.

The scene shifted again. A ravaged corpse stared at her with lidless eyes, its face frozen in a rictus grin of agony or ecstasy — perhaps both. A knife sliced through the skin as easily as butter, blood bubbling from the wound like some hellish spring.

Mara's breath came in ragged gasps. The visions overwhelmed her, threatening to drag her into their macabre dance. She stumbled, her hand shooting out to brace against the cold stone wall. The cultists paused, turning their featureless faces toward her. In that moment of respite, she fought to center herself. But a creeping dread wormed its way into her gut. Whatever waited at the bottom of these stairs, she knew with chilling certainty, would make her long for the comparative comfort of these nightmarish visions.

The cultist's voice cut through the darkness, a whisper that seemed to carry the weight of unspeakable secrets. "Steady yourself, sister. The sight of the Charnel House can be... overwhelming at first."

Mara nodded weakly, her throat constricting as she fought against the rising tide of nausea. She inhaled deeply, the stale air coating her lungs. With trembling legs, she continued her descent, each step echoing in the oppressive silence. At the bottom of the winding staircase, an iron door groaned open, its hinges protesting as if warning her to turn back. She was ushered into a vast chamber, the guttering flames of braziers casting writing shadows on the walls.

The horrors that greeted her defied comprehension. Blood-speckled idols leered from alcoves, their grotesque features twisted into malevolent grins. Mutilated bodies adorned ritual circles, their flesh carved with eldritch symbols that seemed to pulse with otherworldly energy. Robed figures swayed in unison, their chants a cacophony of guttural sounds that clawed at Mara's sanity. The assault on her senses was overwhelming. Mara gagged, turning away from the nightmarish scene. She discreetly retched into a nearby torch sconce, the acrid taste of bile mixing with the coppery scent of blood that hung thick in the air. As her vision cleared, she saw the central dais looming before her. There, bathed in an unholy light, stood Balor, presiding over a complex summoning circle, strange energies crackling and writhing around him like living tendrils of darkness.

With a fluid motion, Balor plunged a dagger into a prone victim lying at his feet. Blood pooled around the lifeless body, but instead of spreading across the stone floor, it began to swirl upward, defying the very laws of nature.

A deafening, inhuman cry shattered the air, causing Mara's teeth to vibrate in her skull. The braziers flared blood red, casting the chamber in a hellish glow that made the shadows dance with malicious glee. Overwhelmed by the sheer madness of it all, she stumbled. Her hand shot out, barely catching herself on a nearby pillar slick with something she dared not identify.

The cultists, unfazed by the nightmarish display, continued to lead her deeper into the heart of darkness. Each step felt like a descent into madness, and she wondered if she would ever see the light of day again.

Her knees buckled, and she crumpled to the ground, her consciousness fading as the world spun around her. The last thing she remembered was the robed figures dragging her limp body away from the unholy spectacle. When she woke, she was alone in her cell, the echoes of distant screams her only company.

She huddled against the cold stone wall of her cramped cell, her body trembling as the echoes of distant screams reverberated through the compound. The harsh fluorescent light flickered, casting eerie shadows that seemed to dance and writhe across the bare concrete floor. With each passing moment, the walls felt as if they were closing in, threatening to crush her.

Exhausted and overwhelmed, she curled into a fetal position on the hard ground, squeezing her eyes shut in a desperate attempt to block out the horrors that surrounded her. But even in the darkness behind her eyelids, the terrifying images lingered, refusing to grant her even a moment's peace.

The door violently gave way, and her captor stood before her once again, ready to drag her back into the nightmare she had just endured. She could only submit to his demands and inwardly curse her stubbornness that brought her to this wretched fate. Her heart raced in terror as she trailed behind him through a narrow passageway lit by flickering torches. The fire's eerie glow revealed sinister symbols and occult markings etched into the rough stone walls, their movements seeming alive in the unstable light. Each step resounded with a foreboding echo, accompanied by the rustling of their dark robes against the frigid floor.

As they progressed deeper into the heart of the ritual chamber, her eyes darted nervously from side to side, taking in the gaping chambers that lined the corridor. Altars covered in dark stains, grotesque relics, and other unspeakable signs of the occult filled these spaces. Half-glimpsed horrors lurked in the shadows, causing her breath to catch in her throat. She forced herself to keep moving, her fingers twitching with barely contained fear.

The Acolyte leading her spoke, his voice low and urgent. "The gathering has begun. Make haste. The master awaits."

Melanie nodded, unable to trust her voice. As they neared an arched entrance at the end of the corridor, a haunting chant echoed out from within. The rhythm was otherworldly, and each syllable seemed to reverberate in her bones. The atmosphere grew dense and oppressive, heavy with the scent of incense and something malevolent lurking beneath.

With each step closer to the doorway, she felt as if she were descending into the maw of some ancient, malevolent entity. The chanting grew louder, more frenzied, and she knew that whatever awaited her beyond that threshold would change her forever. There would be no turning back from the darkness that lay ahead.

Her heart pounded as she entered the ritual chamber, her eyes widening with horror at the scene before her. The cavernous space teemed with black-robed cultists, their forms blurring together in a sea of darkness. At the center, a ritual circle pulsed with an otherworldly energy. Balor stood within, his arms raised high as he chanted in a guttural tongue that echoed ominously through the chamber. The air around him rippled and distorted, shadows flickering and dancing at the edges of her vision. Ghostly apparitions swirled about, their ethereal forms barely visible yet unmistakably present.

As the cultists' chanting reached a fever pitch, she found herself transfixed. Through the veil of the ritual's power, she glimpsed things beyond mortal comprehension. Writhing entities in cosmic voids. Clawed hands tearing at the very fabric of reality. The universe itself seemed to shudder and crack. This was no mere ceremony. This was an apocalyptic event, a fundamental rending of existence itself. Mara steeled herself, ready to act, to stop this madness before it was too late.

Balor's voice cut through the cacophony. "Welcome, Detective. We've been expecting you..."

The cultists turned as one, surrounding Mara in a suffocating circle. She reached for her concealed weapon, but rough hands grabbed her arms, wrenching them painfully behind her back.

"Did you really think your pathetic disguise could fool me, Detective?" Balor sneered.

Mara spat back, "Let me go, you bastard."

"Brave words from someone powerless to stop what

comes," Balor taunted. "You've failed."

Mara locked eyes with the cult leader, refusing to show an ounce of fear despite the terror clawing at her insides.

Balor's lips curled into a cruel smile. "You won't stop the coming cataclysm. The Old One will rise. All is lost."

"I won't let you get away with this," Mara growled through gritted teeth.

Balor chuckled darkly. "My dear, I already have." He waved a dismissive hand. "Take her away!"

Mara met Balor's gaze unflinchingly, her jaw set with defiant resolve. "I'll see you in hell."

"Sooner than you can imagine," Balor replied, his laughter echoing off the chamber walls.

The cultists dragged Mara away, her struggles futile against their iron grip. "Get your hands off me!" she snarled, twisting and pulling to no avail.

Their strength was unnatural, beyond human limits. Arcane symbols glowed on the shackles they clamped around her wrists, sapping her strength further.

"You won't get away with this!" Mara cried out, but her words fell on deaf ears.

The cultists methodically stripped her of every weapon and tool, leaving her utterly defenseless. Mara's stomach churned as they led her deeper into the bowels of the cult's lair. The staircase seemed to descend endlessly, the flickering torchlight casting grotesque shadows on the damp stone walls.

With each step, she felt the weight of her failure crushing down upon her. She had come so close, only to be outmaneuvered at the last moment. Now, as they dragged her into the unknown depths, she could only pray for a miracle — or prepare herself for the horrors that surely awaited.

The cultists manhandled Mara into the cramped cell, their rough hands bruising her arms as they shoved her forward. Ancient markings adorned the walls, their eldritch shapes seeming to writhe in the dim light. As the heavy door slammed shut behind her, darkness enveloped her like a suffocating shroud. Trapped in the inky blackness, she strained against her bonds. They glowed with an otherworldly luminescence, casting eerie shadows across the chamber. Try as she might, the restraints held fast, biting into her flesh with each desperate attempt to break free.

Her eyes adjusted slowly to the gloom, revealing more of the arcane sigils that covered every inch of the cell's surface. Her gaze traced their intricate patterns, a chill creeping up her spine as she recognized symbols of power and malevolence beyond mortal comprehension. A growing sense of dread washed over her, cold tendrils of fear wrapping around her heart. The air grew thick and oppressive as if the very atmosphere sought to crush her spirit. "What have I gotten myself into?" she whispered, her voice trembling in the stillness.

The reality of her situation crashed down upon her like a tidal wave. Rage and frustration boiled up from the depths of her being, erupting in a primal scream that tore from her throat. The sound reverberated off the ancient stone walls, filling the cell with her anguish. But as the echoes faded, only silence remained. The void swallowed her cries, leaving Mara alone with the terrifying realization that no one was coming to save her. In this place of eldritch horrors and forgotten lore, she stood on the precipice of a darkness beyond imagining.

As the weight of her situation sank in, she blinked slowly, her mind struggling to comprehend the reality of her imprisonment. The silence pressed in on her, broken only by the sound of her own ragged breathing. "How deep does this abyss go?" she whispered, her voice barely audible in the oppressive quiet.

The words hung in the air, unanswered. Her breathing quickened, her chest rising and falling rapidly as panic began to claw its way up from the pit of her stomach. Beads of sweat formed on her brow, glistening in the dim light that filtered through the cracks in the ancient stone. "Let me out!" she cried, her voice cracking with desperation. "Please, I can't..." The words died in her throat as the crushing weight of her confinement bore down upon her. Mara began to rock slowly back and forth, her arms wrapping around her knees as she withdrew inward, seeking some semblance of comfort in the fetal position. She squeezed her eyes shut, trying to block out the nightmare that surrounded her.

"This isn't real. Wake up. Wake up!" she whispered repeatedly, her voice a mantra of denial.

But the cold stone beneath her and the musty air filling her lungs refused to fade away. This was no dream from which she could awaken. The reality of her situation crashed over her like a tidal wave, drowning her in despair.

Overwhelmed, Mara curled into a tight ball on the floor, her body shaking with silent sobs. Tears streamed down her face, carving glistening paths through the grime on her cheeks. Her eyes, once full of life and determination, now stared blankly ahead as darkness began to close in around her.

The shadows in the corners of the cell seemed to grow, stretching their inky tendrils towards her prone form. As Mara lay there, lost in the depths of her own mind, the darkness crept ever closer, threatening to swallow her whole in its endless, lightless embrace.

CHAPTER 16
BETWEEN LIGHT AND SHADOW

The ancient wood creaked beneath their feet as Hunter led Father Alex into the shadowy depths of the esoteric library. Hunter's voice cut through the silence. "Welcome to the profane, Father."

Father Alex's eyes darted nervously around the room, taking in the bizarre collection. A display of ritual knives gleamed wickedly, their blades adorned with intricate engravings. Skeletal talismans hung from hooks, their empty eye sockets seeming to follow his every move. An ornate mirror stand stood in the corner, its surface rippling like dark water. He had seen the library once before on his tour of the compound, but he still found it fascinating. He had to admit to being a little uneasy as to why Hunter had brought him here today.

Hunter moved with the confidence of a curator in his own personal museum of horrors. "Here we shall unlock mysteries from Mesopotamia... the Etruscans... Haitian Vodoun..."

With a flourish, he produced a massive tome, its cover emblazoned with the words "Demonic Pacts & Blood Sorcery." As Hunter opened it, Father Alex found himself face-to-face with a grotesque illustration. A horned demon loomed over a robed cultist, its clawed hand extended in a mockery of benediction. The priest recoiled, his stomach churning.

"This is but a fraction of the occult's true span," Hunter continued, his voice tinged with reverence. "I shall teach you its fundamental laws."

Father Alex's gaze was drawn to an etching on the adjacent page. It depicted a sacrifice in excruciating detail — a screaming figure contorted in agony. Below it, descriptions of nightmarish entities and realms beyond human comprehension made his head spin.

Hunter's hand came to rest on his shoulder, steadying him. "Steel your spirit, Alex. This is but ink on a page...formless thought. True mastery lies in action. Remember to beat this thing, we have to fight fire with fire."

Before Father Alex could protest, Hunter guided him to the mirror. The priest's reflection wavered and distorted as Hunter began to chant in a guttural, inhuman language. Alex found himself joining in, the strange syllables burning his throat as they escaped his lips. The air crackled with energy. Suddenly, a shimmering entity materialized within the mirror's frame. It thrashed violently against invisible restraints, its form constantly shifting and reforming. Father Alex's voice grew stronger, more confident, as he continued the eerie incantation.

With a final, piercing shriek, the entity vanished. The sudden silence was deafening. Father Alex staggered backward, his heart pounding in his chest. Exhilaration coursed through his veins like electricity. "By God..." he gasped, "I never imagined such power! Our path is clear. I shall embrace these profane teachings for humanity's sake."

His eyes burned with newfound conviction, a fire that both thrilled and terrified him. Hunter's smile was a dark slash across his face, his teeth gleaming in the candlelight. "Then let us begin your true initiation."

As Hunter's words hung in the air, Father Alex felt consequences settle on his soul. He had taken his first step into a world of darkness, and there was no turning back.

Father Alex stared at his reflection in the ornate mirror, still reeling from the unholy ritual he had just participated in. Though exhilarated by the surge of dark power, unease crept through him. He turned to Hunter, whose gaunt features were thrown into sharp relief by the flickering candles.

"Why have you brought me here, truly?" Alex asked. "You claim to fight the forces of darkness yet revel in their power. I don't understand."

Hunter regarded Alex, his piercing blue eyes seeming to stare right through him. When he spoke, his voice was solemn. "I have not been entirely honest with you, my friend. My origins are...complicated. I tread the line between darkness and light — never wholly embracing one or the other."

He gestured to the leather-bound tomes and occult artifacts lining the shelves. "All of this serves a purpose. I walk among demons and cultists, using their secrets against them when needed. But I have paid a price for such knowledge."

Alex's brow furrowed. "What sort of price?"

Hunter turned, pushing back his hair to reveal a strange symbol etched below his ear. It seemed to writhe before Alex's eyes.

"I was born Jonah Eldritch in a time and place better left unsaid. When I learned my true nature, I chose a new name to reflect the duality within me. Hunter. Predator and prey. Now I move between worlds, belonging to neither."

Father Alex stared at the writhing symbol, mesmerized by its occult power. He hesitated, unsure whether to feel pity or revulsion for the tormented man before him.

"Do not fear me, Father," Hunter said quietly. "I harbor no ill will toward you or your God. But forces beyond your comprehension are converging on this city, and I cannot fight them alone." He closed the heavy tome with an air of grim finality. "An ancient darkness stirs beneath Savannah's genteel veneer. Cultists worshiping long-forgotten gods are gathering, performing profane rituals to shatter the veil between worlds."

Hunter's eyes seemed to glow with an otherworldly light. "Abominations slither up from the depths to walk among us, cloaked in human flesh. An apocalypse brews, yet the city's inhabitants go about their lives in ignorant bliss."

Father Alex shivered despite the library's stifling heat. He opened his mouth to speak, but Hunter raised a hand.

"I know you have reservations. But you are a servant of the light, and I need your help to push back this rising tide of darkness." Hunter placed a steadying hand on the priest's shoulder. "With our powers combined, we can protect this city and its people. We can prevent the annihilation of everything you hold dear. Will you join me, Alex?"

Father Alex hesitated, conflicted emotions welling up inside him. On one hand, he was repulsed by the sinister occult artifacts and rituals. They seemed to radiate an unnatural malevolence that made his skin crawl. But on the other, he could not deny the exhilarating rush of power he had felt while chanting before the mirror. If he could harness that dark energy for good, to combat even greater evil...

"I still have reservations," he said slowly. "The lure of such power is corrupting. How can I be sure I will stay true to the light while delving into darkness?"

Hunter regarded him solemnly. "Faith. Faith in your own convictions. I have seen evil in forms you cannot imagine, both in this world and beyond the veil. I know you have the spiritual strength to resist its call."

He turned and reverently ran his fingers along the spines of the eldritch texts. "These contain wisdom gleaned over millennia by those who walked between realms of dark and light, gathering fragments of forbidden knowledge to maintain the balance. I can teach you to shield your spirit while tapping into forces beyond human comprehension."

Father Alex looked deep within himself, searching for the still, small voice of wisdom. Finally, he gave a single, firm nod.

"Then I shall become your student. Teach me the secrets that will arm us against encroaching darkness."

A faint smile crossed Hunter's pale face. He lifted a gnarled staff from where it leaned in the corner. "We shall begin."

Hunter led him to a secluded corner of the room, where a circle of salt and symbols had been carefully laid out on the floor. "Step inside," he instructed, handing Alex an ornate amulet. As Alex complied, Hunter began to chant in an ancient tongue, his voice echoing through the chamber. Suddenly, Alex felt a pull, as though his very soul was being yanked from his body. Then, everything went black.

Father Alex drifted through the hellscape dimension, his astral form casting a faint glow in the oppressive darkness. Jagged rock formations jutted at impossible angles, their surfaces slick with an oily sheen. Distant screams echoed, carried on fetid winds that whispered of eternal torment. Alex steeled himself, pushing forward through the foreboding landscape.

A billowing cloud of crimson smoke materialized before him, coalescing into a leering demon. Its emaciated form towered over Alex, long, clawed fingers flexing with anticipation. Ram horns spiraled from its skull, framing eyes that smoldered like dying embers. "You've strayed far from your chapel, little lamb," the demon's voice grated like glass on bone. It circled Alex, appraising him with predatory hunger. The priest's heart hammered, but he refused to show fear.

"I've not come unprepared, hellspawn," Alex retorted, his fingers already tracing glowing sigils in the air. A protective circle flickered into existence around him, its ethereal light a beacon of hope in the infernal gloom. The demon's eyes narrowed, lips peeling back in a snarl. With inhuman speed, it lashed out, claws raking through Alex's defenses. The barrier shattered like spun glass.

Pain lanced through Alex as the demon's talons sliced into his aura, drawing streams of ectoplasmic blood. He grimaced, willing himself to stand firm even as his essence leaked away.

"Still clinging to your paltry faith?" the demon taunted. "Renounce your false god!"

"Be gone, demon!" And with his shout, his essence spun away. The hellscape shifted, reality bending like softened wax. Alex found himself standing in a familiar church, sunlight streaming through stained glass windows. The demon now wore priestly vestments, offering him a leather-bound Bible.

"This path leads only to ruin," it crooned, its voice a mockery of compassion. "Abandon your quest and find peace."

Alex's eyes narrowed, seeing through the illusion. "My spirit remains true. Your deceptions fall on deaf ears."

He snatched the Bible, tearing it asunder. The comforting façade of the church melted away, revealing the hellish realm once more. The demon roared, its form twisting into a nightmarish, horned abomination. Waves of maddening whispers assaulted Alex, threatening to shred his sanity.

The priest dropped to his knees, fingers digging into jagged stone as he fought to maintain his grip on reality. The whispers burrowed deep, promising power, pleasure, and an end to suffering — if only he would submit. Alex's resolve wavered, the temptation to give in nearly overwhelming. With monumental effort, he forced himself to stand. His eyes blazed with renewed conviction, lips moving in a torrent of arcane words. The air crackled with otherworldly energy as occult chains manifested, binding the demon.

Alex's hand moved with practiced precision, drawing a glowing pentacle. Celestial fire erupted from the symbol, engulfing the demon in purifying flames. It shrieked, its unholy form imploding into the void. Panting heavily, Alex stood victorious. The ordeal had changed him; his eyes now burned with newfound occult power tempered by unshakeable faith. He gazed into the hellish expanse, his voice barely above a whisper. "I will not falter from my righteous path."

The words echoed through the dimension, a declaration and a warning to the infernal forces that lurked in the shadows. Father Alex's journey had only just begun, and the road ahead promised trials that would test the very limits of his soul.

Father Alex's eyes snapped open, a gasp tearing from his throat as he awoke. An unearthly light flared in his gaze, signaling the onset of a new, terrible phase.

***

Later, in the church basement, harsh overhead lights illuminated a chamber that seemed more befitting a sorcerer's lair than a place of worship. Occult artifacts cluttered every surface, their arcane forms casting twisted shadows. Father Alex, his frame gaunt and his appearance disheveled, hunched over ancient texts. The brittle pages crackled beneath his trembling fingers as he pored over depictions of forbidden rituals and mystical sigils.

"The Sephirothic planes shall be breached," he muttered, his voice a dry rasp. "The blood is the key..."

With a fluid motion, Alex shed his cassock. The garment slithered to the floor, revealing a torso marred by a tapestry of scars. Gripping an obsidian blade, its edge gleaming with malevolent promise, he set about his grisly work. The knife bit deep. Alex carved profane Sanskrit symbols into his own flesh, slicing through muscle and sinew. As blood welled from the fresh wounds, he began to chant in tongues, his voice rising and falling in an eldritch cadence that seemed to warp the very air around him.

Crimson rivulets streamed down his body, collecting in a waiting chalice. Alex repeated this torturous ritual across his limbs and face, each cut bringing both ecstasy and agony. His eyes rolled back, revealing only whites as he pushed himself to the brink of consciousness.

With hands slick with his own blood, Alex lifted the brimming chalice. He used its gory contents to paint a swirling portal sigil on the stone floor, the intricate design pulsing with otherworldly energy. Nearby, a vial of viscous liquid caught the light. Alex snatched it up, downing the bitter herbal elixir in one swift gulp. The effect was instantaneous. His body convulsed violently, muscles spasming beyond his control. The cellar around him began to warp and twist, reality giving way to a howling void that threatened to consume all.

Within this abyssal realm, Alex projected his psyche across forbidden dimensions. Shrieking entities assaulted his mind, their forms too terrible for mortal comprehension. Through sheer force of will, Alex severed these vile visions, clinging desperately to the last threads of his sanity.

The basement snapped back into focus. Alex's mutilated

form slumped against the cold stone, his breath coming in ragged gasps. With trembling hands, he grasped a blade, its tip glowing red-hot. He pressed it against his wounds, the sizzle of cauterizing flesh filling the air with an acrid stench.

Another vial of elixir found its way to his lips. As the liquid burned down his throat, a delirious haze settled over his mind. Alex's eyes, wild and unfocused, gazed upon some unseen horror as he proclaimed, "The old world dies! My faith is now boundless and beholden only to the infinite!"

In that moment, as madness and enlightenment intertwined, Father Alex stood on the precipice of a transformation that would shake the very foundations of reality.

His ritual complete, Alex rose unsteadily to his feet, leaving the cellar behind. He staggered through the winding corridors of the church, his bloodied hands leaving a trail on the ancient stone walls. As he entered the main hall, he began to prepare for the next phase of his unholy endeavor.

The ancient stone walls of the church loomed in the darkness, their shadows dancing in the flickering light of Father Alex's ritual. His hands trembled as he placed each obsidian candle with meticulous precision, forming a perfect circle on the cold floor. The air grew heavy with anticipation, thick with the scent of brimstone and decay.

Alex's fingers curled around a vial of luminescent blue liquid, its glow casting an eerie pallor across his gaunt features. He raised it to his lips, hesitating for a heartbeat before tipping it back. The elixir burned as it slid down his throat, igniting a fire in his veins. "Guide me through the veil," he rasped, his voice barely above a whisper. "Open my inward eye."

Lowering himself to the ground, Alex settled within the circle of candles. His chanting grew louder, more urgent, the ancient words tumbling from his lips in a frenzied cadence. The flames surrounding him surged violently, reaching towards the vaulted ceiling as if grasping for the heavens. In an instant, darkness swallowed the world. The chanting ceased, replaced by a deafening silence that pressed against Alex's eardrums. Confusion etched itself across his face as he peered into the inky void, searching for any sign that the ritual had succeeded.

Just as despair began to creep into his heart, an unseen force latched onto his very essence. Alex's mouth opened in a silent scream as his astral form was violently torn from its physical shell. The boundaries between worlds shattered, and he plummeted into the unknown depths of a realm beyond mortal comprehension.

Alex found himself suspended in a nightmarish void, gazing down upon a hellscape that stretched as far as the eye could see. Ruined buildings jutted like broken teeth from scorched earth, their skeletal frames silhouetted against a sky that bled crimson. Ash choked the air, swirling in eddies that whispered of desolation and despair.

"No...it can't be," Alex breathed, his voice barely a whisper in the oppressive silence.

As if pulled by an unseen force, he drifted over streets teeming with horrific sights. Emaciated figures in tattered rags hunched over charred corpses, tearing at blackened flesh with animalistic fervor. Many of these wretched souls bore grotesque mutations — horns spiraling from misshapen skulls, razor-sharp claws where hands should be, limbs multiplied and twisted into impossible configurations.

Amidst the carnage, pockets of depraved revelry erupted. Mutated forms writhed together in unholy unions, while others performed profane rituals around pentagrams traced in fire. The stench of burning flesh and sulfur assaulted Alex's senses, threatening to overwhelm him.

He recoiled, desperate to escape this vision of hell on earth. Yet an inexorable pull drew him towards a massive citadel that loomed on the horizon. The structure was carved from obsidian that seemed to devour light, pulsing with malevolent energy that sent shivers through Alex's incorporeal form.

Inside the citadel's cavernous temple, robed figures

swayed in hypnotic unison, their chants a discordant drone that set Alex's teeth on edge. At the focal point of their unholy worship stood an altar slick with fresh blood. Human sacrifices were brought forth, their screams cut short as a shadowy demon tore into their flesh with savage glee.

Alex drifted past scenes of unimaginable horror — chambers of torture where victims begged for death's sweet release, laboratories where human bodies were twisted and reshaped into monstrous new forms, ceremonial halls where initiates willingly mutilated themselves in grotesque displays of devotion. The air was thick with the screams of souls trapped in endless torment, their agony a symphony of despair.

"This is madness...a world forsaken," Alex muttered, his mind reeling as it struggled to process the nightmarish tableau.

An oppressive sense of dread settled over him as he approached the inner sanctum. An ethereal veil shimmered before him, promising revelations beyond human comprehension. With growing trepidation, Alex passed through.

Within the sanctum, reality itself seemed to warp and twist. Alex's gaze was drawn inexorably to a massive throne fashioned from countless human skulls. Upon this grisly seat lounged Mephistopheles, his grotesque form defying description, a blasphemous amalgamation of man and beast and things that should not be.

A scream tore from Alex's throat as chaotic visions bombarded his mind. Past, present, and future collided in a maelstrom of insanity. He felt his grip on reality slipping, oblivion beckoning with cold fingers. In that moment of utter despair, Alex's hand found the cross that hung around his neck. The cool metal against his skin sparked a flicker of faith, a lifeline in the tempest of madness. With every ounce of will he possessed, Alex rejected the apocalyptic vision, clinging to that last shred of hope.

Reality shattered. Alex snapped back into his physical body with violent force, breaking the ritual circle as he thrashed and screamed. His eyes, wide with terror, stared sightlessly at the church's vaulted ceiling. The dread glimpse of a possible future had shaken him to his very core, testing the limits of his resolve and sanity.

As Alex lay there, gasping and trembling, one thought echoed through his mind: the battle for humanity's soul had only just begun.

Alex stumbled back into the depths of the basement, his face haggard but his eyes blazing with a newfound focus. His trembling hands gathered an assortment of rare ritual artifacts — ancient bowls etched with forgotten symbols, bundles of mystical herbs that reeked of otherworldly scents, and a yellowed human skull that seemed to grin in anticipation.

With meticulous precision, he arranged the items in a complex pattern, constructing occult circles adorned with arcane symbols of forbidden knowledge. Flickering candles cast dancing shadows on the walls as Alex began to rehearse extraordinarily complex chants. His movements became fluid, almost serpentine, as he entered a trance-like state. His eyes rolled back, revealing only whites, and frothy spittle formed at the corners of his mouth.

"By the seven rings of Aratron, I summon..." The words slithered from his lips in a whispered invocation.

Without hesitation, Alex dragged a ceremonial dagger across his forearm. Blood welled up and dripped into a waiting bowl, sizzling upon contact. The symbols etched on the floor began to glow with an unearthly light, and a howling wind filled the church, seeming to emanate from nowhere and everywhere at once.

Alex's chanting grew wilder, more frenzied, as pulsing vortices tore open the fabric of reality. Through these eldritch portals emerged beings of a nightmare — writhing tentacles that defied geometry, a giant smoldering eye that blinked with malevolent intelligence. Alex channeled their unholy power, testing the limits of his newfound mastery. The very walls of the church groaned and cracked under the strain of forces never meant for this world.

With a final guttural cry that seemed to shake the foundations of the earth itself, Alex banished the entities in an apocalyptic surge of energy. The ritual complete, he stood amidst the chaos, his eyes blazing with eldritch light — a divine-demonic hybrid ready to unleash dangerous occult power against the cult that threatened all he held dear.

The price had been steep. Alex, utterly spent, collapsed to the floor.

In the aftermath, an unnatural stillness settled over the ritual space. Only a few guttering candles remained to illuminate the scene of devastation. Strange eldritch symbols and disturbed salt circles scarred the stone floor, testimony to the unholy rites that had transpired.

In the center of it all lay Father Alex, crumpled and motionless amidst scattered occult tomes and bowls still wet with his own blood. For a moment, all was silent. Then, a groan escaped his lips, and he stirred.

Blinking awake, Alex struggled to sit up, his body visibly drained of vitality. With growing horror, he examined his arms, now permanently marked with arcane brands that seemed to writhe beneath his skin.

The sound of heavy footsteps broke the silence. Alex turned to see Hunter enter the room, recoiling at the nightmarish tableau before him.

"Dear God...Alex, what have you done?"

Alex's voice was hoarse but filled with grim determination. "What I had to. What was needed to have any hope of stopping Balor."

With great effort, Alex straightened himself. His eyes burned with a relentless conviction that seemed to bore into Hunter's very soul.

"I have become...an instrument against the coming darkness. For the greater good."

As Alex spoke, his gaze hardened, fully embracing the sacrilegious apotheosis he had undergone. Hunter watched solemnly, witnessing the last vestiges of his friend's humanity slip away.

"I hope your faith remains strong enough to withstand the consequences of your actions," Hunter said, his voice heavy with sorrow.

Alex's response was chilling in its certainty. "My faith is unbreakable, old friend. But it's no longer that of any benevolent God." With a gesture, eldritch energy coursed through Alex's hands — a terrible fusion of divine wrath and demonic might. "I serve a different power now. One beyond good and evil."

Alex's eyes blazed with terrible purpose, a glimpse into realms of madness and power that no mortal was meant to comprehend. Hunter bowed his head, grieving for the friend he had lost.

"So be it," Hunter whispered, the words falling like a funeral dirge in the oppressive silence.

They stood amidst the remnants of the ritual, the weight of Alex's irrevocable sacrifice hanging heavy between them. The air itself seemed to tremble with the knowledge that something fundamental had shifted in the cosmic order and that the coming days would bring horrors beyond imagining.

CHAPTER 17
THE SEED OF DOUBT

Lilith's heart pounded as robed cultists guided her into a dimly lit chamber. The air hung heavy with the scent of incense and something more metallic. Arcane symbols adorned the walls, their eldritch curves seeming to writhe in the flickering torchlight. At the center of the room stood a stone altar, its surface stained dark with what could only be blood.

Whispered chants began to swell around her, a discordant chorus that made Lilith's blood run cold. Her eyes widened as a hooded figure emerged from the shadows, dragging a struggling victim towards the altar. The poor soul's muffled cries were barely audible above the rising fervor of the cultists.

With a practiced motion, the hooded figure produced an ornate knife. Its blade glinted wickedly in the low light. Before Lilith could process what was happening, the figure slashed the victim's throat. A spray of warm crimson splattered across Lilith's face, and she recoiled in horror, her stomach churning.

A voice boomed through the chamber: "For the awakening!"

What followed was a scene ripped from the deepest pits of hell. The cultists descended upon the victim like ravenous beasts, tearing into flesh with bare hands and teeth. Their frenzied bloodlust transformed them into something inhuman.

Lilith stood frozen, unable to look away from the gruesome slaughter before her. She glanced down at her own hands, now stained a deep, glistening red. The sight made her head swim.

Around her, the chamber erupted in ecstasy. Cultists reveled in their depraved ceremony, their faces masks of rapturous joy. Lilith felt disconnected from it all, as if watching the scene unfold from behind a pane of glass.

As the screams faded and the fervor died down, Lilith felt something shift within her. A creeping darkness seemed to seep into her very being, starting from her eyes and working its way into her soul. New doubts took root, whispers of cosmic truths too terrible to comprehend. In that moment, standing amidst the aftermath of an unholy ritual, Lilith knew she would never be the same.

The last echoes of the cultists' cries reverberated through the chamber, their jubilant faces slowly fading into the shadows. Lilith felt a cold silence settle around her, the metallic taste of blood still fresh on her lips. She stumbled away from the altar, her heart pounding an erratic rhythm in her chest. The world seemed to tilt on its axis, and she steadied herself against the stone wall, her hand leaving a crimson smear on its cold surface.

Lilith drifted through the dim corridor, her eyes unfocused and her mind still reeling from the ritual's trauma. Flickering shadows danced on the rough stone walls, casting eerie shapes that seemed to reach for her with spectral fingers. The air hung thick with the scent of incense and something darker, more primal.

A faint groan, barely audible, pierced the oppressive silence. Lilith's head snapped toward the sound, her senses suddenly alert. She followed the noise, her feet carrying her almost of their own accord until she found herself before a heavy wooden door. Arcane symbols were carved into its surface, pulsing with a faint, sickly light.

Through the door's grated opening, Lilith peered into a holding cell. Her breath caught in her throat at the sight within. Mara, battered and disheveled, hung from the wall, her wrists bound by rusted chains. Despite the woman's obvious suffering, her eyes blazed with an inner fire, a defiance that burned through the gloom.

For a moment, time seemed to stand still. Lilith found herself transfixed, unable to look away from Mara's piercing gaze. In that instant, a connection sparked between them, raw and electric. It cut through the fog of Lilith's indoctrination, igniting a spark of something long forgotten.

Mara's lips parted, words forming on her tongue. But before she could speak, arcane energy crackled through the air. The mystical bonds constricted, sending a jolt of pain through Mara's body. Her words died in a strangled gasp, her face contorting in agony.

The spell was broken by the sudden appearance of cult acolytes. Their hands, cold and insistent, grasped at Lilith's arms, pulling her away from the cell. But as they led her down the corridor, Lilith found her gaze drawn back to Mara. The prisoner's eyes never wavered, holding Lilith's stare with unwavering determination.

As the distance between them grew, Lilith felt something stir within her chest. The seed of doubt, planted by that brief moment of connection, had taken root. And as the shadows swallowed her once more, Lilith knew that nothing would ever be the same.

Lilith was dragged further into the labyrinthine corridors. Alone in her quarters, she replayed the scene over and over in her mind, each time feeling the same jolt of connection, the same stirring of doubt.

Lilith perched on the edge of her bed, the darkness of the sleep chamber mirroring the shadows that haunted her eyes. The silence pressed in, heavy and oppressive, broken only by her shallow breathing. Unbidden, Mara's unyielding gaze flashed before her, seared into her psyche like a brand. The memory pulsed, raw and insistent, refusing to be ignored.

In its wake came a torrent of fragmented images, each more disturbing than the last. Occult rituals played out in grotesque detail, the air thick with the metallic scent of sacrificial blood. Balor's hands, cold and manipulative, ghosted over Lilith's skin, leaving trails of revulsion in their wake. And always, always, Mara's defiant eyes bore into her, accusing and beseeching in equal measure.

But something had changed. Mara's indomitable spirit, even in memory, kindled a spark within Lilith. Long-dormant empathy stirred, pushing against the walls of her conditioning. As the realization of what she had become crashed over her, disgust twisted her features. "What have I become?" The words escaped her in a hoarse whisper, barely audible even in the tomb-like quiet of the chamber.

Lilith's body betrayed her inner turmoil, trembling as if caught in an icy wind. Her face contorted, a battlefield where her ingrained responses warred against the resurgence of her humanity. The conflict etched lines of anguish across her brow, her eyes wide with dawning horror. "I can't do this anymore." The declaration hung in the air, a fragile thing born of newfound resolve and crushing guilt.

In the oppressive darkness, Lilith sat motionless, the weight of her choices pressing down upon her. The path ahead was shrouded in uncertainty, but one thing was clear — she could no longer be the monster they had made her.

Lilith emerged from the chamber, transformed. A newfound resolve coursed through her veins as she navigated the labyrinthine corridors of the cult compound. Her fingers danced across the keypad, inputting the access code that would lead her to Mara's holding cell. The pulsing ward fizzled out, granting her entry.

Inside, Mara stirred weakly, her eyes widening at Lilith's sudden appearance. Lilith pressed a finger to her lips, silencing any potential outburst. "Something in me cracked open when I saw you," Lilith whispered, her voice barely audible. "I have to make this right."

Mara's wary gaze followed Lilith's movements as she worked to undo the bindings. The alchemical suppressants hissed as they were neutralized, and Mara winced as sensation flooded back into her limbs.

They slipped out into the maze of corridors, Lilith leading

the way with practiced stealth. She guided them through back passages, timing their movements to avoid the ever-present cult sentries.

"What's Balor planning?" Mara's whisper was tinged with urgency. "The ritual — what's it for?"

Lilith's face contorted with fear. "I can't...he'll know. The seals... his wrath..."

They crept down a pitch-black corridor, inching closer to their escape route. Lilith's eyes darted around each corner, her hand signaling Mara to follow when the coast was clear.

"If you want redemption, tell me how to stop him," Mara pleaded. "Please..."

Indecision flashed across Lilith's face as she weighed her options, her mind racing. Finally, she spoke, her words dripping with dread. "Balor made a pact...the demon and the cosmic alignment...it will unmake reality."

The color drained from Mara's face as the gravity of the situation sank in. They reached a small side exit, freedom tantalizingly close. But Lilith's outstretched hand halted their progress.

The air turned deathly cold in an instant. An unnatural wind howled down the hallway, snuffing out torches and plunging them into darkness. Mara shivered uncontrollably as Lilith's eyes widened with primal fear.

"You didn't think it would be that easy...did you, Lilith?" Balor's voice slithered through the air before he materialized from billowing smoke, his eyes blazing with unholy rage. The very walls of the compound seemed to crack and bleed at his presence. Mara's scream was cut short as an unseen force slammed her against the unforgiving stone.

Lilith cowered before Balor's wrath. His hand shot out, grasping her neck and lifting her off her feet with inhuman strength.

"You betrayed me! Me! Your master!"

Lilith's tortured gasps echoed in the corridor as Balor's

grip tightened mercilessly.

"I should end you now for this insolence," he snarled. "But no...that would be too merciful." With a casual flick of his wrist, Balor flung Lilith to the ground. She lay there, limp and weeping, as he knelt beside her. His fingers caressed her hair with mock tenderness. "There, there. Your master forgives you." Balor's hand moved to Lilith's chin, forcing her to meet his gaze. Guttural incantations spilled from his lips, and Lilith's eyes glazed over, entranced by his dark power.

"You belong to me," he intoned. "Never forget that."

Lilith nodded slowly, her will crushed beneath the weight of his influence.

"Now beg for my mercy, worm!"

Broken and defeated, Lilith fell to her knees before Balor. "Please...master. Have mercy."

A cold, cruel smile twisted Balor's features. Without another word, he turned and strode away, leaving Lilith shattered in the oppressive darkness.

***

Two brutish figures emerged from the shadows, dragging the limp form of Lilith between them. Her face was a canvas of bruises and blood, her eyes vacant pools of despair. With callous disregard, they hoisted her atop the wooden platform, her body as pliant as a ragdoll.

Mara's arrival was equally unceremonious. Rough hands yanked her forward, securing her to the wall with rusted chains that bit into her flesh. She could only watch in horror as the scene unfolded before her.

Balor's presence filled the room, his imposing figure casting long shadows across the chamber floor. In his hand, a wicked ceremonial dagger glinted malevolently, its blade thirsting for blood. His eyes, burning with cruel purpose, fixed upon Lilith's prone form. "Pitiful betrayer," he intoned, his voice dripping with contempt. "You dared to awaken useless pangs of conscience, like a worm aspiring to become a butterfly. Now, you shall have your wings seared away forever."

Lilith remained motionless, her silence a stark contrast to the growing cacophony around her. Balor began to chant, his words guttural and profane. The very air seemed to warp and twist, reality bending to his will.

Flickering shadows, alive with malevolent intent, crashed over Lilith like dark waves. They bound her to the pyre, their ethereal tendrils tightening with each passing moment. Balor raised the dagger, its edge gleaming in the firelight. With practiced precision, he began to carve vile markings into Lilith's flesh, each cut a desecration of her body and soul.

"With these wounds, I rededicate your hollowed spirit to darkness everlasting!" Balor's voice rose to a fever pitch. "Never again shall you stray from your true path of servitude. This pyre shall consume all lingering weakness within you."

Lilith barely flinched as Balor savagely plunged the dagger into her. Dark blood, thick and viscous, trickled down the blade, each drop a testament to her fading humanity.

The pyre erupted with unholy flame, its heat searing the very air. The cultists, driven to madness by the spectacle, whipped themselves into a frenzied state. Their chants and screams melded into a horrific symphony of depravity.

The ritual chamber pulsed with an infernal glow, bathed in the crimson light of Lilith's funeral pyre. Stacked logs crackled and hissed as flames licked hungrily at the body atop them, consuming flesh and bone with ravenous intensity.

Lilith's body was engulfed by the inferno, the flames seeming to devour her very essence. Balor's voice cut through the chaos. "Thus ends the last flicker of defiance. She is mine forevermore."

Nearby, Mara strained against her chains, forced to bear witness to the macabre spectacle. Her face contorted in a rictus of anguish, eyes wide with horror as she watched the conflagration grow.

As Lilith's body blackened and charred, an eerie

phenomenon took hold. While the rest of her form succumbed to the flames, her face remained untouched, pristine amidst the inferno. Those lifeless eyes, once windows to unfathomable depths, now locked onto Mara's gaze with unnerving persistence.

The pyre roared, its fury building to a deafening crescendo. Lilith's body began to disintegrate, disappearing into the raging inferno as if swallowed by some ravenous entity from beyond. Yet even as her physical form vanished, the weight of her stare lingered, searing itself into Mara's psyche.

The chamber filled with acrid smoke and the sickly-sweet stench of burning flesh. Mara's chest heaved with panicked breaths, her mind reeling as she grappled with the implications of this unholy ritual. What dark forces were at play here? And what role was she, an unwilling captive, meant to serve in this twisted tableau?

As the last vestiges of Lilith's corporeal form crumbled to ash, an oppressive silence fell over the chamber. The flames continued their dance, casting writhing shadows on the walls like restless spirits. Mara's chains clinked softly as she trembled, her eyes fixed on the pyre where Lilith had been — where something unnatural and terrifying had transpired before her very eyes.

Mara's heart pounded in her chest, and the horror of Lilith's unspeakable fate seared into her memory. She struggled against her bonds, desperate to break free from this nightmare. As the flames began to die down, a ghostly figure emerged from the ashes. It was Lilith, or the twisted husk of the woman she once was.

Lilith's charred body hung suspended above the smoldering embers, her long red hair now a twisted mass of cinders. Her once-brown eyes were now voids, windows to the infernal realm that had claimed her. As her charred arms reached beseechingly for Mara, Mara's mind froze in horror, and she slipped into blessed oblivion.

Mara drifted back to consciousness, her eyelids heavy as lead. As awareness crept in, an eerie glow seeped through her closed lids. She forced them open, blinking away the haze. She realized she had been moved from the ritual chamber, but the where of it she was unsure of.

The world swam into focus, revealing a nightmarish scene. Strange symbols and glyphs adorned the walls, pulsing with an otherworldly light that made her stomach churn. Panic clawed at her throat as she tried to move, only to find herself bound by invisible forces that seemed to writhe against her skin.

Confusion gave way to fear as Mara's eyes darted around the dimly lit chamber. The air felt thick and oppressive, as if reality itself was warping around her. She strained against her mystical bindings, muscles tensing and relaxing in futile attempts to break free.

From somewhere deep within the labyrinthine structure, ominous chanting echoed off stone walls. The guttural sounds intertwined with blood-curdling screams that sent shivers down Mara's spine. The horrible realization dawned on her: she was trapped in the heart of the cult's lair.

Determination flashed in her eyes as she gritted her teeth. "Not going to be a sacrifice... I'm getting out of here."

Mara's gaze locked onto a small outcropping near her bindings. She twisted her body, fingers straining to reach it. If she could just pry it loose, maybe she could use it as a tool to escape. As she struggled, the glyphs on the walls began to pulse more intensely. The air shimmered and warped, reality bending in impossible ways. From one of the pulsing symbols, a serpentine apparition emerged, its form flickering and undulating as it approached her.

Mara's heart raced, but she steeled herself against the terror threatening to overwhelm her. "You don't scare me...I know what you are. I'm getting out!" Her defiant words seemed to ripple through the air. The apparition wavered, its form becoming less substantial before fading away entirely. Mara exhaled shakily, forcing herself to calm down. She couldn't let fear paralyze her now.

With renewed determination, she fixed her gaze on the outcropping once more. "I won't let your evil win. I'm seeing this through to the end. You hear me?!"

Her challenge echoed off the walls, seeming to make the very air vibrate with tension. Mara summoned every ounce of strength she possessed, muscles straining as she yanked at the outcropping with all her might. The fate of more than just herself hung in the balance, and she refused to let the darkness win.

CHAPTER 18
ASTRAL INTRUSION

The ancient tomes and arcane artifacts scattered across the antique table cast long shadows in the dim light of Hunter's esoteric library. Hunter and Father Alex huddled close, their faces etched with worry as they pored over the occult texts. Terry stood nearby, his fingers dancing across brittle pages as he assisted their frantic search.

Hunter's voice cut through the oppressive silence. "We haven't heard from Mara in days. She had to have left some trail we can pick up."

Alex nodded, his brow furrowed in concentration as he absently stroked the smooth rosary beads dangling from his fingers. "I'll try a scrying ritual again. There must be some ripple we can trace."

With grim determination, Hunter seized a ritual knife from the table. The blade glinted wickedly in the low light as he pricked his finger, allowing crimson droplets to fall into a black scrying bowl. Alex began to chant, his low voice resonating with power as he waved his hand over the inky liquid.

Terry slammed the tome shut in frustration. "This is taking way too long. We need to get Mara back, now!"

"Try to be patient, Terry," Hunter intoned as he stared into the scrying bowl. "These things take time."

The surface of the bowl churned and swirled, coalescing into horrifying images. Mara appeared, bound and struggling against cruel shackles in a nightmarish cell. Grotesque faces leered at her from the shadows, their malevolent intent palpable. Alex winced but maintained his focus, willing the vision to clarify. Yet, all too soon, the ghastly tableau faded back into obscurity.

Terry's hands trembled as he stared at the bowl in disbelief. "Her cover has been blown!" He started pacing the room and raked his hand through his short-cropped hair in frustration. "We have to do something, guys."

"Still too unclear," Alex growled, frustration etched in every line of his face. "The cult's wards are strong."

Hunter was flipping through pages at a furious pace. He didn't spare Terry a second glance. "Patience, Detective." Terry let out an exasperated sigh as Hunter aggressively jabbed his finger onto the page in the ancient tome in front of them. "Ah! found it."

Hunter's hand found Alex's shoulder, squeezing it in a gesture of solidarity. "Keep trying. I'll project my spirit, see if I can find any cracks in their veil."

Terry looked between the two men. "Wait... What?" The alarm rose in his voice. "What are you doing?"

"What we must, Detective, if you wish to lay eyes on your partner once more," Hunter commanded with a chilling tone, turning his gaze back to Father Alex. "Are you ready, Alex?"

As Alex nodded his assent, Hunter reclined, allowing his body to relax into a meditative state. Strange, guttural syllables spilled from his lips as he began to chant in an eldritch tongue.

The air around Hunter's prone form shimmered and distorted. His spirit, a gossamer echo of his physical self, emerged and drifted upward. It passed through solid matter as if it were no more substantial than smoke, ascending through the ceiling and into the star-strewn night sky beyond.

Hunter's spirit soared high above the city, gliding silently through the night air. Below, Savannah was cloaked in darkness, only the occasional street lamp piercing the gloom. He focused his psychic senses, attempting to detect any occult disturbances that might hint at Mara's location within the cult's compound.

Hunter's astral spirit roamed through the twisted netherworld, desperately seeking any cracks in the cult's occult defenses. The sinister landscape was filled with eldritch horrors

— amorphous shapes that gnashed needle-like teeth and colossal cyclopean structures that loomed ominously over everything.

He could feel the cult's dark magic permeating this realm, fortifying their wards and barriers against all forms of psychic intrusion. The very air seemed saturated with malevolence, pressing in on Hunter's ethereal presence from all sides.

Focusing his will, he managed to push through the oppressive atmosphere, searching for any weakness in the cult's astral fortifications. As he probed further into their compound, hideous creatures assailed him, slashing at his ghostly form with talons and tentacles. Hunter held them at bay, fighting past the demonic guardians that sought to bar his way.

Finally, he sensed a faint crack in the occult defenses — a tiny fissure that led like a thread through the labyrinthine maze of the cult's eldritch stronghold. Hunter dove toward it, pouring his spirit through the narrow opening. His spirit slipped through the crack in the cult's psychic defenses, entering their fortified compound in the eldritch realm. As he floated further inside, the oppressive darkness seemed to grow even thicker, nearly suffocating his astral form. Strange murmurs and unearthly shrieks echoed through the twisted passageways. Hunter steeled himself and pressed onward, determined to find Mara.

Suddenly, a blood-curdling howl rang out, and he felt the aura of the compound shift. The cult members had detected the intrusion. Hideous creatures emerged from the shadows, converging on Hunter's position. Grotesque humanoid forms with pale, sightless eyes and gaping maws, shadowy specters trailing wisps of darkness, amorphous horrors writhing with black tendrils — they swarmed toward the crack in the wards that Hunter had slipped through.

Hunter tried to evade them, his spirit flitting through the horde, but their numbers were too great. The cult's demonic guardians clawed and grasped at his ethereal form, seeking to shred his astral body. As razor-sharp talons raked across him, Hunter cried out in psychic agony. He could feel his spirit-self weakening under the onslaught.

Terrified, Hunter realized he had to retreat — the cult's defenses were too strong. He turned and flew back toward the crack in their wards, the demonic horde pursuing him. Shadowy claws grasped at the trailing edges of his spirit form as he narrowly slipped back through the breach.

The moment Hunter returned to his physical body, he jolted upright with a gasp. Father Alex and Terry stared at him with deep concern etched on their faces.

"Did you find her? What happened?" Terry asked anxiously.

Hunter's face was pale and haunted. "Their defenses are airtight. My spirit barely escaped the demonic guardians." He shook his head grimly. "I'm sorry... I couldn't locate Mara."

Terry slammed his fist on the table in frustration. "Dammit! What are we supposed to do now?"

Father Alex placed a gentle hand on Terry's shoulder. "We'll find another way," he said softly. "But breaching their compound directly may be impossible."

Hunter nodded. "We need to uncover a weakness we can exploit. There must be some crack in their occult armor."

Silence fell over the room. Hunter's words lingered in the air, a haunting reminder of their dire predicament. The trio shared a knowing look, each consumed by their own contemplations. It was evident that a different approach was necessary — one that went beyond sheer strength. They reconvened at the table, determined to devise a new plan.

Hunter slumped back in his chair, rubbing his temples as he tried to process what he had seen in the eldritch realm. The cult's defenses were far more impenetrable than he had anticipated. Simply breaking through by force of will was not going to work. They needed to find some vulnerability, some arcane secret that could unravel the sinister wards protecting the compound.

Terry paced back and forth, his frustration palpable.

"There has to be something in one of these books that can help us," he said, gesturing to the massive collection of occult tomes that littered the table. Hunter had gathered every rare text and forbidden grimoire related to protective rituals and summoning magic that he could acquire. There had to be some obscure bit of lore that revealed the cult's ritual secrets.

Father Alex, meanwhile, had withdrawn to the corner of the room. Kneeling with his rosary clutched tightly in his hands, he prayed fervently for divine guidance. As a man of faith, the priest knew that sometimes salvation came not through man's power alone but by grace from above. He implored God to grant them the wisdom to find Mara and thwart the sinister forces holding her captive.

Hunter grasped another hefty volume from the pile and offered it to Terry. "Do not abandon all hope yet, Terry," he insisted with a sense of urgency. "Continue your search."

Terry slumped back into his seat with a weighted exhale before delving into the timeworn pages of the tome. "Okay, I'll keep looking," he conceded in resignation.

With renewed determination, Hunter and Terry poured over the ancient texts once more. Hour after hour, they scrutinized the arcane symbols and rituals described on the crumbling pages, searching for any similarity to the occult wards they had glimpsed surrounding the cult's compound.

Hunter rubbed his bleary eyes as he pored over yet another crumbling tome, this one so ancient the leather binding was cracked and flaking. It was well past midnight, and he could feel exhaustion seeping into his bones. But he couldn't stop — not when Mara's life hung in the balance.

Terry rubbed his tired eyes and sighed. Another dead end. The text he had been poring over for the past three hours provided no insights on how to breach the cult's defenses. He let out a frustrated sigh, another useless book to toss onto the growing pile. "This is getting us nowhere. We're just going in circles at this point. I need a break," he muttered, closing the heavy tome with a thud. He stood up from the table and stretched, joints cracking. "Anybody else want coffee?"

"No, thank you, Terry." Father Alex looked up from where he knelt, praying in the corner. "Have faith, my friends. The answer will reveal itself in time."

Hunter slammed his book shut, a plume of dust rising into the air. "Time is the one thing we don't have. The longer Mara is in their clutches..." His voice broke, unable to finish the terrible thought.

Terry reclined in his chair, sipping coffee from a sturdy mug. His fingers reached for another ancient tome. "I'll keep looking."

Hunter's deep grunt was a nod of understanding as he snatched a dusty leather-bound book and delved into its secrets alongside Terry.

"Wait a minute." Terry pivoted the book around to show Hunter. "This uses ley lines to pinpoint locations by their energy alignment," Terry explained, his finger tracing the faded text. "Maybe it'll help triangulate where she could be."

Alex's eyes darted across the yellowed page, a flicker of hope igniting in their depths. He nodded, a grim smile tugging at the corners of his mouth. "Good work, Terry. We'll try it next."

With renewed purpose, they scurried about the cluttered space, gathering an assortment of arcane ingredients. Candles guttered in unseen drafts as Alex knelt on the worn floorboards, chalk scratching against wood as he meticulously traced an intricate symbol.

Hunter lay down on the floor, positioning himself carefully within the chalk symbol. He closed his eyes and steadied his breathing, focusing his mind and willing his spirit to detach from his physical form. As he slipped into a meditative trance, he felt the now-familiar sensation of his astral body lifting up and out of his physical shell.

When he opened his eyes, Hunter found himself floating above his own still body. The room around him was muted and hazy, as if he were seeing it through a veil. Turning, he willed himself forward, flying swiftly through the walls of the safe house and out over the shadowy streets of Savannah.

The night sky was an ominous void, the stars blotted out by an unnatural darkness that seemed to ooze and writhe with a life of its own. Hunter could feel the malevolent presence all around him. The astral plane was now fully under the thrall of the Ancient Ones, transformed into a nightmarish domain teeming with eldritch horrors.

In the distance, amid the swirling mists, Hunter could make out the cult's compound. Ethereal walls of dark energy surrounded it, undulating with vile faces that leered and mocked any who dared approach. Strange symbols glowed ominously atop the parapets, warping the fabric of reality around them.

Hunter steeled his resolve and soared towards the foreboding fortress. Monstrous winged beasts screeched and lunged at him, their claws and teeth bared in a frenzy. With graceful movement, he shielded himself from their attacks, his ethereal essence flickering just out of their grasp.

Without warning, a blast of malevolent energy tore through the ether. It slammed into Hunter with the force of a freight train, sending his spirit reeling. Before he could recover, shadowy figures materialized from the darkness. Cultists, their forms twisted and grotesque in this otherworldly realm, surrounded him.

Their hands moved in intricate patterns, weaving spells of binding and entrapment. Tendrils of dark energy snaked towards Hunter, seeking to ensnare his very essence. He reacted on instinct, summoning a shield of brilliant light around himself. The radiance pushed back against the encroaching darkness, but Hunter could feel the strain of maintaining his defense.

The cultists pressed their advantage, their chants growing louder and more frenzied. The air itself seemed to thicken, closing in around Hunter like a vise. He struggled against their assault, his light flickering and wavering under the relentless onslaught.

With a surge of will, Hunter broke free from their circle. He retreated, his spirit form streaking through the astral plane like a comet. The cultists' howls of frustration echoed behind him as he fled, knowing he couldn't maintain this battle indefinitely.

Hunter felt the pull of his physical body, a lifeline in this sea of madness. With great reluctance, he allowed himself to be drawn back, leaving the mysteries of the astral plane unsolved for now. As his consciousness settled back into flesh and bone, Hunter's eyes snapped open, his body jerking upright as a strangled gasp escaped his lips. The dim, book-lined walls of his esoteric library swam into focus, shadowy tomes looming like silent sentinels. Alex and Terry hovered nearby, their faces etched with concern in the flickering candlelight.

Sweat beaded on Hunter's brow as he struggled to catch his breath. The lingering tendrils of his vision clung to him, leaving an icy chill in their wake. He met his companions' worried gazes, his voice hoarse as he spoke. "The cult knows we're searching. They tried binding my spirit. This isn't going to be easy."

The words hung heavy in the air, laden with unspoken dread. Alex's jaw tightened, determination flashing in his eyes. He stepped forward, his hand outstretched to Hunter. "All the more reason we must endure. For Mara's sake."

Hunter grasped Alex's offered hand, his legs unsteady as he helped him to his feet. Their eyes locked, a silent understanding passing between them. In that moment, they both knew the true weight of what lay ahead — a battle not just for Mara but perhaps for their very souls.

The library seemed to close in around them, the arcane knowledge contained within its walls now tinged with a sinister air. As Hunter steadied himself, he could feel an unseen malevolence pressing against the edges of reality, waiting to break through. The search for Mara would continue, but with each step forward, the darkness grew deeper, hungrier.

Terry shifted uneasily, his gaze darting between his companions and the shadows that seemed to writhe in the corners of the room. The night stretched before them, promising secrets and horrors yet unknown. With grim resolve, the trio steeled themselves for the nightmarish journey that lay ahead, knowing that to falter now would mean surrender to forces beyond mortal comprehension.

CHAPTER 19
ECHOES OF DEFIANCE

Darkness enveloped Mara as she huddled in the corner of her cell, knees drawn tightly to her chest. The cold stone floor seeped through her tattered clothes, chilling her to the bone. Her eyes, adjusted to the gloom, darted to the mystical chains encircling her wrists. With subtle movements, she tested their strength, feeling a glimmer of hope as she detected a slight give near the edge of one cuff.

Mara tensed as a muffled boom rolled across the still night air. Her heart quickened — could it be? Had her friends finally tracked her location and come to free her from this wretched dungeon? She strained to listen for any sounds of a scuffle, of keys jingling, or voices raised. But there was only silence. As the echoes faded, Mara's shoulders slumped in disappointment. Of course, it was too much to hope for. She was on her own here.

With a shaky breath, Mara refocused her efforts on the mystical chains. She pressed and pulled, grimacing against the biting metal. The edges were worn smooth from use yet still strong enough to hold fast. Mara refused to give up. There had to be a weakness somewhere. She just needed to find the right spot to give and apply the right amount of pressure. Mara twisted her wrists slowly, feeling along each link. Sweat beaded on her forehead despite the chill seeping from the stones. She was so focused on her task that the next explosion made her cry out in alarm.

This one sounded closer, more violent. Mara's heart thudded wildly. What was happening out there? What fresh evil had been unleashed upon Savannah tonight? Mara shuddered, the cold dread almost stronger than her hope for escape. She redoubled her efforts on the chains. She had to get free, had to find out what new darkness had arisen. The metal edges dug into her skin, and she bit her lip. She could feel the warm trickle of blood as the metal chains cut into her wrists. She ignored the pain, driven by a desperation that coursed through her veins. The muffled booms continued at erratic intervals, seeming to draw nearer with each one. Mara's intuition told her something sinister was approaching.

Each explosive crash shook loose dust from the stone walls, stinging Mara's eyes and coating her hair and clothes in a fine layer of grit. She coughed but did not stop straining against the mystical chains. With a gasp, she felt a link begin to give way. The metal cut deeper, but she persisted, certain that freedom was close.

The sudden echo of heavy footsteps in the hallway outside sent a jolt of fear through her. Mara's heart raced as she steeled herself, knowing what was to come. The cell door creaked open, flooding the small space with harsh light that made her squint. In the doorway stood Xavian, his imposing figure casting a long shadow across the floor. His cold, calculating eyes bore into her, seeming to pierce her very soul.

"I hope you're ready to talk," Xavian said, his voice dripping with malice. "Lord Balor grows impatient."

Mara lifted her chin defiantly, meeting his gaze with a fire of her own. "I have nothing to say to you," she spat, her words laced with venom.

As she held Xavian's stare, Mara's fingers worked discreetly at her bonds, seeking to exploit the weakness she'd discovered. Time was running out, and she knew it.

A cruel smile twisted Xavian's lips. "We'll see about that after today's session," he sneered. "I'll peel your mind open until all your secrets spill out."

Without warning, Xavian lunged forward, his rough hands seizing Mara's arms. She bit back a cry of pain as he yanked her to her feet, his grip bruising. The world spun as he dragged her from the cell, her bare feet stumbling on the cold stone floor.

As they moved down the dimly lit corridor, Mara's mind raced. She knew what horrors awaited her in the interrogation chamber, and fear threatened to overwhelm her. Her heart pounded as Xavian dragged her into the chamber. The air felt thick, oppressive, laden with the stench of ancient evil. Before her loomed a chair that seemed carved from nightmares itself — all twisted angles and grotesque symbols etched deep into blackened wood.

Xavian shoved her into the seat. Cold tendrils of dread snaked up her spine as the occult markings pulsed with an unholy light. She barely had time to register the terror before Xavian's mental assault began.

It was as if a thousand icy needles were piercing her skull simultaneously. Mara's vision blurred, the room spinning as Xavian's probes invaded the sanctity of her mind. Every fiber of her being screamed in agony, but she clenched her jaw, refusing to give voice to her pain. She wouldn't give him that satisfaction.

Mara's mind was on fire, and every ounce of her being was consumed with the burning pain Xavian's intrusion inflicted upon her. Tears streamed down her cheeks, but she wouldn't give him the satisfaction of hearing her scream. She had to find a way out of this, she had to. She closed her eyes, trying her best to block out the pain, and focused on her memories.

Her mother's face swam into focus, smiling at her on her 7th birthday before the cancer had taken her away. The warmth of her embrace, the scent of her perfume, and the way she would sing her to sleep every night. These memories, these moments, they were hers, and no one, not even Xavian, could take them away from her.

Mara clung to the memories of her mother, using them as an anchor against the onslaught in her mind. She focused on the image of her mother's smiling face, recalling the sound of her laugh and the warmth of her hugs. The pain was still there, still intense, but the memories gave Mara something to hold onto amidst the agony.

A particularly forceful probe sent stabbing pain ricocheting through Mara's skull. She cried out despite herself, unable to hold it back. Xavian's cold laughter echoed around her. "Give yourself to the pain," he goaded. "It will all be over if you just surrender."

Mara bit down hard on her tongue, tasting blood. She would not give up. She had to maintain control of her mind, or all hope was lost.

"Tell me what I want to know," Xavian demanded, his voice booming and distorted by the haze of pain.

Mara remained defiantly silent, beads of sweat mingling with tears on her face.

Sensing her continued resistance, Xavian increased the intensity. Abruptly, Xavian broke contact with a snarl of frustration. Mara slumped back, trembling with exhaustion but clinging to consciousness. Xavian glowered at her, chest heaving.

"You can't keep me out forever," he growled. "I'll crack your mind open sooner or later."

Mara raised her head slowly, meeting his glare. "Do your worst," she rasped, her voice hoarse but resolute.

Xavian's lip curled in a sneer. "Oh, I intend to." He raised a hand toward her head once more.

Mara braced herself as Xavian's hand hovered menacingly over her head, ready to resume his mental assault. She focused her mind, trying to shore up her defenses. The psychic onslaught intensified. Mara's body convulsed, her fingers digging into the armrests until her knuckles turned white. Sweat beaded on her brow as she fought against the intrusion. Memories flashed before her eyes — cherished moments and buried traumas alike, all laid bare under Xavian's merciless scrutiny.

But deep within, a spark of defiance burned. With each probe, each attempt to break her will, Mara's resolve only hardened. She met Xavian's cold gaze, her eyes blazing with silent fury. They could torture her body and violate her mind, but her spirit remained unbroken. As waves of agony crashed over her, Mara held onto that defiance like a lifeline in a storm-tossed sea.

Mara gritted her teeth as she mentally braced herself for another assault. She could sense Xavian gathering his power, the air crackling with malignant energy. His eyes glinted with sadistic delight as he prepared to invade her mind once more.

"Ready for more?" he purred, his voice dripping with cruelty.

Mara said nothing, determined not to give him the satisfaction of a response. She dug her fingernails into her palms, using the pain to ground herself.

Xavian's smile faded, morphing into a scowl at her continued defiance. With a snarl, he slammed into her mind with renewed force. Mara's body spasmed against her bonds. It felt as if her skull was being split in two, white-hot knives of agony stabbing through every synapse.

She desperately tried to shore up her mental defenses, but Xavian tore through them like tissue paper. He rifled ruthlessly through her memories, tainting her most cherished moments with his vile presence. Rivulets of blood leaked from Mara's nose as the assault continued. Still, she refused to scream or beg for mercy.

"Tell me what I want to know!" Xavian roared, flecks of spittle flying from his lips. When Mara only glared at him, eyes burning with hatred, he switched tactics. The excruciating pain instantly ceased, replaced by phantom sensations of comfort and safety. Mara found herself enveloped in memories of her mother's embrace, the smell of freshly baked cookies wafting through the air.

Mara's mind reeled, struggling to cling to reality amidst the phantom sensations Xavian was projecting into her mind. The comforting memories enveloped her like a warm blanket, beckoning her to relax into their embrace. But even as her body sagged against the restraints, some part of Mara's psyche remained on high alert. This was nothing but a ruse, a sadistic trick to get her to lower her defenses.

She focused on the rough texture of the armrests digging into her palms, using the pain to anchor herself in the present. Mara forced herself to recall the cold glint in Xavian's eyes, the cruel delight he took in tormenting her. This false comfort was just another form of torture, and she could not let down her guard.

With tremendous effort, Mara pushed back against the pleasant memories, trying to shut out the sensations of safety and home that Xavian was manipulating her into experiencing. It felt like trudging through waist-deep mud, each step requiring enormous exertion.

"Get...out...of my head," Mara growled through gritted teeth.

Xavian's eyes narrowed. The pleasant memories wavered, revealing the stark interrogation chamber once more. Mara panted with exertion, sweat dripping down her face. But her mind was her own again.

"Impressive," Xavian sneered. "But you can't fight me forever."

***

The church basement lay shrouded in darkness, save for the flickering light of ritual candles. Alex moved with practiced precision, his hands steady as he arranged arcane instruments across the stone floor. Each placement was deliberate, calculated to harness energies beyond mortal comprehension.

Hunter stood nearby, his face a mask of concentration as he lit candles and murmured protective wards. The air grew thick with incense and anticipation.

With chalk-stained fingers, Alex etched intricate symbols onto the cold stone. Each line and curve pulsed with latent power, waiting to be awakened. The basement air grew heavy, charged with an otherworldly presence that made the hairs on the back of Hunter's neck stand on end.

Alex took a step back, surveying his work. The chalk

outlines and runic symbols were perfect, just as the ancient texts described. He nodded to Hunter, who moved to stand at the head of the circle, grimoire in hand. They exchanged one last glance, steeling themselves. The time had come.

At last, Alex took his place within the circle of artifacts. The leather-bound grimoire creaked as he opened it, its pages whispering ancient secrets. His voice, low and resonant, began the esoteric incantation. The words seemed to hang in the air, shimmering with an unseen force.

Hunter began the incantation, his voice low but steady, each word dripping with power. The flames of the candles flickered and danced as if stirred by an unseen wind. Alex joined in the chant, the ancient syllables cracking the very air with occult energy.

Suddenly, the candle flames leapt high, casting writhing shadows on the walls. A pulsating aperture tore open within the circle, a wound in the fabric of reality. Through it, glimpses of impossible geometries and alien landscapes flickered in and out of existence.

Outside, the wind rose to a shrieking gale, buffeting the church walls. But within the basement chamber, all was still save for the mesmerizing dance of candlelight. Shadows leapt and cavorted at the edge of the light like living things.

The air grew charged, electric. The chalk lines began to glow, then burn with eldritch fire. Alex and Hunter continued their meticulous recitation, voices rising and falling in a hypnotic cadence. Reality itself seemed to waver, the stone walls melting away to reveal strange vistas and impossible geometries.

The strain was immense. Ritual instruments shook violently, rattling against the stone floor as if trying to escape. Alex's face contorted with effort, sweat beading on his brow as he fought to maintain control over the forces he had summoned.

A rumbling echoed from somewhere deep below, shaking dust loose from the rafters. The flames surged higher, twisting into a column of fire that scored the air with unearthly shrieks.

Then, with an ear-splitting crack, the portal split wide.

Howling winds erupted, threatening to snuff out the candles. But their light held, flickering desperately against the tide of darkness.

With a final, guttural cry, Alex collapsed to his knees. The aperture snapped shut, leaving behind only the acrid scent of ozone and the echo of otherworldly whispers. He slumped forward, utterly drained, his breath coming in ragged gasps.

Hunter's eyes gleamed with a mixture of awe and determination. "We know where she is," he said, his voice cutting through the oppressive silence. "I'll alert the others."

Alex managed a weak nod, unable to summon the strength for more. Hunter's jaw clenched, his face hardening with resolve as he strode out of the basement. The door slammed shut behind him, leaving Alex alone with the dying candles and the lingering presence of powers beyond mortal ken.

CHAPTER 20
CHAINS UNBOUND

The sky darkened to a sickly gray as dusk crept over the horizon, casting long shadows across the cult compound's forbidding walls. Hunter gathered Alex, Terry, and the tactical team for a final briefing. The air crackled with tension as they made last-minute checks on their blessed weapons and occult countermeasures.

Hunter's voice was low and grim as he addressed the group. "It's time. We breach the sanctum at sunset."

Terry's jaw clenched, a muscle twitching beneath the skin. He gave a silent nod, his face a mask of steely resolve. The weight of their mission hung heavy in the air, along with the acrid scent of fear and determination.

As one, they turned to face the looming compound. Its walls seemed to stretch endlessly upward, a monolithic testament to the madness that dwelled within. Somewhere beyond those unyielding barriers, Mara awaited rescue — if she still lived.

The team's breath misted in the chill evening air as they steeled themselves for what lay ahead. Each member knew that crossing that threshold might mean stepping into their own doom. Yet they moved forward, driven by duty and the desperate hope of averting the coming apocalypse.

The last rays of sunlight began to dissipate over the compound's walls, bathing the scene in an eerie, blood-red glow. It was time. With grim determination, Hunter led his team towards the entrance, ready to confront the horrors that awaited them within.

The obsidian walls of the cult compound loomed before them, an impenetrable fortress of darkness against the twilight sky. Hunter's jaw clenched as he led the charge, his fingers wrapped tightly around his weapon. Beside him, Alex's eyes darted from shadow to shadow, searching for any sign of movement. Terry brought up the rear, his weathered face set in grim determination.

Behind them, a tactical squad advanced in formation, their boots crunching softly on the gravel. Each member was armed to the teeth, not just with conventional weapons but with an array of occult countermeasures that glinted dully in the fading light. Amulets clinked against body armor, and vials of holy water sloshed at their hips.

As they approached the imposing structure, the air grew thick with otherworldly tension. The walls seemed to absorb all sound, creating an eerie bubble of silence around the advancing team. Hunter raised a fist, signaling a halt. For a moment, they stood frozen, the only movement the rise and fall of their chests as they drew in deep, steadying breaths.

The compound exuded an aura of ancient malevolence, as if the very stones were imbued with centuries of dark rituals and forbidden knowledge. Hunter exchanged a quick glance with Alex, a silent communication. His pupil had done well, excelling in the dark arts. He hoped it served them well today. With a barely perceptible nod, they resumed their advance, every sense on high alert as they prepared to breach the sanctuary of madness that lay beyond those obsidian walls.

Hunter's hand dropped, and they moved again, their boots crunching on the gravel. The compound seemed to grow even more menacing as they neared, its dark walls closing in around them. They were now at the precipice of the unknown, their hearts pounding in unison with the silent rhythm of impending doom.

The air crackled with tension as Hunter's low voice cut through the eerie silence. "Steady now...on my signal, unleash the full fury of your blessed arsenal."

Alex, his eyes squeezed shut, began to chant feverishly. The words of the entropy ritual spilled from his lips, ancient and terrible. The ground beneath their feet trembled, a deep rumbling that seemed to emanate from the very core of the earth. Before them, the mystical perimeter shimmered and then disintegrated, leaving nothing but empty air where once stood an impenetrable barrier.

"The way is open!" Alex's voice rang out, tinged with a mix of triumph and trepidation. "Obliterate their unholy defenses!"

Terry didn't hesitate. "You heard him! Fire!"

The evening erupted into chaos. The squad's weapons blazed to life, spitting blessed incendiary rounds that burst against the warded walls in blinding flashes of holy fire. Hunter added his own eldritch pyrotechnics to the fray, hurling spheres of profane energy that exploded with thunderous force, shaking the very foundations of reality.

The cultists caught off guard but quick to retaliate, unleashed their own arcane artillery. The air filled with sizzling bolts of malevolent energy, but Alex was ready. His astral form projected forward, weaving celestial shields that shimmered and pulsed, blocking the worst of the bombardment.

Hunter's fingers moved with practiced precision, sketching a complex glyph in the air. As he completed the final stroke, a writhing field of shadow sprang into existence, blanketing their advance. The occult punishment from the cultists' defenses glanced off the inky darkness, deflected harmlessly away.

They reached the fortress walls, looming obsidian barriers that seemed to drink in what little light remained. Alex, his face a mask of concentration, triggered the team's grimoire-created siege engines. Massive spheres of roiling plasma manifested, hurtling towards the walls with unstoppable force. The obsidian shattered, great chunks of stone raining down as the squad surged through the breach.

The moment they crossed the threshold, they were engulfed in a maelstrom of profane retaliation. Banishments tore at their very souls, hexes sought to twist their bodies and minds, and demonic guardians materialized from the shadows, their eyes burning with infernal hatred.

In the heart of this unholy storm, Alex and Hunter's abilities collided. Divine light clashed against umbral darkness, the opposing forces battling for supremacy. The fabric of reality groaned under the strain, hairline fractures spreading through the air like cracks in glass.

"Now, brother!" Alex's voice cut through the cacophony. "Unleash the breach!"

Working in perfect synchronicity, they combined holy relics and cursed artifacts. The air split open, an unstable dimensional rift yawning before them, edges crackling with otherworldly energies.

Hunter's eyes gleamed with a mix of madness and exhilaration. "Advance through the veil! To victory or oblivion!"

With Alex and Hunter at the fore, Terry close behind, the squad charged into the roiling planar tear. They plunged through, leaving the world they knew behind and emerging into the cult's apocalyptic inner sanctum — a realm where the laws of reality bent and twisted, and unspeakable horrors awaited.

The fabric of reality tore asunder, a fiery rift splitting the air with an otherworldly howl. Hunter, Terry, and Alex emerged first, leading their battle-worn occult team into a nightmarish realm that defied comprehension. They found themselves standing on an obsidian plain, surrounded by cyclopean ruins that loomed impossibly large against a blood-red sky.

Strange glyphs pulsed in the air, accompanied by the wailing laments of unseen souls. The team readied their weapons, muscles tense as shadowy forms began to take shape in the hazy distance.

Alex's voice cut through the hellish atmosphere. "Steel yourselves! The darkest depths await."

Hunter's jaw clenched, determination etched into every line of his face. "We've come too far to falter now. Mara needs us."

Before anyone could respond, the air shattered with

horrific screeches. A swarm of winged monstrosities emerged from the haze, their bodies a twisted amalgamation of flesh and shadow. Eldritch fire erupted from their maws, hurtling towards the team.

"Duck!" Terry's warning came just in time.

Alex's hands moved in intricate patterns, invoking divine shields that shimmered into existence around the squad. Hunter retaliated, unleashing blasts of entropic energy that tore through the demonic sentinels, dispelling them in droves. But for every creature vanquished, more cultists and horrors closed in, their eyes gleaming with malevolent hunger.

"Push forward! Cut through their ranks!" Hunter's command galvanized the team into action.

Blessed rounds erupted from their weapons, dropping charging cultists in sprays of ichor and ash. Alex and Hunter found themselves locked in mystic duels with a pair of profane wardens, their abilities colliding in violent explosions of light and darkness.

The ground suddenly trembled beneath their feet. A colossal figure materialized from the swirling chaos — a demonic juggernaut that towered over them like a mountain of corrupted flesh and iron. With a single gesture, it unleashed a shockwave that sent the team flying like rag dolls. The monster lumbered towards them, each step an earthquake.

Alex struggled to his feet, determination burning in his eyes. "This monstrosity cannot be allowed to impede our quest!"

Hunter nodded, a silent understanding passing between them. Together, they channeled their power, launching a combined torrent of divine and forbidden magic. The air crackled with energy as their assault slowly drove the juggernaut back. Under the punishing mystical barrage, cracks began to form in its seemingly impenetrable hide. With a final, deafening roar, the monstrosity collapsed and exploded into nothingness, leaving only a crater in its wake.

Battered but unbroken, the team pressed on. A pulsing

obsidian ziggurat loomed ahead, surrounded by occult symbols that writhed and twisted in the air. The wailing of trapped souls grew louder, a cacophony of torment that threatened to drive them mad.

Alex's voice cut through the din, steeling their resolve. "Mara's prison lies ahead! Steel your hearts! Our final test awaits!"

Hunter and Alex exchanged a look of grim determination. Without a word, they led the charge, their team following close behind. They vanished into the hazy ruins, ready to face whatever horrors awaited them in the depths of this infernal realm. As they approached the towering obsidian ziggurat, the air grew thick with malevolence. Strange whispers and wails echoed from within like the tormented screams of the damned. The structure seemed to pulse with eldritch energy, symbols, and runes carved into the black stone, glowing with an eerie violet light.

Hunter and Alex moved with cautious purpose, weapons at the ready, focused on the goal ahead. Reaching the base of the massive stepped temple, they began their ascent and climbed steadily upwards amidst the swirling chaos.

Halfway up the imposing edifice, Hunter paused, his senses suddenly on high alert. "Do you feel that?" he muttered. Alex nodded grimly. The hairs on the back of their necks stood on end as the atmosphere changed. A powerful psychic disturbance rippled through the air.

Before they could react, the obsidian walls began to crack and fracture. Jagged splits spread across the surface of the ziggurat with an ear-splitting rumble. Chunks of black stone exploded outwards as a shockwave of energy erupted from within. Hunter and Alex were thrown back by the concussive force. Scrambling to their feet, they watched in dismay as a gaping portal tore open the side of the temple.

From the yawning abyss poured forth a new wave of horrors — misshapen creatures seemingly birthed from the darkest depths of madness. Amorphous blobs of writhing flesh, covered in lamprey-like mouths and tentacles.

The team steeled themselves as the horrors poured forth. Hunter gripped his amulet, arcane energy crackling at his fingertips. Alex lifted his cross, divine light radiating around him. Together, they stood against the tide.

The blobs of writhing flesh descended first, pseudopods lashing out hungrily. Alex raised a shimmering shield of faith, deflecting their attacks. Hunter retaliated with lances of eldritch fire, burning through the amorphous horrors.

Next came the insectoid swarms, mandibles clacking menacingly. Terry swung his consecrated baton in wide arcs, crushing through chitinous carapaces. But still, more creatures flooded out in an endless tide. The team was slowly forced back under the relentless assault. Wounds and fatigue began taking their toll. The creatures seemed to attack with renewed frenzy as if sensing weakness.

Hunter and Alex shared a determined look. In unison, they combined their powers, drawing deeply from wells of faith and forbidden knowledge. Divine light merged with umbral fire, unleashing a nuclear mystic blast that atomized the horrors before them.

Panting, they turned to face the portal. The way forward was clear, but they could all feel a sinister presence lurking within the temple's heart. Mara was in there, they knew. And so was the cult's malevolent leader.

"We have to close that portal," Alex shouted amid the chaos. Alex's words rang true. The portal continued disgorging more horrors by the second, an endless tide threatening to overwhelm them.

Hunter's mind raced, analyzing the occult symbols etched around the portal. He recalled an ancient incantation that could reverse the polarity of the gate, sealing it off from the other side.

"Cover me!" he yelled, sprinting towards the portal's edge. Terry and Alex moved to flank him, weapons blazing as they fought back the creatures still pouring forth.

Reaching the portal's rim, Hunter invoked the incantation,

weaving intricate patterns with his fingers. The symbols began to glow, reversing direction as the occult forces shifted. The tide emerging from the portal slowed to a trickle.

With a final flourish, Hunter slammed his palm down on the central glyph. The portal imploded with a deafening roar, sealing shut with a resounding finality. The remaining creatures evaporated, their link severed.

"Well done, my friend," said Alex, clapping Hunter on the shoulder. Terry gave an appreciative nod, eyeing the cultist corpses littering the steps.

Their respite was brief. An inhuman scream echoed from the heart of the temple, filled with rage and frustration. The remaining obsidian walls trembled, cracks spiderwebbing across the surface.

"Seems we've pissed something off," Terry said grimly, reloading his weapons.

"Then let us finish this," said Alex. "Mara awaits."

With Hunter in the lead, the team advanced through the cult compound. Shadows danced along the obsidian walls, cast by an unseen source that seemed to pulse with malevolent energy. The two investigators moved with practiced stealth, their breaths shallow and controlled. Hunter's eyes darted from shadow to shadow, searching for any sign of movement. Alex's hand hovered near his arsenal of blessed weapons, ready to use at a moment's notice.

As they navigated the labyrinthine chambers, the oppressive atmosphere grew thicker. The very air seemed to resist their intrusion, as if the compound itself was a living, breathing entity that sought to expel them. At last, they came upon a massive iron door. Its surface was a canvas of blasphemous symbols, each more disturbing than the last. The metal seemed to absorb what little light there was, creating a void that threatened to swallow them whole.

Hunter withdrew an amulet from his pocket, its surface etched with protective sigils. With a steady hand, he placed it into a recess on the door's face. For a moment, nothing happened. Then, a low rumble echoed through the chamber as ancient mechanisms groaned to life.

The door swung open with agonizing slowness, revealing a darkness so complete it seemed tangible. Hunter and Alex exchanged a look of grim determination before stepping forward into the unknown, the weight of their mission pressing down upon them like a physical force.

The holding cell reeked of despair and decay. Mara lay crumpled on the cold floor, her body a tapestry of bruises and cuts. Glowing chains snaked around her limbs, pulsing with otherworldly energy that seemed to sap her very life force. Her once-vibrant eyes were now sunken hollows, and her clothes hung in blood-stained tatters.

"Mara..." Hunter's voice cracked as he took in the horrific sight.

Alex's fingers traced the sign of the cross, a futile gesture against the darkness that permeated the room. They rushed to Mara's side, the sound of their footsteps echoing in the oppressive silence.

Mara stirred, her movements sluggish and pained. Her eyelids fluttered, struggling to focus on the familiar faces above her.

"You came..." The words escaped her lips in a hoarse whisper, barely audible.

Alex's hand trembled as he brushed the matted hair from Mara's face. Despite the agony etched into every line of her features, she managed to summon a ghost of a smile. "We're getting you out of here," Alex promised, his voice thick with emotion.

Hunter's gaze swept over the chains that bound Mara, his jaw clenching as he took in their unearthly nature. The glowing links seemed to mock him, a reminder of the cosmic horrors they faced. His face tightened, a mixture of determination and barely concealed dread settling over his features as he realized the magnitude of the task before them.

The shadows whispered with malevolence as Xavian's disembodied voice slithered through the air. "She's not going anywhere."

Hunter and Alex tensed, their eyes darting about the gloom. Xavian materialized from the inky darkness behind them, his eyes blazing with unholy fire. He extended his arms, fingers splayed, and summoned a howling vortex of dark energy that crackled with eldritch power.

Instinct took over. Hunter and Alex dove apart as the vortex careened past, slamming into the wall with a thunderous boom. Bricks and mortar exploded outward in a deadly shower. They rolled to their feet, hands outstretched, light and shadow dancing at their fingertips.

Hunter's eyes flashed obsidian, reflecting the void within his soul. He thrust his palms forward, and writhing cords of living darkness sprang forth, snaking towards Xavian with lethal intent. The tendrils entwined Xavian's limbs, but the dark sorcerer merely uttered a guttural chant. The words, ancient and profane, dissolved Hunter's spell like acid eating through flesh.

Alex's fingers traced intricate patterns in the air, leaving trails of golden light. The shimmering sigil ignited, expanding into a shield of radiance that stood between them and Xavian's onslaught. A volley of curses, each more vile than the last, slammed against the barrier. The shield wavered, threatening to buckle under the relentless assault.

Xavian's lips curled into a sneer. "You fools. She belongs to the abyss now."

The ground trembled beneath their feet as Xavian stamped, the very earth responding to his will. A colossal demon construct rose from the fractured floor, its form a nightmarish fusion of shadow and flame. In its gnarled hand, it wielded a mace wreathed in hellfire.

Hunter pivoted to face this new threat while Alex redoubled his efforts to hold Xavian at bay. Mara watched helplessly from her chains, her eyes wide with fear and desperation.

The demon's roar shook dust from the ceiling as it swung its mace in a devastating arc. Hunter rolled aside, feeling the scorching heat as the weapon crashed into the ground where he'd stood a heartbeat before. He retaliated with eldritch blasts that staggered the behemoth, but it recovered quickly, charging at him with renewed fury.

Alex's voice cut through the chaos. "Lend me your strength!"

Mara's eyes clenched shut, her face a mask of concentration. A soft glow enveloped her chains, pulsing in time with her heartbeat. Alex's shield brightened, the surge of power repelling Xavian with such force that he was hurled across the chamber.

In that moment of respite, Alex tossed an ornate relic to Hunter. Xavian regained his footing, his eyes burning with hatred as he unleashed a fresh barrage of dark magic. The very air seemed to warp and twist under the intensity of his assault.

Hunter's voice rang out, filled with grim determination. "This ends now!"

He raised the relic high, and it erupted with blinding luminescence. A shockwave of pure energy burst forth, shaking the compound to its very foundations. Stone cracked, metal groaned, and the air itself seemed to scream.

Mara's chains shattered in a cascade of light, each link bursting like a supernova. She rose, her eyes blazing with molten gold, as mystical power coursed through her veins. The air crackled around her, heavy with potential.

With a primal scream that echoed through time itself, Mara unleashed her newfound power. Xavian was caught in the maelstrom, his body flung like a rag doll into the demon construct. The two forms, mortal and infernal, tumbled together into the yawning maw of the abyss that had opened beneath them.

As quickly as it had come, the light faded. Mara stood tall, her clothing in tatters but her spirit unbroken. She embraced Alex and Hunter, their shared warmth a stark contrast to the chill that permeated the chamber.

Mara's voice was soft but filled with iron resolve. "Let's finish this."

The obsidian chamber shuddered, its walls groaning under the strain of unholy energies. Mara's eyes widened in shock as she stood beside Hunter and Alex, the air around them crackling with malevolent power.

"What's happening?" Mara's voice quavered, barely audible above the cacophony.

Hunter's face was grim, his jaw set. "It's time to go!"

Alex, his features etched with dread, made the sign of the cross. "God help us all."

Reality warped and twisted around them, the very fabric of space-time buckling under some unseen force. Strange, non-Euclidean angles emerged on the walls, defying the laws of physics. Eldritch mists seeped through ruptures in the air, bringing with them the stench of decay and madness.

They took off running down the corridor, their footsteps echoing in the chaos. The gauntlet they had traversed to reach this point was now further deteriorated, crumbling beneath their feet with each step. Ahead, a chasm yawned open, splitting the passage in two. Energies spewed from its unfathomable depths, casting an otherworldly glow on their faces. Mara skidded to a halt at the edge, her heart pounding in her chest.

"Oh god... We're trapped!" Panic clawed at her throat, threatening to overwhelm her.

Hunter's hand plunged into his coat, emerging with a relic that pulsed with ancient power. "Together! Now!"

In that moment, Hunter, Alex, and Mara became one. Their powers intertwined, coalescing into a blinding force that struck the chasm with earth-shattering intensity. The air exploded in a maelstrom of light and smoke, and when it cleared, their path lay open before them.

They pressed on, their desperate ascent a race against time and sanity. Their team was right on their heels as they surged toward the only exit. Behind them, the cult's domain warped and twisted, collapsing into a yawning rift that threatened to swallow everything in its path.

At last, they burst into the open air, gulping down great lungfuls of the crisp night. Mara and Alex doubled over, hands on their knees, gasping for breath. The world around them seemed to spin, the boundary between reality and nightmare blurred beyond recognition.

CHAPTER 21
ROGUE ACTIONS

Ancient maps sprawled across Hunter's worktable, their yellowed edges curling with age. Obscure texts lay open, their pages heavy with forbidden lore. Ritual components — bones, herbs, and crystals — were scattered among the tomes, a chaotic array of arcane potential.

The walls were lined with shelves groaning under the weight of artifacts and relics. Dusty glass cases housed items too dangerous to touch, their surfaces etched with protective sigils. The air hung thick with the scent of old parchment and incense.

Hunter hunched over the worktable, his fingers tracing intricate symbols on a frayed manuscript. His eyes, bloodshot from hours of intense study, darted from one arcane diagram to another. "There's not enough time," he muttered, frustration etching deep lines in his forehead. "We're playing catch-up based on their timeline."

He pushed aside a stack of grimoires, revealing more complex patterns beneath. Symbols and diagrams swirled before him, a dizzying maze of metaphysical connections. Hunter's jaw clenched as he absorbed their implications. "This requires a more aggressive approach," he growled, his voice barely above a whisper. "I can unravel their ritual matrix through strategic metaphysical sabotage...if I act alone. They'll never see me coming."

With trembling hands, he reached for a massive tome bound in cracked leather. Its spine creaked ominously as he opened it, revealing pages that seemed to absorb the room's light. He turned to a specific section, and his breath caught in his throat.

A woodblock print sprawled across two pages depicting a warlock engaged in a forbidden ritual. The image pulsed with malevolent energy, almost alive in its grotesque detail. Hunter's eyes darted to the door, then back to the grimoire. His hand moved of its own accord, reaching for his leather journal.

He began to copy the symbols, his pen scratching against the paper with feverish intensity. Each stroke felt like a transgression, a step further into realms best left unexplored. "While the others are bound by bureaucratic caution and procedure," Hunter muttered, his voice thick with dark resolve, "we are confronted with primal forces that demand primal solutions."

The overhead light danced in Hunter's eyes, reflecting not just light but something deeper — a glimmer of dangerous knowledge, of paths once walked and best forgotten. As he continued to transcribe the forbidden ritual, memories began to surface, unbidden and unwelcome...

The flickering candlelight cast writhing shadows across the chamber walls. Young Hunter's desperate voice echoed through the darkness, a plaintive cry against the inevitable.

"No...stop! You don't know what you're doing!"

His anguished screams reverberated as rows of hooded acolytes surrounded the altar. Their chanting rose to a fever pitch as they positioned a woman upon the cold stone. Behind them loomed a monstrous idol, its grotesque features seeming to twist and leer in the guttering light.

The vision faded, leaving Hunter gasping in the confines of his library. His hands trembled as he steadied himself against the heavy oak table, sweat beading on his brow. The weight of the memory pressed down upon him, threatening to crush his resolve.

Hunter's voice was barely a whisper, rough with emotion. "Never again...I won't fail them this time."

With grim determination, he began to prepare. The ritual garb felt heavy as he donned it piece by piece, each item imbued with arcane significance. Finally, he swept the flowing cloak around his shoulders, pulling the hood low over his face.

Hunter approached the tarnished mirror hanging on the far wall. His reflection stared back, a stranger cloaked in shadows. With practiced strokes, he applied the war paint, dark lines etching forbidden symbols across his skin. As the final mark was drawn, a change came over him. The fear in his eyes hardened into steely resolve.

He turned away from the mirror, ready to face the horrors that awaited. The weight of countless souls rested upon his shoulders as he prepared to step into the night, determined to right the wrongs of the past and confront the darkness that threatened to consume everything he held dear.

Hunter's gaze lingered on his reflection for a moment longer before he extinguished the light, plunging the room into darkness. The only sound was the rustle of his cloak as he moved towards the door, a silent specter ready to face his past. He stepped outside, the cool night air wrapping around him like a shroud as he set off down the path leading into the forest.

The lonely dirt road snaked through the misty woods, a ribbon of darkness cutting through the dense forest. Night had fallen, shrouding the world in an eerie stillness that seemed to hold its breath in anticipation. He headed for the side lot where his bike was parked and waiting.

Suddenly, the quiet was shattered as his motorcycle's engine roared to life. Its thunderous growl echoed through the trees like the battle cry of some mechanical beast. Hunter tore down the road, his body hunched low over the handlebars, every muscle taut with determination.

The bike's headlight carved a narrow path through the fog, revealing glimpses of gnarled branches that seemed to reach for him as he passed. Hunter paid them no mind, his eyes fixed on the road ahead, his mind focused on the grim task that awaited him.

With each passing mile, the forest grew denser, darker, more forbidding. The mist thickened, curling around the tires of his bike like spectral fingers trying to slow his progress. But Hunter pressed on, driven by a fierce purpose that burned hotter than the engine between his legs.

He was racing towards something — or perhaps away from it. Either way, the night air carried with it a palpable sense of foreboding, as if the very darkness itself was aware of the destiny that lay at the end of this lonely road.

As the forest thinned, Hunter's destination emerged from the darkness. The remote compound stood as a stark silhouette against the night sky, still a few miles in the distance. He eased off the throttle, letting his bike glide along the road as he scrutinized the imposing structure. His gaze was drawn to the eerie glow of warding sigils, their otherworldly light stirring a sense of unease within him.

The night hung heavy over the remote compound, its imposing stone walls looming against the starless sky. Hunter crouched in the shadows, his breath catching in his throat as he surveyed the ancient structure. Faint, eerie glows pulsed across the façade — warding sigils etched into the very stone, their eldritch power almost palpable in the still air.

Most of the compound stood intact, a testament to its builders' skill or perhaps to darker forces at work. Only a small section lay in ruin, crumbled stone and shattered sigils hinting at last night's conflict.

With trembling hands, Hunter reached into his pack. The fabric rustled, unnaturally loud in the oppressive silence. He withdrew several objects, each thrumming with occult energy that made his skin crawl. A crystal orb caught what little light there was, seeming to amplify it from within its depths. Beside it, vials of viscous liquid sloshed gently, their contents too dark and thick to be natural.

Hunter's fingers tightened around the artifacts. Whatever horrors lay beyond those walls, he was now committed to facing them. The weight of his mission pressed down on him, as suffocating as the night itself.

Carefully arranging the artifacts on the ground before him, Hunter began to prepare for the ritual. He traced the intricate patterns of the sigils with his fingers, his heart pounding in his chest. The air around him seemed to grow denser, charged with an anticipation that mirrored his own. His lips moved in a silent whisper, ancient incantations flowing from his tongue like dark honey. The artifacts before him pulsed with an otherworldly glow, elemental power surging through their arcane forms as he channeled sorcerous energies into their very essence.

The stillness shattered. Alarm sirens wailed, their banshee screech tearing through the night. The compound's exterior blazed to life, harsh searchlights cutting through the darkness while warding glyphs flickered into existence, their eldritch geometries a silent warning against intruders.

Without hesitation, Hunter sprang to his feet. His hand thrust forward, a roiling ball of flame materializing at his fingertips. It streaked through the air, impacting the wall with a thunderous explosion. Stone crumbled, and flames licked hungrily at the breach.

He didn't pause. Ice shards glittering like deadly diamonds erupted from his palms. Lightning crackled, ozone filling the air. Gale-force winds howled at his command. Hunter became a one-man artillery, bombarding the compound with an arsenal that defied natural law.

Dark-robed figures emerged from the shadows, their movements fluid and unnatural. Cultists. They returned fire, hex bolts sizzling through the air and cursed projectiles leaving trails of corruption in their wake. Hunter moved with preternatural grace, evading their assault while maintaining his relentless barrage.

The earth trembled. Stone golems lumbered into view, their massive forms promising crushing death. Hunter's fingers danced in intricate patterns, and a whirlwind materialized, lifting one of the behemoths as if it were made of paper and tossing it aside like a discarded toy. Pressing his advantage, Hunter advanced. The compound's outer defenses crumbled beneath his onslaught. Yet even as he pushed forward, a chill ran down his spine. The cultists had alerted their elite guard.

Reality warped. Arcane singularities winked into existence around Hunter, gravity itself becoming his enemy. He felt the pull of these cosmic anomalies, each step a battle against forces that should not exist in this realm.

Gritting his teeth, Hunter pushed on. Pulsating eldritch energies assaulted his senses, threatening to overwhelm his very sanity. But his gaze remained fixed, unwavering. The inner sanctum lay ahead, and nothing – not cultist, not golem, not the violation of physics itself – would keep him from breaching its depths.

With a final blast of power, Hunter dispersed the last of the arcane singularities. His body ached from the strain, but he had no time for rest. He scanned his surroundings, spotting a dimly lit entrance to the compound's interior. Ignoring the alarms still blaring in the distance, he steeled himself and plunged into the shadows of the corridor.

The compound's corridors echoed with the piercing wail of another alarm. Hunter moved through the shadows, his footsteps measured and purposeful. The dim emergency lights cast an eerie glow on his face, highlighting the lines of grim determination etched into his features.

As he advanced, he sensed a shift in the air around him. The hairs on the back of his neck stood on end, and a familiar tingle of arcane energy danced across his skin. The warlocks were preparing their defenses, gathering power that crackled and hissed in the oppressive darkness.

A disembodied voice rang out, bouncing off the concrete walls: "Protect the sanctum! Fortify all breaches!"

Hunter's jaw clenched. He knew time was running short. With practiced efficiency, he began to weave intricate patterns in the air, fingers tracing sigils that glowed momentarily before fading. Layers of mystical protection enveloped him, shimmering faintly in the gloom.

The wards settled into place just as a wave of malevolent energy slammed against them. Hunter staggered, but the shields held. Gritting his teeth, he pressed onward into the heart of the compound, where unspeakable horrors awaited.

As Hunter navigated the labyrinthine corridors, he felt the wards around him vibrating with the intensity of the impending onslaught. He paused momentarily, his eyes narrowing as he focused on the pulsating energy ahead. A low growl escaped his lips as he steeled himself, ready to face whatever lay in wait.

He stepped into the massive chamber, his senses assaulted by the disturbing occult artifacts that adorned every surface. Altars strewn with bones dotted the room, while arcane glyphs glowed ominously on the walls, casting an eerie light that seemed to pulse with malevolent energy.

At the far end of the sanctum loomed a towering statue of Mephistopheles, the demonic entity revered by the cult. As Hunter moved through the space, the stone eyes of the effigy seemed to track his every step. Despite his usual bravado, an unsettling feeling crept over him, his skin prickling with goosebumps in the statue's unnerving presence.

The air crackled with dark energy as the warlocks continued their chants, desperately weaving eldritch barricades to block Hunter's advance. But Hunter was relentless, slamming through their mystical defenses with blasts of elemental fury that shook the very foundations of the chamber.

"The unbeliever has breached the sanctum!" cried one of the warlocks, panic evident in his voice.

Another warlock gestured, summoning a stone golem from the very ground. The massive creature's footsteps shook the chamber as it intercepted Hunter, the two clashing in a frenzy of magic and stone that sent sparks flying.

Hunter rolled away from a crushing blow, narrowly avoiding being pulverized. He extended his hand, and a fiery maelstrom erupted around the golem, cracking its body. With a thunderous crash, it fell to the ground, nothing more than molten rubble.

More warlocks joined the fray, battering Hunter with volleys of hex bolts that sizzled through the air. He narrowly deflected them with his artifacts, the magical energies colliding in brilliant flashes of light.

"Your dark magics are no match for my wrath!" Hunter bellowed, his voice echoing off the chamber walls. He sliced his hand through the air, unleashing a shockwave that knocked the warlocks back. But still, they rose again, desperation fueling their determination to defend their lair.

Hunter carved a path through the compound, his mystical arsenal nearly depleted. He swatted aside security teams like flies, arrogance swelling within him with each victory.

"Mere gnats before the storm," he sneered. "This sanctum shall be mine!"

But Hunter's confidence was misplaced. He froze as he realized he'd entered an ornate binding chamber. Suddenly, Balor's elite occult guardians emerged from the shadows, their ceremonial garb rustling as they began to chant.

Eldritch runes blazed to life, activating the chamber's wards. Hunter attacked, but his blows dispersed harmlessly against the chamber's shields, dissipating into nothingness.

"No!" he cried out, desperation creeping into his voice. "Your magics shall not contain me!"

But it was too late. The guardians subdued Hunter with catastrophic bindings, sealing his form into an arcane crystalline prison. He struggled helplessly as the rituals crescendoed, his remaining powers rendered inert by the overwhelming force of the cult's magic.

"Damnable hubris!" Hunter cursed, the realization of his defeat settling in. "I am undone..." The truth hit him like a physical blow. He'd been utterly overmatched, his arrogance shattered. Now, only the cult's mercy could spare him from whatever fate they had in store.

The cultist guards closed in on the mystically immobilized Hunter, his body hanging suspended in glowing sigils and glyphs that neutralized his powers. Despite his predicament, defiance still burned in his eyes.

"You occultist scum are nothing without your parlor tricks," he spat.

The guards laughed, their mocking voices echoing through the chamber. Hunter's fate was sealed, trapped in a prison of his own making, with nothing but regret and the cult's dark intentions to keep him company.

As the last word of his insult echoed, Hunter's defiance was met with silence. The guards merely watched him, their amusement growing as they soaked in his helpless rage. The lead guard stepped forward, his eyes glinting with malicious intent.

Hunter's heart raced as the guards closed in, their eyes gleaming with sadistic anticipation. The lead guard's lips curled into a cruel sneer as he growled, "Let's see what good your bravado does when we peel the flesh from your bones."

Panic surged through Hunter as he strained against the arcane bonds, but they held fast, sapping his strength. The first guard hefted a spiked club, its rusty barbs glistening in the dim light. With a sickening crunch, it slammed into Hunter's ribs. Pain exploded through his body, and a ragged cry tore from his throat.

Before he could catch his breath, another guard unleashed a flurry of brutal punches. Knuckles crashed into Hunter's stomach and face, each impact sending shockwaves of agony through his battered frame. The metallic taste of blood filled his mouth as it sprayed from his nose and lips.

Desperation clawed at Hunter's mind. He reached deep within himself, grasping for the familiar tendrils of his power. But as he extended his trembling fingers, only feeble sparks sputtered and died.

The second guard's laughter echoed off the stone walls. "Not so mighty now, are you mage?"

The assault intensified. Boots slammed into Hunter's prone form, and clubs whistled through the air, finding flesh and bone with sickening precision. The guards' taunts and laughter blended with the wet sounds of pulverized tissue and cracking bones.

Hunter's world narrowed to a haze of pain. His face, a swollen mass of bruises and blood, throbbed in time with his fading heartbeat. Consciousness slipped away, then returned with each fresh wave of agony. Still, the beating continued without mercy.

At last, Hunter lay motionless in a growing pool of his own blood. His body, a broken shell, screamed with every shallow breath. Through swollen eyelids, he glimpsed shadowy figures advancing for the killing blow. Hunter clung to the last threads of awareness, certain his end had come.

Suddenly, the chamber shook. Arcane alarms shrieked to life, their otherworldly wails piercing the air. The guards froze, heads swiveling as they searched for the source of the disturbance.

A blinding light erupted, searing Hunter's retinas even through closed lids. As the radiance faded, he saw Father Alex materialize in a thunderous flash of divine energy. The priest's eyes blazed with celestial fire, his consecrated aura pulsing with power.

"Blasphemer!" one of the guards spat, but fear had replaced the earlier malice in his voice.

Alex's lips moved in an intricate dance, uttering words in no earthly tongue. Astral shields sprang to life around Hunter's broken form. The cultists unleashed a barrage of dark magics and eldritch blasts, but they dissipated harmlessly against Alex's impenetrable aura.

The priest's chanting grew louder, his voice resonating with otherworldly power. Hunter felt a strange lightness overtake him as he rose from the blood-slicked floor, cradled in Alex's radiant protection. Together, they ascended beyond the cultists' reach, their futile attacks fizzling in the wake of Alex's divine might.

Alex's voice boomed, shaking the very foundations of the chamber. "Your profane reign ends! Divine judgment comes!"

In a blinding vortex of light, Hunter and Alex vanished. As consciousness finally slipped away, Hunter heard Alex's voice echoing a solemn vow of reckoning while panicked cultists fired blindly into the empty air where they had been.

With a final surge of energy, Alex thrust his hand towards the heavens, invoking a divine portal. The vortex swirled around them, its iridescent light swallowing the chamber's darkness. As they stepped into the portal, Hunter's world spun, and then there was nothing but the sensation of falling through an endless void.

The night air hung thick with the stench of failure as the getaway vehicle sped through the darkness. In the backseat, Hunter's battered form slumped against the worn upholstery, his consciousness flickering like a dying candle. His once-pristine occult regalia now hung in tatters, edges singed and smoking. Arcane gashes crisscrossed his flesh, weeping crimson tears that spoke of unspeakable horrors.

Through a haze of pain, Hunter's gaze drifted downward. His trembling hand, pale as death itself, reached out to explore the extent of his injuries. As his fingers brushed against raw, seared flesh, he flinched, the physical agony a stark reminder of the catastrophe that had unfolded.

At the wheel, Father Alex's knuckles whitened as he gripped the steering wheel, his eyes fixed on the road ahead. The silence in the car was oppressive, broken only by Hunter's labored breathing and the occasional whimper of pain.

"I was a damned fool," Hunter's voice rasped, barely above a whisper. "Rogue actions that risked us all."

The words hung in the air, heavy with regret and self-recrimination. Father Alex's eyes flicked to the rearview mirror, taking in Hunter's broken form. His response came softly, a lifeline in the darkness.

"We will endure this evil together, with wisdom."

The car continued its journey through the night, carrying its wounded passenger and the weight of unspoken terrors yet to come.

CHAPTER 22
OPERATION NIGHTFALL

Hunter drifted in and out of consciousness, his heavily bandaged body a testament to the brutality he'd endured. The steady drip of the IV provided a rhythmic counterpoint to his labored breathing. Stark-white walls and the antiseptic smell of the hospital room surrounded him, a sterile cocoon far removed from the darkness he'd faced.

The door creaked open, and Terry's worried face appeared. He crossed the room with heavy steps, sinking into the chair beside Hunter's bed with a weary sigh. "You just had to go all cowboy on them, didn't you?" Terry's voice was a mixture of concern and exasperation.

Hunter's lips moved, barely forming words. "Did we get them?"

Terry leaned forward, his brow furrowed. "What were you thinking, man?"

"I wanted to end this." Hunter's voice was a hoarse whisper laden with pain and determination.

"By ending yourself?" Terry's words hung in the air, sharp with fear for his partner.

Hunter struggled to sit up, his face contorting with the effort. "Just get me a car and my weapons bag, and I'll —"

"Absolutely not." Terry's tone brooked no argument. "You're in no shape for a mission. I'll handle the operations from here on out."

A scowl crossed Hunter's face as he sank back into his pillow, frustration radiating from every pore. "You don't know what you're up against," Hunter warned. "This is beyond just police work."

Terry's eyes softened, but his resolve remained firm. "Maybe so. But it's even more beyond just you now, too."

He reached for a folder on the bedside table, thumbing through pages covered in Hunter's cramped handwriting. Arcane symbols and cryptic notes filled the margins, a glimpse into the depths of Hunter's obsession.

"I'll admit, your work here is impressive, if a bit... unorthodox," Terry conceded. "But we need more manpower to take down an operation of this size."

Hunter's eyes blazed with an intensity that belied his weakened state. "Bringing in more souls just exposes them to the cult's evil. This darkness...it stains you. It already has me. Don't let it spread."

A heavy silence fell between them as Terry absorbed the warning. The weight of unseen horrors seemed to press down on the room, making the air thick and oppressive.

"Just rest up," Terry said finally. "We'll talk more when you're back on your feet."

He stood, moving towards the door. Hunter watched him go, helplessness etched into every line of his battered face. "Don't underestimate them, Terry," Hunter called out, his voice cracking. "Please...be ready."

Terry paused at the threshold, giving a small nod before disappearing into the hallway. The door closed with a soft click, leaving Hunter alone with his thoughts and the incessant beeping of medical equipment.

He lay back, staring up at the featureless ceiling. In his mind's eye, shadows writhed and twisted, hinting at the eldritch horrors that lurked just beyond the veil of reality. Hunter knew all too well that the true battle was only beginning, and he feared that even his dire warnings wouldn't be enough to prepare Terry for what was to come.

**

In the subterranean depths of the task force's compound, Terry and his team of cyber analysts huddled around a cluster of monitors, their faces bathed in the eerie glow of screens flickering with arcane symbols and cryptic code. The air thrummed with tension as fingers danced across keyboards, each keystroke a battle against an unseen enemy.

Terry's voice cut through the electronic hum. "Come on, come on...we're almost through their arcane firewall."

An analyst, eyes locked on his screen, called out, "Initiating daemon decryption sequence!"

The monitors convulsed, images distorting as if assaulted by some digital eldritch horror. Occult malware clawed at their systems, threatening to tear through their defenses. Terry's hand slammed down a massive grimoire, its leather-bound cover worn with age. He flipped through pages filled with runic ciphers, his eyes darting across arcane symbols.

"Feed these counter-sigils into the daemon hunter!" Terry barked, desperation edging his voice. "We have to hold the connection open!"

The analysts' fingers flew across their keyboards, streaming the decrypted ciphers into their besieged systems. As if by magic, the glitching subsided, digital wards manifesting in the codescape. A tunnel materialized in the occult firewall, a breach in the enemy's defenses.

"We're through!" Terry exclaimed, a mix of triumph and urgency in his voice. "Hit the data spike now!"

With practiced precision, the analysts triggered remote processes, connecting to the cult's data cloud through the newly formed breach. A torrent of arcane information flooded the monitors, a dizzying cascade of forbidden knowledge. Terry's eyes widened as he took in the wealth of data before them.

"Motherlode..." he breathed, then snapped back to action. "Start the purge! Copy everything!"

The team worked with feverish intensity, with torrents of maps, schematics, and occult symbology pouring in. Terry's brow furrowed as he sifted through the flood of intel, piecing together fragments of a horrifying puzzle.

Suddenly, an analyst's panicked voice cut through the concentrated silence. "Sir! Remote traces detected! The clock's run out!"

Terry's fist slammed down on the desk, frustration and fear mingling in his expression. "Damn it! Purge feeds and kill the connection!"

The analysts scrambled to obey, severing their tenuous link to the cult's systems. As the screens settled, they displayed a vast schematic of global cult sites. Terry stepped back, exhaling heavily as he took in the enormity of what they'd uncovered.

"We've got them," he muttered, a mix of vindication and dread in his voice.

The weight of their discovery settled over him like a shroud. Terry's eyes, haunted by the knowledge they'd gleaned, scanned the faces of his team. They all knew what this meant, the scale of the opposition they now faced.

His voice was low, filled with grim determination as he spoke. "And now...we take the fight to their doorstep."

The words hung in the air, heavy with the promise of battles to come against an enemy that lurked in the shadows, waiting to unleash untold horrors upon the world.

***

Mara stood rigid, her arms crossed tightly over her chest as she stared at the glowing screens before her. Maps flickered with ominous markers, timelines ticking down with relentless precision. The underground compound hummed with tension, the air thick with the weight of impending doom.

Terry's footsteps echoed softly as he approached, his voice barely above a whisper. "The raids bought us some time. But we're still on the clock." He gestured toward the screens, his face etched with worry. "They'll regroup soon. These rituals get completed; we're talking biblical-level shit."

Mara's eyes never left the displays. "How many?" she asked, her voice barely audible.

Terry's response hung in the air like a death sentence.

"Thousands. Maybe more. Mara...we're out of moves here."

Her jaw clenched, a flicker of defiance in her eyes. "There's always moves. Always another way."

The soft shuffle of robes announced Father Alex's approach. His face was ashen, eyes haunted by the weight of ancient knowledge. "I'm afraid not this time. What we face has walked this earth before. Left valleys of bones in its wake." In his trembling hands, he held an ancient text. Its pages were yellowed with age, depicting monstrous figures looming over seas of blood. Alex's voice quavered as he continued, "We stop it now... or not at all."

The door creaked open, and Hunter limped in, his bandages stark white against his battered form. His words carried the weight of grim determination. "He's right. We hit them with everything now...or we lose everything after. No half measures."

Mara's eyes swept across the room, taking in the faces of her comrades. Each bore the marks of battles fought and horrors witnessed. With a sharp intake of breath, she made her decision. "Do it. Hit them all. Level every goddamn site."

Terry nodded, his face a mask of grim resolve. "I'll start coordination with strike command."

As he turned to leave, Father Alex approached Mara. His weathered hands traced the sign of blessing over her, a futile gesture against the tide of darkness that threatened to engulf them all.

Outside, the roar of planes filled the air, a symphony of destruction as they raced toward their targets. Mara's eyes were drawn back to the monitors, watching as payloads detonated in blinding flashes. Cult locations vanished in pillars of fire and smoke, erased from existence in mere moments.

She closed her eyes, unable to watch anymore. The weight of their actions pressed down upon her, a burden almost too heavy to bear. Her lips moved in a silent prayer, barely audible even to herself. "Forgive us..."

The words hung in the air, lost in the cacophony of

destruction that echoed through the compound. The die was cast, and the world trembled on the precipice of change.

***

In the subterranean depths of the task force's clandestine compound, Terry stood at the helm of a high-tech control room. The air hummed with tension, thick enough to cut with a knife. Monitors flickered with ghostly images, tactical maps sprawled across screens like neon spiderwebs, and comm arrays blinked their silent warnings.

Terry's fingers danced across holographic interfaces, coordinating the intricate ballet of destruction about to unfold. The Shadowguard, humanity's last line of defense against the encroaching darkness, prepared for their most crucial mission yet.

Leaning into the headset's mic, Terry's voice carried the weight of worlds:

"Shadow teams, listen up. This is Operation Nightfall. We have one shot to hit these bastards where they live and cripple their apocalyptic plans. You all have your targets and protocols. Follow them to the letter. Once boots hit the ground, it's on. May fortune favor the bold tonight. Terry out."

As the words echoed through secure channels, a symphony of preparation reached its crescendo. In armories that reeked of gun oil and ozone, elite Shadowguard units donned their armor — a fusion of cutting-edge tech and arcane sigils. Each piece clicked into place with practiced precision, a ritual as old as warfare itself.

Mystic artifacts, their surfaces etched with eldritch runes, were secured in lead-lined cases. These were weapons of last resort, forged in forgotten eons to battle horrors beyond mortal comprehension.

Outside, the night air thrummed with the growl of engines. Gunships, their sleek forms bristling with weaponry, stirred to life on floodlit tarmacs. Armored convoys snaked through underground tunnels, emerging onto shadowed streets like metal leviathans.

In a chamber bathed in overhead light, Hunter moved among the strike teams. The occultist's hands weaved intricate patterns in the air, leaving trails of spectral light. Wards of protection settled onto the soldiers' skin like ghostly armor while talismans infused with eldritch power were pressed into waiting palms.

As the witching hour approached, transport choppers lifted into the air. Their rotors cut through the night, carrying squads of grim-faced warriors over a cityscape that slumbered in ignorant bliss. Below, nameless terrors stirred in the shadows, unaware that their doom approached on silent wings.

The pieces were in place. The die was cast. And in the control room far below, Terry watched the operation unfold, praying that fortune would indeed favor the bold on this night of nights.

The night air crackled with tension as the cloaked stealth chopper hovered above the cult compound. Darkness enveloped the scene, broken only by intermittent flashes of gunfire. A team of elite operatives, their faces hidden behind night-vision goggles, slid down fast ropes onto the looming tower below.

Cult guards, their eyes wide with panic, spotted the descending figures and unleashed a hail of bullets. The air filled with the acrid smell of cordite and the deafening report of automatic weapons. Yet, as if protected by some otherworldly force, mystic shields shimmered around the operatives, deflecting the incoming fire in a display that defied natural law.

With practiced precision, the team breached the tower's defenses. The confined space erupted into chaos as they engaged in close-quarters combat. Grunts, thuds, and the sickening crack of bones echoed through the night as the operatives methodically cleared each level.

Elsewhere, the compound's main gate groaned under the immense force of an armored convoy. Metal screeched against metal as the barrier gave way, crumpling like tissue paper.

Cultists, their robes billowing in the night breeze, scrambled to mount a defense. Their frantic shouts mixed with the rumble of engines and the sharp reports of gunfire.

SWAT troops poured from the vehicles, their boots hitting the ground with ominous thuds. They advanced under a blanket of covering fire, the muzzle flashes of their weapons illuminating determined faces and glinting off tactical gear.

A dull thump followed by a deafening explosion rocked the compound. Debris rained down as a grenade blast tore through a heavy door, revealing the entrance to a ritual chamber beyond. The acrid smell of explosives mingled with an older, more sinister scent — one of ancient evil and forbidden rites. As the smoke cleared, the true horror of what lay within began to reveal itself to the advancing forces.

As the chaos outside raged on, the SWAT team's demolitions expert, his face streaked with sweat and grime, set to work. He placed a charge on the heavy door, barring their way, his gloved hands steady despite the adrenaline coursing through his veins. The rest of the team fell back, weapons trained on the door as they braced for the imminent blast.

The SWAT team burst into the ritual chamber, their boots pounding against the stone floor. The air was thick with the acrid smell of gunpowder and the metallic tang of blood. Strange symbols adorned the walls, their eldritch designs seeming to writhe in the flickering torchlight.

Robed cultists scattered like startled rats, their chants cut short by the staccato bark of automatic weapons. Bodies crumpled to the ground, dark stains spreading across their ornate robes. The team moved with practiced efficiency, sweeping the room with their rifles and cutting down any cultist foolish enough to resist.

Amid the chaos stood bizarre relics of forgotten eras — twisted idols with too many eyes, ancient tomes bound in materials best left unidentified. Blood-stained altars dominated the center of the chamber, their surfaces slick with fresh sacrifices.

Discarded ritual daggers lay scattered about, their blades still wet with dark ichor.

As the gunfire died down, an eerie silence fell over the chamber. The SWAT team picked their way through the carnage, their flashlights cutting through the gloom and revealing horrors that would haunt their dreams for years to come. In the corners of the room, shadows seemed to move of their own accord as if some greater darkness was retreating from the light of the living world.

The team leader, his voice hard and steady, radioed for extraction. As the last cultist fell, the team quickly secured the chamber, their movements methodical despite the lingering horror. Their flashlights swept over the room one final time before they began to retreat, leaving behind the grim tableau of their assault.

The night air shattered with the thunderous roar of attack choppers descending upon the cult compound. Their 20mm cannons spat fire, raking across the darkened structures below. Muzzle flashes lit up the sky like artificial lightning.

Cult defenders, their faces twisted with fanatical determination, scrambled to their positions. They hefted RPGs onto their shoulders and manned heavy machine guns, returning fire with desperate ferocity. Tracer rounds crisscrossed the air, a deadly light show against the inky blackness.

Suddenly, a lucky shot found its mark. One of the choppers jerked violently, smoke billowing from its damaged fuselage. It spun wildly, rotors screaming as the pilot fought for control. But it was a losing battle. The chopper plummeted, disappearing behind a cluster of buildings with a sickening crash and fireball.

The remaining choppers pressed their attack with renewed vigor as if enraged by their fallen comrade. Missiles streaked from their pods, leaving trails of white smoke in their wake. They slammed into ornate ritual sites, reducing intricate altars and blasphemous idols to rubble and ash.

Secondary explosions rippled across the compound.

Hidden caches of weapons and unholy relics detonated, sending plumes of green-tinged fire into the sky. The air filled with an acrid stench — a mixture of cordite, burning flesh, and something far more eldritch that defied description.

Through it all, cultists continued to fight, their screams of defiance barely audible over the cacophony of destruction. But with each passing moment, their numbers dwindled, their sacred ground reduced to a hellscape of flame and ruin.

Terry's eyes flickered across the array of displays, watching the assault unfold with grim satisfaction. Green indicators flashed to life as strike teams achieved their objectives, one by one. The underground compound hummed with tension, the air thick with anticipation.

He leaned into his radio, his voice low and gravelly. "Hunter, we've got hostiles dug in at Site Bravo. Can you call in some mojo for our boys?"

Hunter's reply crackled through the speaker, tinged with a hint of dark amusement. "Way ahead of you. Cleansing fire incoming."

Terry felt a jolt of anticipation at the words. He surveyed the ops room, allowing himself a grim smile as he cracked his knuckles. The sound echoed in the cavernous space, a stark reminder of the impending violence. A tense energy settled over him, his muscles coiling in readiness for the coming action.

"Alright, you sonsofbitches," he muttered, more to himself than anyone else. "No more games. Tonight, we take back our city."

The displays before him flickered with an eerie, otherworldly light. Terry's eyes darted from screen to screen, absorbing every detail of the unfolding chaos. He drew in a deep breath, steadying himself for what was to come. With practiced precision, his fingers danced across the keypad, entering the launch code that would seal their fate.

The weight of what he was about to do pressed down on him like a physical force. Terry's hand hovered over the radio for a moment before he grabbed it, his knuckles white with tension.

"Operation Nightfall is a go," he announced, his voice cutting through the oppressive silence. "All units, you have a green light. I say again, you are cleared hot. The night is ours, gentlemen."

As the words left his lips, Terry felt a chill settle over the room. The darkness seemed to deepen as if responding to his command. Whatever horrors awaited them in the city above, they had just unleashed something far worse upon it.

CHAPTER 23
THE END OF TIMES

The ancient sanctum rumbled with a foreboding energy, its massive walls and domed ceiling seeming to vibrate in response to the rhythmic chants of robed acolytes. The deep, guttural tones reverberated through the air, filling the cavernous depths with a sense of dread and power. The flickering torches cast eerie shadows across bloodstained altars, where dark rituals were performed in service to unspeakable gods. Each motion of the swaying figures seemed almost possessed, their bodies moving in a twisted dance as they chanted their unholy incantations. It was a place of darkness and fear, where the boundaries between this world and the next blurred together in a macabre symphony of worship.

At the center of this unholy congregation stood Balor, a towering figure with eyes that gleamed with fanatical fervor. His presence alone commanded both fear and reverence from those gathered around him. In his hand, he raised a goblet filled with a thick, crimson liquid that pulsed with an otherworldly energy. As he brought it to his lips, the metallic taste exploded in his mouth, sending a surge of power coursing through his veins. The elixir's effects were immediate, heightening his senses and connecting him to the cosmic forces now aligning above. With every sip, he felt more in tune with the dark magic swirling around them, ready to unleash its power upon the world.

Balor's voice boomed with an ominous timbre, his words reverberating through the air like a dark incantation. "The hour is upon us," he proclaimed, summoning ancient powers from beyond. "The stars align according to prophecy!" And indeed, the universe seemed to respond to his call. The stars shifted and aligned in accordance with some otherworldly prophecy. In the vastness of space, cosmic forces stirred and twisted, bending to the will of a mysterious and all-powerful being.

Pulsating black holes, their maws agape and ravenous throbbed in time with the cultists' fevered chanting. Swirling nebulae of unfathomable hues writhed and twisted in the void, forming intricate patterns that would surely shatter the minds of any mortal who dared to witness them. The very fabric of the universe seemed to hold its breath, anticipating the culmination of this dark and unholy convergence. The air itself crackled with a palpable sense of malevolence and otherworldly power. It was a scene that would strike fear into even the most courageous of souls as they stood in awe and terror before the cosmic power at play.

As if a veil had been lifted, the boundary between the sanctum and the vast expanse of the cosmos blurred. The acolytes' voices rose to a fever pitch, their words carrying across light-years, resonating with the very stars themselves. Balor's eyes rolled back, overwhelmed by visions of what was to come. The prophecy was unfolding before him, each detail coming to life in his mind's eye. He could feel the weight of destiny resting upon his shoulders, the promise of an apocalypse beyond imagining looming on the horizon. The air crackled with energy as the ritual reached its climax. Time seemed to stand still as Balor braced himself for what was to come.

Balor's gaze focused on the dark expanse above, his heart pounding in rhythm with the chant. The cosmic energy swirled around him, intensifying as if answering his call. He felt a shiver of anticipation surge through his body; the ritual was nearing its apex.

The sanctum trembled, its ancient stones groaning and creaking as they struggled to contain the otherworldly forces at play. Thick, noxious vapors oozed through the crevices in the masonry, filling the air with a pungent stench that burned the nostrils. Balor's eyes rolled back in his head, his entire body trembling with eager anticipation as the frenzied chanting of his devoted followers rose to a feverish crescendo. The walls pulsed and writhed with dark energy, crackling and sparking with each rhythmic beat of the ritualistic incantations. This was no mere ceremony — something powerful and sinister was being summoned within these walls.

As the pulsating starry backdrop above the sanctum neared its apex, the very fabric of reality itself seemed to fray and flicker like a tattered banner caught in a tempest. The stars themselves twisted and contorted, forming sinister sigils in the night sky. The chants of the acolytes reached a feverish pitch, their voices melding into a cacophonous roar that echoed through the dimensions.

Balor, his eyes burning with a maddened glow, felt the cosmic power coursing through his very veins. "Behold, the end of days is upon us!" he cried out, his voice shattering the silence like a thunderclap. "The Overlords have heard our call, and they answer!"

The air was thick with raw, primal energy, electricity crackling through the sanctum like a living, writhing thing. The very air itself seemed to warp and undulate under the weight of the cosmic forces at play. The acolytes continued their maniacal chanting, oblivious to the unspeakable energies they tapped into — or perhaps, they simply did not care, consumed as they were by their twisted devotion.

The sanctum's walls began to convulse and writhe as if alive, ancient glyphs etched into their very substance glowing with an unearthly light. The air shimmered like a desert mirage as reality warped around them. Strange whispers and muted screams echoed from somewhere beyond, rising over the fevered chanting.

As the cosmic energy reached its peak, the very fabric of reality itself seemed to buckle and tear, as if the seams of the universe were fraying before their very eyes. The walls of the ancient sanctum bulged and heaved, ancient glyphs glowing with malevolent power, and in the center of the room, a swirling vortex began to form. The acolytes' chanting reached a fever pitch, their voices melding into a cacophony of hushed whispers and discordant screams. Balor's eyes glowed with an otherworldly light, his grin stretching across his face like a grotesque mask of madness and joy.

Several acolytes, their minds consumed by fanatical devotion, advanced towards the unholy altars. Their eyes glinted with a frenzied zeal as they raised their blades and swiftly drew them across their own throats. Crimson blood spilled onto the stone floor, flowing into intricate channels that had been carefully etched into its surface. The sacrificial offering ignited a dark ritual, the arcane symbols pulsing with malevolent energy as the blood seeped into every nook and cranny of the room. The air was thick with the metallic scent of blood and the oppressive weight of evil power.

With a slow, deliberate movement, Balor raised an ornate urn to his lips and breathed in deeply. The ashes of the damned swirled in the vessel, waiting to be inhaled. As he drew them into his lungs, a sharp, acrid taste coated his tongue. With a raspy voice, he intoned, "Mephistopheles, we beseech thee! Honor our pact!" The words echoed through the dark chamber, the only sound amidst the heavy silence that hung in the air like a suffocating blanket. The flickering flames from the candles cast an eerie glow on his pale face, accentuating the dark circles under his eyes. The room was filled with the stench of sulfur and decay, as if hell itself had seeped through the walls. Balor's eyes glowed with a fiery intensity as he awaited the response from his demonic ally. A sense of terror hung in the air as if something sinister was lurking just beyond their sight. But Balor felt no fear — only a burning desire to fulfill his pact with Mephistopheles, whatever the cost may be.

A sudden, deafening crack echoed through the ancient temple, dislodging centuries of dust and debris from the walls and ceiling. Balor's eyes snapped open, filled with a wild, frenzied look as he gazed up at the ceiling. His face twisted into an expression of religious ecstasy, his voice booming with authority. "The boundaries weaken!" he cried out triumphantly. "The hour of convergence is at hand!" Every hair on Balor's body stood on end as he reveled in the power surging through him. This was the moment he had been waiting for, the fulfillment of his lifelong quest. And now it was finally within reach.

The cultists watched in awe and terror as the fabric of reality tore apart before their very eyes. A swirling vortex of impossible geometry materialized in the air, defying all laws of nature. The edges of the portal shimmered with otherworldly energy, pulsing with an eerie green light. The very air seemed to vibrate with a cacophony of unearthly sounds that sent shivers down the spines of all who heard it.

The cultists were transfixed by the sight, unable to look away from this manifestation of pure chaos and evil. Some screamed in terror, while others fell to their knees in worship. But Balor stood tall and proud as he reveled in the power surging through him.

As he gazed into the depths of the vortex, Balor could feel his mind expanding beyond mortal limits. He saw glimpses of other realms, filled with unimaginable horrors and ancient deities that would make even Mephistopheles seem like a mere mortal being.

But amidst all this chaos and madness, Balor's mind remained focused on one thing — fulfilling his pact with Mephistopheles. He knew that this convergence was just the beginning, a taste of what was to come when their two worlds collided.

With a wild gleam in his eyes, Balor raised his arms triumphantly, reveling in the chaos.

"Behold the void between worlds!" he proclaimed, his eyes now glowing with an infernal light. The sorcerer stood on the precipice of transformation, poised to transcend his mortal form. "All hail the coming of Mephistopheles!"

The swirling portal pulsed, then exploded outward in a maelstrom of dark energy. Eldritch forces engulfed the temple, warping stone and flesh alike. As reality buckled around them, Balor's maniacal laughter echoed through the chamber, a chilling soundtrack to the impending apocalypse.

Balor's voice echoed through the chamber, a dark incantation that seemed to resonate with the pulsating energy of the vortex. The air crackled with anticipation as if the very atoms were waiting for his command. Then, with a final, guttural shout, he thrust his hands into the heart of the vortex.

The world unraveled in a symphony of horror.

Across the globe, screams pierced the air as blood cascaded from countless eyes, painting faces with crimson anguish. Iconic landmarks, once symbols of human achievement, crumbled like sandcastles before an unrelenting tide. The very fabric of reality frayed at its edges, unraveling with terrifying speed.

Ancient ley lines, hidden veins of power crisscrossing the Earth, pulsed with malevolent energy. Their eerie glow cast sickly shadows across landscapes, both urban and wild. Above, the moon hung bloated and sickly, weeping a bloody haze that stained the night sky.

Where the ritual chamber had stood, a void formed. Blacker than the deepest abyss, it pulsed with unknowable hunger. Reality itself tore asunder around its maw, peeling away like burning film — a cosmic projectionist's nightmare made manifest.

Then, as swiftly as the chaos had erupted, it ceased.

An eerie hush enveloped the area, more unsettling than the chaos that had just occurred. The gaping tear in reality snapped shut, erasing any evidence of its presence except for the destruction it left behind. The once-familiar landscape was now twisted and distorted, unrecognizable to those who had called it home. A sense of foreboding hung heavy in the air, a stark reminder that this world would never be the same again.

The once bustling cities lay in ruins, a stark reminder of the arrogance and foolishness of mankind in the face of unimaginable power. Crumbling buildings and twisted metal stood as haunting monuments to the fragility of human existence. The streets were now barren and silent, save for the occasional howl of wind echoing through the desolate landscapes. The only evidence that life had once thrived here was the scattered debris and broken remnants of what was once a bustling metropolis. But now, it was a graveyard of civilization, a bleak testament to humanity's downfall in the face of forces far beyond their understanding.

In the aftermath of the cataclysm, the world seemed to hold its breath. The once vibrant cities were now ghost towns, their streets echoing with the whispers of a life that no longer existed. The moon's bloody tears had ceased, leaving behind an inky darkness that swallowed all hope. Amidst the ruins, the cult sanctum stood defiant, a silent witness to humanity's fall.

A haunting silence blanketed the cult sanctum, broken only by the soft hiss of smoldering embers. Debris littered the ritual chamber, a testament to the unholy rites that had transpired. The air hung thick and oppressive, a miasma of arcane energies that clung to every surface.

Without warning, a deep rumble shook the foundations, vibrating through stone and bone alike. In the flickering shadows, grotesque shapes writhed and undulated, hinting at horrors beyond mortal comprehension. Unearthly cries echoed from distant corners, growing closer with each passing moment.

Amidst the cacophony of screams and destruction, a monstrous figure began to stir. It was an abomination, a merging of two powerful beings — Balor and Mephistopheles — twisted into one nightmarish creature. Its grotesque form twisted and contorted, bones snapping and muscles stretching with sickening pops and cracks as it rose from the ground. The stench of charred flesh and sulfur emanated from its skin, causing all who beheld it to recoil in horror.

The monstrous hybrid creature heaved itself up from the ground, its massive body unfolding and revealing nested limbs that resembled oversized insect mandibles. A guttural roar erupted from its gaping maw, echoing off the crumbling walls and sending clouds of dust billowing into the air. The sheer size and ferocity of the creature were enough to strike fear into the hearts of any who beheld it. Its blood-red eyes glowed with a fierce intensity, daring anyone to challenge its dominance.

Its revolting features took shape, a blasphemous fusion of Balor's primal fury and the endless cosmic horror of Mephistopheles. Cyclopean in nature, its form defied conventional geometry, pulsing with strange energies that lurked just beneath its gnarled hide.

As the monstrosity reached its full height, its immensity became staggering. It dwarfed the ritual ruins, a colossus of nightmare made flesh. Reality itself seemed to decay in its presence, gravity warping and twisting around its impossible form.

Another soul-piercing shriek split the air, a sound that threatened to shatter sanity itself. The hybrid lurched forward, each thunderous step sending violent tremors through the ground. The very earth seemed to recoil from its touch as if recognizing the wrongness of its existence.

Balor/Mephistopheles loomed at its full, unfathomable height, a living embodiment of primordial chaos and the Void itself. It stood as pure apocalyptic terror given form and substance, a blasphemy against nature that heralded the unmaking of all creation.

The abomination's lidless ocular abyss stared outward, promising obliteration to all that fell within its gaze. In that moment, as reality trembled and sanity frayed, one truth became horrifyingly clear: this was not the end of a ritual but the beginning of an apocalypse.

The creature's form began to blur, its edges fraying as if being consumed by the very darkness it embodied. The air around it seemed to thicken, the atmosphere growing heavy with a sense of impending doom. The world watched in paralyzed terror as the abomination started to unleash its true power.

A sinister darkness crept across the face of the Earth, devouring light and hope in its inexorable advance. This was no mere shadow but a cosmic cancer that warped reality itself. Tendrils of entropic energy, like the grasping fingers of some otherworldly behemoth, tore at the very fabric of existence.

Oceans writhed and boiled as the eclipse consumed them, their depths becoming portals to realms best left unexplored. Continents shuddered and split, mountains crumbling like sandcastles before the onslaught of this interdimensional apocalypse. The sky, once a comforting blue, now churned with eldritch colors that defied description and sanity alike.

As the demonic shadow spread, the boundaries between worlds began to blur. Nightmarish creatures slithered through cracks in reality while the laws of physics unraveled like frayed thread. Gravity faltered, time hiccupped, and the screams of the dying were swallowed by an unnatural silence.

In the final moments, as the last slivers of untainted Earth were subsumed, an unspeakable presence made itself known. Mephistopheles, the arch-fiend of infernal legend, stirred from eons of slumber. His rebirth heralded the end of all things, as the world that was became nothing more than a memory, lost in the infinite abyss of his malevolent awakening.

CHAPTER 24
DEFIANCE'S FLAME

The weary survivors of the Shadowguard stumbled into their underground sanctuary, a haven that had miraculously stayed relatively unscathed. As they stepped through the entrance, the darkness seemed to swallow them whole, its malignant aura pulsing with every step they took. The scent of iron and decay hung heavy in the air, mingling with the stench of fear and despair that clung to their battered souls. Their footsteps echoed off the stone walls, emphasizing the lonely emptiness of their once-thriving sanctuary. The only light came from flickering torches, casting eerie shadows that danced along the walls as if taunting them. It was a bleak reminder of how far they had fallen but also a glimmer of hope that they may still persevere against the encroaching darkness.

Mara collapsed against a cold, rough stone pillar, her once-pristine uniform now a tattered and blood-soaked canvas. Her chest rose and fell in desperate gasps, each breath a painful reminder of their crushing defeat. Terry made his way towards her, his footsteps hesitant and unsteady on the debris-strewn ground. In his trembling hands, he clutched a canteen filled with precious water — their only reprieve from the scorching heat of the battlefield.

"Here. You should drink."

Gratitude flickered in Mara's weary, bloodshot eyes as she gratefully accepted the offering of cool water. The clear liquid soothed her parched throat and provided a brief respite from the taste of failure that lingered on her tongue. As she drank, Alex trudged past, his strong jaw set in a determined line as he carried an unconscious soldier toward the medical room. The sight of her comrade's limp form sent a fresh wave of anguish through Mara's heart, weighing down her already heavy steps. She couldn't help but feel a surge of guilt for not being able to protect him and her team better.

She returned the canteen to Terry, her voice barely above a whisper. "How many did we lose?"

"Too damn many," Terry replied, his words heavy with resignation. "If we're going to have any chance now, we need to be smart about this. Strategic."

Mara's eyes hardened. "There's no running from this, Terry. You know that."

As Alex emerged from the medical room, his expression grave and weary, his gaze swept over the pitiful remnants of their once-mighty force. The stench of death and destruction lingered in the air, a constant reminder of the fierce battle that had just taken place. The sight of injured soldiers being tended to by exhausted medics weighed heavily on his shoulders as he spoke. "God willing, some are still fighting elsewhere," he said, his voice heavy with emotion. "But we must accept what sacrifice demands of us." His words hung in the air, a somber acknowledgment of the harsh realities of war.

From the depths of the shadows, Hunter emerged with a steely determination etched into his features. His jaw was set, his eyes blazing with unwavering resolve. "Alex is right. We knew from the beginning that there would be sacrifices on this crusade. But we cannot falter now." He spoke with a fierce conviction, his voice carrying through the darkness like a beacon of hope. "I will gather our forces and search for any weakness in Balor's defenses. There is always a chink in the armor to exploit."

Terry's frustration boiled over. "Haven't we lost enough already, throwing ourselves against this monster? We need to regroup somewhere more defensible and protect who we can."

The atmosphere was thick with tension, the air crackling with energy as Mara and Hunter stood side by side, bristling at the mere suggestion of retreat. Alex, the calm and collected leader, stepped between them, his presence like a soothing balm to their frayed nerves. His strong stance and unwavering confidence served as a calming anchor in the midst of their heated exchange.

"Friends, none of us stand alone. Evil prevails when good souls turn from one another. We must stand united."

Hunter's broad shoulders slumped as he exhaled, the tension in his body loosening. With a nod of reluctant agreement, the atmosphere between them shifted from one of brewing conflict to one of unity. The air was thick with unspoken words and emotions, yet they both understood the weight of their unspoken truce. As they stood facing each other, a sense of understanding passed between them, diffusing any remaining tension and bringing a momentary sense of peace.

Mara's voice was soft but resolute. "You're right, Alex. Whatever happens, we face it together."

A ghost of a smile touched Alex's lips. Mara's attention turned to the ragged band of survivors, her voice carrying effortlessly through the quiet camp. Every word she spoke hung in the air, full of emotion and determination. It was a scene of bravery and resilience against all odds, a testament to the unbreakable spirit of humanity in the face of adversity. "I know how dire this seems. But we're still breathing for a reason. This isn't over. We can't let Balor's darkness win."

The rebels listened with rapt attention, their eyes locked onto Mara as she spoke. Hunter, a towering figure next to her, exuded a powerful sense of support without uttering a single word. His presence alone was enough to give her strength and confidence. The air was tense with anticipation and determination as Mara's words resonated through the group, igniting a fire in their hearts. They were ready to fight for what they believed in, united under Mara's leadership and Hunter's unwavering loyalty. "So long as we keep fighting, there's still hope. We few may be all that's left between the world and the abyss."

Hunter's hand found Mara's shoulder, his touch firm and reassuring. As he stood by her side, his presence conveyed a sense of unwavering strength and solidarity. Alex and Terry quickly joined them, their expressions determined as they formed a united front against the encroaching darkness. Together, they stood tall and unyielding, ready to face whatever challenges lay ahead.

Mara's voice rose, carrying the weight of their shared struggle. "But if we stand as one, our light can never be extinguished!"

As her words echoed across the carnivorous room, a spark ignited in the hearts of the battered rebels. Their weary faces turned towards Mara and her inner circle, their eyes alight with newfound determination.

With a surge of energy, they pushed forward as one, rallying around their leaders. The sound of their cheers pierced through the oppressive gloom like a beacon of hope, a defiant cry against the overwhelming odds they faced.

In that moment, an incredible transformation overtook the rebel camp. No longer were they broken survivors but a force of nature united in their unshakeable resolve to push back against the relentless tide of darkness threatening to consume their world. The air was charged with electricity, pulsing with the fierce determination of these brave souls fighting for their freedom.

As the final word left Mara's lips, a sudden silence fell over the room. The rebels held their breath, the gravity of her words sinking in, their hearts pounding in unison. Then, as if on cue, they all turned to face the ominous night sky, their gaze drawn to the monstrous structure looming in the distance. Balor's ziggurat stood defiantly against the stormy backdrop, a chilling reminder of what they were up against.

The night sky seethed with a palpable malevolence, a dark and foreboding canvas of pitch-black clouds illuminated by fierce bolts of lightning. In the distance, a monstrous structure loomed, piercing the heavens with its imposing presence — Balor's ziggurat, a towering monument to darkness and despair.

Its obsidian spires jutted out like sharp claws, reaching for the turbulent sky above. With each flash of lightning, grotesque carvings and impossible geometries were revealed, etched into the ziggurat's surface like a macabre tapestry. The air was heavy with ominous energy, as if the very fabric of reality was being twisted and distorted by the sinister power emanating from this ancient structure.

The ziggurat cast a vast shadow over the land. The darkness emanating from it seemed to swallow up any trace of hope or joy in its vicinity, casting a palpable aura of dread that permeated the air. A sense of unease and foreboding hung heavy around the structure as if some ancient evil was seeping into everything around it. Even the most confident of passersby felt their courage falter under its sinister influence.

From somewhere beyond the looming citadel, carried on a wind that whispered of otherworldly horrors, came the faint echoes of human voices. They were not cries of fear or anguish, as one might expect in the shadow of such a monstrous edifice, but defiant cheers. The sound was a stark contrast to the overwhelming darkness, a reminder that even in the face of unspeakable evil, some spark of resistance still flickered.

Yet as the cheers faded, swallowed by the vastness of the night, the ziggurat remained. Immovable. Patient. Waiting.

As the last echoes of defiance died down, a sudden silence fell over the landscape, a silence so complete it seemed to drown out even the thunder. The ziggurat's oppressive presence filled the void, its dark energy seeping into the very bones of those who dared to oppose it. In this moment of dread, Mara and Hunter retreated to their command center, seeking solace in strategy amidst the encroaching darkness.

The command center was alive with a grim sense of urgency as Mara stood at the war table, her stance tense and her hands clenched into tight fists. The maps and tactical displays spread out before her painted a bleak picture — the enemy had completely encircled their base, leaving little hope for escape.

Nearby, Hunter paced back and forth, his movements heavy with exhaustion and his nerves strained to their breaking point. Dark circles under his eyes told the story of sleepless nights spent strategizing against an unrelenting foe. Every second felt like an eternity as they awaited their fate in this dangerous game of warfare.

Mara's voice cut through the tense silence. "There's no way we're punching through those defenses again. We'd be throwing lives away."

Hunter whirled to face her, desperation clear in his stance. "So we just let Balor complete his objective and game over for humanity?"

Their gazes locked, neither willing to back down. The air crackled with unspoken fear and determination.

Terry's measured tone broke the standoff. "Look, I hate this as much as anyone, but we have to think about retreating. Regroup somewhere more defensible while we still can."

From the shadows, Alex's melodic voice drifted, laden with otherworldly wisdom. "Perhaps that is what the darkness wants for hope itself to retreat. If the light does not stand firm, how can it ever push back the shadows?"

Hunter and Mara's eyes met in a silent exchange, a wordless understanding passing between them. A shift occurred within the group, a sense of realignment settling over their tense bodies.

With a determined nod, Hunter's conviction returned to his voice, his words now laced with certainty and purpose. "Alex is right. Balor wants us to lose faith. As long as we keep fighting, we have a chance."

Mara squared her shoulders, addressing the team with unflinching honesty. "I won't lie to you all. The odds are against us. But we've defied the odds before. Together, we can do it again. For the future."

A determined energy rippled through the assembled group, their eyes locked in a shared purpose. Heads nodded in unison, jaws firmly clenched with renewed determination. Mara's gaze turned to Hunter and Terry, her eyes ablaze with a fierce determination. Her piercing stare seemed to ignite a fire within them as well.

"Let's go kick their demonic asses."

Hunter spread schematics and occult artifacts across the table, his movements sharp and focused. "The plan is risky, but it just might work. Each team will have a specific part to play..."

What followed was a whirlwind of preparation. Elite Shadowguard units donned specialized gear, their movements fluid and practiced. Terry's voice rang out, briefing military forces on intricate supporting maneuvers. In a corner steeped in candlelight, Alex murmured ancient blessings over weapons and armor. Hunter hunched over equipment, etching arcane wards with painstaking precision, sweat beading on his brow.

Mara gazed out over the camp, taking in the scene. The air was charged with nervous energy as rebels made their final preparations. Some sat in quiet contemplation, steely resolve in their eyes. Others murmured prayers or farewells to loved ones. A few laughed raucously as if in defiance of their fate.

Mara envied their spirit. Doubt gnawed at her, the crushing weight of responsibility threatening to crush her resolve. So much sacrifice, so much still at stake. Each life lost under her command was a new wound on her soul.

A gentle hand rested on her shoulder. "You've done well by them, Mara," Alex said softly. His eyes radiated compassion and wisdom. "Have faith."

Faith. Mara wanted to cling to it, but uncertainty clouded her heart. Still, she managed a small smile. "I'll try."

Alex nodded, giving her shoulder a final squeeze before moving off to continue his blessings. Mara watched him go, drawing strength from his tranquil aura. Come what may, she would face it with her team united behind her.

Hunter appeared at her side, looking haggard but focused. "We're ready." His eyes probed hers as if sensing her inner turmoil. "Mara, listen —"

"Save it," she said firmly, cutting him off. "We've got a battle to win. Balor's not going to kick his own ass."

A hint of a smile played at Hunter's mouth. He gave a curt nod. "Too right." His expression grew serious.

Mara took a deep breath and steeled herself as she stepped out to address the assembled forces. All eyes turned to her, and a hush fell over the crowd.

"Friends," she began, her voice resonating with quiet authority, "I won't lie and say the path ahead will be easy. We face a foe unlike any we've encountered before. But we also face this darkness together, with courage in our hearts and purpose guiding our actions."

Mara met the eyes of each rebel in turn, seeing her own determination mirrored back.

"No matter what comes, remember what we fight for, not just for our own survival, but for the future — one free of shadow and full of hope's light. Keep that flame burning bright within you. With faith in ourselves and each other, we will prevail."

A rumbling cheer rose up, and Mara raised a fist skyward. As one, the crowd did the same, their shouts shaking the very air. Mara felt her doubts burn away, replaced by fiery resolve. At her side, Hunter laid a steadying hand on her shoulder and gave a subtle nod. His eyes said what his voice did not: he believed in her. Believed in them all.

"Right," Mara said, turning to him with blazing eyes, "Let's finish this."

Hunter inclined his head, a fierce light in his gaze. "I'll gather the first team. We'll hit them from the east with full force."

"Good. I'll lead the Shadowguard around and flank them." Mara clasped his arm."

As the others dispersed to their final tasks, Mara pulled Terry aside. She pressed a sealed letter into his hand, her voice low and heavy with unspoken emotion. "If I don't make it back, get this to my sister if she's still alive. Tell her I went down fighting."

Terry's grip tightened on the letter, his eyes meeting Mara's with fierce loyalty. "You'll tell her yourself when this is over."

The weight of what was to come hung in the air between them, unspoken but palpable.

As the sun slowly sank behind the horizon, a feverish energy crackled through the rebel camp. The disparate groups, brought together by a common cause, were bustling with activity as they prepared for the final battle that loomed in the near future.

In a secluded corner of the camp, Shadowguard teams meticulously inspected their weapons and equipment, ensuring everything was in perfect working order. Their faces were hardened with determination, muscles tense and ready for action. Standing before them was Mara, her piercing gaze filled with unwavering determination. Her commanding voice rang out over the gathered warriors, spurring them on and igniting a fierce fire in their hearts. The air was thick with anticipation, each member of the rebellion eagerly awaiting their chance to fight for their freedom.

"This is it, people. The moment we've trained for. Tonight, we make our stand. For the light!"

A thunderous cheer erupted from the Shadowguard, fists pumping skyward in unison. The sound reverberated through the camp, a battle cry that electrified the air and stirred the hearts of even the most hardened fighters.

Miles away, in a misty temple shrouded in ancient secrets, monks moved with practiced precision. Their hands glided over blessed swords and armor, murmuring incantations that imbued the metal with otherworldly power. The air crackled with mystical energy, a stark contrast to the practical preparations elsewhere.

Amid the chaos of the camp, civilians in tattered clothing shuffled forward nervously. Resistance fighters outfitted them with equipment — clothing, gear, and weapons that were unfamiliar to many. The civilians' hands trembled as they grasped the foreign objects, their eyes wide with a mixture of fear and determination. They knew what was at stake — their freedom, their lives — but they also felt the weight of uncertainty and doubt in their abilities to fight against a powerful enemy.

The military forces mobilized with clockwork efficiency. Troops marched in perfect formation, their boots creating a rhythmic drumbeat on the hard ground. Vehicles rumbled to life, their engines growling like awakened beasts. In the sky, aircraft screamed as they took flight, metal birds ready to rain destruction from above.

In a secluded clearing, Hunter addressed an assembly of mystics and seers. Their otherworldly presence sent ripples of unease through the air, but Hunter's voice remained steady. "The arcane arts will play a pivotal role tonight. Do not waver."

The mystics nodded solemnly, their eyes holding secrets of realms beyond mortal comprehension.

As the preparations reached their zenith, everyday citizens watched with growing unease. Forces deployed around them, transforming familiar streets into a militarized zone. Mechanized units rumbled down roads, their metal frames gleaming ominously in the moonlight. Behind them, monks levitated, their robes billowing in an unseen wind.

The Collective Forces marched as one — an army unlike any the world had seen before. Soldiers strode alongside mages, their contrasting energies creating an electric tension in the air. Monks moved with fluid grace, their spiritual power a palpable force.

Suddenly, Hunter's eyes widened. The occult tracker at his side sprung to life, its arcane symbols pulsing with an urgent warning. His voice, when he spoke, was barely above a whisper, yet it carried the weight of impending doom.

"He's here. It's too late to turn back now."

The marching forces continued their relentless advance, resolve etched into every face. They moved forward into the unknown, towards a battle that would determine the fate of all they held dear. The night air grew heavy with the promise of blood and magic as the world teetered on the brink of chaos.

As the Collective Forces surged forward, Hunter slipped away from the front lines. He and Father Alex retreated to the arcane library, their footfalls echoing in the hushed silence. Around them, the world prepared for war, but within these walls, they prepared for something else entirely.

The night air hung heavy with anticipation as Hunter and Father Alex stood surrounded by ancient tomes and esoteric artifacts in Hunter's arcane library. Shadows danced on the walls, cast by flickering candlelight that illuminated their solemn faces. With practiced precision, they etched an elaborate array on the floor, its arcane symbols and geometric shapes forming a complex pattern that seemed to pulse with latent energy.

Hunter's voice was grave as he spoke. "The ritual must be flawless. The fate of humanity depends on it."

Alex nodded, his eyes dark with determination. "Then let us begin. But tread carefully...we channel treacherous forces."

Working in tandem, they began to chant in an ancient tongue, their voices weaving together in an otherworldly harmony. The array came to life, glowing with an ethereal light as supernatural forces stirred in response. Alex, his brow furrowed in concentration, added more symbols to focus the swirling energy.

"Guide the weave, Father," Hunter urged. "This magic transcends life and death."

The air hummed with gathering power, thick enough to taste. But just as quickly as it had begun, the glow dimmed, the array spluttering out like a dying ember. "No!" Hunter's frustration was palpable. "We need more primal energy to catalyze the spell."

Alex's eyes lit up with sudden realization. "The Codex of Azathoth...it spoke of relics from elder epochs. Artifacts that resonate with the song of creation itself..."

Hunter's jaw clenched, his resolve unwavering. "I'll not

utilize anything tainted by darkness. We walk the noble path."

As they spoke, visions of preparation flashed through their minds. Resistance fighters donning armor and checking weapons. Military forces organizing convoys, the rumble of tanks and thrum of helicopter blades filling the air. Occult orders performing rituals, blessing relics and armor with whispered prayers.

Alex turned back to the ancient texts, his fingers tracing faded symbols as he searched feverishly. He stopped suddenly, his breath catching as he found an etching that mirrored their array.

"Anaxagor's Celestial Essence!" he exclaimed. "Anaxagor was imprisoned eons ago by the Ancients...it alone could ignite the ritual."

Hunter considered this, weighing the risks. "A dangerous gambit...but we've no other options if we're to stop Balor."

Without warning, Alex clutched his head, overcome by a vision. A massive, crumbling prison loomed before him, guarded by a slumbering titan of impossible proportions. An ancient voice whispered: "Come...renew our covenant."

Alex's eyes snapped open, filled with renewed conviction. "The way is clear. We must journey to the Vault of Relentless Eons."

Hunter placed a steadying hand on Alex's shoulder, concern etched on his face. "Mara and I will go retrieve what you need."

The array flickered briefly, a surge of power coursing through it before fading once more. Alex nodded, his jaw set with grim determination. "With the grace of God, you shall return in time," he vowed.

As Hunter hurried out into the night, Alex turned back to the unstable array. The weight of their task settled heavily upon him as he resumed his occult incantations, praying they would be enough to hold back the encroaching darkness.

CHAPTER 25
PATHS OF THE FAITHFUL

The subterranean chamber yawned before them, a cavernous maw lit by the flickering dance of torchlight. Strange occult symbols adorned the stone walls, their eldritch forms seeming to writhe in the unsteady illumination. Hunter and Mara stood transfixed, their eyes unable to break away from the mesmerizing sight before them: A swirling vortex of primordial energy that pulsed at the chamber's heart. It was as if they had stumbled upon a portal to another realm, a place where the laws of reality no longer applied.

From the depths of that otherworldly maelstrom, a towering phantasmal form coalesced. Anaxagor, the fallen celestial god, loomed over them, his massive figure casting a shadow that seemed to devour all light around it. The air trembled and distorted in his presence as if reality itself could not withstand his power. When he spoke, his voice boomed with an otherworldly resonance, shaking the ground beneath their feet and causing their bones to vibrate with fear. The sheer magnitude of his being left them feeling small and insignificant in comparison.

"Why have you awakened me from eons of slumber, mortals?"

Hunter and Mara exchanged an uneasy glance, the weight of their mission pressing down upon them like a physical force. Hunter swallowed hard, his throat dry as desert sand, before finding his voice. His voice came out strained and hoarse, betraying his nerves and the overwhelming pressure they were under. "Great Anaxagor. We humbly seek your aid. The mortal realm faces apocalyptic ruin. Your celestial essence could turn the tide."

The god's piercing, otherworldly eyes narrowed, their ephemeral gaze sweeping over the mortals before him. With intense scrutiny, he seemed to see through their very beings, his disdain for them radiating like a noxious cloud of ancient disgust. It was as if he could peel away their flesh and peer into their very souls, judging them with an authority beyond comprehension. The air around him crackled with power and malice, a chilling reminder of his divine nature and the insignificance of mere humans in his eyes. "And what is the fate of this fragile mortal sphere to me? I care not for your plight."

Desperation clawed at Mara's insides, her body trembling with a mix of fear and hope. She took a hesitant step forward with wide, pleading eyes that reflected the inner turmoil she was feeling. The quiver in her voice revealed her inner turmoil, a delicate balance between fear and hope that threatened to spill over at any moment. "Please, Anaxagor. We will offer anything in return. But without your power, all is lost. Have mercy!"

The god-form's gaze shifted, fixing on Mara with a curious intensity that was somehow more terrifying than his previous indifference. The air around them seemed to grow heavy and charged with an unspoken power as if the entire world was holding its breath in anticipation of what would come next. Every fiber of Mara's being tingled with a mix of fear and awe, unsure of what consequences may follow this encounter with a deity. "Perhaps...for profound sacrifice, I would grant my waning celestial might. But the price will be steep for distorting fate's weave..."

A weighty, foreboding feeling settled over Hunter and Mara. It draped itself around their shoulders, pressing down on them with the gravity of the moment. As they shared a somber glance, they understood the dire implications of the pact they were about to make. The consequences could be damning, but with the looming threat of apocalyptic destruction, what other choice did they truly have? Their breaths came in short, nervous bursts as they steeled themselves for what lay ahead.

Hunter's voice was steady, belying the terror that gnawed at his gut. "We accept your terms, Anaxagor. For the greater good, we must risk the price."

As Hunter's words hung in the air, an eerie and otherworldly chant began to reverberate through the chamber. The sound seemed to emanate from the very depths of the vortex before them, causing reality itself to warp and twist with its intensity. Anaxagor, his ghostly form shimmering with power, stretched out a spectral hand towards the vortex, his voice booming like thunder within the cavern. The combination of sound and sight was both mesmerizing and terrifying, leaving Hunter and his companion frozen in awe and fear before the powerful being before them.

"Then it shall be done! But heed the cost..."

The ritual's power crashed over them like a tidal wave. Mara gasped, her eyes widening in shock as arcane markings etched themselves into her skin, burning like brands. Hunter gritted his teeth against a pain beyond mortal comprehension, feeling as though his very essence was being rewritten.

With a flick of his godly hand, Anaxagor summoned forth two glowing vials of celestial essence. The ethereal liquid swirled and sparkled in the light, emitting a faint humming sound. As the god's magnificent form slowly dissipated into the swirling vortex, Hunter and Mara felt a powerful surge of energy course through their bodies. It was as if they had been touched by divinity itself, leaving them with an indescribable feeling of transformation and destiny. They knew that their lives would never be the same after this encounter with a god.

Mara's voice was barely a whisper, fragile and filled with doubt. "Have we damned ourselves, Hunter? Was the price too high?"

Hunter met her gaze, his own eyes haunted by the weight of their decision. "Only time will tell, Mara. But we do what we must."

With solemn purpose, they departed the chamber, the precious vials clutched tightly in their hands. Each step echoed with finality, leaving them to wonder if their pact with the fallen god had not doomed them all.

As they left the chamber, the world outside seemed to have changed along with them, reflecting the dread they felt inside. Climbing into their convoy, they set off, the celestial vials their only hope in this forsaken world.

The convoy rumbled through the desolate streets of what was once a thriving metropolis. Mara gripped the steering wheel, her knuckles white as she navigated the treacherous terrain. Crumbling buildings loomed on either side, their jagged silhouettes stark against the night sky.

Hunter clutched the vials of celestial essence as if his life depended on it. His expression was a mix of awe and trepidation, fully aware of the power they carried and the high price they had paid to obtain it. The weight of their decision hung over them like a dark cloud, casting a pall on the already bleak landscape. Mara could feel his unease, her own insides churning with the same apprehension.

"Where do we go now?" Mara asked, her voice cracking, barely audible over the rumble of the engine and the chilling wind whistling through the bullet-ridden windows.

Hunter consulted the frayed, blood-stained map and ancient tomes that now glowed an otherworldly hue, a grim reminder of their pact with Anaxagor. "According to these coordinates, we need to head east. There's a hidden sanctuary, a last stronghold of researchers and mages desperately trying to stave off the apocalypse." He paused, his eyes reflecting the hopelessness that surrounded them. "It's our only chance, Mara. Our only hope to save what's left of this world."

Mara swallowed the lump that had formed in her throat and nodded, her jaw clenched in determination. "Then east we go."

The convoy pressed onward, the roar of its engines the

only sound besides the howling wind that cut through the desolate city streets. The headlights sliced through the darkness, illuminating the rubble and decay that now surrounded them.

Mara's gaze remained fixed on the road ahead, though her mind was far away, lost in thought. The weight of their actions pressed heavily on her shoulders. Had they done the right thing? Or had they damned humanity to a fate worse than the apocalypse they hoped to prevent?

Hunter studied the ancient texts intently, memorizing each intricacy of the incantations they would need to unleash the celestial essence. Dark bags hung under his eyes, evidence of the sleepless nights since this mess all began. He could not afford to fail, not with so many lives hanging precariously in the balance.

As they drove deeper into the gloom of the dying city, an unnatural fog rolled in, obscuring their view of the road. The convoy slowed to a crawl as Mara struggled to navigate through the soup-like haze. She could just barely make out the outline of a bridge looming ahead.

"This is it," Hunter said, his voice grave. "The bridge to the eastern precinct."

Mara's hands tightened on the wheel. According to the map, this bridge was their only passage across the wide river separating them from the sanctuary. She took a deep breath, steeling her nerves. They had come too far to turn back now.

The convoy inched forward. Demonic creatures swarmed the streets, their grotesque forms illuminated by bursts of gunfire from the armored vehicles. The air was thick with the acrid smell of smoke and the metallic tang of blood.

"Stay tight! We're almost through!" Mara's voice crackled over the radio, a beacon of determination in the chaos.

The convoy pressed on, engines roaring in defiance of the hellish landscape. Soldiers leaned out of their vehicles' windows, their weapons blazing against the encroaching horde. The staccato of gunfire was punctuated by inhuman shrieks and the sickening crunch of bodies being torn apart.

SHEIN DAVIS FULLER

Without warning, the ground erupted in a shower of concrete and twisted metal. A massive demon, its hide glistening with otherworldly ichor, burst forth from the rubble. It towered over the vehicles, its maw gaping wide to reveal rows of needle-sharp teeth.

Time seemed to slow as the behemoth slammed into one of the armored transports. Metal screamed as it crumpled under the impact, and the vehicle careened sideways, flipping onto its roof in a shower of sparks.

Mara's reflexes kicked in. She wrenched the wheel, desperately trying to avoid the carnage. But in her haste to evade one danger, she veered straight into another. The sickening crunch of metal on concrete filled her ears as her vehicle collided with a pile of debris.

The impact threw her forward, the seatbelt digging into her chest. As the world spun around her, Mara's thoughts raced. They were so close to safety, but now, trapped in the heart of this nightmare city, their fate hung by a thread.

Mara shook her head, trying to clear the stars from her vision. The headache that pounded behind her eyes was nothing compared to the knot of dread that had formed in the pit of her stomach. They had no time for this. They needed to reach the sanctuary, and fast.

"Hunter!" she called, twisting in her seat to check on her partner. "You alright?"

He groaned in response, but other than a few cuts and bruises, he appeared unscathed. The vials of celestial essence were miraculously unharmed, their glow pulsating softly in the dimly lit interior.

"We need a new ride," Mara said grimly, unbuckling her seatbelt and grabbing her shotgun.

Hunter nodded in reluctant agreement, slipping the vials into a reinforced pack. "Get the others. I'll cover you."

Mara nodded, her heart pounding in her ears as she opened the door. The stench of death and rot hit her like a physical blow, and she fought the urge to gag. The night air was alive with the shrieks and cries of the hellish creatures that now outnumbered the city's original inhabitants.

"Over here!" Mara shouted, her voice carrying over the din of the battle.

Her remaining teammates, battered but alive, rallied around her. Together, they fought their way through the hellish landscape, fending off attacks from all sides as they made their way to the nearest functioning vehicle. The deafening roar of gunfire mixed with the guttural howls of the demonic horde, but Mara and her team pushed forward with single-minded purpose.

Reaching a battered Humvee, they quickly dispatched the mutated creatures clinging to it, and their small group piled inside. Hunter took the wheel, flooring the gas before Mara and the three men in the backseat had even closed their doors. The tires spun, spewing gravel before gaining traction. They shot forward, weaving through the debris-strewn streets at breakneck speed.

"Did we lose them?" Mara shouted over the growl of the engine, glancing back anxiously as Hunter careened around a sharp corner. Shadowy forms seemed to loom up at every turn, only to vanish into the swirling fog as they sped past.

"For now," Hunter replied tersely, his knuckles white on the steering wheel. His foot did not ease off the gas.

Mara leaned her head back against the seat, trying to slow her breathing. The landscape became more desolate as they left the outskirts of the city. The bridge couldn't be far now.

A thunderous crash jolted Mara from her thoughts as the rear window exploded in a hail of gunfire. Chaos erupted in the backseat as the three men scrambled for cover. Mara spun to see several motorcycle-mounted creatures in hot pursuit, their gnarled features twisted in bloodlust.

"Friends of yours?" Hunter quipped grimly, wrenching the wheel to avoid the barrage.

Mara seized her shotgun and maneuvered over the men

crouched in the backseat. Leaning out the shattered rear window, she took aim at the pursuing demons. The recoil jarred her shoulder as she fired, her first shot blasting a creature off its bike in a spray of dark ichor. Quickly chambering another round, she fired again. The second shot struck the front wheel of the next motorcycle, sending it into a violent flip. The bike careened into its fellow demons, tangling their vehicles into a heap of twisted metal.

"Got 'em!" Mara shouted triumphantly. But her victory was short-lived. More creatures emerged from the fog, racing to join the chase. Mara fired until her shotgun clicked empty.

"I'm out!" she yelled to Hunter. "Floor it!"

The Humvee's engine roared as he coaxed every last ounce of speed from it. The bridge was just ahead, a hulking silhouette through the mist. Hunter tore onto it at reckless speed, weaving between abandoned vehicles. Mara's heart leaped into her throat as the edge of the bridge whizzed by only inches from her window.

Halfway across, the bridge abruptly ended, sheared off where something massive had torn through it. Only a few steel girders remained, jutting out over a yawning chasm.

"Hold on!" Hunter yelled. Before Mara could even process what was happening, he turned the wheel sharply. The Humvee shot off the edge of the ravaged bridge, launching into empty space. For a heart-stopping moment, they were airborne. Mara felt the breath leave her lungs as the Humvee crashed onto solid ground once more. Her teeth clacked together painfully, and she tasted blood in her mouth from where she had bitten her tongue. For a moment, all she could do was gasp for air, her fingers digging into the seat beneath her until her knuckles turned white.

Beside her, Hunter let out a shaky laugh, almost giddy with adrenaline and disbelief that they had made it. "Everyone still alive back there?" he called out, glancing in the rearview mirror at their battered teammates.

A chorus of pained groans answered him. Nothing seemed

to be broken, at least not severely. Mara steadied herself with a deep breath. They were alive. That was what mattered.

Peering through the cracked windshield, Mara could see the sanctuary up ahead, a crumbling cathedral perched on a lonely clifftop. Iron gates swung open to receive them, revealing a courtyard filled with haggard soldiers and civilians. The last remnants of humanity banding together in this forgotten holy place to make their final stand.

Mara allowed herself a small smile. After everything they had suffered, all the friends and loved ones lost along the way, they had made it.

The Humvee rolled to a stop inside the sanctuary's courtyard, and Mara stepped out onto the cracked pavement, shotgun still clutched in one hand. She surveyed their new surroundings, taking in the soaring Gothic architecture of the cathedral, worn by time and circumstance, into a kind of decaying grandeur.

Makeshift shelters and supply tents crowded the courtyard, a ragtag collection of humanity's remnants. Their faces told stories of hardship and loss as they watched the newcomers warily. Mara felt the weight of their stares, sensing the fragility of the hope these people clung to in this place.

She turned to Hunter as he came up beside her. "We made it, but this is no paradise," she said quietly. "These people are hanging on by a thread."

Hunter nodded, his face grim. "We need to speak to whoever's in charge. Find out just how safe this sanctuary really is."

They were directed inside the cathedral, whose cavernous interior echoed with hushed voices and footsteps on the cracked marble floor. Scarred wooden pews stood empty, the altar bare. Any ornamentation or finery had long been stripped away or destroyed. Mara felt a pang at the desecration of this once-holy place.

Near the altar stood a makeshift command post, with

maps, radios, and other equipment scattered across tables. A gruff, bearded man in combat fatigues stood conferring with a few other officers. As Mara and Hunter approached, he turned to greet them.

Mara studied the commander as he approached them. His face was weathered, his beard streaked with gray, but his eyes were sharp and alert. He carried himself with a quiet confidence that spoke of experience commanding men in the field.

"Welcome to the Sanctuary," he said, shaking their hands firmly. "I'm Commander Easton. We don't get many visitors making it this far."

"We appreciate you taking us in," Mara replied. "I'm Mara Lawson, Savannah PD. This is my associate, Hunter Eldritch."

Hunter gave a curt nod, his gaze sweeping over the cathedral pensively.

"Savannah, eh?" Easton said. "That city's gone straight to hell, pardon my language. We've been hearing some demonic things coming out of there."

"You don't know the half of it," Mara said darkly. She quickly summarized the fall of Savannah — the spreading evil, the loss of communication, and finally, the total descent into chaos.

Easton's face was grim as he listened. "I wish I could say you'll be safe here," he said finally. "But we've had breaches too. Whatever evil is brewing out there, it's getting stronger."

He turned to glance back at the maps and radio equipment. "We're cut off from the outside world. Just barely holding this position while we try to gather intel, figure out what the hell we're dealing with."

"No need to figure it out," Hunter interjected suddenly.

Mara glanced at Hunter, but he remained silent, his eyes fixed intently on Commander Easton. After a heavy pause, Mara spoke up.

"What my partner means is that we have some crucial information that could help explain the situation." She shifted her shotgun and pack, steeling herself. "We know the root of what's happening. And we think we may have a way to fight back."

Easton's eyes narrowed, equal parts skeptical and intrigued. "Alright, you have my attention. Let's talk somewhere more private." He led them to a small room off the main sanctuary that had likely once been an office. Hunter carefully set his pack on the desk, the glass vials inside clinking faintly.

Once the door was closed, Mara launched into their story. She told Easton about the ancient prophecies Hunter had unearthed, foretelling the rise of a demonic horde that would herald humanity's end. How they had sought answers in the occult underworld of Savannah, making contact with beings no mortal was meant to reckon with.

Finally, she revealed the bargain they had struck: the vials of celestial essence they now carried, gifted by the enigmatic Anaxagor in exchange for their souls should they fail to turn back the apocalypse.

Easton's brows furrowed as he listened. "Celestial essence? Anaxagor? You're telling me this is some kind of...occult end of days scenario?"

Hunter stepped forward, his eyes blazing. "Your enemy is older than this world. But we can stop it. The essence is the key." He unslung his pack, reverently retrieving a small glass vial filled with shimmering silver liquid.

Easton stared at the vial in Hunter's outstretched palm. Mara could see the internal struggle on his face as he weighed their story. His eyes reflected both disbelief and desperation.

Finally, he shook his head. "I don't know what game you two are playing here. But I've got good men and women relying on me to keep them alive. No fairy tales or magic potions are going to save us."

There was a commotion outside. Easton stormed out onto the balcony and looked into the courtyard. "It seems someone else has arrived." He turned to Hunter and Mara. "Expecting anyone?"

"Our comrade from Savannah radioed he'd meet us here," Hunter turned to Mara before continuing. "Alex must have arrived."

Mara nodded. "He must be anxious to get started."

The doors opened and Father Alex entered the room, his priestly robes billowing behind him as he strode purposefully into the room. Though he had come from battling the darkness to reach this haven, his eyes were clear, and his expression serene.

"I'm sorry I'm late," he said in his gentle, warm voice. His gaze moved between Hunter and Mara, sensing the tension in the room. "I came as quickly as I could. The evil has spread so far now."

He stepped forward, placing a comforting hand on Mara's shoulder before turning to address Commander Easton directly.

"I understand your skepticism, my friend. But I assure you, every word they have spoken is true." Alex's voice rang with sincerity. "I have witnessed the prophecies myself. The celestial essence is a gift, our only chance to push back this darkness."

Easton searched the priest's honest face, then sighed heavily, shaking his head. "So you vouch for their story, Father? Are you telling me you believe this — this occult rapture is upon us?"

"I wish with all my heart that it were not so," Alex replied gravely. "But yes, I believe."

The commander turned away, gripping the back of a chair with white knuckles. The room was silent for a long moment before Easton nodded slowly, considering their words carefully. "If what you say is true, then we'll need to move quickly. This sanctuary won't hold forever."

He turned to Hunter. "I'll gather my top officers and scientists. Tell them everything you know about this...essence. If we can find a way to turn it into a weapon, we may just have a fighting chance."

Hunter's eyes gleamed. "Yes, it must be fashioned into the proper occult implements to channel its power most effectively. I have several designs in mind..."

Mara cleared her throat, shooting Hunter a meaningful look. "Let's take this one step at a time. What we need now is more intel. We should do some reconnaissance, try to gauge the enemy's numbers and movements."

She glanced at Alex. "Father, perhaps you could provide spiritual support here to the people. Your wisdom would be invaluable."

Alex nodded. "Of course. My place is here with our flock, keeping their hope alive."

Easton headed for the door. "I'll have my scouts prep for a mission. We'll track the enemy's activity and search for any weaknesses." At the threshold, he paused, looking back at the trio with newfound respect.

"For the first time since this nightmare started, we have a plan. That's thanks to you." His voice turned grim. "But if your celestial essence can't turn this war around, God help us all."

He departed, leaving Mara, Hunter, and Alex alone among the maps and radio equipment.

As Easton's footsteps receded, the room fell into a tense silence. Hunter and Mara exchanged a glance, their minds already racing with strategies and contingencies. Alex stood by the window, his gaze lost in the encroaching darkness, his hands clasped in silent prayer for the battle ahead.

The trio spent the next hours poring over maps, discussing potential strategies, and sharing what they knew about the essence. As night fell, Hunter and Mara left to retrieve the containers they'd hidden earlier, their hearts heavy with the weight of their task. Alex, meanwhile, found solace in prayer, his thoughts consumed by the looming battle.

The door creaked open, and Hunter and Mara entered. Their faces were etched with a mixture of dread and determination as they approached Father Alex. In their hands, they carried two containers that pulsed with an otherworldly glow, casting eerie shadows that danced across the room.

As they drew near, Father Alex's eyes widened. He reached out with trembling hands, his fingers brushing against the smooth surface of the containers. A flicker of hope ignited in his weary gaze.

"Bless you both!" he exclaimed, his voice thick with emotion. "We may have a chance yet."

The containers hummed softly, their unearthly light seeming to intensify in response to his words. The air in the room grew heavy, charged with an electric tension that made the hairs on the back of their necks stand on end. Whatever was contained within those glowing vessels held the power to tip the scales in their desperate fight against the encroaching darkness.

With a solemn nod, Father Alex blessed the containers, his voice resonating in the silent room. As he finished, the trio looked at each other, their resolve hardened by the gravity of their task. Hunter, taking a deep breath, rallied his occultists and prepared to venture into the Stygian Domain.

Hunter led the procession of occultists through the nightmarish landscape. Reality twisted and warped around them, bending in ways that defied comprehension. The air itself seemed to ripple and distort, creating a disorienting effect that threatened to overwhelm the senses.

The chants of protective spells echoed through the surreal environment, a desperate attempt to maintain some semblance of safety in this realm of madness. Hunter's eyes darted from side to side, constantly vigilant for threats that could emerge from the swirling chaos.

Suddenly, he felt a shift in the atmosphere. The distortions intensified, and Hunter sensed the approach of something sinister. His voice cut through the chanting, urgent and commanding. "The veil is thinning! Hold to the Path!"

No sooner had the words left his lips than a monstrous form burst forth from the warped reality. A shadow beast, all gnashing teeth and writhing darkness lunged at the group with primal ferocity.

Hunter's hand moved with practiced precision, brandishing a glowing artifact. The object pulsed with an otherworldly light, its power clashing against the creature's shadowy form. As the two forces collided, the beast let out a bone-chilling screech that seemed to reverberate through multiple dimensions.

The shadow beast recoiled from the artifact's radiance, its form dissipating like smoke in a strong wind. It retreated into the swirling chaos, leaving behind an oppressive silence broken only by the ragged breathing of the occultists.

Hunter's grip on the artifact tightened as he scanned the nightmarish landscape. He knew that in this place, survival meant constant vigilance. The Path ahead remained treacherous, and the thin veil between realities could tear at any moment, unleashing horrors beyond imagination.

***

The acrid stench of corruption hung heavy in the air as Alex and the Faithful gathered on the sacred grounds. A sickly miasma swirled around them, threatening to choke out their very existence. Yet, they stood firm, their voices rising in unison as they chanted ancient prayers of protection and banishment.

Tendrils of light emanated from the group, piercing through the oppressive haze. The illumination carved a path through the darkness, a beacon of hope in a world consumed by shadows. Alex's voice rang out above the others, clear and unwavering. "By the Light, we banish this evil!"

As if sensing the challenge, the miasma thickened, pushing back against their efforts. The murky vapors coalesced, forming grotesque shapes that writhed and twisted at the edges of perception. Lesser souls might have faltered, but Alex pressed forward, undaunted by the nightmarish display.

His eyes blazed with an inner fire, a testament to the depths of his conviction. Each step forward was a battle, the ground beneath his feet seeming to shift and buckle. Yet, he advanced, leading the Faithful deeper into the heart of the corruption. The light that surrounded them flickered and wavered but refused to be extinguished, a fragile barrier against the encroaching darkness that threatened to devour them all.

CHAPTER 26
AT THE GATES OF HELL

The sky writhed with sickly celestial phenomena, casting an eerie twilight over the primordial battlefield. Vast armies converged across the hellish landscape, dwarfed by the colossal silhouette of Mephistopheles's ziggurat temple. The ominous heavens bore down on the ancient structure, its malign edifice looming like a caldera leading into the depths of hell itself.

Amid the devout, Mara stood firm and unwavering, her jaw set in determination as she braced herself against the encroaching darkness. Hunter's collection of occult amulets glowed with a pulsing, otherworldly light, each tiny spark a beacon of hope against the oppressive gloom that threatened to consume them. The air was thick with an eerie stillness, broken only by the faint hum of magic and the distant cries of unknown creatures lurking beyond their sight.

Strange energies undulated outwards from the temple in concussive waves, shaking the heroes' resolve. Many clutched holy symbols, steadying themselves against the onslaught of otherworldly power.

Terry's stern presence commanded the military assets, his voice booming with authority as he barked orders to fortify their defenses. Hunter and Alex, masters of the arcane, conducted protective rituals with a commanding tone and powerful incantations, summoning mystical barriers to hold back the encroaching darkness.

At the front line, Mara's voice rang out, rallying the forces. "Today, the world's soul hangs in the balance. What we do now will echo through eternity!" Her words cut through the oppressive atmosphere, igniting a fire in the hearts of those gathered. Soldiers hardened their gazes, gripping weapons with white-knuckled determination. Police officers bowed their heads in fervent prayer, lips moving in silent supplication. Acolytes traced mystical sigils of protection in the air, their fingers leaving faint trails of luminescence.

From within the temple's abyssal depths, rumbling chants grew louder, a discordant symphony of madness. In the hazy distance, the first signs of unholy abominations began to manifest — twisted forms that defied description, their very presence an affront to reality.

The brave warriors stood amidst a shroud of mysterious shadows, an eerie calm enveloping them as they braced for the coming storm. Their unbreakable resolve shone like a flame in the encroaching darkness, a guiding light for those facing unspeakable horrors. They stood poised, ready to battle for the very existence of a world on the brink of annihilation.

As the last echoes of Mara's rallying cry faded, the warriors steeled themselves for the imminent onslaught. The air crackled with anticipation, a palpable tension that seemed to draw the shadows closer. Then, as one, they retreated, falling back to the Shadowguard bunker. Their retreat was not one of fear but of strategy — a momentary respite to regroup and prepare for the battle that lay ahead.

In the depths of the Shadowguard bunker, darkness clung to every corner like a living shroud. The cavernous armory echoed with the metallic clicks and clacks of weapons being checked and loaded. Elite operatives moved with practiced efficiency, their faces grim masks of determination as they donned occult armor festooned with arcane symbols. Ancient artifacts of power were distributed, each item thrumming with barely contained energy.

Across the city, in hidden sanctuaries and forgotten places of power, preparations of a different sort unfolded. Hunter's voice cut through the tension, his words heavy with the weight of impending doom. "We face the end of all things. This night decides the fate of every living soul." He stood at the center of a circle of warrior monks, their eyes closed in concentration as they chanted in languages long dead to the modern world. The air around them shimmered and pulsed, coalescing into translucent spheres of protective energy that slowly expanded outward.

In a nearby cathedral, Father Alex moved among a group of crusader knights. The scent of holy oils filled the air as he anointed each warrior in turn, his weathered hands steady as he traced sacred symbols on gleaming armor and razor-sharp blades. The knights knelt in solemn reverence, their expressions a mix of fear and fierce determination as they prepared to face the horrors that awaited them in the coming darkness.

As the warriors and monks continued their preparations, word of their impending battle spread throughout the city. The news was met with a mix of dread and determination as every citizen understood the gravity of the situation. The city's religious leaders, too, began to prepare in their own way, calling upon divine intervention to aid in the coming conflict. Meanwhile, the military forces stationed around the city readied their weapons, steeling themselves for the fight that would determine their world's fate.

The night sky loomed ominously over the assembled military might, a dark canvas against which the gleaming metal of tanks and artillery pieces stood in stark relief. From above, the vast array of firepower stretched out like a lethal tapestry, each weapon a deadly thread in the fabric of war.

Mara stood before the assembled troops, her figure silhouetted against the backdrop of destruction. Her voice carried across the field, filled with a mixture of determination and barely contained fury. "The darkness rises against us." A pause hung heavy, pregnant with anticipation. The soldiers held their breath, hanging on her every word. "But we shall meet it head-on!" Mara's voice rose to a crescendo, her fist punching skyward. "For the light!"

The response was immediate and deafening. A roar erupted from the assembled forces, a primal war cry that seemed to shake the very earth. It was a sound of defiance, of rage, of fear transmuted into furious resolve. The cry reverberated across the battlefield, drowning out the distant rumble of engines and the metallic clink of readied weapons.

As the sound faded, an eerie silence settled over the troops. They stood ready, eyes fixed on the horizon, waiting for the darkness Mara had spoken of — a darkness they could all feel creeping toward them, inexorable and hungry.

As dawn broke, a staggering sight unfolded across the battlefield. Humanity's last stand against the encroaching darkness had amassed in numbers beyond comprehension. The heroic forces stretched as far as the eye could see, a sea of determined faces and gleaming weapons.

In the eerie half-light, frontline warriors methodically checked their gear. The metallic clicks of weapons being loaded echoed across the field, a menacing counterpoint to the heavy silence of impending doom. Each soldier's face was a mask of grim resolve, eyes haunted by the knowledge that this might be their final stand.

At the forefront stood Mara, her features etched with unwavering determination. Her eyes, hard as flint, scanned the horizon where an unspeakable horror lurked just beyond sight. She drew her weapon, the gesture a silent signal. A ripple of movement passed through the ranks behind her as thousands followed suit.

The air grew thick with tension, charged with the collective fear and resolve of the assembled forces. As Mara took her first step forward, the army surged behind her like a great tide of humanity, ready to crash against the shores of darkness that threatened to engulf their world.

The desecrated lands swelled with Mephistopheles' corruption, a blighted wasteland of jagged obsidian shards and sulfurous miasma. The once-sacred ritual grounds had been twisted into a nightmarish hellscape, an affront to nature itself.

A massive aerial armament soared overhead, its engines

screaming defiance against the unholy silence. Salvos of concentrated light erupted from its underbelly, blasting craters into the tortured terrain. Gunships swooped and strafed, their weapons spitting death at unseen foes below. Across the battlefield, glyphs of banishment detonated in brilliant flashes, momentarily illuminating the chaos.

The Shadowguard task force breached the perimeter, moving in tight combat formation. They engaged the cult hordes in vicious close-quarters battle, a frenzied dance of steel and blood.

"Lay down suppressing fire! Push to the central spire!" a Shadowsoldier bellowed, his voice barely audible above the din of combat.

Hunter's cabal of mystics traced glowing sigils in the air, their fingers leaving trails of ethereal light. An aetheric shield blossomed into existence, a shimmering barrier that blocked the incoming firestorm of demonic energy.

Cultists screamed as Alex's holy warriors cleansed them with consecrated blades. The righteous fury in their eyes matched the unholy madness of their foes. Mara, her face a mask of grim determination, led a daring teleport gambit. Squads of warriors materialized deep within the enemy ranks, sowing confusion and death.

The two armies clashed in an apocalyptic frenzy. Cult hordes swarmed from all sides, threatening to overwhelm the defenders' position. Alex hovered protectively over injured warriors, his hands weaving restorative magic. Flesh knit, bones mended, and the fallen rose to fight again.

Hunter hurled arcane spears of liquid light, each one piercing through hordes of horrors. The abominations shrieked as they were unmade, their corrupt forms unable to withstand the purity of his assault. He rallied his war mages, his voice carrying over the cacophony of battle. "Hold the line! Our realm depends on it!"

Terry led his tactical teams in scaling the spire's face. They moved with practiced efficiency, but even their skill couldn't save them from the cyclopean defenses that rained death from above. Men and women fell, their bodies tumbling into the abyss below.

The coalition forces gained ground, inch by bloody inch, only to be battered back by a relentless demonic advance. Hope dwindled as they stared up at the central spire, its impossible geometry a mockery of sanity.

Atop its peak, the nightmare vision of Mephistopheles's ascension loomed. His voice boomed across the wasteland, a sound that shook the very foundations of reality. "My hour is at hand!"

Deep, ominous rumblings echoed through the earth, accompanied by screams of torment as Balor's demon form first manifested atop the central ziggurat. The armies of light stared up in horror as Mephistopheles's massive frame towered over the ritual site, blotting out the moonlight. His horns scraped the night sky, a corona of unholy energy crackling around them. A sulfurous miasma poured from his maw, choking the air and clouding the minds of those who dared to look upon him.

In that moment, as the full enormity of their task became clear, even the bravest warriors felt their resolve waver. They were ants before a god, and the god was angry.

The corruption emanating from Mephistopheles pulsed outward in nauseating waves, tainting everything it touched with Mephistopheles' foul essence. The ground beneath their feet bubbled and churned, transforming into viscous tar pits that threatened to swallow them whole. Jagged spikes of obsidian erupted from the earth, encircling the ziggurat in a lethal ring.

Mara recoiled, her face contorted in revulsion. "My God..."

Alex's voice rang out, filled with unwavering conviction. "Have faith, child! We must repel this evil!"

Hunter's urgent cry cut through the chaos. "Focus your wards westward — the rift lies there!"

The acrid air melted flesh from bone, causing soldiers and mystics alike to retch and stumble. Vehicles sank into the liquefying terrain, disappearing into the bubbling mire with sickening gurgles.

The night air crackled with tension as Terry surveyed the chaos unfolding before him. Civilians scrambled in panic, their faces contorted with fear as they rushed toward the evacuation zone. In the distance, fiery explosions bloomed like hellish flowers, painting the sky in shades of orange and red. The apocalyptic forces were drawing near, their approach heralded by the screams of the fleeing masses.

Terry's squad stood at attention, their eyes fixed on their leader. He could see the doubt, the fear, and the determination etched into their faces. They were the last line of defense, the thin barrier between salvation and annihilation for the innocent lives behind them.

Drawing a deep breath, Terry steeled himself for what was to come. His voice rang out, cutting through the cacophony of panic and destruction. "We'll buy them as much time as we can. This is the moment we swore an oath for. No retreat!"

The words hung in the air, heavy with the weight of their implications. Each member of the squad knew what this meant — they were prepared to lay down their lives for the greater good.

With grim resolution, Terry's squad moved into position. They locked down the entrance to the evacuation zone, their weapons at the ready. The air grew thick with anticipation as they braced themselves for the impending onslaught.

In the eerie calm before the storm, Terry's mind raced. He thought of the oath they had taken, of the lives they were protecting, and of the horror that awaited them. As the distant rumble of approaching doom grew louder, he silently prayed that their sacrifice would not be in vain.

The squad stood firm, a bulwark against the encroaching darkness. They were the last hope for the terrified masses behind them, and they would hold the line until their last breath. The night stretched on, pregnant with dread, as they waited for the inevitable clash that would determine the fate of countless souls.

Once-reliable tactics crumbled in the face of Mephistopheles's overwhelming power. Bullets ricocheted wildly, striking friend instead of foe. Missiles looped back on their launchers in impossible arcs. Protective wards flickered and died, leaving their casters exposed and vulnerable.

A fiery pentagram blazed to life around Mephistopheles as he unleashed his devastating assault. Hellfire rained from the sky, incinerating soldiers where they stood. Fissures tore open, revealing glimpses of nightmarish realms beyond human comprehension. The very fabric of reality warped and twisted at his command.

Mara's eyes widened in horror as she watched their position become engulfed in the onslaught. Her heart pounded in her chest as she screamed into her radio, her voice tinged with desperation. "Fall back! Fall ba —" Her words were cut short as a massive chunk of debris hurtled towards her. In a blur of motion, Alex tackled Mara, sending them both tumbling to the ground. The projectile missed them by mere inches, showering them with dust and rubble.

As the dust began to settle, Terry and Hunter scrambled over, pulling Mara and Alex from the wreckage. Terry's face was etched with concern as he helped Mara to her feet. "Mara! Are you alright?"

Mara's head swam, her vision blurring as she struggled to focus. Her voice came out weak and dazed. "We have to retreat... it's over..."

Before anyone could respond, Hunter's voice cut through the chaos. "Look!"

They turned as one, their eyes widening in collective horror. Mephistopheles had manifested an enormous profane colossus, its massive form burning with hellfire. The towering monstrosity exuded palpable darkness as it marched across the battlefield, each step crushing the remaining resistance with terrifying ease.

Utterly overwhelmed, the few remaining heroes

gathered behind Alex. His lips moved in desperate prayer, a final plea to powers that seemed to have abandoned them. As Mephistopheles's demonic hordes descended upon them, the last vestiges of light were blotted out, plunging the world into suffocating darkness.

Amidst the chaos, Mara's battered Shadowguard unit took cover behind crumbling ruins. The air was thick with the stench of sulfur and death as swarming demonic forces closed in from all sides. Ammunition ran low, each shot more precious than the last as they made their desperate last stand.

Mara's voice rang out, a beacon of defiance in the face of certain doom. "This is it. We knew the risks. Make every shot count! For the light!"

The unit fought bravely, their weapons blazing in the darkness. But for every demon they felled, ten more took its place. The endless hordes pressed in, their inhuman shrieks drowning out all else.

Atop a crumbling mesa, Hunter and Alex combined their mystical knowledge in a desperate bid to hold the evangelistic forces together. Waves of cleansing energy pushed back against the tide of chaos, but for how long?

Hunter's face was a mask of strain. "Just a little longer! Hold the line!"

Alex's voice rang with fervent belief. "By the grace of God, we shall prevail!"

Across the battlefield, resolve wavered as warriors watched their light being extinguished by the demon's blight. Despair warred with duty on grim faces. A temporary respite came as leaders rallied their troops with rousing words about shining their light against any darkness. Beleaguered warriors found a second wind, determination kindling in their eyes.

But their renewed hope was short-lived. Mephistopheles unleashed a cataclysmic new attack, tearing at the very fabric of reality as his dominion over this realm grew. Mara and her allies braced against the onslaught, steel entering their gazes. This battle was far from over; it was only just beginning.

As the battlefield fell into a brief lull, Mara found her footing on the ruins of an ancient tower. The remaining warriors rallied around her, their desperate gazes reflecting the ethereal glow of her raised blade. The air stilled, holding its breath for the next command, their eyes fixed on their leader. She raised her blade, its ethereal glow cutting through the darkness. The air crackled with anticipation. "Unleash oblivion!" Mara's voice rang out, echoing across the battlefield.

In an instant, chaos erupted. Futuristic cannons hummed to life, their energy building to a crescendo. Mystics, their eyes rolled back in concentration, summoned storms that raged overhead. Agility teams launched themselves into the air, their forms blurring as they soared.

The sky ignited with arcane missiles, their guided trajectories weaving intricate patterns as they streaked towards Mephistopheles's army. Sorcerous strikes tore the earth asunder, leaving smoldering craters in their wake. Ethereal beams, focused and relentless, saturated the area in blinding light.

For a heartbeat, Mephistopheles's presence vanished, swallowed by the magical onslaught. Mara pressed binoculars to her eyes, scanning the devastation. She barked orders, directing concentrated fire on weak points in the demon's defenses. Hope flickered in her chest, a dangerous spark. But as the dust settled, that hope was crushed. Mephistopheles emerged, untouched by their most potent attacks. His aura of miasmic corruption rippled, mocking their efforts.

"Impossible!" Mara's disbelief cut through the din of battle.

Mephistopheles's retaliation was swift and terrible. He raised his arms, and the very fabric of reality bent to his will. The battlefield twisted and warped, transforming into a nightmarish volcanic wasteland. Lava bubbled from newly formed fissures, and noxious fumes choked the air.

Mara's squads scattered, their formations shattered. Cut

off and overwhelmed, they sought whatever cover they could find in the hellish landscape.

"Fall back! Regroup!" Mara's command was tinged with desperation. She watched in horror as their carefully planned assault crumbled. The relentless artillery barrage, their trump card, only served to further enrage the demonic entity. Mara's scream of frustration was lost in the cacophony of destruction, a futile cry against the encroaching darkness.

Mara's heart pounded in her chest as she watched her troops struggle against the twisted landscape. The once familiar terrain had become a treacherous enemy, its molten veins claiming the lives of those too slow to react. She felt a cold dread seep into her bones as Mephistopheles laughed, his mirth echoing ominously across the battlefield.

"We're trapped, Hunter," Mara bellowed amidst the pandemonium.

"I shall attempt to lead us to safety," Hunter roared to those still standing. With a dramatic sweep of his arms, he joined his palms and slowly withdrew them, conjuring a portal. His body quivered, every sinew pulsating with torment as he poured the final remnants of his essence into sustaining the shimmering gateway for their escape. The atmosphere crackled with arcane force, existence itself warping under the immense pressure of the collapsing dimension.

Shadows danced at the edges of his vision, threatening to consume him entirely. Yet he held on, watching through gritted teeth as his allies scrambled through the flickering gateway. Each passing figure sent a fresh wave of pain coursing through his veins, the portal's stability waning with every heartbeat.

The realm around them groaned, great chunks of what passed for matter in this twisted place breaking apart and dissolving into nothingness. Time itself seemed to stretch and warp, seconds lasting eons as Hunter fought against the inevitable.

His legs buckled, knees slamming into the ground that

was no longer truly there. The portal flickered violently, its edges fraying like an old photograph left too long in the sun. Hunter's lips, cracked and bleeding, parted in a hoarse whisper. "Go! It's... closing..."

With monumental effort, he forced his eyes open one last time. The final ally's silhouette passed through the unstable threshold, and Hunter allowed himself a moment of grim satisfaction. His mission was complete, even if the cost would be his very existence.

The portal snapped shut behind Hunter as he dove through. He tumbled roughly onto the marble floor of the sanctuary, its pristine interior a stark contrast to the hellscape they had just escaped. He collapsed to the floor, his energy spent.

Breathing heavily from the exertion, Mara gave Hunter a thumbs-up for the save. Then she rose on unsteady legs and took in the battered team that had made it through. Less than half their number stood before her, their eyes hollow, their hope wavering. She steeled herself and spoke, her voice raw but firm.

"We have lost much. But we must press on. This is not the end — it is only the beginning. Mephistopheles may have won this battle, but the war still rages. We will rest, rebuild, and prepare to take the fight to him once more."

The words rang hollow, even to Mara's own ears. How could they hope to prevail against a foe of such unfathomable power? She pushed the doubt down; it would do no good now. Their only chance was to have faith that good would somehow triumph over evil.

Mara met each survivor's eyes in turn. "We will remember those we've lost. Their light will guide us in the darkness to come."

Alex stepped forward, placing a comforting hand on Mara's shoulder. "Have faith, my child. The light still shines, even here." He gestured to the stained glass windows lining the sanctuary.

In the quiet that followed, Mara felt a hand on her shoulder.

It was Hunter, his eyes reflecting the same pain but also a glimmer of hope. He guided her to the sanctuary's windows, their vibrant colors muted by the smoky haze outside. The sight of the ruined grounds hit her like a punch in the gut, but she steeled herself, knowing there were still those who needed her strength.

The survivors ventured back out into the destruction. The once verdant ritual grounds had been transformed into a blasted, smoldering hellscape. Mara's boots crunched over scorched earth as she supported a wounded soldier, his arm draped across her shoulders. The acrid stench of burning flesh and melted metal assaulted her nostrils. "Steady now. We've got you," she murmured, her voice hoarse from shouting commands.

They navigated through a maze of mangled military vehicles and makeshift barricades, the rubble a testament to their failed defense. Ash hung thick in the air, coating Mara's lungs with each labored breath. An oppressive sense of dread settled over the battlefield like a suffocating blanket.

Ahead, Father Alex knelt beside the fallen form of a mystic warrior. With a gentle touch, he closed the dead man's eyes, a final act of respect amidst the chaos. Nearby, Terry frantically worked to save his battered squad, his hands slick with blood as he applied tourniquets and pressure bandages.

Mara lifted her radio, her voice cracking as she spoke. "Bravo team, status?"

The response crackled through, each word a hammer blow to her dwindling hope. "Completely routed in Sector 4. Took heavy losses. Falling back to rally point."

Her face fell, the weight of their losses etched in the lines of her brow. She guided the limping soldier towards Alex, who had set up a makeshift triage area among the ruins.

Hunter looked up, his eyes haunted. "I've done all I can for now. We must retreat, regroup."

"No," Mara insisted, her jaw clenched. "We have to keep pushing forward, whatever it takes."

Alex rose, placing a gentle hand on her shoulder. "Look

around you, child. We're decimated. Balor has unleashed forces beyond our control."

Mara's gaze swept across the hellish landscape. The proud ranks of their army had been reduced to a handful of haggard survivors. Her shoulders sagged under the crushing weight of responsibility, the mantle of leadership suddenly feeling too heavy to bear.

In the distance, violent flashes lit up the horizon like a macabre fireworks display. Each burst of light marked another line of defense crumbling, another group of allies falling to Mephistopheles's onslaught. Mara drew in a shuddering breath, steeling herself against the tide of despair threatening to overwhelm her.

"Then we make our stand here," she declared, her voice low but resolute. "Prepare the counter-ritual."

Alex nodded solemnly, understanding the gravity of her decision. Together, they turned to rally their remaining allies. Overhead, apocalyptic clouds gathered, roiling with unnatural energy. The air crackled with tension as they prepared for their final, desperate gambit against the forces of darkness.

CHAPTER 27
THE LIGHT'S LAST STAND

In the cavernous throne room, Mephistopheles stood at the window, his imposing figure silhouetted against the dim light filtering through the stained glass. An eerie, crackling energy danced around him, casting flickering shadows on the stone walls. Outside, what remained of the gathering forces of his enemies swelled like a rising tide, but their numbers only served to fuel Mephistopheles's malevolent confidence.

A twisted smile crept across his face, contorting his features into a mask of demonic glee. His eyes, once a dull gray, now flared a deep, malevolent red that seemed to pulse with an unholy light.

"Let them come," Mephistopheles growled, his voice dripping with contempt. "My power shall eclipse their light."

The air in the room grew heavy and thick with the stench of brimstone and decay. As Mephistopheles's power surged, the very foundations of the fortress seemed to tremble as if cowering before the dark entity that resided within its walls. The approaching army, unaware of the true horror that awaited them, marched ever closer to their doom.

As the first tendrils of dawn crept over the horizon, they illuminated a scene of utter devastation. The landscape surrounding Mephistopheles's fortress was a testament to the apocalyptic battle that had raged through the night. Smoldering craters pockmarked the earth, their edges still glowing with residual heat. Debris floated eerily in the air, defying gravity and reason alike.

For miles in every direction, the destruction stretched on, a grim tableau of otherworldly carnage. Yet amidst this ruin,

Mephistopheles's stronghold stood resolute, its dark silhouette etched against the lightening sky. The fortress seemed to sneer at the heavens, a defiant monument to powers beyond mortal comprehension.

The air hung heavy with the acrid stench of smoke and something else — something ancient and malevolent. As the light grew stronger, it revealed more horrifying details: twisted metal fused with organic matter, pools of iridescent liquid that seemed to whisper and move of their own accord, and shadows that lingered far longer than they should have in the growing daylight.

Mephistopheles's fortress loomed over it all, a dark sentinel guarding secrets that man was never meant to know. Its walls, untouched by the devastation around it, seemed to absorb the dawn's light rather than reflect it. The stronghold stood as a stark reminder that whatever eldritch horror had been unleashed here, its source remained undefeated, waiting within those impenetrable walls for the next foolish soul to challenge its dominion.

In the depths of a pitch-black abyss, Mara's frantic calls reverberated off unseen walls. Her voice, raw with desperation, searched for any sign of her missing squad. The oppressive darkness seemed to swallow her words, leaving only a deafening silence in return. With each passing moment, the dread in her gut grew heavier. Time was running out. Reluctantly, she retreated, her heart heavy with the weight of abandonment.

Across countless realms, defenders rallied for their last, valiant stands. The air crackled with a mixture of fear and resolve as they faced the oncoming apocalyptic tide. Blood-stained weapons glinted in the fading light, wielded by hands that trembled but did not waver. The cost would be great, but every second bought was a second of hope for those they protected.

As twilight descended, a somber silence fell over the realms. Occult warriors, their faces etched with grim determination, embraced loved ones for what they knew might be the final time. Whispered words of farewell mingled with choked sobs as families clung to each other, reluctant to let go. These brave souls were about to make their stand against Mephistopheles's relentless armies, a sacrifice that would echo through eternity.

Amidst the chaos, Alex stood like a beacon. Eyes closed in concentration, hands outstretched, he summoned forth a divine nova of light. The radiance burst forth, a shield of pure energy enveloping a crucial extraction point. Those within its protective embrace felt a moment of respite from the encroaching darkness.

Alex knelt at the heart of a glowing mandala, its arcane geometries pulsing with eldritch energy. He was surrounded by crumbling pillars and enigmatic glyphs. The air hung heavy with anticipation as he began his esoteric invocations, his voice a low murmur that seemed to resonate with the very stones beneath him. He retrieved the two containers of pure white essence that Mara and Hunter had acquired for him. He consumed their contents, feeling the power surge through his veins. Rising, he led a solemn procession of mystics, their ritual vestments rustling in the chamber's stillness.

"Brothers...sisters...the hour is nigh. Invoke the rites of exorcism!" Alex's voice echoed off stone walls.

As one, the mystics began to intone, their eldritch syllables reverberating through the air. Alex guided their chanting, his hands weaving intricate patterns that seemed to conduct the very fabric of reality. A strange humming filled the chamber, growing in intensity as the ritual progressed. Suddenly, the ground trembled. The glyphs etched into the weathered stone ignited with an otherworldly radiance, casting eerie shadows across the chamber. The acolytes who had gathered to witness the ritual gasped in awe, their eyes wide with a mixture of fear and reverence.

The mystic formations pulsed with gathering energy, their sonorous chanting drowning out the distant explosions of battle. Alex raised fetish idols high, their grotesque forms catalyzing the ritual's power. The air shimmered with harmonics as the chanting reached a fever pitch.

The mystics began to falter. Their life forces were being siphoned away, fuel for the cosmic furnace that opposed Mephistopheles's darkness. Alex steeled himself, knowing what must be done. "By the Covenant of Azrael, I invoke the Rite of Ruin!" he cried out.

With deliberate movements, Alex donned a sacred breastplate. Its metallic surface caught the unearthly glow, seeming to pulse with a life of its own. As he continued his chant, his voice swelled, filling the chamber with forbidden names that had not been uttered for millennia.

Flames erupted around the altar, licking at the air with hungry tongues. Alex's eyes blazed with unwavering conviction, reflecting the inferno that raged before him. The very fabric of reality seemed to crackle and warp as he summoned the fires of creation itself.

Sweat beaded on his brow, trickling down his face as he strained against the immense power he was channeling. Yet he persisted, his voice rising to a thunderous boom that shook the very foundations of the ruins.

"By the Throne and First Dawn," Alex intoned, each word resonating with terrible purpose. "I invoke the Seven Seals and un-Names. Let the upwards path be opened!"

As the final syllable left his lips, a blinding flash exploded from Alex's form. Heavenly rapture bathed the ruins in its terrible glory, scouring away shadows and leaving those present feeling raw and exposed.

When the light faded, Alex stood transformed. His eyes glowed with an inner fire, his posture radiating an unshakeable resolve. He faced the impending darkness, backed by a faith so absolute it bordered on madness.

With a swift motion, Alex sliced his palm, blood spilling onto the mandala. The profane pact was sealed. The mystics convulsed, their souls consumed by the ravenous ritual. Sigils burned into their flesh, searing patterns that spoke of sacrifice and terrible power.

The stage was set. The ritual was complete. And in the depths of those ancient ruins, something primordial stirred, awakening to Alex's call.

***

The faithful gathered in a hallowed circle outside Mephistopheles's Citadel, their chanting a low, hypnotic drone that seemed to vibrate the very air. At the center stood Father Alex, his presence commanding and otherworldly. An aura of serenity radiated from him, casting an ethereal glow in the darkness. Alex's voice rang out, clear and resonant. "Brothers, sisters...lend me your light."

The chanting intensified, growing more urgent with each passing moment. Ghostly tendrils began to emerge from the bodies of the mystics, snaking through the air toward Alex's outstretched hands. The spectral streams intertwined, coalescing into an orb of hallowed light that pulsed with an otherworldly rhythm.

As Alex channeled the orb's celestial energy, his feet slowly left the ground. He hovered, suspended by an unseen force, his eyes blazing with divine purpose. The orb throbbed, unleashing shockwaves that rippled through the air in perfect synchronization with Alex's chanting.

His voice echoed in the minds of all present: "With this vessel, I invoke the Creator's will..."

The faithful screamed, their voices a cacophony of ecstasy and agony as they poured their very essence into Alex's conduit. The air crackled with eldritch energy, and those watching could see Alex's humanity visibly separating from his mortal form. His eyes, once warm and compassionate, were now filled with an infinite light that seemed to stretch beyond the boundaries of reality.

In a blinding flash, the orb exploded with radiance so intense it seared the retinas of those who dared to look directly at it. When the light faded, Alex stood transformed — a mortal shell now imbued with the raw power of Creation itself.

His voice boomed across the citadel, shaking the very foundations of the ancient structure. "Mephistopheles! Your profane anchors shall not prevail against the Creator's infinite grace!"

Alex extended his arms, his fingers splayed wide. A concentrated beam of searing divinity erupted from his palms, tearing through the air with a sound like reality itself being rent asunder. The faithful cowered, shielding their eyes from the unholy brilliance as the fabric of the world around them began to rupture and fray.

The void shuddered, a tremor rippling through the very fabric of nothingness. Alex's light, a beacon of hope in the endless dark, pierced the abyssal gloom. It struck Mephistopheles' eldritch anchors with the force of a thousand suns, each ray a sword of divine judgment.

The anchors, once unassailable bastions of otherworldly power, began to crack. Fissures spread across their surfaces like spiderwebs, each one a testament to the light's purifying might. Fragments of corrupted essence splintered off, disintegrating into the nothingness from whence they came.

Mephistopheles, the ancient entity of unfathomable evil, felt its grip on reality weakening. Its corrupted essence writhed in agony, unable to withstand the revelation brought forth by Alex's light. The truth of its existence, laid bare by this metaphysical onslaught, was too much to bear.

From the depths of the void came an unearthly shriek. It was a sound beyond human comprehension, a cacophony of a thousand dying stars and the death throes of reality itself. The noise reverberated through the non-space, threatening to tear apart the very seams of existence.

As the light continued its relentless assault, Mephistopheles' form began to unravel. Tendrils of darkness, once so sure in their dominion, now recoiled from the purifying radiance. The battle between light and dark, good and evil, raged on in this timeless, placeless void — with the fate of all creation hanging in the balance.

The beam's intensity crescendoed, engulfing Alex's mortal form in a blinding cosmic radiance. The faithful stood transfixed, tears streaming down their faces as they witnessed the awe-inspiring spectacle. The demon's hold shattered, but in its wake, a vacuum formed — one that stronger, more insidious forces might rush to fill.

The chamber quaked violently, showering dust and debris upon the onlookers. As the supernova of light faded, an oppressive silence descended, heavy and foreboding.

In the aftermath, a writhing mass of darkness hovered, tethered to the material plane by gossamer threads of malevolence. It howled mutely in the void, its very essence an affront to reality. Mephistopheles' malformed being corroded the space around it, a cancerous blight of utter corruption that screamed soundlessly against its fragile anchors.

The demon's grip on reality began to slip, its nightmare body glitching and flickering like a corrupted video feed. But as it faltered, the light intensified once more. This time, it was an all-consuming radiance, unbearable in its purity, scouring away the shadows with merciless intensity.

Mephistopheles raged in silent fury, desperately clawing for purchase through the vessels and souls still chained in its unholy thrall. Yet Alex's divinity shone ever brighter, a beacon of hope in the face of infernal darkness. The chorus of the faithful reverberated, building to a crescendo that shook the very foundations of reality.

A deafening psychic crack split the air as Mephistopheles' anchors finally gave way. Divine light erupted in a catastrophic wave, engulfing the demon's essence. The corrupted form unraveled, atomized utterly in the celestial fire. Mephistopheles' final, soundless scream echoed in the minds of all present, a psychic death rattle that would haunt their dreams for years to come.

As the last vestiges of the demon dissipated, Father Alex collapsed to the floor, his mortal form spent by the cosmic battle. The faithful rushed to his side, their faces a mixture of awe, fear, and uncertain hope. The threat may have been vanquished, but the scars it left behind — both seen and unseen — would linger long after this day.

The ancient citadel trembled, its walls quivering and sending cascades of dust down upon the assembled soldiers. Stones tumbled from the ceiling, clattering across the floor as a tumultuous wind howled through the halls. In a frantic rush, Mara and Hunter burst into the room, their eyes wide with terror as they saw the crumbling walls. "Quickly!" Mara commanded, her voice strained with urgency. "We must evacuate immediately before the entire structure collapses!" As chaos erupted around them, Hunter and Mara bravely carried Father Alex to safety, determined to save him from the crumbling fortress.

A cosmic tempest raged, its primordial power engulfing Mephistopheles's citadel. The once-imposing structure buckled and groaned, its foundations crumbling under the onslaught of uncontrolled forces. Matter and energy collided in a cataclysmic dance, annihilating everything in their path.

Blinding light pierced the darkness, accompanied by a deafening roar that shook the very fabric of reality. The maelstrom swallowed Mephistopheles's domain whole, its apocalyptic fury leaving nothing untouched. Ancient stones disintegrated, reduced to cosmic dust in mere seconds. The air crackled with otherworldly energy, charged with the potential for both creation and destruction.

As the storm intensified, reality itself seemed to warp and twist. The boundaries between dimensions blurred, allowing glimpses of nightmarish realms beyond human comprehension. Eldritch horrors lurked at the edges of perception, their forms too terrible for mortal minds to process.

In the heart of this chaos, Mephistopheles's citadel continued to crumble. Towers toppled like a child's blocks, swallowed by the insatiable maw of the cosmic tempest. The very ground beneath the fortress heaved and split, revealing abyssal chasms that threatened to devour what little remained.

As the last vestiges of Mephistopheles's domain disappeared into the swirling vortex, an eerie calm descended. The storm's eye passed overhead, offering a momentary respite from the devastation.

CHAPTER 28
IN THE AFTERMATH

The hushed tranquility of the sanctuary enveloped Mara as she lay in a simple bed, her wounds swathed in bandages. A faint hint of color had begun to return to her pallid cheeks, a small victory against the darkness that had nearly consumed her. Father Alex sat vigil beside her, his gaze fixed on the world beyond the window, lost in contemplation.

A soft rustling of sheets broke the silence as Mara stirred. Alex's attention snapped back to her, weathered features softening into a gentle smile. "Welcome back," he said, his voice resonating with familiar kindness.

Mara managed a weak smile in return. "You didn't have to stay," Mara's voice was barely above a whisper. "But thank you."

The warmth of Alex's smile seemed to chase away some of the lingering shadows in the room. "I wasn't about to leave you alone. Not after everything."

Gratitude flickered in Mara's eyes as she nodded, wincing slightly as she shifted her battered body. The weight of recent events pressed down upon her, threatening to suffocate her newfound hope. "I came so close," she murmured, her voice thick with unspoken horrors. "Closer than I care to dwell on."

Alex's hand found hers, his grip firm and reassuring. "But you made it through the darkness. As I knew you would."

The unspoken names of the fallen hung heavy in the air between them. Mara's voice cracked as she spoke, "So many didn't. Lilith...Serafine..." Her words trailed off into the oppressive silence. Alex bowed his head, the weight of their losses evident in the slump of his shoulders.

"I know," he acknowledged, his voice heavy with sorrow. "The cost was far too grave."

Doubt crept into Mara's eyes, mingling with the trauma that still lurked beneath the surface. "Was it worth it? What we sacrificed?"

Alex met her gaze, recognizing the internal struggle that mirrored his own. "I've asked myself the same, in weaker moments," he admitted. "But our cause was just. Is just. We did what was necessary."

A ghost of a smile flitted across Mara's face, but it vanished as quickly as it had appeared. The weight of their actions bore down upon her, threatening to crush what little strength she had regained.

"Tell that to the survivors," she whispered, her voice laced with anguish. "The ones left to mourn. Who still face horrors in their dreams."

Alex nodded slowly, his brow furrowed in contemplation. The silence stretched between them, filled with unspoken regrets and painful memories.

"When my faith wavered," he began, his voice low and measured, "I forgot those we helped. The ones who found peace. Who can sleep at night again, untroubled by darkness."

A spark of hope ignited in his eyes as he continued, "I visited a family yesterday. Their little girl was plagued by nightmares...until Mephistopheles was banished. They can finally live without fear. That is worth any price."

Soon, there was a soft rap at the door, and Terry entered, his haggard face breaking into a grin at the sight of Mara awake and alert. "About time you got up, sleepyhead," he teased, though his eyes shone with affection for his long-time partner. Mara rolled her eyes in mock annoyance, then winced slightly at the motion. Terry's smile faded into concern as he surveyed the toll her ordeal had taken.

"I'm alright," Mara said. "Just remind me not to make any deals with devils again."

Mara tried to push herself up in the bed, gritting her teeth against the pain that flared through her body. Terry was at her side in an instant, gently easing her back down against the pillows.

"Take it easy," he cautioned. "You've been through hell and back. Literally."

Mara let out a weak chuckle at Terry's attempt at humor. Even now, after everything they had endured, he was trying to keep her spirits up.

"What's the latest with the Council?" she asked quietly. Terry's expression grew serious, his mouth set in a thin line.

"Still deliberating," he said. "Debating whether we went too far."

Mara closed her eyes, fresh doubt and guilt churning within her. She had acted on instinct, done what she thought was needed to eliminate the threat. But at what cost? How many laws and oaths had she broken to banish Mephistopheles back to the depths of Hell?

She felt a gentle hand on her shoulder. Opening her eyes, she met Father Alex's compassionate gaze.

"You did what you felt was right," he said softly. "What you had to do to protect the innocent. Have faith that goodness will prevail, whatever comes next."

Mara looked from Alex to Terry, seeing the unspoken question in their eyes. Were the ends enough to justify the means? When this was over, could she live with herself and what she had done?

Mara tensed, her eyes darting to the window as the shadow passed. Terry's hand went reflexively to his hip, but his holster was empty.

"What was that?" Terry asked sharply, moving towards the window. He peered out cautiously.

The shadow was gone. Only the moss-draped oaks swayed gently in the humid evening air. Somewhere in the distance, thunder rumbled.

Terry shook his head. "Must have been a trick of the light." But the furrow between his brows remained.

Alex stood, crossing himself quickly. "Perhaps just a cloud passing over." But his voice lacked conviction.

Mara slowly sat up, wincing against the ache in her ribs. She felt it, too — a sinister presence lurking nearby. Mephistopheles may have been banished back to Hell, but his demonic allies still stalked the shadows of Savannah.

"We should leave this place," Mara said urgently. "It's not safe here anymore."

Terry turned to her, eyes dark with worry. "You're in no shape to travel. You need to rest and recover your strength."

Mara shook her head vehemently. "I'll rest better far from here. We all will." She met Alex's gaze. "You feel it too, don't you, Father?"

Alex hesitated, then nodded grimly. "I fear the evil we battled has not been entirely vanquished. Dark spirits remain in Savannah."

Mara slowly eased herself out of the bed, wincing as her injuries protested. Terry moved to help support her, slipping an arm gently around her waist.

"We'll go back to the Shadowguard," he said. "Hunter is there. He mumbled something about needing to see something in his library."

Mara nodded, leaning into him gratefully. Her strength was returning, fueled by determination. They had survived the demonic onslaught, but the war was far from over.

Father Alex gathered up his holy water and crucifix, tucking them securely into his bag. His weathered features were grim but resolute. He met Mara's gaze and gave a single, solemn nod. They would make their stand together, whatever came next.

The three slipped silently into the inky night, keeping to the shadows as they made their way towards the edge of town. The darkness seemed to press down on them, carrying whispers of unseen threats. Somewhere, a raven cawed ominously.

"Damnable birds," Father Alex grumbled under his breath. "Damn things give me the creeps."

Mara glanced back at the looming silhouette of the abandoned cult compound, its arched windows like sightless eyes. It was there she had faced the yellow-eyed horror that haunted her nightmares. There, Lilith, Serafine, and the others had sacrificed everything to turn the tide against the demonic horde.

"We won't forget them," Terry said quietly, following her gaze. "Or what they gave up for us."

Mara turned away, steeling herself. The weight of the dead was heavy, but the living still needed her protection. She would honor their sacrifice by carrying on. She moved slowly down the dark street, leaning on Terry for support. The wounds on her body still ached, but it was the deeper trauma that weighed most heavily on her mind. Flashes of the horrific ritual, of Lilith's desperate cries as the unholy fire licked at her body, haunted Mara's thoughts.

They reached the parked car, its black paint seeming to melt into the shadows. Mara eased herself gingerly into the passenger seat, letting out a soft gasp as her bruised ribs protested. Terry started the engine, the rumble seeming unnaturally loud in the still night air. He glanced over at Mara, his eyes filled with concern.

"We shouldn't stay in Savannah long," Mara said quietly. "It's not safe here."

Terry nodded. "We'll see what Hunter found in his texts, then get you out of here to recover."

Mara shook her head. "I can recover later. We need to keep moving, stay one step ahead." She turned to look out the window, her breath fogging the glass. "Whatever comes through from the other side...we need to be ready."

The car glided through the empty streets as a light rain began to fall. Father Alex sat silently in the back, one hand resting on his battered leather bible. His face was etched with weariness.

They should soon arrive at the Shadowguard headquarters.

The rain fell harder as they drove through the empty streets, the windshield wipers barely keeping up with the deluge. Mara gazed out into the night, watching rivulets of water streak across the glass. Somewhere out there, just beyond the veil of rain, sinister forces were conspiring against them.

She shivered, drawing her jacket tighter around herself. The wounds on her body had mostly healed, but the psychic scars remained raw and aching. She could still hear the screams as the demonic hordes swarmed through the city and could still smell the stench of their sulfurous blood. So much death and destruction in their wake.

Mara closed her eyes, fighting back the memories. Lilith's agonized wail as the flames licked her body when Balor enforced his infernal punishment on her. Serafine's screams as Balor plunged the dagger into her chest, her blood spraying the unholy symbols painted upon the floor. So much given, so many lost. And yet, they had succeeded in driving the demons back through the veil, at least for now.

The car pulled up outside the unassuming brick façade of the Shadowguard headquarters. Mara opened her eyes, steeling herself. There would be time to mourn later. Right now, they needed answers.

***

The flickering candlelight cast long shadows across Hunter's esoteric library, painting the walls with an eerie, dancing glow. Ancient texts and yellowed scrolls lay scattered across the mahogany desk, their musty scent mingling with the acrid smell of melting wax. Hunter's eyes, wide and feverish, darted across the pages before him, his fingers tracing arcane symbols and eldritch diagrams.

"It's all falling into place," he whispered, his voice raspy from hours of intense research. "The prophecies, the warnings. Mephistopheles was but a mere introduction..." Hunter's hands shook as he flipped through the delicate pages, revealing diagrams of celestial beings and depictions of otherworldly creatures that surpassed human comprehension. The gravity of his revelations weighed heavily on him, threatening to shatter his sanity, but he couldn't stop now. He was on the brink of understanding everything.

His voice was barely a whisper, drowned out by the sound of pages rustling. "There is an order to it," he murmured. "A hierarchy of wickedness. And we have only just begun to conquer the first." As his fingers delicately traced the illustrations of ancient deities wielding unimaginable power, Hunter's mind was flooded with visions. He saw the fabric of reality torn apart, dimensions colliding in a symphony of chaos. Vile creatures slithered through the void, their very presence distorting all that they touched. Hunter stumbled back, gripping the desk for support as he gasped for air. The revelations were both mesmerizing and terrifying.

"Seven cycles," he croaked, his throat parched and strained. "Seven harbingers to pave the path."

The gravity of this revelation draped over him like a cloak. Hunter's broad shoulders slumped, yet unwavering resolve glimmered in his gaze as he squared his posture.

"Mephistopheles...just the first transcendental vanguard," he said, his voice growing stronger with each word. "Six more still lie ahead."

Hunter took a deep breath, steeling himself against the cosmic horrors that awaited. His jaw clenched, resolve hardening his features. "We can only confront that which we are willing to know."

With a resounding thud that echoed through the library, Hunter slammed the ancient tome shut. The sound hung in the air, a finality that marked the end of one chapter and the beginning of a far more terrifying journey.

As Hunter prepared to leave the library, he heard a sinister whisper coming from one of the texts. The whisper started off faint, barely audible over the crackling of the candles. But it steadily grew louder, more insistent, until the voice seemed to fill the room.

"Stay...read...learn..."

Hunter's blood turned to ice in his veins. That voice — it couldn't be. He turned slowly, eyes scanning the shelves. There, on a high shelf, one of the books shook ever so slightly. Hunter reached for it with a trembling hand. The leather cover was icy cold to the touch. He opened it slowly, heart pounding.

The pages flipped rapidly in the still air, settling on an ominous illustration of a horned demon, eyes glowing malevolently. The whisper returned, stronger now.

"Let me in...I can show you power beyond imagination..."

Hunter slammed the book shut with a gasp. This was no ordinary text — he could feel the dark energy pulsing from it. The insidious voice chuckled.

"You cannot resist...your curiosity will be your undoing..."

Jaw clenched, Hunter wrapped the book in a cloth and shoved it deep into his bag. He had to get it out of here — figure out what sinister entity it contained. As he turned to leave, a cold breath tickled the back of his neck.

"We will meet again, Hunter Eldritch..."

Hunter felt the ominous presence fade as he strode from the library, the ancient tome secured in his bag. His mind raced as he made his way down the dim hallway to meet with the others. What sinister revelations was this dark artifact keeping secret? And what unholy dangers would be unleashed if he dared delve deeper into its vile pages?

The answers would have to wait. Right now, there were more pressing matters at hand. Hunter entered the main room of the safehouse where Mara, Terry, and Father Alex awaited. Their faces, etched with exhaustion, turned to him as he entered.

"Were you able to find anything useful?" Mara asked, her voice tinged with desperation. In the candlelight, the bruises on her face looked like dark shadows.

Hunter chose his words carefully. "I've uncovered more

about the hierarchy we face. But this is only the beginning."

Terry's eyes narrowed. "What exactly does that mean?"

"It means the forces we defeated were only the first wave," Hunter replied grimly. "There are more powerful entities behind the veil, orchestrating these attacks. We have merely bloodied the hands of their foot soldiers."

Father Alex's shoulders slumped, the graveness of this news clearly weighing on the priest. But his eyes remained resolute. "Then we must have faith. Faith in our cause, our mission. Faith in the light that will guide us through the darkness."

Hunter suppressed a cynical chuckle. He had never been one for faith. "I'm afraid, Father, that faith might not be enough. The signs are unmistakable. The Overlord's legions amass as we speak."

Alex's head hung low, his sigh heavy with defeat. "We've given up so much...how can one possibly oppose such an ageless malevolence?"

Hunter turned, his face a mask of grim determination. With practiced precision, he etched another rune into his scarred flesh, the pain barely registering in his haunted eyes. "I don't know, old friend. But stand, we must."

He crossed the room with purposeful strides, his fingers tracing the worn leather spine of an ancient tome. As he feverishly translated the archaic text, his voice took on a hollow quality. "All my studies, all the battles fought...they were merely the prelude."

Mara's eyes darted around the room, assessing their meager resources. "If this thing is as bad as you say, we'll need an army."

Hunter's head snapped up, his gaze piercing. He shook his head, a humorless smile twisting his lips. "Armies are meaningless. This is a war for realities...fought in nightmares and dying stars."

Terry's voice quavered, betraying his fear. "So what do we do?"

Hunter's hollow stare fixed upon them, his eyes bottomless

pools of despair and resolve. "We go on the offensive for once. Take the fight to The Overlord before its victory is assured."

Mara's brow furrowed, her skepticism evident. "And how do we fight something we can't even comprehend?"

"By revealing its form...pulling back the veil so it stands naked before us. Then we strike without mercy." With a dramatic flourish, Hunter yanked back a heavy velvet curtain. The group collectively gasped as a hidden sanctum was revealed, its walls lined with occult relics and ritual tools of unimaginable power and provenance.

"I've prepared for this battle since I uttered my first warding. But I cannot triumph alone."

The others absorbed the sight before them, a mixture of awe and terror etched on their faces. Slowly, resolve began to harden in their eyes.

Alex's voice was barely above a whisper, but it carried the weight of a solemn vow. "God help me...I will walk with you into the valley of shadow."

Terry squared his shoulders, drawing strength from a lifetime of duty. "We took an oath to protect this city...well, the world now, I guess. It's time to extend that oath."

Mara's gaze locked with Hunter's, a silent understanding passing between them. She nodded, her jaw set with grim determination.

Hunter's voice resonated with newfound strength. "So be it. We few stand against the encroaching oblivion."

With practiced ease, he drew a ritual knife from its sheath. The blade glinted ominously in the dim light, a silent promise of the ultimate sacrifice that lay ahead. "By my works and will, I vow to see this through. The Overlord's unmaking shall be our legacy!"

The air crackled with tension as the group's resolve hardened. They stood united, facing fates both terrifying and necessary. Together, they would challenge the ancient evil that threatened to consume all of existence.

Erik Daniel Shein, originally born as Erik Daniel Stoops in Northfield, Ohio, emerges as a visionary storyteller deeply captivated by the paranormal and a fervent champion for animal welfare. His artistic flair spans various genres, seamlessly merging his love for storytelling with a profound commitment to animation and the welfare of animals.

Erik's odyssey in the realms of publishing and animal welfare commenced alongside editor Sheila Ann Barry at Sterling Publications. Together, they crafted six non-fiction children's books about animals, presented in an engaging question-and-answer format. His exploration extended to the fascinating field of herpetology, where he refined his expertise as a trained authority on reptiles and amphibians.

As a consultant for both local and federal fish and wildlife services, Erik immersed himself in the intricate world of these creatures, contributing invaluable insights to conservation endeavors. This rich background served as the bedrock for his eventual transition into the enthralling realms of written and visual storytelling.

Melissa Davis is an accomplished multi-genre author with over 50 novels and numerous screenplays to her credit. Born in Southern Illinois, her lifelong passion for reading inspired her to begin writing creatively at the age of seven. She further developed her talent while attending the prestigious Illinois Summer School for the Arts during high school. Melissa went on to graduate with a Bachelor's in Education from Illinois State University. She initially worked as a teacher before leaving to focus on raising her children and pursuing her dream of becoming a full-time writer.

As a multi-genre author, Melissa's novels span a diverse range including contemporary and historical fiction, fantasy, mystery and more. With over twenty years of experience, she is an expert in crafting intricate plot lines and multi-dimensional characters that resonate with readers across genres. Her writing has been praised by critics and readers alike for its warmth, insight, and ability to capture the full range of human emotion. When not writing her next book, Melissa enjoys connecting with her loyal community of readers.

Karen Fuller is an award-winning and accomplished multi-genre author with over 30 novels and numerous screenplays to her credit. A graduate of Pensacola State College with an Associate of Arts degree in Business Management, Karen has turned her creative passion into a successful writing career spanning over two decades.

Born in Alabama, Karen began writing at a young age, inspired by her voracious reading habit. After starting a family, she devoted herself to raising her children while continuing to write in her free time. In 2011, Karen took her entrepreneurial spirit further by founding her own publishing press, World Castle Publishing, to provide support and guidance to aspiring authors.

When not crafting intricately woven plotlines brimming with multidimensional characters, Karen enjoys traveling the country to meet her loyal readers at book events. She also loves experiencing the outdoors while camping and watching auto races. Married for over 40 years, Karen now splits her time between writing novels, running her business, and visiting her two grown children and young grandchildren, who provide endless inspiration.

Karen writes in a diverse range of fictional genres, effortlessly transitioning from thriller to romance, dystopian to fantasy. Her novels have received numerous accolades for capturing universal emotions and showcasing the breadth of the human experience. Driven by her imaginative spirit, there is no literary terrain Karen Fuller cannot expertly explore.

www.ingramcontent.com/pod-product-compliance
Lightning Source LLC
Chambersburg PA
CBHW021505240626
47154CB00002B/507